# Greyson Gray:

## *Deadfall*

B.C. Tweedt

# DEDICATION

This novel is dedicated to those who have devoted their lives, in part or in whole, to the wellbeing of children. It is true that children are the future, and that as they go, so will our world go. Those who see children as the foundation and expend so much effort to build them up often don't see immediate fruits of their labor, but they labor still, working for little money or acclaim. I give a special *thank you* to the teachers, parents, pastors, mentors, and others who lend compassionate hands to the hurting, words of wisdom to the curious, dollars to the impoverished, discipline to the rebellious, and guidance to the lost.

# ACKNOWLEDGMENTS

This book, like the others before it, has grown to maturity only because of the many people who have given it water or pruned its unruly branches. My mother has used her editing skills like a master gardener, but in fact, there have been a dozen others who have nurtured the book through its various stages. Thank you to the beta-readers, who, as young as twelve years old, have pointed out typos, given wise suggestions, and otherwise planted many seeds which sprouted in the final version. Finally, I truly appreciate the grass-root efforts of each reader who chooses to tell a friend about the series or writes a review online. Each one contributes to Greyson's story blooming for the world to see. Thank you!

# Prologue

The abandoned cruise ship lurched to the side. The ship was reeling on the rolling waves, cracking under pressure, weakened by the fires that burned at its core.

Gripping Sydney's hand tighter, Greyson pulled her up the tilting flight of stairs as the staircase churned beneath them. Suddenly their next stair snapped apart. Tripping on the gap, Greyson stumbled to his knees, pulling Sydney down with him.

Nick and Jarryd were right there, bleeding from their wounds and yanking them onward. "Get up or we die!" Nick scolded.

Suddenly splinters blasted over their bodies as a giant chasm ripped a path across the wall mural of an underwater castle. They covered their faces but didn't stop their frantic staggering up the shifting stairs. The plumes of dust and debris seemed to cave in around them, but amidst the chaos, the tiny, yellow emergency lights flickered, revealing the only path to safety.

"Keep going!" Greyson commanded.

Greyson led the group, coughing at the smoke and stumbling with the floor tilting at nearly impossible angles. Navigating with only the fuzzy yellow rectangles glowing at his feet, his head swam, numb from pain and dizzy from blows to his head. Reaching another landing, Greyson glanced at the sign dangling from a screw somehow keeping a grip in the plaster.

*The Empress Deck.*

"Two more!" Sydney rasped, red welts vivid on her neck.

No reply was needed. They saved their energy for the last two flights, ignoring the heat wave and crackling fire coming from the landing. Greyson gritted his teeth, feeling the pain spasms coming from his ribs, face, and legs. He wanted to shed his soggy shoes, but there was no time to stop. Looking back, he saw the lobby of the Empress Deck crack in two, devoured by the level below with a plume of flame and smoke rising from beneath.

Suddenly another lurch sent them sprawling into a wall.

"Come on!"

Greyson tugged on their arms until they were back on their way.

"Through here!" Sydney pushed the door against the storm that raged with lashing wind and stinging rain; but it was friendlier than what was behind.

1

They stepped into it, onto the sloping main deck, trailing single file as the wind whipped at their clothes.

As the kids stumbled against the railing, they were suddenly very aware of the fact that the sinking was almost complete. The waves, once twelve floors down, were now splashing over balconies of the rooms beneath, only a few floors down.

Greyson searched for an escape route, but the lifeboats were already gone.

"Watch out!"

A deck chair came sliding toward them, but Greyson grabbed it just in time, pushing it away.

More chairs came careening toward them with a rush of water overflowing from the deck's pool.

"Hold on!"

They grasped the railing, rocking with the waves as if standing up on a roller coaster. Nick and Greyson battled with the deck chairs, but the others saw something. Their eyes went wide, their fists clenched white to the railing. They shared a look as another blast of lightning bathed the storm clouds with a blanket of light. But there was something else illuminated. Massive. Powerful.

"Greyson!"

The ship tipped the other direction, sending the chairs back toward the pool. Greyson managed to stagger over one last chair to join the others at the railing.

"We have to..." he trailed off, catching a glimpse of the massive battleship, its guns gleaming with rainwater, its steel hull piercing the hurricane's waves like they were nothing. The orange lifeboats had gathered near it, bobbing in the storm swells.

Greyson's mouth hung open and fear stole his breath. The realization cut at him, slicing an icy blade along his spine.

*It can't be. All of it. All of it for this.*

Greyson gulped, letting the rainwater wash over his trembling lips as the words formed and reformed.

"It's...it's a deadfall."

# PART 1

# Chapter 1

*Seventeen days ago. Iowa.*

Everything about the cemetery reminded Greyson of the haunting pictures he'd seen of the bomb's aftermath. The clouds hung low over the cemetery's trees, like the mushroom cloud that had hung over Des Moines for hours. The cemetery's grass was covered with dew, like the layer of ash and dust that had settled on roofs and yards and cars for days after the blast – and lingered even now. The stiff breeze, like the wind that flowed through house-less, tree-less Ground Zero, forced the families attending the funeral to stiffen and shiver. But the graves were much neater here, memorialized by rounded gravestones and covered with mowed grass and flowers. The graves in Des Moines had been the rubble of homes, a charred car thrown into the air, or a blood-soaked cot in a tent-hospital for radiation victims.

After the bomb, there had been frequent funerals at this cemetery. Though the attack was four weeks old, bodies were still being recovered from around Ground Zero; and many other cemeteries had been closed due to concern over radiation. While there was often more than one funeral at a time, there was only one this early in the morning – a handful of people surrounding the hole in the ground, backed into a corner by the trees.

As the breeze blew at the brown hair sticking out from the sides of his red hat with a white 'G' on the front, Greyson glared at the coffin like it had wounded him. And it had. It had taken his mother from him. Swallowed her, hid her from him. And it would never let her go. It wouldn't let her hug him, comfort him, kiss him. It would keep her trapped, below the earth, even if he needed her. Even if he wanted to say he loved her. Even if he could tell her that he had found out where Dad was. There was nothing he could do – and that made him angry.

He knew he was supposed to be sad – others told him so by saying he could cry, telling him that tears were okay, like he needed their permission. They meant the best, but they didn't understand. Sure, he was sad. But he was even more furious.

He felt the urge to punch someone or something, but he knew the FBI would step in and whisk him away. They had agents all over the cemetery. Four he could see – but he knew there were more. They hadn't wanted to let

4

their key witnesses out of their sight, not even for a private funeral for his mother. They feared that those who had committed the worst terrorist attack in history would seek to tie up loose ends. And the loose ends had names – Greyson, Jarryd, Nick, Sydney, and Sammy. There would be another funeral tomorrow – for Liam – but that would not be private; and the loose ends would not be able to attend it for security reasons.

Greyson's friends stood in the last row, and their parents in front of them, all of them stoically watching the unknown balding pastor ramble on, delaying the inevitable lowering of the casket into the ground to "rest in peace."

Greyson sighed and sighed again, trying to fight the tremble of his lips. And then he smelled something and blew out even more air, not wanting to breathe it in. It couldn't be the smell from the casket, could it?

Standing in the back of the small crowd and wearing a suit and tie too small for him, longhaired Jarryd leaned in toward his twin brother and whispered. "That was me."

Nick rolled his eyes toward his neatly gelled blonde hair and new red-framed glasses. While Jarryd and Nick had once only been distinguished by Jarryd's big front teeth, Nick's haircut, weight loss, and new glasses now made them appear to be mere brothers rather than twins.

"What?" Jarryd complained in a gruff whisper, grimacing at the smell himself. "What was I supposed to do? Hold it in?"

Nick nodded and eyed him as if saying, "Duh."

Jarryd sneered. "Nah man, if I held it in, it would come out my tear ducts."

Nick leaned in and whispered. "Well, at least something would be coming out of your tear ducts."

Jarryd paused, squinting at the coffin and then at Greyson, whose lips wavered and eyes glistened as he did his best to hold the tears at bay. Sydney had tears streaking down her cheeks. Even their parents were crying in front of them. Maybe he *should* be crying.

"Gosh," Jarryd elbowed his brother, still whispering. "Should I cry?"

Nick gritted his teeth. "Shh!" They were at a funeral. His brother didn't have an ounce of sentimentality in his bones.

"Should I fake it?"

"Shh!" Nick sighed and glanced nervously at the back of the other mourners' heads.

Jarryd leaned close. "Pull my armpit hair."

"What? No."

5

"Do it. It'll work. They're right in the middle. Six of them."

"Shut…up."

"Do it."

"No."

"Fine. I'll do it myself." A moment passed. "Ow!"

Nick rolled his eyes and shifted uncomfortably in his chafing dress shoes. When he looked over at Jarryd, tears were welling in his eyes and dropping toward his lips. Jarryd added in a few sniffs with a huff or two for good measure.

Hearing his sniffs, Sydney leaned toward him, pressing her blonde hair against his cheek and cuddling his arm with hers. "It's alright." The compassion in her voice made his pain go away and together they listened to the pastor conclude his message. And then Jarryd turned to his brother – and winked.

"We now commit her body to the ground," the pastor prayed. "Earth to earth, ashes to ashes, dust to dust, until the sure hope of the resurrection of the dead. Amen."

*Resurrection of the dead?* "Dude, she'll be a zombie?" Jarryd mumbled.

Sydney squeezed his bicep until she heard him whimper.

"Greyson." The pastor looked at him. "You may now place the first dirt on the coffin."

The comment struck Greyson from his daydream, and he stood, confused. The others began to murmur and look at him, but he couldn't believe he had to do what the pastor had said. They'd make him bury her? After all he'd been through?

Sydney's mother took a step forward and whispered in his ear. "It's…it's a symbol, Hun. I'll go with you."

She ushered him to where a small garden spade was stuck in the pile of dirt that was to bury his mother. Sydney's mother pointed at it, nodding at him. "Say your goodbye." She then averted her eyes, crying, like everyone else.

He looked back at his friends. Even Jarryd was crying.

And then he caught eyes with Liam's parents. They had come to pay their respects. But why should they pay anything? It was he who owed them. A rush of emotion made him shake. He wanted to run to them – to hug them and cry out that he was sorry. *I'm sorry! I'm sorry! I let him go! It was me!* But something stopped him. And now they were staring at him – not knowing that he had

6

signed off on their son's death, just as he was now signing off on his own mother's.

But he had to. The pastor was getting impatient – fidgeting; this pastor was nothing like Pastor Whitfield, who he had met just after the fair attack, and who was also most likely dead. This pastor looked and sounded as if he were ready to go home – a victim of the dozens of funerals he had been compelled to lead since the bomb. And now all the adults were nodding at him, as if he were a small boy afraid to get on Santa's lap at the mall. But he was no longer a boy. A boy would not pull the trigger with a shotgun pointed at a man's chest. A boy would not pummel terrorists with ball bearings or do half the things he had done.

And a boy should not have to bury his own mother.

But *he* had to.

Fighting the lump in his throat, Greyson stabbed the spade into the dirt and walked the spadesful of dirt to the coffin. For a moment he hesitated, letting the spade hover above. He thought the words in his head – hundreds of them – but let the emotion speak for itself. If she were really dead, she wouldn't hear him anyway.

But then again. If there were an afterlife, maybe she was watching him now. Right now. From somewhere above. Right next to him, even.

Suddenly the world around him seemed to blur. He retreated into himself and fought the pain that clinched his lungs, hindering his speech. Choking it down, he spoke to her as if she were lying in front of him. They were alone.

"It's just me now, Mom. Just me."

He clenched his chin and sucked in a breath, the tears fighting to win.

"But I promise you. I'll do what I can." His eyes focused past the casket to where he could imagine her face. "No matter what. They'll try to stop me. They can try to kill me – they killed you. They killed Kip and Liam." He clenched his fist around the spade. "But I promise. The next time I see you – I'll be dead, or I'll be here with Dad." He closed his eyes and took in a few more breaths. "I'll find him for you, Mom. I'll find him."

He held out the spade and turned it over, letting the dirt crumble over the top of the coffin and into the hole. Then he threw the spade to the pile of dirt and held out his hand with his pinky stretched toward the coffin. "I promise."

He took in a deep, shuddering breath and shook it with the air.

---------------

7

American flags were everywhere. They lined the streets from the highway to the square downtown; they topped light poles leading to the stage at the steps of the capitol building; they were even in handheld form for the masses to hold and wave. As the crowning achievement, the largest one flew high above the capitol building's golden dome. Though the residents of Iowa City knew the building as the "Old Capitol," it was once again the state's capitol. Des Moines had lost more than thousands of its citizens; it had also lost its status as Iowa's capital city.

Standing before a throng of supporters who stood before a legion of television cameras, the Governor – and presidential candidate – stood at a patriotic podium, solemnly staring over the crowd, drawing out a dramatic hush before beginning the last part of his speech.

"There are no words that can give to those who we have lost, the measure of devotion and respect they deserve. There are no words, but we must continue trying. Some have criticized me for making speeches during the crisis. They say I'm taking advantage of the situation – of the victims." He fought back the anger clenching his fists. "I say, how dare they! They seem to have forgotten that we are at *war*. And I was *in* the war zone, a target of the enemy's cruelty. My son was kidnapped…tortured…by the enemy." He drew in a sharp breath and took another pause to contain himself. Crying on stage may win him more voters, but he still had his dignity.

Inside the Old Capitol, Sam, Governor Reckhemmer's son, sat on a step of a beautiful spiraling staircase, listening to the muffled speech through the set of massive double doors that would be his entrance to the stage. Impatient, he fidgeted with a small, black thumb drive and scratched at the edge of an itch on his back. But he knew better than to scratch the itch fully. The scars were still forming. The doctors said the best thing to aid the healing was to keep applying the ointment day and night. And he had done so, watching himself in the mirror, too proud to let someone else do it for him. He'd look right at the jagged letters, hatred biting at him – fresh and painful. He hated Emory for cutting a message into his back. And he hated the terrorists – even more than his dad did.

"…I have the right to speak out as much as anyone, to provide a voice for other victims just as I tirelessly labor for the good of this great state. I am Governor first, candidate second."

The crowd erupted in whoops and hollers, cheering him on. The contest was getting heated, and his supporters increasingly saw the other candidates as weak and incompetent. There was no one as qualified to run for their party's nomination as Governor Reckhemmer. It would still be another ten months before he could be appointed his party's nominee at the national convention, another four after that before he could be elected President, and another two months after that before he would be inaugurated, but they were already anxious, zealous even. The stakes of an election had never been higher.

"But if they want to make this about the election, you know what? I don't care *who* we elect. I don't care what his or her name is. But we must make sure that whoever the nominee is, he or she will not rest until there is justice, until the victims and the victims' families are taken care of, and until Des Moines is rebuilt."

He pointed to the west, where he imagined the scene of destruction, where he had witnessed firsthand the horrors of the blast. Experts had said the explosion had been equal to 20 kilotons of TNT – as big as the bomb that destroyed Nagasaki. Almost a mile in every direction, blocks and blocks of houses were laid flat, demolished and scattered over the streets. Cars were nearly incinerated and blown hundreds of feet from their garages. And now, besides those they still found under rubble, countless radiation victims packed the hospitals, losing their livelihoods or their lives.

"We must make sure that this person is willing to do anything…to *sacrifice anything* to protect this great country from terrorists – those who wish to destroy or divide – and there is little difference between destroying and dividing."

He scanned the crowd again, hoping there were a few Pluribus sympathizers out there, listening. "There are real enemies in our midst. They are wolves in sheep's clothing – out to devour us. And this country deserves a shepherd, who after experiencing the evil and danger of the wolves' fangs firsthand, is especially vigilant – who has every nerve and muscle primed to take a knife to the wolves' throats in order to save the flock."

He paused as the crowd once again erupted into cheers, their faces lit with a mixture of excitement and the same anger that he felt himself. "I hope you find that person. And I hope each one of us are those shepherds – in our homes for our families, in our communities for our neighbors. And where we shop or dine or are entertained – we will watch for wolves. To protect those we love."

That was Sam's cue. He pushed open the double doors before the flashes of lights, waving flags, and applause. He smiled wide and waved back, striding upright and confident beside his dad, who embraced him for the crowd to see. They hugged and then stood and waved even more, hand in hand. Ever since Sam's mom had passed away years ago, they had been an inseparable pair. In troubled times, the ads said, the country needed a courageous man in office – one who would do anything for his country. And most knew what that meant. The 'anything' was ordering the jets to destroy the Pluribus truck carrying the nuclear device before it could reach downtown – even when he thought his son was inside. If he would do that for his country, what wouldn't he do?

Sam smiled and waved – a symbol of what his dad would sacrifice for the country. He had to be perfect for them, otherwise, how significant was the sacrifice?

His dad looked down on him with a smile that could have been a mirror. "I love you, son."

"I love you, too."

-----------------------

*Beep. Beep. Beep.*

Orion watched the heart-rate monitor with glazed eyes, itching at the cast on his left arm. The other teenaged boys beside him were growing impatient. They had been watching for several minutes now and there had been no change. She was in a coma. There wasn't *supposed* to be any change.

But Orion kept watching, the hatred burning in his face and crooked nose, flushing it red – but not as red as his cousin's hair. Her beautiful hair. Usually long and luxuriously curly, it now seemed ragged and greasy, flattened against the hospital pillow. Her eyes were closed – her mouth choking down the breathing tube. Of all the Pluribus children, he'd known her the longest. Jacob had rescued her shortly after Everett had rescued Orion. He couldn't stand to see her in pain – to see the stitches on her forehead where they had operated on her to stop the hemorrhage that the ball-bearing from Greyson's slingshot had caused.

*Brain damage.*

The words from the doctors had struck him like a hammer. If she awoke – if – she would have permanent brain damage.

The doctors were told it had been shrapnel from one of the explosions, but Orion knew what had caused it. So did the boys next to him – the tall one, the one with buzzed hair, and the one with the broken glasses.

"He did this to her," Orion said, unmoving.

Buzz nodded, grimacing. "If he wasn't dead, I'd –"

"We don't know he's dead."

The boys glanced from Orion to RedHead's seemingly lifeless body.

"I – I thought you said he jumped into the river," Buzz asked.

"The StoneWater team found his chip. They never found his body."

"They haven't found a lot of bodies."

Orion sneered. "He's alive."

"But how?"

"I jumped, and I'm alive, aren't I?" He glared at Buzz until he backed down.

Orion had broken his nose and arm, but he was alive. Once he'd called his dad to tell him that the kids had escaped from the back of the moving truck, his dad had ordered him to leave the bomb with the Russian and to escape himself. Not long after Greyson had jumped, he too had thrown himself off. The water had been deep enough to break his fall, but shallow enough to break his arm as he submerged. He had barely made it to the shore and caught his breath before the shockwave knocked him back into the water among downed trees.

He knew it was a miracle that he was alive. If he'd jumped a moment later, he would have hit land. And if he'd decided to stay on the truck, he would have been incinerated when nuclear device went off.

He was alive for a reason. And he knew what it was.

With a sudden rage, he flung a food tray across the room, kicked a wheeled cart into the wall, and stormed into the hallway. Nurses stopped to stare, and the other boys joined his march out of the hospital.

"I'm going to find him. And I'm going to kill him."

# Chapter 2

*The next morning*

Greyson swung as hard as he could, over and over, delivering powerful blows. The sweat flew off his forehead and he was growing tired, but he knew he couldn't stop. Now was the time when the battle was won – when his enemy grew weak and he stayed strong.

"Aaaaagghhh!" he pounded the punching bag again and again, rocking it side to side as it hung from the basement's rafters. The chain had begun chafing at the wooden beam above, sending tiny wood fragments whirling below like tiny snowflakes. Some stuck to Greyson's sweaty chest and back, but he didn't notice.

*DOOF! DOOF! DOOF! DOOF-DOOF-DOOFDOOF!*

He paid extra attention to his breathing. His last bodyguard, Kip, had said that it was crucial in any fistfight. If the fight lasted longer than the first blows, the winner was often the one with more endurance. Endurance had always been one of his strong suits.

*DOOF-DOOF-DOOFDOOF!*

Especially if something was driving him to keep going and it all depended on him. He'd die before failing.

*DOOFDOOFDOOFDOOF!*

And that's what hurt the most. He'd failed so many people even though he'd tried so hard. And it hadn't been fair. How did it all come to be on his shoulders? Why was he the one who could have stopped the State Fair attack? Why was he the one who could have stopped the bomb, who could have saved Liam?

*DOOF! DOOF!*

Why hadn't God, or Fate, chosen someone who would have succeeded?

*DOOF! DOOF!*

Why did God let so many people die?

His arms were on fire, his heart racing faster than he could land punches.

*DOOFDOOFDOOFDOOF!*

*Why did God let Mom die?*

"Aaaagghhh!"

*DOOFDOOFDOOFDOOF!*

"Greyson!"

A man's voice. Angry.

Greyson turned rapidly, his hands held up, ready to fight, but his body sagged, dripping sweat to the concrete floor. When he realized who it was, he heaved out a breathy sigh and wiped at his mess of hair. "What? I said I wanted privacy."

The man took a step forward, frowning. He towered over Greyson and had dark stubble along his chiseled jaw. Though he was dressed in a plain button-down shirt and khakis, it was clear he meant business – and not business like most think of it. He was a killer of killers. One of the FBI's most elite. And he didn't look happy.

"Screaming – when you have four men upstairs on edge, protecting you – not smart."

Greyson swiped his shirt from the floor and dabbed his face with it. "Sorry, dude." He was unstrapping his punching gloves and heading toward the shower when the man pressed his fingers against his sternum. Greyson looked up at him.

"And your punches get sloppy when you're tired," the man said. "Conserve your energy and make them count."

For a moment he relished the advice. It was good. He wanted to say, "Thank you, Agent Gavin." But he didn't. Gavin could probably train him as well as Kip had, but there was no way he was going to get close to another bodyguard only to find out either that Gavin was using him or to watch Gavin die – or both, like had happened with Kip.

Gavin arched his brow at him, as if offering himself as trainer or friend.

Greyson scoffed. "Whatever." If all went according to plan, Agent Gavin wouldn't be around much longer anyway.

He waited for the man's hand to retreat and then made his way to the shower's spout jutting out from the concrete wall behind a thin curtain. Greyson figured the FBI was running out of money just like the government was and couldn't afford to finish their safe house basements.

Even so, the basement had worked well as his little sanctuary. The Hansens had even brought down a couch to make it his own room. And everybody knew to give a boy privacy in his own room.

Greyson put his hands on his waistband and stared at Agent Gavin. "Now, if you wouldn't mind…"

Gavin turned on his heels and left up the stairs, shaking his head.

---------------------------

Sydney opened cupboard after cupboard, frustrated. "Where're the stupid glasses?"

The safe house was nice, bigger than the house she had grown up in, and it had a lot of perks. But it wasn't the home she had grown up in. That alone made her hate it.

Her mother found the glasses and poured her some orange juice. "We'll get used to it soon enough, Syd."

"You sure?"

They shared a look – her mother's eyes sparkling beneath heavy eyelids. "We don't have a choice. We will."

Sydney sipped her orange juice and sat down as her parents sipped their green tea on the bare dining table. Some days an FBI agent or two would join them for a drink, but this time they were alone. Two of their FBI guards sat together on the front porch, one was following Greyson, and the fourth was somewhere on the perimeter – which, in a suburban neighborhood, wasn't too far away either. Still, it was one of the first private moments they'd gotten in a few days. There were many things Sydney wanted to talk about, but she didn't know how to start.

It was like there was something in the air, preventing them from having an ordinary, everyday conversation. Normally they'd be discussing the day's activities – her day at school for instance. But she wouldn't be starting at her new school with her new identity for a few more days. And today's activity consisted mostly of Liam's funeral, which only her parents would be attending. That didn't make the best conversation. Other topics could include the updated body count, her memories of the terrorist attack, or…

"How's the orange juice?" her mother asked.

Sydney sipped again, as if she had forgotten. "Good. Pulpy."

Her mom attempted a smile. Another awkward moment and her dad tried. "How's Greyson, honey? Yesterday had to have been tough."

Sydney descended into thought. She couldn't cry, no matter what – not in front of her parents. And she'd cried enough – more than Greyson. *Had he even cried at all?*

"I don't know. Same I guess."

"He had a nightmare again last night," her mother said, concerned etched on her brow. "Poor thing."

"Think he needs help?" her dad asked. "I mean, professionally?"

"Just 'cuz he doesn't cry?"

"That's just part of it. Most boys refuse to cry because they're afraid. They're afraid it makes them less of a man. But they get it all wrong. Being a man is not about what you don't do – it's about what you do – whether you humble yourself and whether you take on responsibility for yourself and for others. He's not the only one to get that mixed up."

"I think they already tried talking to him about that stuff. He hated it."

"I wouldn't like it either, but he *should* talk to someone. He needs someone."

*He talks to me.* "Just saying, if you tell him that, he might run away." *Faster than his current plans...*

Her parents descended into thoughts themselves, stirring their tea with the bags. "Well," her father started, "I guess it's not up to us, anyway."

Sydney nodded. "Are they going to make him?"

He shrugged. "They could."

"Then they'll have to make me, too, right? Why not? They've made us tell the story a dozen times already, why not force us to relive it all again? What's one more time?"

A sudden memory flashed in her mind.

*She sat in a cold, metal chair in a bare room. Greyson and Jarryd were next to her and a table separated them from two suited FBI agents. One of them, Agent Feldkamp, she had met before, after the incident at Morris. She was nice, and Sydney trusted her.*

*"I know it is hard, with all you've been through," Agent Feldkamp said, leaning her elbows on the table, "but it is vitally important that we know all the details. I don't think I have to explain to you why your testimonies are essential for us in finding the truth."*

*They had been speechless, curling into themselves as if they were cold.*

*A small camera on a tripod was capturing it all – every facial movement – or the lack of them.*

*"So, I hope you understand that we must keep you safe until the investigation is complete. As far as we know, Pluribus and Emory are not aware that you are all alive. We will have to keep it that way. That means you will all need new identities. New lives."*

*They nodded, blank-faced. Sydney glanced at Greyson, but he gazed into space, as if in a daydream.*

15

*"What if we refuse?" Jarryd asked. "I mean…my parents. What if they…refuse?"*

*Agent Feldkamp glanced at her colleague. "We will discuss that with your parents. Now, before we end today, is there anything else that you haven't told us? Anything at all?"*

*Sydney stared at the camera — its retina just inside the lens seemingly focusing on her, zooming in and out. She turned to Greyson and examined him, waiting. He hadn't shared everything — almost everything, but not all. He was holding something back. Agent Feldkamp looked trustworthy, but apparently not enough so for Greyson.*

*He wouldn't tell her what Emory had whispered into his ear before loading him into the truck for what seemed to be a sure death — "Your father is in Nassau."*

Sydney's mother patted her daughter's hand. "Are you okay, dear?"

Sydney took a deep breath and suddenly smiled as if it were all perfect again. She could be good at pretending if she tried hard enough. "I'm fine."

Her mother furrowed her brow but chose not to pry further. "Where is Greyson, now?"

Part of Sydney had wanted her mother to pry. But she shook it off. "I heard the shower turn off a while ago."

Her dad took a silent prompting from his wife and started abruptly. "We've been meaning to talk to you about something, Syd."

"Okay."

"Greyson's a nice kid…"

Sydney felt a wave of embarrassment wash over her. They were going to have this talk *now*?

"…we like him a lot."

"Okay…"

"And just so you know," her mother interjected, "We weren't so sure to begin with. He's one of those bad-boy eye-candy types with no regard for authority, doing what he pleases."

"Mom!"

"And he takes his shirt off willy-nilly…"

"Mom! He's a good guy! He 'disregards authority' when it's bad. He does what he does to help other people. And he's funny, disciplined, smart, and…and…"

Her parents were giving each other a knowing look. She hated that look — like they thought she was cute. Finally, her mother elbowed her father, prompting him to continue. "Anyway, we just wanted to say that, though we have discouraged you to befriend boys in the past…we think it's good for you to be with Greyson during this time. To be close friends."

*Friends?* They were giving their approval for her to be friends with him?

"Okay. That's what we are." *Is it? Are we just friends?*

Her parents nodded at each other. "Good," her father said, relieved. "Glad we talked. Maybe you could find him now – do friend stuff."

"I bet he's in the computer room with his shirt off again," her mom said with a faint look of disapproval, leaning in toward Sydney. "You know what he's been looking at dear?"

"You – you've spied on him?"

"No – well, just over his shoulder. He was looking at the Bahamas – some tourist site."

Sydney's heart dropped in fright. "He's just dreaming, Mom," she lied, trying to keep her composure. "We've been talking about places we'd rather be."

Her mother nodded to herself, thinking. Much to Sydney's relief, she seemed satisfied with the explanation. "Oh, that makes sense, I guess. Letting him dream couldn't hurt."

"Right," her dad said with a smirk. "Sometimes I look at our old wedding photos and dream of what could have been."

Before his wife could retaliate, Sydney's dad looked at his watch and shot up from his chair. "It's about time to go!"

Sydney breathed a silent sigh of relief but realized something as she pushed in her chair. If her parents did catch on to Greyson's escape plan, and they stopped him…he'd have no choice but to stay. They'd have more time together…as friends.

*Friends.* Sure, they'd half-kissed under the missile. And then there was that almost-kiss at the Ye Ol' Mill. But both times they hadn't been in their right minds – with people trying to kill them and all. It was almost as if they had been about to die, and they'd been given one last chance at getting kissed before kissing the world good-bye.

But that didn't make them girlfriend and boyfriend. That title involved more than kissing. She wasn't exactly sure what else it needed, but they didn't have it, whatever it was. Jarryd had made a stupid joke about him being in love with her, but that's all it was. A stupid joke by a stupid boy.

So, as a just-a-friend, she was supposed to let him escape, and he was supposed to go find his dad.

They only had a few more days together.

"Dear, you sure you're okay?"

Her mom was staring at her. Sydney shook free from her thoughts and smiled her perfect 'I'm okay' smile. "Yup! Have fun at the funeral."

Her mother gave her a skeptical look.

"I mean…you know."

"I know. We'll video-call you when it's about to start. And we'll put you on mute, just like you showed us, so you don't interrupt the service if you speak."

"Thanks."

"Keep talking to him, honey. Get him to laugh." Her mother came over to her and held her arms. "He needs a friend like you."

# Chapter 3

"Where is my *frickin'* hairspray?" Jarryd asked, his chest puffing out almost as far as his lips. He was looking directly at Sammy, who was hunched over the largest of dozens of cardboard boxes around the living room. Sammy shrugged and went back to dumping the contents of the smaller boxes into a bigger box.

"Don't...ask me," Nick said, doing push-ups amidst the boxes. "I packed...all my things...already. Besides...who...would steal...hairspray?"

Jarryd swung his bangs out of his eyes. "I don't know, genius. Maybe someone who wants some?"

Nick scoffed and kept going, beads of sweat starting to drip from his brow onto his glasses. The new frames were a pain, but he had returned home from his time with the Pluribus faction to find out he was out of contact lenses; and now with the move, his mother had said they'd have to wait until they got to Texas to get more. Until then, his childhood red frames would have to do.

But maybe he would keep them. They covered the eyebrow mark the Plurbs had given him while he'd been one of them. After the two Plurbs had rescued him and Sammy from the fake cops in the SuperMart, they'd taken the boys to their headquarters – a church's basement. They'd stayed there a week, where half a dozen Plurbs had taken care of them despite the hazards that came with the bomb's aftermath. The Plurbs had explained their beliefs in a way that really made sense to Nick, but after a week, he realized that he wasn't quite ready to give up his life for the fight. They had obliged his wishes, sending both him and Sammy to a nearby FEMA refugee shelter.

In the meantime, Nick's family had nearly given him up for dead. But once he'd showed up at the shelter and explained himself, the FBI and Homeland Security had interviewed him and his parents repeatedly, as if they were suspects. It was the incessant interrogations that pushed his family over the edge, convincing them to rid themselves of FBI protection with a move to Texas.

"Thirty!" Nick collapsed to the carpet and let his limp arms rest.

"Wow! More than twenty-nine!" Jarryd mocked. "I could do thirty while clapping."

Sammy smirked, pushing his mess of curly hair back out of place. "Do it and I'll give your hairthpray back."

19

"You took my hairspray?"

His lazy eye rolled away, like it was hiding. "No. I mithpoke."

Jarryd glared at him. He'd punch Sammy's stubby face, but his parents would find out, as they always did, and he could kiss his video game privileges goodbye. Plus, they would lecture him on being nice to their new brother, because it's been oh-so-hard to be Sammy – who had lost his parents long ago and now his Grandma. And now, being adopted to another family, he supposedly deserved a little compassion. But Jarryd knew what Sammy really deserved, and it wasn't compassion.

"If I find that hairspray in one of your boxes, I'll eat your soul."

"I'm turning on the TV," Nick said abruptly, punching at the remote. He clicked through the channels.

"You can't do any puthhups, can you Bucky?" Sammy asked Jarryd, sucking at his saliva.

Jarryd scowled, and pushed his lips over his front teeth. "I don't feel like it. But what about you? You were Plurbing-out with Nick. Why aren't *you* doing pushups?"

Sammy shrugged. "They told Nick to get thtronger. They told me to never come back. We're both doing what we were told." He stuck out his tongue and went back to dumping a box full of silverware into his own box.

Jarryd sighed, still angry. "Dude, that's our silverware."

"What else will I eat with?"

Jarryd jumped up and investigated Sammy's box. "Nick! He's put our pantry in here. All the peanuts of course, but also the Cheez-Its, Oatmeal Crème Pies, and yeah...even the Spam."

"Thpam's for the war," Sammy explained.

"The war?"

"Yeah," he whispered through the saliva pooling on his lips, as if it were a secret. "The Civil one."

"There's not going to be a Civil War, you Dipwad."

Nick tapped Jarryd's leg from where he was doing sit-ups. "Don't be so sure." He gestured toward the TV and turned up the volume.

The news anchor spoke over images of jammed-pack roadways and airports with ridiculously heightened security. The anchor told of the thousands of people who had been displaced by the bomb and how several states had offered the refugees homes, including Texas. He also mentioned that others besides refugees were heading south in increasing numbers.

"Just like us," Jarryd said. Nick nodded, continuing his sit-ups. Even Sammy was watching the screen.

The anchor explained that there were many possible reasons for the migration south. Many reasons were political or religious, with citizens choosing to live in states that were battling much of the newer policies of the Foster Administration. Some cited feeling safer further away from population centers, others noted the southern economies were faring far better than their northern counterparts, but a small percentage of travelers gave a very disturbing reason – fear of secession and a coming war.

The boys gave each other a grave look and then followed Nick's glance toward the window where a U-Haul had pulled into their neighbor's house. Another 'For Sale' sign was only a few houses down. Eyeing their moving boxes, Jarryd asked the question he hadn't directly asked his parents yet. "Why are *we* moving?" He moved to the window and peered out.

Nick shrugged. "Judging by what I've heard - all of the above."

Jarryd scanned their safehouse's peaceful neighborhood. A kid rode past on a bike, and a man was tending to his gutters across the street. War seemed the last thing that could happen there. "It's kind of scary, you know? Just think of it."

Sammy and Nick both nodded, thinking. They both found it difficult to piece together the images of war they'd seen on the news with the peaceful images of their American homes. They didn't mesh.

"It's not really going to happen, is it, Nick? They won't let that happen."

The TV droned on as Nick collected his thoughts. His brother was actually scared. It was a rare moment. "Not any time soon, Jarryd."

"How soon? Like ten years?"

Nick chuckled, but Jarryd kept looking to him as if he really knew.

"I don't know! At least one or two. The Plurbs don't even have an army, and the states haven't…"

"Good! So, I still have time!"

"Time for what?"

"To make-out with a chick."

Nick rolled his eyes and quickly turned up the volume. The anchor was introducing a guest. The title at the bottom of the screen read *Corwin Greer: Pluribus Congress member*. He appeared smug with small glasses hanging on the end of his nose, a short beard, and a skinny tie accentuating his tweed suit coat.

The grey-haired anchor looked to his papers and cleared his throat. "Thank you for joining us, but I have to begin with the pressing question. "What do you have to say regarding the suggestion that Pluribus be labeled a terrorist organization by the federal government, the infamous SDN list, which of course would lead to the arrest of anyone – including yourself – who has worked for or funded the organization – including those who harbor Plurbs in their homes?"

The Pluribus Congressman smiled, paused to collect his thoughts, and then spoke calmly. "Frankly, I'm surprised it didn't happen after the Foster Administration accused Pluribus of backing the failed terrorist attack at Morris College. It doesn't surprise me then, that they would accuse us of the August attacks as well – even the sickening accusation of trying to destroy one of our own cities."

"But there is evidence –"

"Please let me finish. Of course, there is evidence when the investigation is run by the very administration that is accusing us. And what do they give us as evidence? A few amateur videos and testimony of unidentified juvenile witnesses. But you know what? There very well could be Plurbs who backed the attack."

"Really? On the record?"

"Of course. Pluribus is not just an organization. Pluribus is an idea. It can't be bound by a title. Everett Emory, though he may claim such on his internet videos – is not our leader. There are many out there who may call themselves a Plurb, but who want to *destroy* the government – like Emory. I, along with most Plurbs, despise those who would do such a thing and give us a bad name." He sighed. "Just as it would have been wrong to label all Muslims as terrorists after the attack on the twin towers, we can no more call all Plurbs terrorists for the actions of a few."

"Isn't Pluribus calling for violence when it's calling for secession? Do you remember what happened in the Civil War?"

"Secession can be achieved without war, and that's what Pluribus was created to do. This idea, of a new American Republic of the Constitution, or ARC, is a natural consequence of our current government's actions. The Pluribus declaration, just like the Declaration of Independence, states that whenever a government deprives its people of their right to life, liberty and the pursuit of happiness, it is the right of man to alter or abolish the government, and to create a new one."

"The Declaration of Independence was written shortly before the Revolutionary War...."

"Don't keep spewing the same fear that the government is spewing. Listen, if there were a war, we'd lose. The government's taken from us every type of weapon that could possibly stand a chance against their drones and tanks – and we know it. It'd be a slaughter. We're not calling for war – we're calling for a new government."

"Getting back to what you said earlier – you say Everett Emory is not your leader, but the FBI says otherwise. His videos get millions of hits..."

The Pluribus Congress member shook his head. "Emory is a soulless, lunatic arms dealer wanted by every lawful government. He tortures, recruits child soldiers, and murders for the highest bidder. While he has an attractive face and an attractive message, his tactics are despicable."

The anchor smirked. "Some of your tactics are debatable as well. While our debt is ballooning and our foreign enemies smell blood, when we seem to need unity most, why do you incite protests and boycotts?"

"On August 17th, we woke up to a different world, where people felt as if their lives could be taken from them at any instant. They were afraid. But Brother government was happy to open their arms wide. The problem is, they won't let go. The Never Again Act restricts our freedom. Pluribus wants the government to let go. We want security without sacrificing our freedoms to attain it. And that's why this southern migration is only a trickle. The government will find that if they label all Plurbs terrorists, despite their support of violence or not, that the ensuing chaos will only lead to a fire that will burn until they, too, plead for secession."

The anchor was struck speechless and an awkward moment of silence spilled over into the boys' living room. Nick had stopped doing his sit-ups, but he suddenly turned off the TV and started again.

"Uh...I don't think I understood half of that," Jarryd said. "But the half I did sounds frickin' scary. But how can that Pluribus guy lie like that? We've told 'em that the Pubes did it all! I mean come on! Every Pube I've met is a psycho!"

Nick's brow furrowed, and he shared a knowing look with Sammy. He stopped his workout to talk with Jarryd. "It's not that simple. He's right. Pluribus is...well...it's not what you think."

Jarryd sucked in air and crossed his arms. "Oh, yeah? You a Pube now? Hang with them for a week and now you're on their side?"

Scoffing, Nick tried to calm his brother. "No, it's just…the ones me and Sammy were with didn't want anything to do with what happened."

Jarryd smiled. "Ah. So, you were with the good Plurbs. That's like saying 'I was with the good Nazis'."

"No, it's not. The Nazis were Germany's *government*. And that Pluribus guy didn't even mention half of what *our* government's doing. Do you know that the Never Again Act allows the government to launch drone attacks inside the US on United States citizens if a secret council thinks it will stop an attack? They'll kill us to protect us."

Jarryd rolled his eyes. "Whatever. Keep doing your sit-ups. You'll need a lot more to catch up to Greyson."

"*What?*"

Jarryd laughed. "You heard me."

"I am not trying to…whatever."

"You're wearing a fanny pack."

Nick looked down at his fanny pack. "So? It's practical! I can keep all my—"

"You're pretending." He pointed at his fanny pack. "You're like a kid. You keep your toys in there and pretend to be Greyson."

It took a few moments for Nick to restrain himself. Despite having a similar face, his twin brother couldn't be more different. Jarryd was thicker all around, especially in the cheeks and calves, and would almost always come out on top in physical fights. But he also had a thicker skull. Verbal fights wouldn't achieve much either.

Instead, Nick drifted into thought.

He imagined himself with the Pluribus faction. The leader, Thomas, handing him a stack of books. His cot in the church's basement. The fast-food meals they brought him and Sammy. The nightly discussions. The knife, cutting hair from his brow, drawing blood.

"You're right. It's easier being a kid and pretending."

Jarryd swung his hair out of his eyes and pumped his chin. "You said I'm right. That's weird."

"But there comes a time you can't pretend anymore."

"Oh, yeah? When?"

"When we need to step up and do our part to stop tyranny."

Jarryd nodded. "Stop tyranny? Geez, dude. Remember when doing our part meant staying in school and not doing drugs?"

Nick laughed. "Yeah."

"Now I can't even do that – the staying in school part. Can't even have friends. Saw a kid coming over the other day – the FBI dolt turned him away." Jarryd gulped. He'd stopped packing, holding a stuffed ostrich in his hand.

Nick eyed his brother. He'd slipped back into his old self for a while – when things were not always a joke and they could be real with each other.

"We should just adopt Greyson, too," Jarryd said. "He'd protect us from the terrorists – I mean the *bad* ones."

"He says he already has a real family – and he's about to go find him."

Jarryd was only half-heartedly rearranging a box, distracted. He gazed at the stuffed ostrich for a moment and then turned to Nick. "Why does he got to run away? It's like he's always looking for trouble."

Smiling, Nick knew he was worried about Greyson, as they all were. "Helen Keller once said, 'Life's either a daring adventure, or nothing.' He must think the same."

Jarryd nodded thoughtfully – so thoughtfully that Nick felt like they had taken a step forward as brothers. In the span of a few minutes, his brother had been inquisitive, vulnerable, and concerned for others. His brother had matured.

And then Jarryd laughed. "Helen Keller? She was deaf and blind! *Crossing the street* was an adventure for her!"

Nick rolled his eyes with a sigh.

*Baby steps.*

# Chapter 4

Agent Gavin greeted Sydney with an uncomfortable stare outside her room. The new house wasn't that large, but this was the last place she had looked for Greyson – the second-floor landing with her bedroom, her parents' bedroom, and a bathroom. Why Greyson would be up here was beyond her.

"Hey. Greyson in my room?"

Agent Gavin nodded without a hint of a smile, standing still as a soldier in front of her closed door. He was serious about his job, but not about her privacy. She took the last step to the landing slowly, waiting for Agent Gavin to move.

"Can I get in, please?"

"Stay clear of the windows."

"Sure."

He opened the door for her and closed it behind. And there was Greyson, sitting in the window's nook, holding a pillow. His red hat was tipped upwards as if he had been laying his head down on the pillow. Creases had formed on his cheek and temple, but he smiled at her. Perhaps it was his best 'I'm okay' smile.

"Agent Gavin said to stay away from the windows," Sydney whispered.

"Agent *Murray* said to stay away from the Security Building."

Sydney sighed, remembering Secret Service Agent Murray's sincere face as he lied to them, telling them that there was nothing going on at the State Fair. It turned out he was a Plurb and a traitor. Kip had been his mentor, yet had brought him as bait to the fair. And then there had been Everett Emory pretending to be his dad. No wonder Greyson didn't trust anyone.

"You okay?" She sat down on her own bed, suddenly glad she had decided to make her bed this morning, and then even more suddenly afraid that she was alone in her room with a boy. Her nighttime clothes had been put away – thankfully.

"Yeah," he said, still clutching a pink pillow – her pillow. "You?"

"I'm alright."

"Really?" he asked with piercing eyes, examining her face.

The question caught her off guard. Sydney didn't know how to respond, taking in a deep breath.

"You sure you're okay?" he asked again.

He was asking for real, like he really cared. Could she tell him how she really felt? Should she dump her entire emotional anguish on him? He couldn't really want that, could he? No. She was supposed to be comforting *him*. Besides, she hadn't really lost anything except a home and some friends. He was the one who lost his mom. "No, really, I'm fine," she lied.

For a moment, they stared into space or searched the room for something interesting to look at. Greyson eventually found his shoes and chose to examine them. Sydney's eyes had landed on her nightstand, where a picture of Greyson had been framed where she could see it each night. She casually got up and set it facedown.

"Why are you up here?" she asked as nicely as she could.

A glimmer of amusement nipped near his eyes, and he glanced out the window. Pulling a notebook from underneath the pillow, he wrote something down and hid it again. "Timing the guard dressed as a gardener outside. Makes a round every ten minutes. Takes him anywhere from ninety seconds to a hundred and ten to make it around."

"Gotcha."

He was planning his escape. Always. He was always thinking of it, bouncing ideas off of her and obsessing on the details. She hated it, but it was the only thing that animated him. If she crushed it, she was afraid he'd think there was nothing else to keep him going.

*Get him to laugh.*

"Hey. Forget about the plan for a sec. Let's do something normal kids do."

Greyson's stare was blank. "What?"

"You know. Something fun."

"They won't let us leave."

"We can do something fun in here." As soon as she heard herself, she wanted to take back the words. "Or, somewhere else in the house."

"Like what?"

They'd forgotten how to be normal. "Umm…" She looked around her room and found what she was looking for. "There!" She raced to a box she had yet to unpack and came out with a hunky, black device.

"What's that?" Greyson asked.

27

"It's an old Polaroid camera my mother had when she was a kid. She gave it to me."

"Polaroid?"

"It prints the picture as soon as you take it. They don't make them anymore, I don't think."

"Okay…"

"Let's take a selfie!"

He made a face. "No, thanks."

She pumped her eyebrows at him. "I dare you."

"Oh, come on. That's not fair."

"Why not?"

"You can't just dare me to do anything you want."

"Why not?"

"Because I'm not your slave. And dares are for hard things."

Sighing and hanging her arms loose, she walked to the nook and sat next to him. "Isn't it hard for you to smile? I know it is for me."

Greyson avoided eye contact, plucking at the fringes of one of her pink pillows. "I guess."

"Then I dare you to smile."

He bobbed backward with a contemplative sigh.

"Don't make me tickle you."

He stiffened and fought back a smile. "Fine. Then we get back to the plan."

She shrugged. "If it's a good one."

They shook on it, and she held the camera up in the air, clumsily pointing the lens at Greyson. She scooted closer to him. She felt his bicep against her side, and the smile came a little more naturally.

"Three…two…one…"

He poked her ribcage just as she snapped the picture. In an instant she retaliated with a barrage of pink pillows and pokes of her own. He fought back, landing pillow punches to her face, but she heard laughs escape from his mouth. She laughed, too, tackling him on to the nook and pressing her fingernails into his sides.

The door creaked open and Agent Gavin stood dumbfounded. The kids stopped mid-wrestle, and Greyson peeked out from under Sydney's body. "Privacy – geez!"

Agent Gavin raised his brow, glanced around the room, and slowly closed the door.

Sydney held herself up, hovering over Greyson with the hair from her ponytail falling around her face. They stared at each other for a moment, but the awkwardness soon won out.

"Let's see the picture."

"Good idea."

They sat up and straightened their clothes. Sydney grabbed the picture from the camera's printer and shook it. "Hey! It's great! Well, you look good. Just ignore the half with the ugly girl on it."

She showed Greyson and then acted as if she was doing something else. But out of the corner of her eye she saw him his gaze linger at the picture with a smile pricking at his lips. Sure, she'd been fishing for compliments, but would he take the bait? Nope. Just when it seemed like he wanted to say something, something else seemed to pain him, and he dropped his hands. "Can we get back to the plan now?"

She tried to hide the disappointment. "Fine. I guess it's better than this other one." She walked to her dresser and slid the Polaroid into a silver frame, covering the picture of her and her old friend, Melinda, who she'd probably never see again.

"What have you got so far?" Greyson asked.

Taking one last look at the Polaroid, she spun around and reached into her pocket. "These." She held out a handful of ball-bearings.

"Whoa! Nice," Greyson exclaimed, happy to see more slingshot ammo. He was especially grateful since they weren't allowed to go to the store. "Where'd you get 'em?"

Sydney hesitated for a moment. The plan was distracting him. She had to keep it up for his sake. "The skateboard wheels and a yo-yo," she said, walking toward her closet. "Just where that site said we could find them. Apparently, my childhood toys are still worth something." She didn't want to mention that she had still liked the skateboard – and the yo-yo. It was tough being a single child.

"Good work. You're the best."

*The best?*

Sydney tried to not smile too big, but her heart was suddenly set racing. If her mom had said that, she'd have groaned. But when Greyson said it, she felt warm and giddy. "By the way, you've *got* to be more careful on the computer. Mom saw you looking at the Bahamas. Did you delete the history at least?"

Greyson shook his head, dismayed at his lack of foresight. "Yeah. But I should've been more careful."

"You never know how much she might snoop."

"Do they…"

"No," she answered before he could ask. "For now, they just think you're dreaming of possibilities or whatever."

He nodded. "At least she hadn't been looking when I was researching how to make homemade bombs using household cleaners."

Sydney shook her head, debating whether to argue with him about the stupidity, uselessness, and danger of making bombs. Instead, she just took a more general tact. "You know this is crazy, right?" she blurted as she swung a heavy backpack out of her closet and hid it behind her bed, just in case Agent Gavin snuck a peek inside. "We have my parents and the FBI here to protect us. Why leave? They could help."

"Syd…" he sighed, disappointed. "We've been over this."

"So?"

"The FBI won't let me go – and if I ask for help – who knows if there's another mole? The less attention I bring, the better. And your parents…what would they be able to do? About as much as my mom could do when she was trying to help. I can't waste another year or another day. Who knows how long he'll be there? I have to go."

She shook her head, failing to find some way to convince him to stay. "Fine. Look what else I've got."

He nodded and left the nook for her bed. Crawling over the side, he plopped stomach-first on the bed and peeked into the bag.

Trying to ignore the fact that he was now lying on her bed, Sydney unzipped it and showed him what she had collected during the last few days.

"First of all – you've got tons of cash. Thank my parents later. Your mom's research papers. Box of granola bars, beef jerky, a blanket, a raincoat. Um…some Skittles, all your clothes."

"Don't look too closely at those."

Sydney chuckled. The last thing he probably wanted was a girl examining his boxer briefs for size and stains.

"Don't worry. Nothing's worse than my dad's whitey tighties. You only had one pair of mesh shorts, so I also threw in one of mine."

"I'm not wearing girl clothes."

"Really? Come on."

"Girl shorts are just....short...you know?"

Sydney smiled. "True. But don't you fear – my parents don't let me get the super short kind, even for dance. These are my basketball shorts. You could try them on."

"Nope. Not happening. If they happen to be too big on me, you would think you're fat. If they happen to be too small on me, you'd get an eyeful of my buns."

"Your *buns?*"

Trying to hide his red face, Greyson began rummaging through the bag as a diversion. "That's what my mom used to...never mind. What else you got?"

Sydney shrugged, also trying to shake off the images in her head. His cute, embarrassed smile didn't help.

"Creamed corn? Really?" he asked, grabbing a can from the bag. "That's like a cat ate a corn cob and vomited it out."

"That's why my parents won't miss it."

"And it's heavy."

"So? Too hard to carry on and off the bus, huh?"

Greyson shrugged. "I think I'll be eating enough fast food that I won't need to eat cat vomit."

"It's good for you."

"Healthy stuff is usually gross."

"No, it's not. Not always."

"Yeah? Give me an example," Greyson demanded.

"Granola bars."

"If they're coated in chocolate."

"Strawberries."

"Coated in chocolate."

"Milk."

"Chocolate milk."

Sydney growled in frustration. "Ugh...you..."

"*I'm* good for you?"

Sydney nearly choked, trying to hold in her laughter and embarrassment.

Greyson laughed, too, thankful for the levity. "I think I proved my point."

Sydney shook her head, surrendering, and they locked eyes for a moment – but the look lasted a bit too long. Breaking it off, Greyson pushed the creamed corn back into the bag, snatched the jerky, and pushed himself off the bed.

"Got to keep this handy," he said, putting the jerky in his pack. It was now nearly full of food and the homemade device he'd need if he were ever chased again.

He also swiped the ball-bearings and dropped them in their own side pouch. "These, too."

Sydney sighed. "Let's hope you don't have to use those."

# Chapter 5

"I've seen enough." Greyson retreated to the nook and re-clutched the same pillow. Why should he be forced to rub more guilt in his face by watching Liam's entire funeral? He'd already watched hours of endless TV coverage, listened to visiting pastors pray, and suffered through counselors telling him how to grieve. And when thousands had gathered at the edge of the radiation zone by the Des Moines River to light floating candles, he'd been miles upstream adding one for his mom and one for Liam in his own private vigil.

He'd had enough.

Sydney didn't push him. "That's fine. I'll keep it on over here if you change your mind." She sat cross-legged on her bed with the laptop on another pillow.

Once her parents had video-called from the back of the church and put them on mute, they'd been able to see and hear the funeral's opening minutes without worrying about disrupting the service – and without being seen. Just to make sure, Sydney readjusted the piece of tape the FBI had placed over their laptop's webcam long ago.

Judging by the video, the church was full and Sydney's parents were awful with technology. The camera was jumping up and down or wandering toward the ceiling when Sydney's mother forgot about it. Every now and then she pressed a wrong button and switched from her phone's front camera to the back so that they'd be looking at her black dress rather than the funeral. Still, it was better than nothing.

Greyson's phone buzzed in his pack, and he fished it out. It was Nick.

"The call's been cleared," came Agent Gavin's voice.

Greyson glanced up to see Agent Gavin looking at him from a crack in the door to Sydney's room. He didn't know how it worked, but somehow the FBI could intercept any calls going in and out. Perhaps they were even monitoring them. Security was important. Privacy was not.

"Thanks."

Agent Gavin closed the door and Greyson answered the call. Nick's face appeared, and he knew Nick could see his. Suddenly he was self-conscious. Could Nick see something in his eyes? Would he see how he fought back the tears?

*"Hey, man. How you holding up?"* Nick asked.

"Fine. You?"

*"Good."*

"Good."

*"Got the funeral on?"*

"Yeah. Wanna watch?"

*"Yeah. I got Jarryd and Sammy here, too."*

"Cool. I'll hand you off to Sydney. Just a sec."

When Greyson held the phone out to her, she couldn't help but to shake her head in amusement.

"What?" Greyson asked. "What did I do?"

"Boys," she said, grabbing the phone. "You act like you're watching a football game. Hey, Nick."

Greyson watched as Sydney held the phone up to the computer so that Nick could see what her parents were seeing. For a moment Greyson was lost in thought, amazed at the situation. He had to wonder, had someone ever watched a funeral that was being transferred from phone to computer to phone? If not, they were making history.

But then his mind darted back to reality and he averted his eyes out the window. Half of him wanted to think about Liam, to remember him, to memorialize him, but the other half had to fight against it. He didn't *want* to remember. Every time he did was like a stab to his heart. Liam's eyes would stare at him through the water, disappointed, afraid, and accusing. But if he didn't remember, if he fought back the memories by distracting himself, he could forget – at least for a little while.

"Greyson?"

He shot a look at Sydney, startled.

She was watching him from the edge of her bed. She had propped the phone against a pillow, allowing the twins to watch the laptop. "It's okay to cry, you know? Boys can cry, too. It's manly."

*Manly? To cry?* "No, it's not. Then chicks would be more manly than men. And that'd be weird."

Sydney smiled and moved to sit by him in the nook. He scooted over and hoped the moisture in his eyes would not overflow to his cheeks. Even if she thought it was manly.

"So, what's a man then? Someone who doesn't cry?"

"I don't know. I guess."

"You don't know?"

"I mean, of course I do. Duh. It's just…"

"Dad says manliness isn't just about *not* being a girl. It's about *being* something. Not *not* being something, you know?"

Greyson made a face and shrugged. He knew what she meant, but he couldn't give her an impression that she knew more about being a man than he did.

When he didn't respond, she went on. "Stuff like being responsible and humble and strong."

"Okay, okay. I know that already. And I'm fine. Just tired."

"Come on. Why are you lying? You're not fine, and that's okay. That's what's great about you – you love people so much, you're willing to do anything for them! You loved Liam and still do. Who wouldn't cry after losing someone they love?"

Greyson's lip was quivering again. He had to fight it. And anger always worked. He wanted to yell but held that back as well. He couldn't take it out on her. "If I cry, I'd have to cry for 8,000 people, not just Liam. Eight thousand! I'd never stop crying – and that's definitely not manly."

Sydney stifled a laugh. "True. You'd eventually have to stop blubbering."

Greyson smiled. "I wouldn't get anything done."

"But that doesn't mean you can't start, or cry just a little bit. You know? Just, like, wail for an hour straight and get it all over with. It can't be good to hold it all in."

After taking a deep breath and examining the compassionate sparkle in Sydney's eyes, Greyson turned. "You can cry *for* me, okay?"

"I already have."

He paused, not knowing how to respond. Choosing to ignore it, he looked out the window again. "Crying doesn't make anything better. I have to *do* something. I have to make their lives mean something. I have to make their…*deaths* mean something."

A sudden gasp coming from the bed startled them both. *"Greyson! Did…are you seeing this?"*

Hearing the urgency in Nick's voice, Greyson threw the pillow down and ran to the laptop. "What?"

*"Look! Do you see him?"*

35

Greyson looked from Nick's frightened face on the phone to the laptop's shaking image of a bunch of shifting heads and backs. People were milling about, but besides that, he couldn't see anything or anyone in particular.

*"Tell your parents to keep it steady…and to…"*

"We can't," Sydney declared. "Until they unmute us."

"What is it, Nick? Who'd you see?"

Jarryd's face popped on the screen. *"It was Orion!"*

Greyson and Sydney dropped the phone on the bed and peered at the laptop. Her parents were now walking down the aisle. They could see the backs of several heads – some with long hair, others with short hair or even bald – but none were recognizable. Not until one of them turned.

"Is it?" Sydney asked, pointing at the screen.

*"Guys?"* Nick started from the phone below. *"This isn't a pleasant view."*

Greyson looked down where the phone was pointed up toward his and Sydney's nostrils. "Sorry."

When he brought the phone up again, they all gasped in astonishment. It was *him*.

"Orion." Somehow, he was alive. *How?* "We have to warn them," Greyson said. He'd seen what Orion could do. He'd taken his punches. He'd seen him kill Kip in cold blood. Greyson hated his guts.

"How?" Sydney asked. "My parents can't hear us or see us."

"Then get their attention. Take off the tape."

Sydney pulled it off and the two of them waved at the webcam, hoping their mother would notice.

*"Wait,"* Nick warned from the phone's screen. *"I bet he's fishing right now."*

*"Fishing?"* Jarryd said. *"In a church?"*

*"For clues, moron. He was seeing if we'd show up."*

Sydney nodded. "That's why the FBI wouldn't let us go."

*"Right. Pluribus thought you guys were dead. But now…maybe they're not so sure."*

Looking at the laptop, they could see Sydney's parents make their way down the steps to where Liam's coffin was being loaded into the long, black hearse. A small crowd gathered with them on the steps. They scoured the crowd for Orion's face, but he had disappeared.

Greyson stood up suddenly, still gripping the phone. He stared at Nick. "We have to go get him."

*"Don't be stupid. Tell the FBI to go get him. They'll be a hundred times faster."*

Greyson watched Sydney's door for any movement or shadows of someone listening. They had experimented with phone calls before, to test if the FBI could listen in, but he still wasn't sure. He'd have to be careful.

"I don't trust them."

*What harm will it do? If the FBI wanted to, they could have killed you already.*

"Only a few of them know where we are. But if I tell Agent Gavin about Orion, he'd have to tell someone else. Emory said he had men in the FBI. If a bad one finds out about us…"

*We have to do something.*

Greyson sighed. "Fine. Call the Shepherd line or whatever they call it – so it's anon…anoma…so they don't know who's calling." He turned the laptop toward him and eyed the crowd again. "But if Orion's snooping around, he already thinks I'm alive. And now the FBI will clamp down on us again. I better get started."

*Now?* Nick knew Greyson was referring to his escape.

"Yeah."

Nick and Jarryd's face were sullen, crammed together on the other side of the little screen. Even Sammy was looking over their shoulders, his lazy eye just as dismayed as the other one. *This stinks,* Jarryd whined. *Why can't we all…together, you know?*

"You have parents," Greyson said matter-of-factly.

The boys nodded, a sudden and tense silence covering them. Suddenly the moment was too emotional.

"I like your glasses, Nick."

Nick smiled, a little embarrassed. *Thanks.*

An awkward silence.

"Well, goodbye."

*Bye, dude.*

"I'll talk to you in a few days, I hope. Call them right away!"

They faked smiles again. *Will do. Bye.*

Sydney leaned toward the phone. "Bye guys!"

Greyson ended the call and hung his head for just a few beats before the urgency returned. Turning toward the laptop, he was about to close it – but he froze in fear. Sydney's mom had pressed the wrong button again and the laptop's screen was filled with her black dress – and the boy lurking behind her shoulder. Greyson locked eyes with him across the great distance of cyberspace, but the hatred burned just as hot. Orion smiled with surprise just before he darted away.

*He saw me. He knows I'm alive.*

Greyson gulped down the welling emotions and slapped the laptop closed, staring at Sydney. "It's time. Right now."

# Chapter 6

The campaign office seemed busy, but Sam's dad said it would be twice as busy in January – when Iowa had the nation's first caucus of the year to start deciding their party's nominee for President. Since President Foster had already served his two-term limit, their party needed to elect someone new. There were half a dozen others fighting with Governor Reckhemmer for the nomination, but the field would narrow and narrow until there was only one to run against whomever the other parties chose as their nominees.

Until then, the campaign office in Iowa City would be furiously calling, fundraising, creating yard signs, and a hundred other tasks that, to some, were the most important things to do in the world. To Sam, something told him his dad would be the nominee no matter what. How could the nation reject the exact person it needed?

Sam watched out the large office window into the main room where lines of volunteers cold-called citizens from tables filled with phones. Others rushed around without looking at the campaign slogans draped on the walls, the statistics written on wall-sized marker boards, or the map of Iowa that detailed their strategy almost street by street. It was rather intense – almost like a miniature war. And soon, with primary season coming up, it would be fought from state to state until his dad would be officially appointed the party's nominee next August.

But it's not like that would make things normal again. Sam dropped his head to the homework on the table. He didn't really have a home for the next year or so, they'd be traveling so much; so maybe he shouldn't call it homework – maybe it was just 'work.'

He'd scrawled in a few answers he knew off the top of his head, but he hadn't worked up the ambition to open the textbook yet. His tutor would be upset; he'd be upset with him no matter what. No amount of effort was enough.

*Buuuuzzzzz. Buuuuzzzzz.*

The phone vibrated in his pocket and he welcomed the distraction. Flinging the homework to the side, he glanced at the caller ID and ran to his laptop. After connecting a cable to the phone and a few clicks, he answered.

"Hello?"

"This is Greyson."

Sam paused. He had expected Sydney's voice. "Hi."

"Hi. We need to talk. Privately if possible."

"Um…" Sam peeked out the window and typed in a few more commands on the computer. "The line's secure, both ways. Is Sydney there?"

Greyson paused. "She's here. Look. I need to go right now."

"But I thought you said you'd be going —"

"I know. But Orion was snooping at Liam's funeral and…he saw me."

"Orion? Did you report it?" He was already typing in the search on the Shepherd Database.

"Yeah."

"Okay. Yeah, I see it. Nick and Jarryd call it in?"

"Yeah – wait. Wait. I thought the line was supposed to be anon…anomy…private or whatever."

"Right. It's withheld from normal citizens. But…nothing's really anonymous anymore." He took pride in pronouncing anonymous correctly when Greyson couldn't.

"Okay. But anyway, today. I need to go."

"Alright. How soon?"

"As soon as possible. An hour? Less?"

"Wow. Okay."

"Sorry," Greyson said.

In the background, Sam could hear Greyson and Sydney whispering.

"Just a sec." Sam typed furiously and continued glancing toward the window. He could hear his father in the adjacent office, still in a meeting. If he heard their chairs being pushed in, he would know his father would check in on him soon.

After another minute of frantic computer work, he was nearly done. "The taxi will be in the block behind your house in an hour. Have him take you to the bus station. I'll have your ticket at the Will Call window. Your name is Nolan Willis. Thought you might want to keep the first name."

"Not really."

"No, it's better so you don't slip up. Now, you're going to have refugee status. That allows you to travel as an unaccompanied minor without an ID. The password is Blue Ribbon."

There was a pause and a scoff. "Got it."

Sam heard chairs squeaking in the adjacent room and men's loud voices. He had to hurry.

"Remember – don't show your face. Cameras will pick it up, anywhere. Facial recognition software is –"

"Yup."

" – and only use cash. Don't use a phone – don't even bring it. It can be tracked. They probably have your voice recorded somewhere, so maybe just avoid all calls. Anyway, now that Pluribus knows you're alive, the government won't be afraid to tell everyone you're missing. You might have to adapt. It will make it even harder to stay hidden."

The government, Pluribus, and the nation will be looking for him. *Harder* was putting it lightly.

"I'll manage."

"The bus will get you to Florida. You can't fly, remember. Security is too tight. You'll have to use the money to hire a private ship. Or something. That part's on you for now. I'll keep thinking."

"Got it."

The door to the other office opened and suited men and women poured into the main room.

"Gotta go." He watched his dad say goodbye to the entourage of adults. There was silence from the other side of the phone.

"Thank you," Greyson whispered finally. "For your help."

"Of course. You helped me escape once."

By pushing him out of a moving vehicle – but it still counted.

"Yeah."

"Oh, and one more thing. Tell Sydney that security will probably be increased at the house – or they'll move her again."

"Okay. Hopefully they don't know she's alive. And they'll be too busy looking for me."

For a moment, both boys were nodding their heads in agreement. For all their past disagreements, they had always had one thing in common – an affection for Sydney.

Sam's dad greeted the tutor at the front door. In a second they'd be making their way straight to him. "Got to go." In a flash, Sam hung up, pulled the cable, and closed the laptop. When the tutor and the Governor walked in, Sam was busy scribbling an answer on his worksheet.

Greyson hung up the phone and returned it to Sydney. "We have an hour."

"An hour?"

"Yeah. I think I'll need sunglasses to cover my face. And something with a hood."

Sydney shot to her closet, searched for a bit, and came out empty handed. "I have a hooded sweatshirt, but it's downstairs in the coat closet. And my dad's sunglasses are above the keys."

Greyson nodded to himself, thinking through the plan. A sudden wave of fear prickled his skin, but it passed quickly. There was no use being afraid. It would only tempt him to change his mind. In a few days, he would be in the sunny warmth of the Bahamas with his dad. Fear wouldn't stand in his way.

"Do you need me," Sydney began coyly, "to get the transponder out?"

Transponder was the word Agent Feldkamp had used to refer to the GPS tracker the FBI implanted in his shoulder. At least this time they had told him they were tracking him – to keep him safe, of course.

"No, I got it. Used a mirror."

"You check for other ones?" she asked awkwardly. "You know? In case the first was like a diversion or something."

Greyson rolled his eyes. "Yes, of course. Like a hundred times."

"That's a lot of checking."

He smiled. "They're really small."

"Did you find any?"

Greyson shook his head, pointing to his fanny pack. "Just the one. I'll ditch it as soon as I get out. Put it in someone's car or something to throw them off. But anyway – you go first, then later bring the bag down the back stairs when no one's looking. I'll do my workout routine, so he'll give us privacy."

"Got it. Then we sneak out the basement window right after the guard makes his rounds."

Greyson's shoulders slumped and he blinked an extra time or two to illustrate his disapproval. "*We?* We've talked about this."

"Yeah, but things have changed. The Plurbs will be looking for all of us now. Orion saw my parents."

"So? They didn't see you. They saw me. Plus, Sam will help to increase the security here. You'll be safer here than out there with me."

"But –"

"Fifty-five minutes. We don't have time to argue," he averted his eyes to her dresser. "Plus, we couldn't carry all your clothes and make-up and shoes."

It was Sydney's turn to show her disapproval. "Meet you in the basement in twenty minutes."

He glanced at his watch. "Sounds good."

She left, leaving the door open long enough for Agent Gavin to see Greyson still inside, staring at the Polaroid picture in the silver frame.

Thinking there was something about Sydney's smile that was especially attractive, he suddenly had second thoughts about leaving her behind.

-------------------------

*"Dad?"*

"Yes, son?"

*"He's alive."*

"He?"

*"Greyson. I saw him. Not at the funeral, but on a video call."*

"Whose video call?"

*"Parents of the girl."*

"Did you follow them?"

*"I am now."*

"Good."

*"What do I do? If he's there."*

Emory thought for a moment. "Take him. We can use him."

*"Take him? But..."*

"I can send the Fisherman."

*"No. I'll handle it."*

"With a team. Call Bartlett. He'll follow your orders. Tell no one else."

*"Got it."*

"I trust you'll get it done."

*"I will."*

"Good."

Everett Oliver Emory tapped his smartwatch, hanging up the call as he smiled to himself. The boy *was* alive. And as they suspected, he was one of the witnesses the government was hiding.

Emory put his ever-disguised face in his hands and thought. The fact that a few extra children had survived presented complications. Yes, they were witnesses, placing Emory as the man behind the bombings, but he didn't care about that. They would only tell the world what they already wanted to think – the Plurbs had nuked Des Moines. They hadn't witnessed anything else beyond that. They didn't know what he had originally planned to do with Sam, or his connection with StoneWater, or who was really behind everything. Besides, the government and the media already had their narrative, and they would keep telling it. The child witnesses would only reinforce it.

The problem was, with Greyson alive, the government had a witness who may know something no one else did. Greyson may know where the next attack would happen.

Emory remembered whispering in the boy's ear. "Your dad's in Nassau."

But perhaps Greyson didn't know the significance of what he knew.

Perhaps he actually thought Nassau was where he would live happily ever after with his father. He was just a child after all, with lofty dreams and a wild imagination. A child wouldn't have caught an adult's macabre sense of humor and irony.

And finally, Emory wasn't the only one who wanted the boy. There were others. The others were powerful and deceptive, two things Emory prided himself on being. But Emory's desires and the others' desires didn't always align. They were *too* powerful, *too* deceptive. They would have to learn that Emory could only be outpowered, outdeceived for so long.

So, if the boy could be captured, he could be useful. But if not, Emory would rather he not fall into the others' hands. He would have to fall into no one's hands. He would have to die.

Either way, nothing could get in the way of this attack. He'd put a lot of effort into training Orion, and Orion was one of the few people he could trust were not loyal to the others. He'd do Emory's bidding and tell no else. So, he'd give him his shot. But if he failed, the Fisherman wouldn't fail.

# Chapter 7

*DOOF-DOOF-DOOFDOOF!*

"Good," Greyson praised quietly. "Just like that. Make it noisy. He has to believe it's me." Agent Gavin was just up a flight of stairs, giving Greyson the privacy he desired in the basement during his familiar routine.

Sydney smiled, but had to shake out her knuckles. The punching bag was more solid than it had looked when Greyson was punching it.

While Sydney fought the bag, Greyson put her hoodie over his shirt. "Fits well."

"That's wonderful," she huffed.

"See? You're offended."

"Not at all." Sydney hit the bag again a few more times, a little more gingerly.

Greyson tried on the sunglasses and smiled at Sydney. "How they look? Like I got swag?"

Sydney smacked the bag. "Swag? Sure. Greyson, we have to talk."

"I won't use that word again."

Sydney laughed briefly, and then stopped herself for fear of being too loud. "No, it's not that."

Glancing at his watch, he went to the basement's window, which was head level and just big enough to crawl through to the back yard. In a minute or two, the FBI agent would be making his way around the perimeter. As soon as he passed, Greyson would be free to go. "Ok. What's up?"

"You're happy, aren't you?"

Greyson felt his smile pushing at his cheeks and pulled off his sunglasses. *She's right. I am. Why?*

Greyson shrugged, which was difficult with the backpack weighing his shoulders down. "I guess so."

Sydney punched again. "Because you're leaving."

Dropping his eyes to the concrete floor, he thought. He *was* happy. Happier than he'd felt since he was at the fair before the attack. *Why?* Because he had hope, and finally, after weeks of waiting, he was able to pursue it. His daring side had been trapped, and now it was about to be released.

"Yeah. But I'm sad, too. Leaving you guys."

*DOOFDOOFDOOF!*

Sydney's knuckles were red. "I want to go with you."

He shook his head and took another glance at the window. "But you'd leave your parents."

"But you're leaving me."

Greyson's smile faded into an embarrassed smirk. His cheeks flushed with heat. He didn't know what to say to that. Maybe if he'd watched more movies he'd know exactly what to say – or if he'd learned more from Jarryd – but he hadn't. He was just standing there, stupid, letting the bag swing between them as a barrier. Suddenly sensing the silence, he vented his embarrassment into the bag.

"My turn." *DOOFDOOFDOOFDOOFDOOF!*

"I want to go with you," Sydney pleaded over his punching. "I won't have any friends here when the twins leave. Plus, it's our *thing*. We can be daring – find your dad, and then come back, and be happy."

"It *was* our thing…" Already regretting saying it, he averted his eyes to the window, hoping to see the man's legs pass by outside. None came.

Sydney frowned and took over the punching. *DOOFDOOFDOOF. Doof. Doof.* She began breathing more heavily, both from the exertion and the impatience. "You blame me, don't you?"

Both of them let the bag swing, creaking against the rafters. More sawdust sprinkled into their hair from above.

*Do I? Blame her? Maybe. If she hadn't fallen off the moving truck, I would have stopped the bomb. But either way, I can never tell her.*

"No. Duh!" he whispered briskly.

She blew at a piece of her hair that had fallen over her face. Greyson thought back to the time he had pulled that same strand back over her ear before going into Cattlemen's Steakhouse.

*DOOF!* He added another punch into the mix. "Why would I blame you? You didn't do anything wrong."

She hadn't. But was it still her fault? *DOOFDOOF!*

He suddenly remembered pounding her chest as she lay dead in front of him. He had screamed at her: *"I'll dance with you, whenever you want! Wherever you want! I promise. I'll never leave you out of anything. I'll never…leave you behind."*

Greyson gulped down a lump in his throat and looked guiltily at Sydney. Had she heard him make that promise to her? "I – I…I'm sorry," he said solemnly. And he meant it. He didn't want to leave her. It was the last thing he wanted to do. After losing so much, it hurt to lose anything else at all – especially her. "I have to do this…alone."

A sudden urge to comfort her, to make things right, made his foot take a step toward her, to the side of the bag. She eyed him cautiously, taking a few more half-hearted punches to the bag and blowing again at the strand of blonde hair. A faint glow of sweat had formed around her hairline and at her temples. There was something about that glow that made him want to put his fingers on her face and stroke her cheek.

Sydney's eyes examined him. "You okay?"

He took another step toward her. *That's it,* Jarryd would say. *You can do it, bro. Chicks are nuts for confidence.*

But he wasn't that confident.

He could see her gulp a lump in her throat as well. She was dressed in short-sleeved athletic clothes, not good for a long trip, but good for running or fighting – two things that she was considering.

"Greyson?"

"Is it okay if I…if we…"

They were close now. Sydney's eyes bounced around, and Greyson suddenly found the confidence he hadn't had in this way before. Certainty strengthened his gaze, but his hands still shook as he raised them to her.

Just before his fingers found her arm, a shadow shifted over them and Greyson and Sydney's eyes snapped to window. Something had passed by the window. It was time.

They looked back to each other, and Greyson took a small step back. For a moment, they could only look past each other.

"Can I…hug you?"

Sydney peered at his vivid, green eyes, which were usually topped with intense, pensive brows, but were now wide open, shining with a shy desire. She couldn't help but smile. "Sure."

He smiled back and they embraced. Sydney buried her face into Greyson's hood, and he let her golden ponytail fall against his cheek. The hug felt comforting and real to them both.

"You didn't need to ask," she said, already dreading when the hug would end. "Friends can hug whenever."

Sydney instantly regretted the word. *Friends?*

Greyson let go first, eyes averted to the window. He glanced back at her, smiling. "Thanks. But I got to go."

47

He scuttled to the shower, turned on the water, and returned to the window. Agent Gavin would definitely not come down to check on them now.

He turned to the window and stood on his tiptoes to check for the agent dressed as a gardener. He was gone. Then, turning the lock and pushing outward, he opened the window to its fullest. Judging the opening's limited size, he took off his backpack. "Alright. I'll need a boost."

Sydney rushed to him and suddenly understood the hug. It had been a ruse, to convince her to let him go by himself. It was his goodbye.

"Is this goodbye?"

"Quick," he whispered, in a rush.

She held out her interlaced fingers, and he put his left foot in the cradle, pushing off and guiding himself through the windowsill without a word. Squirming though, he crawled onto the grass. It was only after he turned around to look down at Sydney that he responded.

"Now's our goodbye." His head poked from the window at Sydney's head level. He was smiling, waiting for her response. She grabbed his backpack and dragged it to her feet.

She pouted. "Goodbye?"

Greyson smirked for a few seconds, debating with himself. *Do it. You'll regret it if you don't. I dare you.* A cold chill made him shake and his voice waver. "Can friends…kiss whenever they want to as well?"

Sydney smiled, too, and took a timid step toward him, leaning her face upward to meet his.

Footsteps interrupted their goodbye. Coming from the ground floor, there were two sets. And then voices. It was Sydney's parents, returning from the funeral. They'd be looking for them at any moment.

"The backpack, quick!"

Snapping to action, Sydney slammed the backpack into the windowsill, but it was too big. The bloated bag wouldn't push through.

"It's too big!" she whispered franticly. "I have to take stuff out."

"Hurry!"

She pulled the bag back down and yanked at the zippers. Out came the blanket, the flashlight, and her mesh shorts. When she pushed it back to the windowsill, Greyson pulled from the other side.

"Push!"

"I am!"

The footsteps were loud above, and they were calling her name. It wouldn't be long. He had to go, now!

Sydney jumped and pushed the bag until it popped free. Greyson went tumbling with it into the backyard, out of view.

A quiet rushed in as her panic washed away, the only sound being that of the shower splashing on the concrete and dripping into the drain.

Sydney stood, breathing heavily, staring at the empty windowsill where the sun's rays glowed in a golden-white square. It took a moment for it to sink in. At first, she expected him to come back, to beg for a kiss, or to at least say goodbye, but there was nothing but the sun.

He wasn't coming back.

# Chapter 8

When Sydney's parents pulled into a driveway, Orion quickly took a right turn. He'd been following them for almost an hour, and as far as he knew, the FBI driver hadn't noticed him. Tailing someone wasn't as easy as he had imagined it. He had almost lost them a few times, but his personal Hornet drone would track it down until he could re-establish visuals.

When launched out the window like a paper airplane, the fist-sized drone would follow his GPS position at whatever hover height he determined. Its birds-eye camera feed appeared on his phone and could easily send him directions to intercept the car. It had served its purpose two times, but now that they were approaching the final destination, the Hornet was signaled home. It zipped through the window into Orion's waiting hand.

Not wanting to ruin his surveillance at the last moment, Orion began a lap around the suburban neighborhood, sniffing out the security. As he turned to the street behind, a taxi passed him, going the other direction. He glanced at it but thought nothing of it. His thoughts were on the house itself, and how to infiltrate it.

After the lap, he found an inconspicuous parking spot on the street behind the house and turned the car off to wait for his team to arrive – and to plan. If Greyson weren't in the same house as the parents, he'd have to use the parents to find the boy. There were many options to do so. He could kidnap them and torture them elsewhere; he could kill all the security guards and torture them there; or he could also take the stealthy approach, sneaking in and keeping them quiet at the barrel of a gun. Perhaps their daughter, Sydney, was still alive. If so, that would make it even easier. And more fun.

Whatever he did, he had to do it wisely. His father had given him the mission, knowing he craved vengeance and that he wouldn't expose their real mission with Greyson. Orion couldn't disappoint him. Failure would not only mean losing his chance at revenge, it also meant his father would be in danger of losing everything. There was a lot at stake, and...

A flash of movement startled him. A suited man with gun drawn came rushing toward him from the direction of the target house.

Panic swarmed Orion's senses; he fumbled with the controls and rolled down the window. The suited man ran into the street, looking left and right, afraid. If Orion had thought clearly enough, he might have realized that the agent had been looking for someone else, and perhaps the taxi had been carrying that very *someone* away. But Orion didn't notice – he was pulling his gun from his ankle holster. When he looked up again, the FBI agent was staring at him, perplexed.

The guns fired at each other, nearly simultaneously.
*BANG-BANGBANGBANG!*

------------------

Sydney's family heard the gunfire inside the house, followed by squealing tires. The worst thought popped into Sydney's mind. *They took him.*

Two FBI agents rushed with guns drawn to Sydney and her parents; they pushed them toward the garage as they assessed the situation. Her parents were frightened, her mother crying and holding her, and her father holding her mother – but Sydney was numb. The shots still seemed to hang in the air, ringing in her ears. Who had been shot? Had he made it?

"What's going on? Is he okay? Is he okay?"

The FBI agents refused to answer, speaking instead to the agents outside as their eyes and guns pursued every corner, every window. Soon they had been herded to the garage and into an SUV. She hugged her mother and her mother hugged her back.

Her thoughts flashed to her last conversation with him. This was what Greyson had wanted, wasn't it? For her to be in her parent's embrace under FBI protection. Safe. Secure.

*But Greyson...*

# PART 2

# Chapter 9

*Eight hours later…*

Greyson's head bobbed with the movement of the road. His eyes were open, but his mind was elsewhere – drifting with the mechanical hum of the bus's engine and the whine of the road. The yellow lights running the length of the bus lit the middle aisle for late-night bathroom runs, but there were few others awake. They had turned off their lights, snuggled into blankets, and found the most comfortable positions against headrests and windows.

He pressed his forehead against the window, letting the bobs of the road move his skin up and down, massaging his skull. He had a headache, but he'd gotten used to it. It hurt to think so hard, but he couldn't stop. The thoughts were haunting him like demons. And he dreaded them. It was whenever he shut his eyes that they would attack.

Though there wasn't much to look at, he kept himself awake by watching the night's scenery through the large sunglasses that covered much of his face. There were outlines of houses along the highway, but road signs and headlights mostly. He wondered where the others were going. South? Along with the other thousands? North? To Canada? Or maybe they were just going about their business. Returning to normal.

That's what many were wondering. Was it okay to return to normal? How long until it was okay to throw a party without getting scorned? Before laughing at comical violence on a TV show? Could kids return to school? Learn about Hiroshima? How much time is enough after a nuclear catastrophe?

His forehead grew sore, so he pulled his hoodie further over his head and used it as a pillow rather than the cold glass. Plus, it would hide more of his face. No one could know who he was, or they'd bring him back – or worse. Depends on who found him.

The bus driver slowed for a turn, and the streetlights spilled through the windows like a disco ball on one last spin, dancing on the heads of the sleeping passengers. Greyson's thoughts again played through his mind, memories he didn't want to remember. But his guard had gone down – he'd gotten too comfortable. His eyes had shut beneath the aviator sunglasses and his jaw drooped. Soon his cheek pressed against the side of his hood and his arms curled into his jacket. After some time, thoughts drifted into dreams. Timidly at first. Then building in story and depth. Ones he cared about. Things he feared. Memories he dreaded. And the demons attacked.

"Ugh!" Greyson jerked awake, his right hand tensed and white, almost skeletal.

But the bus was silent – and still. It had stopped, but no one had woken. Greyson glanced around, still regaining his senses, and spotted the bus driver outside, working a gas pump. Bright fluorescent lights poured down to the gas station's cement and made Greyson squint, even with his sunglasses.

In a moment he was out of his seatbelt, padding softly down the yellow-lighted aisle and exiting the bus, carrying his backpack with him. The air was chilly, like it was most late September nights. At least the bomb hadn't changed the seasons.

He nodded at the bus driver. "Bathroom."

"Right," the bus driver squinted, but decided not to mention the boy's sunglasses or backpack. "Five-minute stop."

Greyson nodded again and watched his breath escape toward the fluorescent lights. Still shaking off the sleep, he blinked heavily and let out a yawn. It felt good to get off the bus, stretch his legs, and clear his mind. But a gas station at night wasn't the best place to linger. Especially when no one else was around.

He eyed the neighborhood. Not far off the highway. A darkened strip mall to the right, a high, wooden fence to the left, blocking off a neighborhood of apartment buildings with barred windows and chipping paint.

The door jingled as he opened it, and the first thing he noticed was the security camera pointed directly at him.

He pulled the hood further down and eyed the lanky, male cashier who looked up from a small television screen. The cashier eyed him back.

"Hi," Greyson said.

"Hi," the lanky cashier replied, watching him closely.

Greyson looked over the aisles and found the restroom sign. He couldn't help but to overhear the television as he made his way to the back of the store.

"…south of Des Moines today. The suspects were caught looting in the Yellow Zone, only eleven miles from Ground Zero. Officials took the opportunity again to warn citizens to stay clear of all Radiation Zones unless one has obtained proper identification tags. Without the need to patrol the safety border, government and aid workers would be able to spend more time in rescue operations…"

*Rescue operations? They meant body recovery.*

Greyson finished his business in the bathroom and then took a long look at his face in the mirror. He pulled at his upper lip, examining a scar that ran halfway to his nostril. Not too horrible-looking, and perhaps even something other boys might brag about, but to him, it would only be a reminder of what had happened. He pulled at the skin around his eye. The black and purple and sick yellow had finally faded entirely.

At least the visible marks were going away. He put the glasses back on.

"…over 8,000. Asked about the unsettled death toll, Governor Reckhemmer lauded the efforts of the emergency personnel and volunteers who had devoted much of the last month to their country. Lashing out against the focus on the death toll, he said, 'At this point, it cannot increase our love for those who were killed nor increase our hatred of terror. Let us focus on the things that do.'"

Ignoring the cashier, Greyson left the building and the television. He was watching the bus driver put the gas nozzle back when he heard the footsteps. He stopped.

To his right, three teenaged boys approached him with long strides. To his left there were two more, one a girl. They were not dressed to impress, and their faces were dirty – and angry.

Options burst into his mind. *Go back into the station. Run to the bus. Confront them. Attack them before they get the chance.*

Making his choice, he turned to face the three and looked over his shoulder at the other two. They stopped and glanced at one another like they hadn't expected him to stop.

"What do you want?"

"Just…just give us your money, and we'll let you go," the biggest one commanded. His cheekbones were clearly visible, and he licked at his chapped lips. Perhaps he was weakened by hunger. Perhaps he needed the money.

Greyson hesitated and shifted the backpack on his shoulders. He was analyzing them. The two boys next to CheekBones were wide-eyed and fidgety. Scared. The ones behind were probably the fast ones, meant to keep him from running. But they looked younger – more of an even match.

55

"Hurry up!" CheekBones snarled. And he pulled out a knife, letting it hang by his side.

Greyson's heart dropped, and the tension jerked at his muscles.

"Don't," the girl gasped. "If your dad finds out…"

"He won't! Shut up!" CheekBones snapped. He turned back to Greyson. "Give us your bag, now!"

Greyson gulped and glanced toward the bus. The driver was watching them, slowly reaching for his pocket. The thugs caught his glance and turned their attention to the driver.

Slowly dropping one hand from his backpack strap, Greyson reached and pulled the bottom of his jacket up and over his worn, red fanny pack. His fingers quietly worked the zipper.

"I'll give you some money. Just put away the knife."

CheekBones turned back to Greyson and noticed his hand at the zipper. He took a step closer. "Give us everything. Drop your bag. No funny business!"

One of his friends shook his arm. "The driver, man. He's calling the cops!"

"I know, I know! Hand it over, kid! You have three seconds! Three…"

Greyson eyed the distance between him. There wouldn't be enough time. "Two…"

There were too many of them. He had to give them what they wanted. At least for a little while.

"One…"

"Okay!" he yelled. He swung the backpack to his front and held its hulk in his hands. It had everything he needed for days. Hundreds of dollars. Food. Clothing. It was all he had.

"The money's in the top compartment."

*I hope this works…*

He took in a deep breath and threw the backpack at CheekBones as hard as he could. In a flash, he snatched his slingshot, loaded two balls at once with one finger separating the two.

*SNAP!* The balls flew in a V and slammed into the necks of the two boys next to CheekBones, sending them reeling backwards and to their knees, gasping for air. Greyson swung around and put the lunging boy down with another ball. The girl was frozen in her tracks. He let her be, deciding instead to deal with CheekBones.

But he was gone – already sprinting toward the fence with the backpack in hand, abandoning his friends. Greyson loaded and fired a ball into

CheekBone's calf, but he staggered on, climbing onto a dumpster and then the fence beyond.

*My backpack…*

"Stop!"

He burst after him, but he was suddenly dragged down from behind. The girl had latched onto his back and flailed her fingernails at his neck and around to his face.

With a jab from his elbow she was off of him, but the damage was done. CheekBones had disappeared over the fence. Panic jolted into his lungs at the thought of losing it.

Growling and rushing to his feet, he sprinted to the dumpster, the hoodie falling from his head in the wind, reminding him, too, that his hat was also in the backpack.

He deftly pushed himself onto the dumpster and over the fence. He surveyed the landing while in the air. A backyard, a swing set, a large, leashed dog barking hysterically, grass to break the fall. But no sign of CheekBones.

Greyson landed in a roll and was thinking through his next steps when suddenly something slammed into him from behind, sending him face-first into the grass and dirt. Before he could right himself, someone had seized his jacket, swung him around, and planted his forearm to his throat.

*CheekBones.* He'd been hiding just behind the fence. Waiting for him. Greyson had been outsmarted. And now he was outmatched.

The dog wouldn't stop barking – loud, frightening, and only a few feet away. CheekBones eyed it but felt satisfied with the chain keeping it at bay.

"Gotcha, kid." CheekBones smiled to himself and held the knife against Greyson's cheek.

"Take it! Take the bag!"

"Oh, I will. And your weapon, there. Pretty effective. It might come in handy."

CheekBones kept the knife pointed toward Greyson's face while finding the slingshot with his other hand. All the while the dog kept nipping at the air, its jaws snapping and snapping, flinging slobber. Its chain jerked at its neck, but it didn't seem to care. It wanted their blood.

*RUFFRuffRuuuUFFRuRRUFF!*

"I'm taking the bag and you're not going to follow!"

"Wait! Just…just take the money. There's hundreds. But I need the bag. I'm…I'm…"

*RrrrUFF! RrrrUFFF!*

"You're what? A refugee?" Suddenly CheekBones tugged at Greyson's hair and pulled at his lips so that he could examine his teeth. "No radiation – so you're either lyin' or got off easy. Half the world loves you. You get free food, housing, sympathy cards from all over the frickin' world." He stood up and grabbed the backpack.

Greyson sat up, eyeing the boy's knife.

"What about *me*?" CheekBones continued. "And *my* family? We've been poor for years – before the bomb! But they don't give a crap about *us*. They say the recession will end soon? Unemployment will level out? They lie…"

*RUFFRuffRUUUFFRuRRUFF!*

CheekBones rifled through the upper compartment and found the envelope. He fingered through Sydney's parents' money and his eyes lit up. For a moment his eyes glazed with daydreams, his mouth curling in a fateful smile, but another loud bark from the dog shook him awake and he heard the sirens. Police. Suddenly fear crossed CheekBones' brow and he glared at Greyson.

"You've seen my face. You'd lead them to me."

*No…* "I won't…just don't."

*RrrrUFF! RrrrUFFF! Grrrr…*

CheekBones pulled the knife up and stuffed the envelope in his jacket. He took a step toward Greyson. The knife's blade shone with the motion-sensing light from the apartment building. Greyson's shallow breaths were lost in the dog's frenzy.

*RUFFRuffRUUUFFRuRRUFF!*

CheekBones stepped over Greyson and bent his knees. Greyson could see it in his eyes. He was desperate enough. He was going to do it.

"Sorry," he said, a catch in his voice. "But I have to…"

He pointed the knife at Greyson's chest and lunged.

# Chapter 10

With a guttural roar, a flash of black blazed over Greyson, sweeping CheekBones and the knife away. Startled and too stunned to move, Greyson watched as the dog latched on to CheekBones' arm and shook horribly, rattling the length of broken chain that hung from its collar. The boy went down in an instant, screaming for his life.

Taking advantage of the opening, Greyson scrambled to his feet, grabbed his backpack and the slingshot, and raced to the fence. Sirens competed with the sound of vicious growling and CheekBones' anguished screams. None of the sounds were good. He didn't want any of it – especially the cops.

He peered through a hole in the fence. Cop cars pulled into the station and the bus driver was waving them in.

Greyson turned to the dogfight and searched for an alternate exit. For now, the dog was still occupied with CheekBones, but there was no telling when it would suddenly sense the other intruder.

Not wanting to give the dog any more reason to notice him, he tiptoed across the yard to the back gate, keeping watch as the dog mauled the boy's arm.

"Help!" CheekBones' cry came just as Greyson was about to leave; a sudden wave of compassion hit him like a sledgehammer. The boy had been desperate – and the dog could kill him. And again, it would be his fault. CheekBones was reaching out as Liam had.

"Hey!" Greyson yelled at the dog, his left hand gripping the gate. "Stop!"

To his alarm, the dog dropped CheekBones' arm and snapped to Greyson, bloodlust still in its eyes. Its pointy ears were alert, watching him, analyzing its next victim. Now that Greyson got a good look at him, he knew. German Shepherd. A breed preferred by police and the military. A breed known for its ferocity.

Greyson gulped. The dog kept watching.

During the hesitation, CheekBones whimpered, pushed away, and crawled toward the fence. The dog ignored him; its eyes still locked on to Greyson.

"G-g-good boy. Stay…"

CheekBones staggered to his feet in a state of panic, tried to climb the fence with one good arm, abandoned the idea, and ran to the corner where a board was broken at the bottom of the fence. He kicked at it haphazardly, his eyes still on the dog. Finally, the boards were broken enough that he began to crawl through.

And then Greyson remembered. He still had the envelope.

"Wait! My money!"

He took a step toward CheekBones and so did the dog. Greyson stopped. The dog's jowls were slobbering – its eyes still locked on Greyson – though it cast sideways glances at CheekBones as he slid through the small opening. CheekBones was a tempting target, yet the dog was still watching Greyson. Why? Was he the bigger threat?

A banging sound resonated in the direction of the dumpster and a policeman's head suddenly popped over the top, shining a flashlight in the yard. The light landed on Greyson.

"Freeze! Police!"

Greyson eyed the dog, the flashlight, CheekBones' disappearing shoes – then made his choice. He bolted.

"Freeze!"

He expected a gunshot, but there was only the bark of the dog behind him. His feet pounded pavement as he swerved into the street. He was heavy with the backpack. Its bulk swung back and forth, giving his stride an awkward waddle, and most definitely decreasing his mobility. He wouldn't be able to outmaneuver the cops very long. He had to find a hiding spot – soon.

The neighborhood was dark. Most everyone would be asleep – it was nearly 2 a.m. Did he dare try to break into someone's home – or just knock and hope they would hide him from the police?

He couldn't risk it.

He swerved into an alley between apartment buildings and took a quick glance back. The cop wasn't following. But the dog was, gaining on him, zipping through the streetlight.

Greyson let out a yelp and sprinted between the buildings, breaking through a few shrubs into a larger open area with a wide-open gate and black fencing. There weren't any lights here, but there were a few trees ahead and lots of small statues to hide behind. He ran and ran, the sound of the backpack smacking against him, reminding him of how slow he was.

And then he heard its footfalls. It was right behind him.

Taking a deep breath, he slowed to a stop. For a moment he couldn't turn around. He had a thought that if he confronted the beast, it would feel threatened enough to attack. Maybe if he just lay down in a sign of submission, it would pass him by. Or he could play dead. He'd heard you were supposed to do that in case of a bear attack, though his dad had said it depended on the type of bear. If a Grizzly were hungry or protecting its young, it'd do the deed whether or not you chose to fight back. German Shepherds were the Grizzlies of dogs.

He turned slowly, his arms outstretched as if to show he was unarmed. For now. His slingshot was still an option.

The dog stood erect only five feet from him – ears alert, eyes dark and direct. But its tongue was out, panting. It wasn't growling, but a slight whimper escaped its loose lips that hid all but the sharpest fangs.

*Now's my chance…*

Breathing heavily, Greyson reached into his pack. The dog watched. His fingers found what he was looking for. When the dog took a step forward, Greyson startled, throwing the object from his pack at the dog's feet.

In an instant, the dog snatched up the beef jerky and swallowed it whole. As if thanking him, the dog let out a soft bark – though it still sent a chill down Greyson's spine. And then it drooled.

Suddenly a wave of relief forced Greyson to smile. And he laughed a little. "You…you hungry?"

Greyson found another jerky nugget in his pack and threw it to the dog. It caught it in mid-air and didn't even chew.

Greyson laughed again and knelt, hands open and toward the ground. Like it had seen an opening, the dog burst forward knocking Greyson into his backpack and rolling to his side. Laughing out of shock and relief, Greyson let the dog lick his face and hands.

"Hey! Gross! Sick!"

Like a switch had jolted the dog into action, it jerked erect and searched the darkness.

It took a moment for Greyson to realize what it had done, and a sense of awe overtook him. The dog was trained. "No, it's okay. We're okay. Don't *sic*. There's nothing to sic."

He didn't really know what it meant to "sic", but he'd heard other people command their dogs to "sic" this or "sic" that, as a command to attack.

Before the dog could think to sic him, Greyson found another nugget and watched as the dog inhaled it with pleasure.

"Good boy…" he praised, petting it as it sniffed at his fanny pack. He had to zip it shut to keep it from eating all his jerky in one gulp.

Faint light from the street revealed the gorgeous beast. It had a sleek, black coat swirled with a caramel brown, like delicious hot cocoa – not to be confused with something sweet, though. Its muscles were taut, especially around its legs and jaw; and its teeth, especially the fangs that hung over its lips, could simply rip through flesh like paper.

And he'd seen it in action.

But its eyes, at least right now, were like puppy eyes, round as quarters and full of love.

Greyson pet it a few more times, still more than hesitant that it would suddenly find him empty of beef jerky and try to satisfy its hunger in some other way.

"Now what, boy?"

He looked around. The police weren't anywhere close, and they could hide here. In the…cemetery.

Looking around, it finally sunk in. Graves were everywhere – big and small stones, crosses, and angels – all rolling over the gentle hills into the darkest dark. Spooky, but a great place to hide. He'd make his way to the tree line and plan his next move there.

He got up, staring at the dog. "Time to go home. Okay?"

The dog stared at him.

"Shoo. Go home. Understand?"

The dog bounced on its hind legs.

"What? No. Not *stand* - understand! You have to go home."

The dog sat and cocked its head.

Greyson sighed and knelt to the dog's collar. Finding its nametag, he read the name.

He grimaced at the name. "What? Really?"

The dog whimpered.

There weren't many worse things to call a dog. Whoever owned the dog was obviously cruel. And worse yet, there was no address or phone number.

Suddenly, the dog growled and turned to face the road. Greyson followed its gaze. Beyond the cemetery's fence, Greyson glimpsed a patrol car slowly making its way down the street, shining its spotlight in the alleys between buildings. Farther away, a tiny spotlight shone down from a moving object above. Police drone.

"Frick!"

He jerked to his feet and jogged toward the graves. "Go home, mutt." He couldn't call it by its name.

It followed him, matching his strides with two or three of its own.

"Ugh...fine! But I'm not stealing you. If you follow me...frick! Hide!"

He slammed himself to the grass and shifted behind a gravestone just as the spotlight swept through. He was hidden well, and so was the dog. Somehow, the dog had gotten the sense to sit behind its own gravestone. It panted, staring at him out of satisfaction. He could swear it was smiling.

The spotlight made another sweep but kept moving, scouring the next neighborhood one alley at a time.

Greyson watched the drone until it was out of view, took a few more breaths, and then pushed himself to his feet. The backpack felt like a hundred pounds, digging into his shoulders and scrunching his spine; it couldn't be that heavy, but it felt like it. In fact, everything seemed worse suddenly. He looked around. Darkness. Lurking cops. A strange dog, staring at him from on top of a grave.

A grave. Where a coffin had been buried with someone's mom or someone's dad. Where some kid had been forced to pour the first shovelful of dirt over his dead mom.

An urgency pushed him forward, toward the back of the cemetery where trees hovered over a black, metal fence. Greyson ran to it, grabbed the bars, and shook. The metal laughed at him with its creaks and squeals, and it wouldn't let him out. He was trapped.

He took a few steps back, beginning to stagger as thoughts caught up to him in the silence. A mournful, haunting voice seemed to wail inside of him. It had been wailing for days, but he finally had the time to listen. He was too tired. Too alone. After so long, it was just him, with no one watching.

He fell back, his guard came crashing down, and the tears came flooding in.

At first, they were for himself. He was hiding from the cops in a graveyard hundreds of miles from home. No money. No phone. Helpless. He couldn't afford bus tickets. It was ruined. Everything. In a matter of minutes, he'd gone from being only a few days from his dad, to ruin. He had failed.

He let the sobs grow, even as the dog sniffed at his hair and neck. Death was all around him. Death had seemed to follow him recently – haunting him, perhaps forcing him to confront it – to give it what he owed. Tears.

63

Memories assaulted him full force – both good and bad. His mother's face, his last goodbye. Liam's cold, dead eyes – pleading. Kip's body, rocking with the bullets. Orion, standing over Kip, smirking. The mushroom cloud. The staggering refugees. The panicked people. Memorials. Speeches. Funerals. Leaving Sydney.

He was sorry. For his mom. For Liam. For the 8,000 and counting. More than this cemetery could hold. Far more. It was his fault. All of it. He deserved this.

He hated himself. He'd never been angrier. His fists clenched at the grass and pulled up wads of dirt. He started to yell, but he couldn't alert the cops. What came out instead was a husky, head-pounding gag that pulsed at the veins in his neck and forehead. How could he have let it happen? How many had been children, or had children? How many other moms had died? And the orphans were now asking why. He was the answer. *He* was why.

Suddenly the dog's tongue slapped his cheek, interrupting his thoughts, its tongue pleasant and gross at the same time – like therapy. Eventually the dog found more sensitive spots, like his ears. And then it caught a taste of the salt in his tears and the tongue swiped at his cheeks, nostrils, and mouth.

He pushed angrily at the dog's face. "Get off!" The anger swelled over his sadness, and he lashed out at the dog. It whimpered and backed up. But only for a moment. It took another cautious step forward, like it was testing the water, and came at him again.

Feeling bad for shoving the dog, this time he let him back in for more licks. Odd enough, it felt good, and he'd already forgotten that he'd been crying. Soon, he hugged the dog close, both to keep him from licking, and for the comfort it gave. It felt good to hug – human or not. And he was tired. The dog's fur was like a warm pillow, and he didn't move. Maybe he liked the hug, too.

But a breeze blew through and gave him a chill. The reality came back again.

"Okay, okay," he sniffed and wiped at his tears and the slobber. He held the dog at arm's length, suddenly returning to the situation at hand. He was lost, alone, and far from his goal. But he wasn't finished.

*"You've got a long way to go, buddy."*
*His dad leaned out the car window, watching him as he shuffled along the gravel road, wearing a backpack full of sweet corn. The dare had been ten miles, and he had gone three.*

*But he was tired. His feet dragged through the gravel, his shoulders ached, and he'd slowed to a shuffle.*

*"Put your shoulders back, chin up – eyes forward. Keep your form or it'll keep you down. You can do it."*

Greyson rolled his shoulders back and lifted his chin.

*Enough crying, Greyson.* He had to admit that it had made him feel a little better, but now wasn't the time. The cops could come back at any moment. "Think, Greyson. We've got to get out here and find somewhere to sleep – well – I've got to." He turned to the dog. "You do what you want, but you should probably stay home where you're safe and stuff. I only have so much jerky."

The dog cocked its head again and pawed at his pant legs. He wanted to come with. "No. Well, you know what? I'm not taking you back. What do I care? It's your own dumb fault. You broke the chain."

He eyed the chain, still connected to his collar. "And it's not doing you any good anymore."

He took off the animal's leash and threw it toward the graves. But he left the collar. The nametag gleamed in the faint moonlight.

*KITTY.*

"You're free, Kit," he said, deciding on a suitable name the dog would still recognize. "I don't know where I'm going. I'm just going. And I don't have much food. You have a bowl of food back home, but with me you don't need a chain. Your stupid choice."

Greyson trekked toward the gate, turned the corner, and headed south. Kit followed at his heels.

# Chapter 11

"I'm home!"

The sharply dressed man set his briefcase and Redmond Aerospace Defense badge on the entry table, hung his keys next to his wife's, and closed the door behind him. There was no response. That was odd. She had said she was looking forward to him coming home.

"I'm home! You here, babe?"

No response. He sighed. *Should have got the intercoms.*

He set his shoes in the coat closet. The maid got a little too miffed when he would leave them in the hall, but she was better than the last maid by far. The hardwood floors were polished and bright, the chandelier sparkled, and he could understand her despite her accent. He didn't want to ruffle her feathers any more than he already had.

Walking through the dining room, he checked the hedges outside, wondering if his wife was talking with the neighbors. He walked past the pictures on the china cabinet, peeked inside the study where she would read late into the night, and made his way to the kitchen.

For the first time, he began to worry. There was a half-eaten ham sandwich and a lip-stained glass of milk.

"Heather?" He turned from the dishes and rushed to the glass door that led to the back yard. "Heather?"

The birdfeeders were swaying with the breeze. The garden was empty, except for a shovel and a pair of gloves.

He took out his cell phone and dialed Heather as he paced from the kitchen to the main hall. It rang once. Twice. Three times.

"Geez!"

He stopped and jerked back. He'd been so distracted, he'd nearly run into it. But what was it?

He leaned closer, inspecting it. A long string – no – fishing line dangled from the second-floor balcony above. And at his eye level, there was a golden fishing hook, sharp and dangerous.

And on the hook was something that made him smile. Something his wife knew he liked very much.

A ripe strawberry.

At first, he had thought it was a few of his coworkers playing a prank on him, but the strawberry sent a very different message. Maybe she had seen him coming home.

He hung up the phone and reached for the strawberry. But it yanked upwards, just out of reach and then slowly rose to the second level's railing and disappeared, pulled by some invisible force.

"Oh. That's how it is?" he asked playfully, turning at the bannister and padding up the stairs with a goofy smile. "I can play along."

He was whistling for her when he made it to the landing. The strawberry seemed to be stuck by the bedroom door. For a second he was surprised she would risk the stains on the carpet, but he let it slip his mind. Instead, he quietly snuck to the door and peeked inside.

The Fisherman, a leather-skinned man with a scraggy beard and a drooping fishing hat, watched from the other end of the hall as the prey approached the bait.

He raised the harpoon gun and aimed its arrow tip. It would expand after entering the prey and stick, like a hook in a fish's mouth. The thin rope trailing from its end allowed him to reel in whatever it had hooked. It was a beautiful contraption. Practical, reliable, and deadly if he wanted it to be. He pulled the trigger.

*SHINK!*

The Fisherman watched with a blank expression as the rope rippled from his gun like a streamer, and the harpoon found its target. Setting the gun down, he opened his rusty, green tackle box and helped himself to a strawberry. Then, humming to himself, he pulled on the rope, reeling the flopping prey in one foot at a time.

But he stopped. He was getting a call through his smartwatch. With a gruff Spanish accent, he answered. "Hola?" He listened to the man on the other line. "Sí…sí. Un niño? Nassau? Sí. No problema."

He ended the call and continued pulling the line. "Here fishy, fishy, fishy."

# Chapter 12

*The next morning*

The sun beamed onto Greyson's face as he bent back and threw the cornhusk. The dog zipped through the field, kicking up soft dirt in its wake. Kit had been the perfect companion throughout the long night and into the morning. He provided fun with fetch; he made Greyson feel a little safer – like Kit was his very own bodyguard – and he was easy to talk to.

"I'm just confused," Greyson divulged when Kit returned the mangled and slobbery husk. "It's not like I blame her for everything…but in a way it's totally her fault, right? I mean, if it weren't for her escaping with Sam, we would have gotten out of the fair with no trouble. Reckhemmer would have made a deal with Emory to get Sam back and maybe the bomb wouldn't have gone off. And…and the whole thing with Liam. I know it's not right to think so, but if she hadn't been there, I would have saved Liam, you know? Can I blame her for all that?"

Greyson looked down at Kit and Kit looked back at him with his wet nose and flopping tongue.

"You're a good listener," Greyson said, smiling. "But don't be afraid to speak."

*RUFF!*

"Yeah. That's life." Greyson smiled and patted him on the head. "But this isn't so bad, right? We're free of the bus…I don't have to hide my face. I can do this, Kit. *We* can do this."

Greyson adjusted his hat, rubbing his forehead. They walked on together through the corn graveyard, where stalks stood up as foot-long spikes from the sprawling fields of western Illinois. Mud was sticking to the soles of his feet, but it was better to stay off the main roads. He hadn't seen any signs of being pursued, but he also didn't know how madly the FBI would be after him.

He took in a deep breath and raised his face to the sun. A smile fought with his heavy cheeks, powered by the feeling of the sun and a new kind of fuel that invigorated him. Whenever the fear of the unknown crept at him, or anger at himself drew him to grit his teeth and kick at the ground, the new fuel would counter it. The fuel was hope. It was no longer the faint, fake hope he used to have when he would wait at home for a phone call or a letter. This was hope he could feel. It was based on something true – that he knew was real.

"See that horizon, Kit?" he pointed to the fields beyond, pockmarked with only a few gravel roads and farmhouses. "My dad's over there. You'll like him." He smiled at Kit for a few moments and then tripped on a stalk. He turned back to kick it and sighed sheepishly. "Just a little farther."

Once they reached another gravel road, he kicked at the gravel to clean off his shoes and did his best with Kit's paws. Taking a breather, he swung his backpack to the ground, pulled out a map and unraveled it on the side of the road.

Finding the small town where he'd been robbed on the map, his finger moved only an inch to the exit he'd seen when the sunrise had given them their first light. It was only another inch or two to where he thought they were now – just a half-mile off the main highway. His eyes glazed over as he saw how many more inches he had to go – just to get through Illinois.

He couldn't walk the whole way. Without money, without an ID, and being something like a fugitive were a few factors limiting his options. And he couldn't risk asking anyone for help. He was completely on his own. There was no flying, no bussing, and no driving. A railroad would be nice, but they weren't on the map. Perhaps he could find a bike? Or a horse?

The map's lines and scrawl marks grew blurry; he was suddenly feeling very lost and very tired. His feet were already sore, and his back was aching from carrying the pack for hours. Though he still had a few swigs of water left, they were already running low. The beef jerky, trail mix, granola bars, and a few other goodies were going fast. The dog was an eater. The food could last them for a little while. But how long was a little while?

Breathing a heavy sigh, he let his head sag to his chest. He would need to find a place to sleep tonight. He could skip one night, but he was nearly spent.

Kit growled.

At first, he just put his hand on Kit's head and gave him a few pats. "I'm okay, buddy. Just thinking."

But Kit kept growling; Greyson looked up and matched his gaze. The fright jerked him to action. He scrambled to fold the map, but the folds weren't right. Quickly abandoning the idea, he balled the map and shoved it in the backpack, glancing toward the oncoming vehicle. They had to have spotted him already. He was toast.

But suddenly he had an idea. Since he was already spotted, it was the only thing he could think of doing.

Greyson pointed his thumb toward the highway. He was shaking, imperceptibly from the vantage of the passenger, who seeing him, pleaded with the male driver to pull over. The four-door sedan drove past, sending a plume of dust washing over him, but stopped soon after with a little squeak of the brakes.

Smiling at Kit out of relief, Greyson picked up his backpack and ran to the car through its dusty trail, pulling his hood over his hat and low on his brow. This was a risk, but he had to take it. There was no way he was walking to Florida.

The woman's window rolled down and she leaned out. "Hi! Need a ride?"

Greyson inched a little closer, not wanting to show his face. "Uh…yes, please. South?"

The woman leaned toward the driver and whispered something to him. Greyson eyed Kit, and he let out a small whimper.

"We're going to St. Louis. That okay?"

He recalled St. Louis on the map. It would take him a few inches in the right direction at least. "Yeah. Thanks."

He reached for the door handle, but it clicked locked. The driver leaned over the passenger. He was young – thirty maybe. "You running from home?"

Greyson gulped and shook his head 'no'. The less he said the better. He was a horrible liar.

"We can't just pick up a kid. We'd be accused of –"

"I'm a refugee…and…and an orphan."

The couple shared a look.

"You carrying any weapons?"

"Eric," the woman scolded. "He's just a boy."

Eric shook his head, ignoring her, and kept staring at Greyson. "*Are* you?"

"No, sir," he lied. "But my dog needs a ride, too."

"Does he bite?"

"Only to chew."

The man chuckled and raised his eyebrows at the woman. She gave him pouty lips and it was all over. The lock clicked undone and he opened the door for Kit. He jumped in; the backpack went in next, and then Greyson. It took an extra ounce of courage to close the door behind him, but he did, slamming the interior into silence.

"So," the woman said, breaking the silence. "What's your name?"

"Nolan. And this is Kit."

"Ah. I'm Alyssa, and this is my husband, Eric. He's sorry about all the questions."

"Okay."

An awkward silence finally led to a longer period of quiet where Greyson could think and the couple could whisper their private conversations. Petting Kit, he watched the field whizz by, imagining the time he was saving each second that passed.

Minutes passed and Greyson would catch Eric glancing at him in the rearview mirror, still wary of having an unknown passenger behind him and his young wife. Greyson couldn't help but to think that he was right to be nervous. He himself had just been robbed by a kid only a few years older. And he also had a weapon in his pack that had severely injured several people. Perhaps it had killed one. At the fair, he had seen RedHead drop like she had died, but she might have just been knocked out cold.

"You bored back there?" Alyssa asked with a tone that told she was smiling.

"Um…not really."

"You aren't playing any games or anything. Most kids would have their game tablet or whatever out, killing zombies or throwing birds at pigs or whatever."

Eric laughed at her between glances at the road.

"I don't have one."

"Really? No phone either?"

"Nope."

She turned in her seat as much as her seat belt allowed, trying to look at him to make sure he knew how weird he was. "Can I ask you something? What's your story? Why are you heading south?"

A few stories popped in his head, but he was no Jarryd. Maybe the best story would be the truth.

"Mom died in Des Moines. I have family down south, but they can't travel."

*That was actually pretty good.*

"Oh. Sorry." She paused and turned back to the front with a sympathetic look toward Eric. After another long, awkward silence, she tried again. "How about the radio? You like country, Nolan? Or are you more of a pop kinda kid?"

71

"Uh…whatever."

Alyssa shrugged and turned the radio on.

When the pop music clicked on, he gave Kit a regretful look. How much more of a drive did they have until St. Louis?

Suddenly a buzzing siren interrupted the music from the radio, followed by an announcement from a soothing female voice. "This is a government broadcast. Please be on alert for a missing child in your area. He is a male of 13 years old with short brown hair. He was last seen wearing a red baseball cap with a white 'G' on the front. If you have seen this child, please call 911 immediately. We repeat, this is a government broadcast…"

"I-I'm sorry. T-turn it off," Greyson said, his slingshot loaded and pointed at the back of Eric's head. The band creaked as he held it back as far as he could in the narrow backseat.

*I have to. There is no other option.* But he still hated himself. "Pull off the road…and let us out."

Kit growled, sensing Greyson's alarm.

"Whoa…easy kid. Don't do anything stupid."

"You, either."

Before long, Eric pulled onto another gravel road. There was an uneasy silence in the car. Greyson was so ashamed, so nervous, that his hand trembled; he felt he might lose grip of the slingshot's ammunition pocket.

"Nolan – we can help. Whatever's going on, it doesn't matter. We can-"

"Throw your phones, wallet, and keys out the window – passenger side. Please."

*I have to!*

"What?"

"I'm sorry! Just…just do it."

"If you're in trouble, we can help –"

"NOW!" The scream startled them, and Kit growled ferociously. His voice had cracked and come out like he had two different voices. It had startled him as well.

Once the items were thrown out, Greyson eyed Eric in the mirror. "I'm going to leave now. You can't let anyone know you've seen me. Just let me go."

"Sure," Eric said coolly. "Whatever you want."

Releasing the pressure on the slingshot, Greyson pushed the car door open and exited with his backpack and his dog. Finding the phones, he smashed

72

them on the ground and put the car keys in his fanny pack. They couldn't turn him in. And they couldn't follow.

What if they knew how to hot-wire the car? Or they had a spare key?

Just to be sure, he pulled out his slingshot to put a ball into the tire.

*ZIP! PLING!*

The ball bounced off. *Should've remembered.* Frustrated, he pulled a multi-tool from his fanny pack and stabbed a back tire with its knife; with a blast of air, the car's corner leaned to the ground. Inside, Alyssa was crying; Eric was trying to comfort her.

"Now, get out and…and walk away! Down there," he pointed into a cornfield with a wavering finger. "And don't stop."

After some debate, Eric held Alyssa's hand and tread into the muddy field. Greyson watched them for some time, until they were small figures in the distance, and then decided it was time for him to leave as well.

As he walked away, he felt horrible pangs of guilt. They'd been nice to him, just wanting to help. And he'd repaid them by destroying their stuff.

But he'd done what he had to. If he had to do that again – he would. Maybe someday he'd be able to find them and explain it all to them – or pay them back somehow to make it all better. Maybe he could make up for a lot of the bad he'd done once he found his dad. His dad would know what to do – how to make the guilt go away.

But if he didn't find his dad, this trip would be in vain, and he would have ruined a couple's phones and tire for nothing.

He *had* to make it.

He picked up the pace, eyed them over his shoulder one last time, and set out for the tree line with his shoulders back, chin up, and eyes forward.

# Chapter 13

Sydney threw her clothes from a trash bag into the bottom drawer of her new room's dresser. She was angry. This house smelled like mold, and the wallpaper looked moist. But that was minor. The majors were two things. One, the FBI hadn't let her call anyone since Greyson had left. They'd even destroyed her phone. And two, her parents were just lying down and taking it all from the FBI like submissive little dogs with tails between their legs. Why couldn't they just tell them they didn't want protection, like the twins' parents had?

"It's for the best, honey," she mocked under her breath now that no one was around. "They're looking out for us, honey. They'll find him, honey."

After Agent Gavin had died trying to save Greyson from his captors (that was the story the FBI was going with, for now), the FBI had driven them in seemingly random directions for a long hour to escape any terrorists who may have followed. Once satisfied they weren't being tailed, the agents had been given directions from their superiors. They were to relocate. Again.

At least she had that in common with Greyson. Now no one would know where either of them was.

After sleeping in the new house with borrowed pajamas and toiletries, her possessions had come packed ever so nicely in trash bags. They'd even thrown the picture frames in with the clothes to protect them.

Sydney rolled her eyes, but then jumped when the door opened.

"What?"

The agent held out a phone to her. "For you."

Skeptical, she reached out for it, half-expecting him to pull it away and laugh. He didn't.

"Hello?"

*"Sydney. This is Sam."*

"Sam!" She probably sounded too excited.

*"Hey! How are you doing? You know…considering."*

Sydney eyed the FBI agent who was watching her. She shooed him away, and he obeyed with a condescending smirk. "I'm okay. New place sucks. But they haven't let me call you; do you know —"

*"I'm here on speakerphone with my dad, Syd."*

74

Then came the Governor's voice. *"Hello, Sydney. I apologize for the place…and for everything. It – it really is unconscionable that we failed to protect you, Greyson, and your family after you've done so much for us. I just talked to your parents and expressed my deepest regrets."*

"But it was the Feds' fault," Sam added. *"Dad'll fix them when he gets elected."*

Sydney smiled. It was good hearing his voice again.

*"Sam,"* Governor Reckhemmer sighed. *"It won't happen overnight. So, until then, I wanted to ask you, Sydney, if there is anything I can do to –"*

"Tell me about Greyson," she blurted. Suddenly she realized what she had done. "S-sorry. I didn't mean to interrupt."

*"Oh, well, I understand your concern. What do you know so far?"*

She had to be careful not to indicate Sam's help in Greyson's escape. "Nothing, really. That they took him."

*"Syd – he got away,"* Sam interjected. *"He was on a bus, but he ran from some police in Illinois. Then someone reported that they had picked him up hitchhiking, with a dog."*

Her breath caught in her lungs as the sensation of relief traveled to her smile. He'd made it out. But what had happened? Why had he hitchhiked? Had he run out of money already? He had a dog with him?

*"He punctured one of their tires, stole their keys, and ran,"* Sam concluded.

*"That was this morning,"* the Governor added. *"There's been no sign of him since. His transponder was found on the side of the road half a mile from your old residence."*

Sam was excited. *"Nothing on security cameras, credit cards – nothing."*

Sydney took in a deep breath, trying to put it all together.

The governor sighed as well. *"We're trying to understand why he's still running. Perhaps he thinks Pluribus is still chasing him."*

Sydney imagined Sam playing it cool, trying to avoid eye contact. "Yeah. I bet that's it. After having that tracker put in him, he's been a little paranoid ever since."

*"I understand that. He's probably skeptical of the FBI as well."*

Had she said too much? "Yeah, I bet."

There was a brief pause on the other line. *"Sydney, did you happen to notice a red backpack go missing from your things before Greyson was taken?"*

The air sucked from her lungs. She had to respond quickly, or risk being suspicious. "Uh…no. I have one, but I just got my things today. I can look for it."

*"No, no. Just wondering."*

"Okay."

Another pause. *"The FBI will keep looking for him, but their resources are spread thinner than they've ever been. He should show up soon. I'll make sure you know as soon as I do. Is there anything else I can do for you?"*

Nodding to herself, she worked up her courage. "Yeah. Could I get another phone?"

The governor laughed. *"Oh, they took that from you? Hard to be without one of those nowadays. I feel naked without mine."*

"Dad!" Sam moaned.

Sydney laughed, too, mostly at Sam.

*"Sure thing,"* the governor agreed happily. *"And you know what? I'm going to step out of the room here and let you two catch up. It was nice talking to you. Again – anything you need."*

"Thank you, Governor!"

*"You're welcome. Take care."*

She listened for his footsteps and the closing door. When the sound came, there was a pause. *"Just a sec, Syd."*

As Sydney waited, she knelt by a trash bag and began taking her picture frames out one by one, laying them carefully on the stained carpet. There were several pictures of her with her mom and dad and one of her friends – though these friends were from her old school and would never be her friends again. The next picture was the one of Greyson she had kept by her bed.

*"Line's secure."*

"That was close. Think he knows?"

*"That he ran away on purpose? No. But they still don't know how he got the bus ticket."*

"What is Greyson doing? Has he tried to get ahold of you?"

*"He got robbed. They caught some of the robbers, though they wouldn't admit to it."*

"Geez." Sydney's shoulders slumped as she held the broken picture of Greyson. The glass was cracked over Greyson's face, like he'd been caught in a spider web. But he was still smiling that perfect smile. Her mother had taken the picture the first day of the fair, before it had all gone wrong.

She stood up, carrying the frame to her new bed, which creaked under her weight. "We've got to help him, Sam."

*"With helicopters, drones, and all, I think they're going to find him. I don't know what else we can do."*

---

The moonlit trees hurtled past to the left and right as he weaved between them, sprinting as fast as his lumbering backpack allowed. His breath came out in cold, airy gasps, filtering into the orange and yellow leaves where he imagined the helicopter hovering in the night sky.

Greyson could hear the *whupwhupwhupwhup* of its blades, but he'd lost track of its spotlight. He had panicked when he'd seen it – which had been almost a full minute after he'd heard it.

Kit had been walking beside him in the field at the edge of the trees, and they'd begun to get complacent, hours after escaping from the couple in the car. They were just beginning to look for a place to hunker down for the night when Kit's ears had perked up, near-perfect triangles of antenna-like radar. Before long he'd heard it, too, and they were off, trudging through the field and into the trees.

"Here, boy! In here!" Greyson knelt at the roots of a tree that hung over a dried riverbed, eroded beneath except for the roots that kept it upright. Cowering within its roots, he hid within the small dirt cave.

Kit ran to him, and Greyson pulled him closer. If he was as scared as Greyson was, he didn't show it. Kit even gave him a lick and watched him while panting, as if they were just taking a break from a game.

*WhupwhupwhupWhupWhupWhup!*

Greyson clutched Kit closer, suddenly afraid that he'd dash away, chasing the helicopter like it was the mail truck or a rabbit.

*It's the government, right?* The Plurbs didn't have helicopters. If anybody caught him, it was best the government be the captors. They'd take him back and never let him go; but at least they wouldn't kill him or torture him like the Plurbs would.

But then again, maybe the Plurbs *did* have helicopters. If they could get an atomic bomb, they could get a helicopter.

*WhupWhupWhupWHUPWHUPWHUP!*

The spotlight found their hiding place.

# Chapter 14

The helicopter's spotlight beamed through the gaps in the leaves above, a golden-white glow – like a sudden, piercing gaze of the sun. Greyson pushed himself deeper into the dirt and the roots, letting them hang over his shoulders and around his knees. For a moment they felt like snakes, but he shrugged off the irrational fear and hugged them tight.

Kit growled at the spotlight as it jerked through the trees further along the riverbed and away from their little cave.

*WHUPWhupWhupWhupWhupwhupwhupwhupwhup.*

Only after the last sound of the blades had echoed away in the night was Greyson able to breathe fully with a sigh of relief. Exchanging a look with Kit, he released the roots and snuggled closer to him.

From his vantage point at the edge of the creek bed, he scanned the dark trees that stretched for miles as a boundary between two empty fields, like a reef in an ocean of dirt. And he had fallen in.

Mud streaked his face and clotted in his hair. He swiped at his arms and then his hair and face, but that only made it worse. Only after wiping the mud from between his fingers, using the inside of his hoodie, was he able to feel clean enough to pet Kit again. Together they listened to the night, reluctant to move from their cave.

---

Sydney lay down on her bed, determination seeping into her eyes the more she looked at Greyson's picture. "Sam. Find us a way to the Bahamas."

Sam scoffed into the phone and laughed a little to be more polite. *"Vacation would be nice, but I'm pretty busy."*

"Then just me. And maybe the twins and Sammy. We can all go – even our parents." Her eyes lit up as the idea implanted itself. "Vacation is exactly what we need."

*"Well, that would be nice, but –"*

"Your dad said I could ask for anything, right? What's the difference between waiting for the terrorists to find me again in Iowa, and waiting in the Bahamas?"

"Well, I don't think —"

"Can you ask him, Sam? We'll meet Greyson there and help him find his dad."

There was a long pause. Part of Sam didn't want to get interrupted again, and the other part didn't want to disappoint her. *"I'll ask. But it won't happen overnight."*

She nodded at his governor-like response, turning over on her stomach with the frame on the pillow. She would have to replace the glass somehow. "Thanks."

*"But you've got to do me a favor, then."*

Sydney smiled coyly at his suggestion, imagining his dimples as he smirked. "Okay. What?"

*"Tell me about yourself. Honestly."*

Her brow furrowed. "Huh?"

*"I want to know you better. Without talking about terrorists or running away."*

Her smile grew and her worries were replaced with a kind of curiosity. "Okay. What do you want to know?"

*"Well, let's start easy. What's your favorite color?"*

*Red.* But she couldn't say that. "Yellow. Yours?"

*"Red, white, and blue together."*

"So, is that like brown or something?"

He laughed generously. *"Your turn."*

"Uh...what type of music do you listen to?"

*"Classical mostly."*

"Yeah, right."

*"No, really!"*

"Why?"

*"Because I like it. And it gives me a better ear. I play piano and violin."*

"No way," she whispered, as if it were a secret. "For real?"

He chuckled. *"Yeah. For real. I take lessons and stuff, but I'm not going to be a professional or anything. Dad said it develops the mind and gets the ladies...uh..."*

"The *piano* does? Maybe if you played the guitar..."

They laughed together and her bed squeaked.

*"What was that?"* he asked.

"The bed. It's got to be thirty years old."

*"Yikes. Can I see it? Want to switch to video call?"*

Sydney looked at what she was wearing. "Uh...sure. Call me back?"

*"Yup."*

She ran to one of her trash bags, found a better shirt and changed quickly. When the phone began to buzz, she jumped back on the bed stomach-first. The picture frame with Greyson's picture fell from the pillow and into her hands. Using the spider-webbed glass as a mirror, she tidied up her hair and straightened her heart necklace.

But she stopped. She looked beyond the cracks to Greyson's face.

Guilt gnawed at her heart as her phone continued to buzz.

*He left me. It's okay. He'd want me to have another friend – to be happy. I'm tired of pretending to be okay. I need someone, too.*

She swallowed the guilt and put a strand of hair back in place.

Satisfied, she put the frame face down on the bedside table and answered the call with a beaming smile.

------------------

Greyson began to shiver even though he was huddled with Kit. Now that he was fully satisfied that the helicopter hadn't spotted him, the cold finally motivated him to move.

Pulling his backpack out of the root-cave, he tried to wipe some of the mud off its exterior, but it was futile. Instead, he zipped it open and fingered through the contents.

*Where's the blanket?* The answer dawned on him, and he shook his head in disgust. He dug in deeper and frantically searched but came up without a flashlight. *Really? What else did she take out?*

And then he found the can of creamed corn.

He looked at Kit and showed him what he had found. Kit cocked his head and Greyson cocked his as well. "Exactly." At least she hadn't grabbed his extra underwear. That would have been awkward. Though he would trade all his extra underwear – even the ones he had on – for a blanket.

At least *she* had the blanket and a warm house. At least one of them was comfortable and safe.

Shivering and rubbing his arms, Greyson thought through his options. Being so tired, and still a little worried there were more helicopters out looking for him, he decided to stay. Putting on every piece of clothing he had, he began constructing a makeshift shelter over the root-cave.

Not really knowing what to do, he found a few fallen branches long enough to lean against the overhang that formed a little roof. He then weaved a few more branches horizontally through the longer sticks. Finally, he gathered what leaves he could find on the ground and piled them inside the cave.

Greyson rubbed his hands on Kit for friction. He supposed he could start a fire right now, but it wouldn't be smart. What if he had started a fire before the helicopter had flown over? He'd have been spotted and nabbed before he could have put it out.

Alternating feelings of despair and exhilaration bit at him like the chill. Shivering, he crawled to his leaf bed, called Kit to him and snuggled into his fur. Though it felt frigid outside, it only had to be about fifty degrees. What if he had waited a few more weeks to leave? What if he had taken Sydney with? Would they have been robbed? What if he had not told Kit to stop attacking the boy? Would Kit have killed CheekBones? What if Dad is in Nassau, like Emory said, but he isn't alive?

Another chill shook the thoughts away. He could ask himself a hundred 'what if' questions, but most wouldn't help. What mattered now, right now, was getting some sleep.

And for that end, he quickly took the hat from his head and found his multi-tool in his fanny pack. After a few delicate slices, he had freed the picture from the pouch sewn into his hat. It had been folded and pressed against his scalp for more than a year – ever since Kip had told him and his mom to burn any belongings that could help the terrorists trace them. Together they had burned album after album, but this picture he had kept hidden.

Now, staring at his dad's face, he felt guilty. He hadn't looked at it since he had hidden it away. Part of him had begun to forget what he looked like. It only took a second to rearrange the picture he'd had in his mind to match the picture, but it had taken a second still.

He took another few seconds looking at him. They shared the same wide smile – the same bold, green eyes – and the same thick brown hair, though Greyson's was now matted with mud. He smiled at him, imagining them together. He slid the picture into a groove in the stick wall.

Desiring even more company, he searched the front pocket of his fanny pack and unraveled a folded photograph. Shivering, he held the Polaroid into a stream of moonlight, admiring her smile. The picture had caught her just as she had reacted to his poke. It was an unfiltered, un-posed smile like the one he knew and loved. She had said earlier to ignore the ugly girl in the picture.

81

He had wanted to argue. She was far from ugly. She was naturally beautiful. He knew she wanted him to tell her so, but something held him back. His own smile had made him feel guilty.

But now he wished he had said it.

"Goodbye, Beautiful," he said softly to Sydney. "And good night." Then, kissing her photograph, he folded it back up and stored it away safely.

# Chapter 15

*Three days later…*

Kit nuzzled closer to Greyson's restless, sleeping frame. The boy's eyelids fluttered, and his brow creased with intense concern. Sensing his distress, Kit whimpered and pawed at his side.

*The mushroom cloud towered overhead, blinding Greyson and scorching his clothes. He felt his skin burning, sizzling, and pain tore through him in jagged, metal waves. But just as he felt he would burn to ash, Orion punched him, and he was powerless to defend himself. Emory laughed from behind, approving Orion's work – immune to the blast still roaring on the horizon, toppling trees.*

*Greyson swung around and saw the crusty cowboy, SnakeSkin, reaching toward him, dripping wet with a deathly glare. Greyson turned to run, but Liam was grasping his legs, pulling him toward the shore. The trees were on fire all around him. Liam was crying out, and SnakeSkin advanced, drawing his serrated knife.*

*Greyson was helpless, stuck, screaming out. He screamed for his dad, but he didn't come. Who could help him? No one was there. No one was ever there.*

*He felt the blade enter his stomach.*

Greyson woke with a gasp and grabbed at his slingshot as Kit pawed at his side with sharp claws. He ignored the claws, collecting his thoughts as he struggled to wake fully. He put his face in his hands until his breathing slowed.

Kit nuzzled him with his wet nose.

"Okay, okay," he said, pushing Kit's snout away and beginning to pet him. "Good morning to you, too."

Though he felt he could sleep another day, he had to get moving and stay moving. The dusk was fading into night, and the sun's heat would go with it. Out of necessity, he had become nocturnal – traveling during the cover of night and sleeping through the heat of the day. It didn't make for the best sleep, but he didn't have much of a choice.

Groaning painfully, he managed to stand, rubbing at his sore legs and shaking off the nightmare – whatever it had been. He tried to pull at some of the clumps of dirt that had matted his hair, but it was useless – and painful. Instead, he slipped his hat on over the mess.

He took a swig from his water bottle he'd filled from a farmer's watering trough. The water had been meant for the farmer's cows, but Greyson had been desperate. Though his lips were still cracking from being so chapped, his head no longer pounded as bad as it once had.

Kit smiled at him, panting. Remembering Kit's needs, he poured him an inch of water in the bowl he'd made from two pieces of curved bark. With a little carving from his knife, he'd made two notches for them to fit together just right. It leaked a little bit, but Kit would drink from it so fast it didn't have time to leak much.

Finally waking fully, he took a long look at the map and walked to the edge of the trees. Fields stretched both in the direction he had come and in the direction he was headed, though there were hills to the east finally offering an alternative to southern Illinois' expansive plains. On the horizon, he could barely make out the light of a town beginning to glow with the new night, and listening closely, he could still hear the distant hum of a highway.

Though it had been a long few days, some of the longest he'd ever had, they had only traveled a few dozen miles. Sure, treading along the dried creek bed was not the fastest route, but he'd thought it was the safest by far. But now, he wasn't so sure. Safety from captors was one thing, but safety from hunger and cold was another.

He had to find a faster way south. He'd lay awake for hours, just thinking. A bike. A horse. Jumping on the back of a semi. Finding a train. Even trying hitchhiking again had crossed his mind.

Kit whined and pawed at his fanny pack. Greyson gave in and rummaged through the remnants. Sadly, his fingers came out with the last beef jerky nugget. It was not only the last nugget – but the last of all their food. Six granola bars, trail mix, Skittles, and a package of jerky could only be rationed for so long with a ravenous teenager and a sizable dog.

*Enjoy it, mutt.*

He threw it to Kit and smiled as he ate it in one gulp.

"No more," he said, holding up his hands, wondering if he knew what the gesture meant. "All out."

Kit cocked his head and Greyson shrugged. *Well, there is one more thing of food.* But he hadn't reached that point yet. The creamed corn was only for extreme emergency.

Suddenly his stomach growled at Kit so loudly that Kit growled back. The way Kit glared at his stomach made him laugh for a while, but the pain that followed sobered him. His stomach and Kit's were in competition in a way that scared him. What if they didn't find food soon? Would Kit walk until he couldn't anymore, or would he turn on Greyson – making him dog food? Or…would Greyson ever eat Kit?

Shaking the stupid thought from his head, he destroyed his stick-shelter and scattered his leaf-bed. Once the evidence was gone, he swung his backpack around his shoulders with another painful grunt. The straps rested perfectly on the blisters from yesterday.

"Let's go, boy. Maybe we can find some burgers tonight…with hot fries and ketchup. And a Dr. Pepper."

Kit licked his chops.

"Have you ever had Dr. Pepper, Kit? No? Well, it's frickin' good. It's even good hot. Tastes like cider. Did you know that?"

Greyson trucked along the edge of the field, eyeing the lights from the farmhouse up ahead. A thought perked in his mind, tempting him. If he'd already stolen someone's dog and someone's water, what would a little more matter?

--------------------

Orion ran his fingers along his crooked nose as if stroking a beard. Lost in thought, his brothers examined the scene with him. Tiny rubber fragments from where the tire had been punctured, a few plastic pieces from the remains of the two phones, and four sets of footprints. Two sets headed out to the fields but had returned to the same spot – the same size and sole marks. Another set headed diagonally, into the fields, but south. Smaller prints – size 10s. And then there was another set of print next to the size 10s. But they weren't human.

"This is where it must've happened."

One of Orion's friends, Glasses, sided up to him. "I agree. He could be close if he kept walking. Thirty miles maybe."

"He'd keep heading south."

Emory had been surprisingly calm when he had found out what happened, but Orion could tell that he was disappointed. Killing an FBI agent had been an unexpected spark to add to an already flammable situation. His father had gone into intense planning mode for hours, finally returning to him with a plan of action.

"Launch the Quad drone," Orion commanded. "Follow that tree line. He'll stay close to the highway for a reference point."

His tall brother, Lanky, pulled open the trunk of the SUV and removed a large suitcase. The biggest brother, Buzz, joined him, taking the small vehicle from its protective packaging and unfolding its four rotors. Buzz switched it on as Glasses took the remote-controls and checked the highway not far behind them. They waited for a few cars to pass, hiding the drone from traffic until the proper time.

"Now."

Lanky and Buzz lifted the drone into the air, and it whirred to life, hovering above their heads like a hummingbird. It was the size of small pizza and only armed with a central camera surrounded by the four rotors, but something about it was intimidating. When someone would see it, they wouldn't know who controlled it or what it would do to them.

Most Americans hadn't experienced a fear of drones yet. To them, they were hobby items, toys, or just another delivery option. It was the terrorists overseas who were afraid of drones with names like Predator and Reaper. But things would change soon enough. America had let drones in, trusting their government to keep them safe. But what would happen when it was the government they had to fear? And what would happen if those drones fell into the wrong hands? Soon enough they would be afraid of blue skies.

With a sudden jerk, the drone burst away, into the night. Its silhouette was only visible as it blocked out the stars, whisking away at thirty or forty miles per hour.

"Infrared's working," Glasses said, watching the video feed from the tablet.

"What are those?" Buzz asked, pointing at red and yellow blobs on the screen as the drone zoomed over them.

Glasses scoffed. "Cows, genius."

"Let's go," Orion commanded.

As they turned their SUV around to follow the path of the drone, Orion slowly stroked the curve of bone on his nose where Greyson had struck him. The jagged look had ruined any beauty he'd had. He looked forward to returning the favor.

--------------------

The jagged scars looked like melted wax had dribbled down his skin and hardened. Sam pushed at them, testing them for healing while watching in the hotel's mirror.

Thin, leathery letters. Crinkled to the touch.

*Ex Molo Bonum.* Latin for 'out of evil comes good'.

It was his back he was reading. His body was a message given to his dad – a scroll, written by knife with blood.

He smashed his eyelids down to try to hide the sparks of memory that haunted him. The knife that so easily sliced through his flesh. The searing pain. The bonds that tied him down, cutting at his wrists and ankles. The feel of his blood dripping down his sides and around to his abdomen.

He opened his eyes to stare at his face in the mirror as it hovered above the scarred back. His face was youthful, but his back looked so old. If he turned to the side, he was just another half-Asian boy. But when he exposed his back, he was a withered scroll. He was both at once. Boy and message.

He turned to face the mirror. This is what he wanted people to see. Even the mole on his cheek. Nothing hidden. He was just like everyone else. Happy. Confident. Proud. Handsome and winsome.

Politician.

From following his dad, listening to his campaign managers, and conversing with the other candidates' kids, he was learning what politics was all about. Facing the public with your best foot forward. Showing them the side of you or the side of the issues you wanted them to see, and not so much the other side. You were supposed to talk about your opponents' scars, but never your own. It's not like you would lie about them – his dad said he never lied – but you were supposed to *hide*.

His dad didn't have much to hide, though. The only thing he would hide was something he thought the public did not need to know – like Emory's message. If Emory had wanted to world to hear the message, Sam's dad wanted the opposite.

Sam kept his front to the mirror, listening to the faint voices coming from outside the bathroom where his dad was speaking on the phone. He was talking to someone about the economy – one of President Foster's major scars. And the scar was getting deeper. So deep that there had been tons of protests and riots – until the bomb. Even the rioters had sensed it wasn't right to fight the nation while it was under attack. They had stopped rioting as if to honor the victims with a week of peace. But with the bomb had come a plummeting stock market and more bad news about the national debt. And they'd started rioting again.

*Debt.* That word came up all the time with numbers so large he could barely fathom them. His dad would strategize on how to show the public the scars, but also how to heal them. He was a problem solver, a doctor.

Maybe someday his dad could think of a way to heal his scars – to make his back clear, the color of the rest of his skin – the color his mother had given him with her Chinese ancestry. He didn't want to have to hide half of himself.

"Sam?" His father's voice came from the other side of the door.

"Uh – yeah? J-just a second." He was frantically putting on his shirt and flushing the toilet to make it sound like he was finishing up.

"We need to talk about your new tutor. I'll be waiting for you in the conference room."

He ran the faucet, also buttoning his shirt. "Okay! Be right out."

Before leaving, he took another look at himself in the mirror. His back was hidden again, beneath a pleasant exterior. Adding a smile helped even more. But it didn't change what he felt about himself. He was hiding something besides his scars – the fact that he'd helped put Greyson in this mess. And hiding things wasn't fun.

Whenever he had played hide and seek as a younger kid – mostly with babysitters – he had wanted to be the seeker. The one in control. Sometimes he hadn't even looked for the hider. He'd helped himself to a cookie in the kitchen or got into things he wasn't supposed to. He looked for them on his own time. In a way, the hider was at the mercy of the seeker.

Hiding was not who he was.

---------------------

Hiding behind a rusted grain bin, Greyson eyed the farmhouse, watching for any movement through the lit windows. There were only two lights on now, both downstairs in the two-story house. He might be able to sneak a peek in the windows to see how many were awake, but it would be smarter just to wait for them to go to bed and turn off the lights.

Until then, though, there was the dilapidated red barn to his left. It probably had a wealth of tools – and maybe, if it were still in use – it would have animals and their food. Maybe there would be blankets, or…if there were cows…there'd be milk.

Licking his lips, he worked up the courage to sneak to the barn through the thick grass, his eyes still latched on to the windows, ready to hit the deck if a figure would appear.

Kit strode confidently through the grass and approached the barn first. There wasn't a back door, so they curled around the outside where some rusted equipment threatened to gash their shins. Thankfully there was enough moonlight to paint the tops of everything with a dull, blue hue, and they managed to avoid them with no trouble. They wouldn't have that moonlight for much longer, though. A wall of thick, tumbling clouds hovered in the west, rolling closer every minute.

Finally, working their way to the barn's front door, they found it open. Suspicious, he glanced toward the house. Empty porch. Lights still on. A long driveway stretched out to a gravel road that lay bare in both directions. No one was watching.

"Looks clear," he whispered.

It happened in a flash. Kit went in first, and with a yelp, fell to the dirt as his legs were taken from under him. Greyson had just turned to follow when the trap barreled toward his face.

# Chapter 16

Greyson's face was frozen, staring at the wooden beam that had almost slammed into his teeth. He had jolted back just as the beam came down from the rafters like a pendulum. But his reaction would have been too late if it hadn't been for Kit.

Looking down at Kit, who had gone before him, Greyson knew that Kit had saved his life or at least his teeth. The dog had tripped over the trip wire as it came through the doorway, triggering the trap that swung down over the dog's head, but straight toward Greyson's. If Greyson had gone in first, the heavy beam would have bashed his skull.

Though the trap itself had shocked him, it was the two words scrawled into it that had frozen him.

*GO AWAY!*

Whoever had etched those words had meant it.

But Greyson glanced toward the farmhouse. There was still no sign of anyone. Whoever had set the trap may not have heard the banging of the beam against the doorway. And more than likely, there was something inside the barn that he didn't want trespassers to see. He would have to be quick, but the risk was worth it.

Satisfied he wasn't being watched, Greyson ducked under the beam and stepped inside to examine the trap. Loose fishing line snaked on the dirt and wound up both sides of the doorway. Kneeling to pick up a strand in his hand, Greyson's eyes followed the line to the ceiling where two dowels were still swinging. Scrunching his head in thought, he drew himself a mental picture of how it had worked. It was so simple. The tripwire was tied to the dowels that had held up the wood beam like a swing. It had only taken a little push to jerk them free from their holes, releasing the beam to gravity.

A hint of a smile played at his lips as he gathered all the fishing line in his fist. In another minute he had found a dusty horse blanket with dinosaurs and the name *Max* on it, a small roll of twine, and some nails.

Stopping himself before zipping his bag closed, Greyson sighed. His conscience was creeping at his heart, reminding him of what he was doing.

Stealing.

Taking a glance at Kit, Greyson nodded to himself. He wouldn't steal. He would *borrow*. He could give it all back and more – once he had enough money to do so. He would come back and repay whoever owned these things – even though it was obvious the owner was not using them anymore.

He just needed a way to keep track.

Reaching into his fanny pack, his hand came out with a small Bible – the Bible that Pastor Whitfield had told him to give to Liam. It was a pretty convenient writing pad. He opened it and fingered through the thin, leafy pages. He felt guilty writing anything on the pages themselves, so he scrawled a few notes into the inside of the front cover. "One blanket. Twine. Four nails. Farmhouse.'

On his way out he would need to peek at the house's address. He'd keep track of anything he had to borrow, and then, someday, he would pay them back for everything. It would be his payback list.

In bold, capital letters, he wrote PAYBACK LIST on top of the page. Suddenly he regretted writing so big. His handwriting was horrible and almost filled half of the first page already. He flipped to the second page to make sure he'd have more room but stopped.

*What's that?* There was a message in someone else's handwriting.

*Liam, I suggest starting with the book of Luke. I hope you get to know Jesus more and more with each year.*
*- Pastor Whitfield*

*With each year…*

Suddenly irritated, Greyson closed the Bible and pushed it into his fanny pack. He couldn't think about Liam anymore. If he just pushed him out of his mind, it wouldn't hurt as much.

*CHUCK-CHICK!* The distinct sound of a shotgun pump. Behind him. Just outside the doorway.

Kit was growling, his lips shaking over his sharp teeth as he lowered his eyes past Greyson's shoulder. For a moment, Greyson debated his options, muscles tight as a spring as he knelt over his backpack. His fingers slowly wrapped around his slingshot.

# Chapter 17

"Stand up slowly! And turn around."

The voice was older – gravelly – but leaving no doubt to its confidence. Still kneeling, Greyson abandoned the idea of going for his slingshot. It would take far longer for him to load, draw, and shoot than it would for the man to squeeze the trigger.

Instead, he stood up slowly and held his hand up to Kit with the motion to 'stay'. Both were edgy, hungry, and tired. But that was no excuse for being stupid.

"Turn around!"

Greyson turned to face the man. He stood in the darkness outside, just a silhouette, but still distinguishable as an elderly man, with a drooped back and a wobbly grip on the shotgun.

"I was just looking for –"

"I DIDN'T ASK YOU!"

Greyson startled at the booming voice that echoed in the musty barn.

"You all are the same. You're not looking for shelter – you're *trespassing*. Not looking for food – looking to *steal*."

Fear gripped his throat, but its grip was much looser than he remembered it being. He'd been held by gunpoint before – and he'd lived to tell about it.

"How old are you?" the man asked, taking a step closer.

He had to sound innocent. Unafraid. "Thirteen. You?"

"Are you blind? You got a seeing-eye dog, and you don't seem to see this here shotgun pointed at you."

"No, sir. Just hungry."

The old man paused, the shotgun's barrel still making a trajectory toward Greyson's abdomen. "Are you alone?"

Greyson dropped the tension in his shoulders, trying to appear even more confident, though his heart pounded against his ribs. "Just me and the dog."

"Are you armed?" The man's eyes came into view as he stepped up to the doorway where the beam formed an upside-down cross. His eyebrows were bushy and gray, and he was indeed wrinkled, but not as much as Greyson would have guessed.

Greyson swallowed the fear and took in a deep breath. "Yes," he answered. "Two of them. Plus my dog's four."

The man sneered. "Think this is funny, do ya? I'd kill ya if I wanted. Bury you in the barn. Who'd miss ya?"

"Why kill me? You'd just have a mess to clean up and a body to bury. And less ammo."

For the first time, the man seemed to lose his angry composure. But it was just a glitch. He quickly ducked under the beam and re-aimed the shotgun at Greyson's chest. "I've killed before, son."

"So have I."

They examined each other in the light through squinted eyes like an old western duel, right before the cowboys would draw their weapons. Greyson's hands were at his sides, but too far from his slingshot to stand a chance in this duel.

*Mental note. Keep slingshot closer to hand.*

"You that boy they're looking for?"

Greyson kept his face blank. He had to lie better. "No, sir."

The man jerked his shotgun up, now pointed at Greyson's face. "What they want you for?"

His strategy was failing. *He might actually shoot me.* "I…I…don't know who you're talking —"

The man took another step forward. "Terrorism?"

"No."

"Running a checkpoint?"

"No. I don't…"

The man's eyes had lost their kindness. "Then tell me!"

*Tell. Tell.* The word gave him an idea. It might be the only way out.

"Okay, okay. I'll *speak*."

At the command, Kit let out a sharp bark that reverberated in the barn. The old man jerked out of fear, turning to face the dog and raising the gun out of instinct to block the dog's attack. But it was Greyson who attacked.

His left hand grabbed the gun's barrel. His right found the man's soft belly like a punching bag. In an instant, the man had doubled over and fallen to the dirt and straw. He coughed and grasped at his stomach; for a moment his eyes sparked with anger, but the longer Greyson stood over him, holding the shotgun away from him like it was a stinking diaper, the softer the man's gaze became.

93

With gusts of wind sifting through the doorway and banging at the sides of the barn, the rain began as a soft patter against the wooden roof and then turned to a rushing downpour.

"S-Sorry. But I didn't know if you were going to shoot."

It took another few deep breaths for their adrenaline to fade. Their fears softened and the man sat up, supporting his elbows on his knees. "Well, now you got the gun. What you going to do with it?"

"I'll give it back to you. Just promise to let me go. I'll repay you for the blanket and the rope and the nails. I promise."

The man stared him down, thinking. He didn't know what to make of this boy.

Greyson took the opportunity to eye Kit. The dog had saved him twice now. "And some food for the road, please. Dog and human."

The man laughed – an odd mixture of scoffs and guffaws – like he couldn't believe what was happening. Greyson smiled and even laughed a little with him until he had finally settled down. "Fine. You earned it. Last time I got played like that was in 'Nam."

*Nam? Should I know where that is?*

"Uh…thanks."

Not eager to hold on to the shotgun any longer than he had to, he laid it on the dirt and reached his hand out to the man. His heart began racing again, hoping he was right about him.

They grasped hands and, with a great struggle, he pulled the man to his feet. For a moment they were right next to each other. He smelled of smoke and old wood, but his grip was still strong enough to crush Greyson's hand. If there were a fight, it wouldn't end well.

But there wasn't one. The man bent over to the shotgun, eyeing the dog. "Just in case you'd like to know, if the Feds want you dead, I want you alive. If they want you in custody, I want you free." He got real close and put his shaky hand on Greyson's shoulder. Kit growled, but the man ignored him. "If I can take something back from the government, I'll do it. They always take what they want; I'm getting sick of it."

Greyson nodded, suddenly conscious of his chapped lips and his own body odor. But the old man didn't seem to care.

"Now, let's get you and Fido some food."

Kit and Greyson smiled at each other. *Food!*

Greyson snatched up his backpack and followed the man to the doorway; but the man stopped suddenly and turned.

"How'd you avoid the deadfall?"

Greyson cocked his head. "Huh? The trap?"

"Dog set it off?"

"Oh, yeah. It almost got me."

"Almost hit ya right in the Georgia."

"It's not a Georgia hat."

"It looks like one."

"Well, it's not."

The man shifted on his feet, still in the doorway. "Then what does the 'G' stand for?"

Greyson gave an annoyed look. "I don't know. Everyone asks that."

Squinting as if he were examining the hat, every scuff mark, every frayed edge, the man finally shrugged. "Then make something up! 'What do *you* stand for?'"

Letting the question descend into his thoughts, Greyson nodded to himself. He'd always guessed the 'G' stood for 'Gray', but he had never asked his dad. When he saw him next, he'd ask him.

"It might be for my dad's name. I stand for my dad."

The old man nodded and gave a surly frown. "I was expecting 'Guts', 'Glory', or 'Good'. But there're worse answers." He turned and put a hand on the trap's beam. "Next time I'll hook an extra arm on the bottom of the beam. It'll swing up and out, right at the groin – just like Charlie did in 'Nam."

Greyson nodded like he knew who Charlie was.

"No more babies," the man whispered with a smile. He muttered something else to himself as he ducked under the beam and into the rain. His figure hobbled toward the farmhouse.

Gritting his teeth as he imagined the pain of a beam to his groin, Greyson followed the old man into the darkness. His stomach was burning and hollow, but something nagged at him even worse. He stopped and turned toward the barn as the rain matted his hair and dripped down his brow.

"What did you call the trap again?"

The old man kept walking, speaking into the rain. "A deadfall. There's bait, a trigger, and the trap. Bait shows the prey something it wants – in this case, the open door to shelter. The trap falls, then you're dead. Deadfall. It promises life, but gives death."

The man, seemingly unaffected by the rain, continued his walk toward the comfort of his home, leaving Greyson staring at the doorway.

"Come on. I have more inside. I'll show you."

A voice inside told Greyson to run. If a deadfall lured its prey by showing it something it wanted – then maybe he was being lured right now. *Bait – food. Trigger – the house. Trap – who knows?*

Shaking off the thought and ignoring the voice, Greyson quick-stepped to the man and followed him through the door.

# Chapter 18

The plane shuddered with a brief spat of turbulence, but Sam wasn't concerned. He was too busy observing his new tutor, Calvin, at the table across from him. Calvin was odd, to say the least, but friendly. Sam couldn't quite place what his oddities added up to be, except maybe immaturity. For example, he held his laptop to his chest in a death grip with every vibration of the plane. His small eyes were hidden behind small glasses, eyelids clenched tight like he was expending great mental effort to close them.

There were more examples – the way he drank Mountain Dew religiously, the time he blushed when Sam asked him about his girlfriend, and the skinny jeans he wore – and they all pointed to him being lost in his teenage years despite being almost thirty.

"So, you worked for the NSA?" Sam asked, trying to stall the lesson as long as he could.

The tutor's eyes unclenched and, being embarrassed, he gulped and released some of his grip on the laptop. "Uh…work, actually. I still do, I'm just on leave to help you."

"On leave?"

Calvin's eyes darted around. "Right. Temporary lack of employment."

"Just to tutor me?"

His dad had told him that he was going to get someone younger, smarter, and more techy, and he'd kept his word. Only the best for his son.

"Well, sort of. I uh…am not really allowed to talk about it. Not able to talk about anything, really." He glanced around the plane, though there were only a few other people around, and all were absorbed in their computers. It was a private flight – a fancy one reserved for the governor and his campaign team.

"That makes sense. You probably know most of our nation's secrets."

That was a line he'd heard somewhere before. Most of what he knew about the NSA was that they were a highly secretive agency who many thought were spying on everyone – including Americans. Many, including his dad, loved them for protecting the country. Others hated them. But what was new? There wasn't much in the country anymore that *someone* didn't hate.

"No, not really. They keep it pretty limited. I just meant they are pretty strict on what you say, what you do, what friends you have, what questions you ask…"

"Gotcha. Like when I ask my dad, 'Can I please not waste my life studying lame stuff?'"

"Right," he laughed. "May I ask to what stuff you were referring?"

Sam smiled and glanced out the window. The cloudless night sky and brilliant stars cheered him up, despite having to fly to D.C., and despite having to be tutored the entire way. "Grammar is horrible, but my dad says I need it for speeches. And history can be cool, but dad said my old tutor spent a little too much time focused on the Nazis. He got concerned."

Calvin nodded and began to relax, though he was the type that seemed to always be a little on edge – a little paranoid he was going to say the wrong thing or look at someone the wrong way. "The Nazis *were* a little lame, though I can't blame your last tutor for wanting you to know about them. Don't want history repeating itself…"

The seatbelt light went off with a ding and it was like a switch went off in Calvin's head. "Anyhoo, don't you worry," he said, unfolding his laptop on the table and starting it like a well-worn habit. "We're going to focus on the stuff that makes this world go round. The stuff that can take down nations and militaries with a click of a mouse. Kabam! It's math, it's art, it's poetry, and yes, even a little grammar. But it's computer language – not boring English."

"Sounds cool." Sam unbuckled his seatbelt and leaned in. "Did Dad tell you I know a lot already?"

Calvin ran his hand through his squirrely black hair and adjusted his glasses. "Yes, he did. And I'm quite aware of all you've done." He smirked.

Sam squinted at him. *What does he know?* "Wh-what?"

Calvin jerked up, intently peering over his glasses. He paused, letting the seriousness of the moment come to a head. "Oh, everything you do online can be tracked. I know every site you've visited, every message you've sent, every image you've seen. I know everything you've done."

Sam's mouth sunk open and his mind raced as his tutor's eyes drew even more serious. And then Calvin laughed and snorted, smacking himself on the knee over and over. Sam scrunched his brow, watching Calvin laugh and laugh. A few other men and women in suits watched them with sideways glances, and the stewardess gave him a nervous smile.

"Your face! It gets them every time!" He kept laughing, and Sam felt a weight come off his shoulders. He didn't know. His secret was safe...for now.

"But dude..." Calvin said, taking deep breaths to calm down. "You seriously shouldn't look at that stuff. It ruins your mind. Truuuuust me."

---

Greyson still didn't trust the old man. He kept his distance, even as he offered him a seat at his kitchen table.

"Here. Dry off," the old man said, throwing him a bath towel from the bathroom around the corner.

He'd need more than a towel to earn Greyson's trust. Still, Greyson would use him as long as he could.

Greyson patted Kit's face with the towel and then swiped at his fur, muttering something about making him feel better.

The old man had stopped outside the kitchen, watching them. He found it odd that the boy wiped the dog before drying himself. A hint of a smile worked at his lips before he returned to his permanent scowl and searched for a type of food a boy would eat. It had been too long.

Kit suddenly erupted into a full-blown dog shake, sending water spraying over the kitchen tile. Greyson laughed and finally used the towel on himself.

"You'll clean up after yourself," the old man said matter-of-factly.

Greyson finished drying his hair and instantly went to using the towel as a mop on the floor, crawling after Kit as he left muddy footprint after muddy footprint on the tile.

"Sorry, sir," Greyson apologized.

The old man didn't respond, as if he were lost in a memory.

---

"What do you think it could be, female parental unit?"

Jarryd's mom shook her head and glanced at him through the rearview mirror. "Jer-Bear, call me Mom or I'll need to call you an ambulance."

Jarryd pumped his chin at her. "Oh, I'm scared! But no, seriously. What's with the traffic?"

It had been stop-and-go traffic for half an hour. They had been watching their GPS's estimated time of arrival grow later and later. Most of the half hour they had tried sleeping, but only Sammy had been successful. He was leaned forward onto his lap, drooling into his half-empty peanut container.

Nick was too concerned to sleep. Though he'd gotten out of the car to scan past the moving van that their stepdad drove ahead of them, he'd spent the last few minutes examining the lighted billboard along the highway. The picture was of a half-burnt teddy bear lying amongst rubble. Behind the unfortunate bear was the silhouette of a ruined cityscape, smoking and burning. Big, bold letters stretched to the right of the teddy bear. NEVER AGAIN.

"Again, I don't know," their mother replied. "It might be another tollbooth, but it might be the Oklahoma border. Your dad said there are rumors of traffic stops…"

Nick rolled his eyes and shook his head to himself, gazing out the window into the dark Kansas plains. He knew they weren't rumors. This *was* a traffic stop. But he couldn't tell them that he knew. They would ask how he knew and then he'd have to lie again. If they knew he was still in contact with the Plurbs who he'd met at the SuperMart, they'd freak.

"Look, a warning sign," Jarryd blurted.

Their car rolled forward another ten feet, slowly revealing the sign as it came into view from behind the moving van: *Do Not Turn Around. Violators Will Be Fined.*

The traffic stop was just like Nick was told. First the traffic jam. Then the signs warning them not to turn around. And then would be the drones.

"Aagh!"

His mother had screamed as the first drone appeared at Jarryd's window, its stubby camera pointing, scanning through the windows. It didn't appear to be armed – just a surveillance drone – but there were certainly more above them, out of sight, monitoring, waiting.

The drone seemed to focus on each one of them for a mere moment before hovering to the next car. Nick had been more amused than afraid, but it was his mother who was hyperventilating. Adults seemed to have a harder time with drones, having not grown up with them. But the kids had seen enough of them in person, and had watched enough videos of the newest, more sophisticated drones, that seeing one didn't bother them much.

On the other hand, if they had seen a Bradley Fighting Vehicle parked nearby, it may have given them pause.

At one traffic stop, there had been rumored sightings of one such vehicle.

It had supposedly been hidden in a dark green cargo container plunked in the middle of a farmer's field, ready to defend against any attack with its distinct tank-like treads, short-barreled gun turret, and box-like missile launcher. Nick saw one such cargo container right now. Perhaps it was the same one that had spurred the rumors. But he imagined the rumors were probably just that. Still, what if it was there, concealed inside a green cargo container in a barren Kansas field instead of the war zones in the Middle East? Was the government really that scared? Would it ever really be necessary?

"Someone's talking with Dad."

Nick leaned over Sammy's slumped back to where Jarryd was watching a soldier talking with their stepdad through the driver's side window. Leaning back to his side, Nick noticed there was another soldier on the passenger side holding something like an electronic squeegee, dragging it along the side of the moving van's cargo hold. In the soldier's other hand was a computer tablet that he was examining intently.

"They're x-raying our stuff," Nick explained.

"Cool!" Jarryd took his turn leaning over the sleeping Sammy, using him as an armrest.

Together they watched the soldier make another sweep with the device, this time holding it higher. After the second sweep, the first soldier came to the back, unlocked the padlock with the key their stepdad had given them, and rolled up the door to all their belongings.

"We have nothing to hide, boys," their mom comforted. "Just stay calm and –"

"Speak for yourself," Jarryd interrupted. "I've got things to hide. Valuable things."

"What? All your bomb-making supplies?" Nick remarked.

"Shh!" warned their mother.

Jarryd rolled his eyes and lowered his voice. "The FBI took that already. My whole chemistry set! But hair-spray's got flammable propellant in it."

Nick nodded. If there was one thing his brother knew, it was mixing things together to make new things. It was too bad he spent most of that knowledge on making new hair styles.

"True. And you do have a whole box of that kind of stuff."

"Yeah. Secret stuff."

"Right. Concealer, exfoliating cleanser, toner…what else?"

"There's like ten steps." Jarryd waved over his face. "You think *this* just happens? While you and the sun are still sleeping...I'm creating handsome."

"If I were you, I'd keep that secret, too."

The soldiers finished their search quickly, secured the door, and waved the van on. Jarryd caught a glimpse of his stepdad in the driver's side mirror. He looked frustrated to say the least. But he knew better than to flip the bird at a soldier – whether or not they had a Bradley Fighting Vehicle pointing a missile launcher at them.

"Our turn," their mom said, driving to where the soldiers were waving them down. "Be calm."

The first soldier had the typical short camo hat and a nameplate bearing the name Williams. Setting his jaw as if he were bored, Williams waited for their mother to roll down the window. "Mrs. Aldeman, correct?"

*The drone must have fed their facial identifications to his tablet.*

"Yes, sir."

"Sorry for the delay. We are conducting a few routine traffic stops just as a precaution, keeping the terrorists on their toes," he explained as if he'd done it a hundred times – and he probably had. "Reason for traveling?"

"Moving to Texas with the refugee housing program. I'm following my husband, and he has the papers. He was in the moving van –"

"Who is the third child?"

"Uh..." their mom looked back at the sleeping Sammy, as if she had forgotten about him. "That's our adopted son. It's not finalized yet, but..."

As his partner scanned their trunk, Williams took a step toward the back window and motioned to Jarryd to roll down his window. Jarryd pressed the button and tried not to tremble. "Hey."

Ignoring Jarryd, the soldier glanced at his handheld device and examined each one of the boy's faces, comparing it to the picture he had on his device. *Looking for Greyson?*

"You are Jarryd?"

"The one and only."

William's face didn't change. "And him?" He pointed to Sammy.

Jarryd slapped at him until he woke with a gasp, his lazy eye floating around, and the line of drool flopping to his t-shirt. His hair looked the same as it always did – like a hyena had been electrocuted.

"Sammy. He's talking to you."

102

Sammy sucked at his slobber and rubbed at his eyes until he could focus on the soldier. "Whoth the buff dude?"

"Who are you?" Williams asked, getting impatient.

"Your *wortht* nightmare."

"Sammy!" their mother scolded.

Nick shook his head and laughed. "He's so funny. Our new brother."

"Are these your brothers, Sammy?"

Sammy swung his gaze from Jarryd to Nick to Jarryd, and back to Nick again. "They *do* look familiar."

Jarryd and Nick laughed and shrugged. Jarryd leaned into the skeptical soldier. "He's a little slo-oooow."

"Right. You," he looked to Nick. "Why are you moving to Texas?"

*Why is it your business?* "Uh...'cuz my parents are taking us there? I'm just a kid. But, boy, I can't wait to see the Alamo, where rebels stood up to a much superior force." Nick adjusted his glasses, making sure the frames covered the scar over his eyebrow.

"Right. Before they were all slaughtered," Williams replied snidely. He then typed something into his device, exchanged a look with the other soldier, and waved them on. As fast as it had started, it was over. The traffic picked up and nothing was said for several beats, as if they didn't want to jinx it. Sammy drifted back to sleep, and their mother called their stepdad. Her voice was strained, and they could hear their stepdad's anger. He said something about being justified in leaving, telling her they'd made the right decision.

Soon enough, a sign welcomed them to Oklahoma. Nick watched it fly by, getting lost in his thoughts as the power lines drooped up and down between each pole like drapes. His thoughts were just about to fade into a daydream when another sign caught his attention. At the edge of a fence, just visible in the starlight, was a homemade sign made of plywood and painted white. In red spray-painted letters it read:

*Future Home of the ARC – Where You're Free Again.*

The drooping power lines dipped and rose, dipped and rose. Nick's lips did the same, until the smile won out.

103

# Chapter 19

Greyson tried to eat slowly, but he had never been so hungry. It seemed like he grew hungrier with every bite. As soon as his first bowl of soup had only a few drops left, he wanted another; but the old man was occupied making something else for him.

"There, you have yourself your very own sling-bow." The man, who had asked to be called John, held up Greyson's slingshot. He had provided two new bands of his own, connecting one band to each side of the slingshot's Y frame. He had said that two bands were needed to stabilize the new ammunition.

John held up the homemade arrow he had fashioned in only a few minutes. It was a six-inch bolt as thick as a marker and threaded like a screw. The tip was sharp, and the other end had a nut screwed on for a grip. Toward the back, two tiny wings, like an arrow's fletching, were made from duct tape and would keep it steady in the air. And finally, a wingnut was threaded up to the middle of the bolt for the bands to hold.

"So, just put one band around this side of the wingnut, and the other around the other side," John narrated as he showed Greyson what to do. "Then, you pull it back, and…"

Greyson scooted his chair back.

John pulled it back until the rubber creaked, then he released it slowly, still holding the nut of the arrow. "I think it'll do what you want it to do."

After John had asked whether or not he really was armed, Greyson had shown him his slingshot. One thing had led to another, and Greyson had mentioned its failure to pierce car tires. After a quick trip to his basement workbench, the man had returned to the kitchen with a vigor and purpose.

"How'd you know how to make that?" Greyson asked, impressed. He had a guess, but he wasn't sure. While John had made his run to the basement, Greyson had perused the pictures on the wall. One had been taken of John in full military uniform from a long time ago. It wasn't very good quality, but he could see what looked like a jungle behind him. The jungle, combined with the automatic rifle he had slung over his shoulder and the cigar hanging from his mouth, made him look like an impressive man.

"I've always been good with those type of things. 'Suppose engineers should be. You keep it and the supplies. Should be able to make one on your own."

"Really? Thanks. So cool." Greyson put the bolt-arrow and the supplies to make another one into his fanny pack and immediately removed his Payback List. He scrawled in the supplies.

John eyed the book and Greyson's writing skeptically. He started to say something but changed his mind. Instead, he stood and pushed in his chair, making his way to a side door. "You asked about the traps, right?"

Greyson had to smile. He'd never had a grandpa before, but if he had, John would have been a good one. Maybe John had never had a grandson before either. He sure seemed to enjoy teaching him things.

Though his belly still felt empty, Greyson listened intently as John showed him another deadfall he had built for the side door, explaining each mechanism and how it worked. Most of the time, Greyson was intently listening, but at times his attention would fade, and he would find himself admiring the wrinkles folding into each other at the corners of John's eyes. It made him wonder what the old man's eyes had seen. He had seen war. Real war. If what Greyson had seen gave him nightmares, what did John have to deal with? He eyed John's shaking hand as he pointed at a notch he'd cut into the trigger plank. What had that hand done? How many times had it pulled a gun's trigger while pointed at another man?

"But it's the idea behind a deadfall that makes the booby trap work."

Jarryd would be launching into a laughing fit with this talk of booby traps. Greyson smiled at the thought, but when John turned his gaze to him, his smile vanished. It wouldn't be smart to get on John's bad side.

"Deadfalls play on whatever drives you. Food, water, love, duty. In 'Nam they knew we had to do our duty, and the Viet Cong used that drive to make traps for us - deadfalls. For one, they knew we never left a man behind. So, they'd give us a perfect opportunity to do our duty – lay out the body of an American soldier with a live grenade primed to go off when we moved him. We'd think we were doing the right thing by retrieving our friend. A good thing. But duty left us open to deadfalls."

*Vietnam.* Of course, that's what he had meant by 'Nam. The jungle picture was taken during that war. And from what Greyson could remember from his history lessons, it was an awful war that led to an American retreat. Tens of thousands of Americans had died, and hundreds of thousands of Vietnamese.

He remembered fragments about massacres, napalm, and pesticides that caused disease. John had lived through all that?

"The traps ever get you?"

John grunted and gestured Greyson back to the dining table where he pulled out a chair. The old man groaned as he sat, both hands on his knees. "They got me. Just not my body."

Greyson squinched his brow.

John rocked in his chair. "They're still getting me to this day. I see them take my friends. Worse, I see what I did to 'em after we caught 'em. That was another trap I fell into. Revenge. I did some bad things I regret. I wish I could take 'em back, more than anything."

The old man sighed. "But I can't. I'm stuck with them. My demons."

*Demons?* The word struck Greyson. It was an odd word – and it evoked a twinge of fear. He watched John as his eyes closed, crinkling the wrinkles on his cheeks into more folds. "You…you said 'demons'?"

John looked up, suddenly out of his reverie. "Oh. Yes…I did, as metaphor. You know much about them?"

Greyson shook his head.

"Well, then. Let me tell you a story."

"About demons?"

"Yes, about the non-metaphor kind. It took place many years ago. It's a story even older than I am."

Greyson gave him a polite laugh and leaned back, preparing for the story. He eyed Kit who lay in a corner, stomach full and ears perked.

"A long time ago, there was a small town by the lake. Some of the townsmen fished on the lake, but others kept pigs in the vast countryside, to eat or to sell for their livelihood. It was quiet back then – no electronic gizmos or cars or what not; but still, their world was not immune to crazy."

John nodded with a smirk. Greyson smiled back.

"There was a man, known by all in the town," John said with a sinking voice, leaning forward with intensity, "who was possessed by demons."

Greyson winced. He didn't like the word.

"Many of them. So many that the man called himself Legion – the name for a Roman army made up of over five thousand men."

"He had five thousand demons in him?"

He nodded. "The townspeople were so afraid of him, they often tried to chain his hands and feet; but he would break through the iron chains with

106

incredible strength. No one in the town was able to subdue him – even the strongest of the strong. Eventually he escaped, tore off all his clothes, and lived in the tombs outside of town where he would cut himself with stones and cry out day and night…a chilling sound."

Kit lifted his head and looked at Greyson. Perhaps he could smell Greyson's fear. "Geez. Naked dude cutting himself? That *is* crazy."

"Yes, though the man was still human just like us, he was haunted, controlled by those demons that did awful things to him. Made him act horribly. Hurt him. Just like our metaphorical demons can do. And no one could help the poor man. He was shunned – too dangerous and full of evil to let close to the children. Then, one day a traveling teacher came from the other side of the lake. The demon-possessed man saw him coming and ran at him."

Greyson listened intently, ready to hear what happened to the teacher. He imagined the violence the man could do, the fear on the teacher's face, the…

"But as soon as the man got to the teacher, he fell on his hands and knees and begged – *begged* – the teacher not to torture him."

Greyson drew back. "Wait. The demon-guy asked the teacher not to 'torture' him?"

"Right. The demon-guy was afraid of the teacher. The demons asked the teacher, 'What do you want of us?' And then they begged him over and over to let them go, because they knew the power the teacher had."

"But he's a teacher? He sounds kind of beast for a teacher."

John smiled. "And the demons knew it. Finally, the teacher commanded the demons out of the man and gave them permission to enter the herd of pigs. The poor pigs, now possessed, ran themselves into the water and drowned. But the man…he was freed."

Greyson alternated between a frown and a smile. It was the weirdest story he'd ever heard – but he liked it.

"The man was himself again. The townspeople came out and were surprised to see him in his right mind; but they were also afraid. They'd seen what the teacher had done to the herd of pigs – their livelihood. He'd changed everything they knew, and that scared them. When they asked the teacher to leave, he agreed, getting into the same boat he came on."

"What? That was dumb. He just like…saved that guy."

"You're right. And the guy was thankful for it. He wanted to go with the teacher on the boat, but the teacher said no."

"Well, I wouldn't want to be on a boat with a naked guy either."

John's laugh caught Greyson off guard, but he laughed along. "No, no. The guy is clothed now, and he is so grateful, he travels to city after city to tell everyone how amazing the teacher was."

"Cool. That's a happy ending, I guess. What does the teacher do after that?"

John stretched his back and pointed at Greyson's fanny pack. "You'll have to read to find out. That story is one of many in that little book of yours."

Greyson felt at the pack, thinking. "Really?"

"Yeah. You read it much?"

"Uh…no. Not yet. It's not even mine, really."

"No? Whose is it?"

John's question hit a nerve. "It's…" Greyson started, his eyes darting around the room. He grew nervous. "My…friend's. He…never mind."

John took in a long, deep breath. "I understand. We all have demons of our own."

Greyson's eyes shot up with a glint of fire. "I don't have demons."

"You don't?" he asked with surprise. "That's great. But, tell me then. What are you running from?"

"I'm not running from anything." Offended at the thought, Greyson shot to his feet and began pacing about the kitchen, suddenly anxious to leave. He'd forgotten his mission. "I'm *not* running. I'm not. I'm looking for my father. And I gotta go. I'm going to find him no matter what it takes!"

John kept calm during the outburst. "I believe you."

"No matter what!" Greyson started putting away his dish, but he felt lost in his urgency, pacing back and forth.

John shifted in the hard chair and rubbed the ends of his knees, examining Greyson's determined face. "You're determined. Strong headed. I get it. But be careful. Remember those traps? They work best on the strong headed ones."

Greyson stopped his pacing. "What's wrong with being strong headed?"

John thought to himself, folding his hands together. "Nothing. It's a very good thing. But just be careful; don't lose *yourself* while finding *him*."

Greyson let the words sink in, fighting his conscience. A flash of memory passed before his eyes – a memory of leaving Sam in the abandoned house, giving him to the terrorists so that they would tell him where to find his dad. The guilt that never seemed to go away nagged at his insides. Maybe he *did* have demons.

He turned with a wavering chin. "What happens if I do…lose myself?"

The old man stood with a groan and a few creaks from his knees. He joined

Greyson by the refrigerator, placed a rough hand on his shoulder, and spoke softly. "Then you'd need a new self."

*A new self?* John was as bad as Pastor Whitfield had been when he'd said Greyson was sick, infected with a disease with a mystery cure. It's as if they had teamed up against him, rubbing his guilt in his face – pointing out his demons and saying he was so beyond fixing that he needed to start over.

Suddenly, Greyson had had enough of his new teacher. He'd distracted him from the mission.

"Thank you for the soup and the milk and the arrows." He swung his backpack onto his shoulders and headed toward the side door; but he stopped suddenly. "What's your address?"

John seemed about to say something else, but instead gave his address. Greyson took the small Bible and pencil from his fanny pack and jotted it down. "I'll put you on my Payback List."

John cocked his head and stared at the book. "But – you can stay. You'll need more food and…if I said anything…"

Greyson had already disabled the trap; he turned to look at John as he opened the door, but John's face curled into horror. Greyson's heart leaped into his throat as he turned to the open doorway.

Ten feet away, illuminated in the motion sensing light and pointing its camera straight at his face, was a hovering drone.

# Chapter 20

*BANGGGGGGGGG!*

The gunshot exploded inside the kitchen and rung like crashing cymbals in Greyson's ears. At the same time, the drone ripped apart in a burst of sparks, two of its rotors whirling into the darkness in directionless retreat. The rest of its body collapsed onto the mud, whirring and twisting as if in agony, shaking off the rain. Greyson was stunned motionless.

"Get in!" John grabbed his shoulder and yanked him inside.

Greyson backed away as John reset the trap and turned to him wildly, still gripping the shotgun. "I knew it. You are the one they're looking for."

Greyson nodded, gulping, the sight of the drone still seared into his mind.

"They sent that after you. You have to leave. Now."

John grabbed his backpack's strap and shoved him through the house, ignoring Kit's growls as the dog followed close at his heels.

"But they'll be coming here. You'll be –"

"Shut up! Ol' Steve – my neighbor – has horses, to the south. Head to the hills and stay off the roads. I'd give you my car, but they'll be watching the roads."

He shoved him toward the backdoor and planted his feet, holding his shotgun at the ready. For a moment they didn't say anything, and Greyson fought to think of the right words to say.

"I – I'm sorry."

"I said shut up! Just go!"

Greyson nodded and motioned for Kit to follow. As the door shut him out in the rain, he took one last look at John through the back window. Then, turning toward the neighbor's house, he ran as fast as he could, not looking back.

---------------

"Alright, squirt," Calvin said, typing furiously at his laptop while Sam watched from across the table, bored. "We need a project. You'll read books for homework, but when we're together, we're working on something challenging."

Sam shrugged, snapping out of his boredom. "Okay. Sounds cool. What's the project?"

Calvin shrugged back. "Don't know. Got any ideas?"

Sam raised an eyebrow. "Me? Aren't you supposed to come up with that stuff?"

He shook his head. "I could, but you'll be more engaged if you come up with it. Just for fun, think of anything you wish you could do with a computer. Hack the Chinese embassy, look through your girlfriend's webcam, change traffic lights…"

The idea hit Sam in a flash. "I got it!" Sam blurted. "I want to send my friends and their families to the Bahamas."

"That's nice of you. But too easy."

"Under different names."

"Ah, that's better."

"And they're under FBI protection."

"Oh. Wow."

Sam nodded, smiling. "But I understand if you can't do it."

Calvin laughed. "I can do anything, but you're being very specific. If this is something you want to do for real, I'd get fired for sure. Maybe worse."

"Couldn't you do it without getting noticed – if it were for real?"

"I think the FBI would notice when the people they're protecting are no longer there."

"Then we convince them that they're not supposed to be there anymore."

Calvin grabbed his can of Mountain Dew and took a long swig. Then, after glancing around at the others on the plane, he turned back to Sam. "I know the situation your little friends are in, you know?"

"Okay."

"So, I just want to make sure that you know we're playing games here. That's what you're saying…right? Not for real."

Sam leaned in and his eyes grew serious, examining Calvin's face for clues to how he should proceed. And then he laughed. "Haha! Your face! No, not for *real!* Geez! But we can pretend; you can show me how you would do it if it *were* for real."

Calvin wiped his sleeve against his forehead, relieved. "Whew! I thought you really wanted to do it. That would have been crazy stupid and risky. It would even require forging your dad's signature."

"Oh, leave that to me. His campaign manager hands him a packet of papers needing his signature every morning. Slip it in there and he wouldn't notice."

Calvin stared at him.

"I mean…" Sam winked at him. "If it were for real."

Calvin's sly smile grew. "This is going to be fun."

---------------

The horse whinnied and reared up, as if it could sense the danger coming. Greyson fought with the bridle from below and just managed to slip it on before it reared again. Cinching the saddle was easier.

Checking the straps one more time and dodging the horse's flank as it jerked in the stable, he mounted it and bounced his heels against its side, guiding it through the door and into the storm.

Kit trotted behind nicely, but not right behind, as if he knew what a horse's hooves were capable of doing.

Sweeping the neighbor's land for any signs he was being watched, Greyson maneuvered to the back, dismounted to unlatch the gate, and stared across the overgrown field to John's farmhouse.

"He'll be fine, Kit. He's probably going to turn us in anyway."

His conscience nagged at him, and so did John's question. *What do you stand for?* It was his dad's hat. His father had dared him to keep it until he was able to give it back to him, so it only made sense that Greyson would stand for Gray. That was what he was living for now. But 'Good' and 'Guts' and 'Glory' were all fitting as well. He wanted to stand for them all.

*Enough thinking. I finally have transportation. Dad's waiting.*

He found the stirrup with his foot and launched himself onto the anxious horse. "Yah!"

Mud flung from the horse's hooves as it galloped toward the forested hills.

------------------

John had loaded his pockets with shotgun shells, taken off his shoes, and steeled himself inside the protective walls of the staircase leading from the ground floor to the bedrooms that had once been filled with his wife and children. He never went up there anymore. Not since he could sleep on the couch downstairs. The house had outgrown him.

But his new guests were not welcome. Ever since the economic recession started, there had been strays. Then there were the ones that would wonder in from the roadblock, looking for a hotel or a bathroom. He used to help them as he could. But then there had been the ones who broke in, beat him, and robbed him. They had been dirty. Ruthless. Yet, he had come out of it alive – and determined to never let intruders do that to him again.

But these intruders were different. They were government goons who flew a drone onto his property, spying on him. Sure, they were after the boy for whatever reason, but it was about time they found out that they could not take whatever they wanted from him.

They'd taken all his guns they knew about after he saw a Veterans' Affairs psychiatrist who had promptly diagnosed him with Post Traumatic Stress Disorder. They'd basically taken his wife when her government-mandated insurance forced her to wait months for a transplant. She had passed away, still waiting. And they'd taken his sons. They were now the government's very own. He didn't blame his sons. The government had deep pockets. But they were no longer his.

He heard tires on gravel approaching from the driveway. Though he was hidden from any windows, the headlights reflected on the wall like a passing wave.

As car doors closed and the headlights extinguished, John told himself to calm down. If they knocked, he'd disable the trap and would answer normally. But he knew they wouldn't. That wasn't their style anymore. Their drone had already provided enough evidence for an automatic search warrant, and he'd provided them with enough reason to suspect he was armed and dangerous.

He waited, pressed against the wall, listening over the sound of his old heart feeling more alive than it should be. Flashbacks of Vietnam slapped hard at his eyes. Hiding in the tall grass, listening for footsteps and the enemy's steady breath. Darkness and death all around. His rifle the only thing protecting him. Finger on the trigger. Eyes closed, blocking it out, controlling his own breath. A click of foot on twig. A rush of grass on pant-leg.

A twist of a doorknob.

They weren't knocking.

# Chapter 21

The traps worked their wonders.

The side door and front door opened at the same time and delivered blows to the intruders, breaking one's nose and striking the other one senseless with a log to the forehead.

John snapped to action and whirled from the staircase to the kitchen where he fired a shell into the one holding his bloody face. His lanky body flung backwards like a battering ram had slammed into his chest.

He turned and hobbled swiftly to the front door, barely making a noise in his socks. The shotgun shook in his hands, but his eyes were focused and knees steady.

Another one was going for the window. John's shot blew the window apart, shattering it in the intruder's face, sending him staggering and screaming.

The one at the front door was still lying on the ground, out cold.

*How many more?*

He kept his aim at the one by the front door, waiting for someone to come to his rescue, and backed toward his staircase refuge. He had five more shots before he had to reload.

And then he heard movement again from the kitchen. Glancing in that direction, he shifted his aim and approached the tile floor.

He listened long and hard before making his move.

He swung around the wall. He pointed the gun at the side door, at a window, and again at the doorway.

No one. Except for a tiny, buzzing drone hovering over his table.

It wasn't armed. It must be a distraction!

When he swung back toward the front door, an incredible bang startled him. A wave of fear and cold hit him so hard he dropped his gun.

His mind raced and confusion wracked his eyes as they searched for an answer. When the gunman stepped forward from the doorway, he knew what had happened.

He'd been shot.

Looking down to his stomach, he saw the wound and his hands gravitated toward it. Suddenly his legs felt weak and he had to kneel. He thought about reaching for his gun again, but the gunman was striding toward him, his pistol still leveled and ready to fire.

Another surprise took him off guard. His vision was blurred, but he thought the gunman was a kid. A teenager with a crooked nose and hateful eyes.

"Where is he?" the teenaged gunman asked, putting the gun barrel up to the old man's forehead.

John clutched at his stomach and gritted his teeth as the pain began radiating up his spine. He wanted to throw up. "Go to h –"

The gunman cracked John over the head with the butt of his gun. Blackness erupted inside his head as he lost consciousness, but the bottom of the staircase blinked into view a few seconds later. He heard voices like echoes from a distance. A boy's deep voice in the room. "My face, man! I'm bleeding. There's glass in it! We got to go!"

A cool response. "Shut up. Almost done here."

John just wanted a few seconds to fall asleep, here on the floor, but the gunmen rolled him over and stood over him, the pistol pointed at his head.

"I'll ask one more time. Where. Is. He?"

John closed his eyes, wondering where death would bring him.

But in an instant, a flurry of sounds erupted around him. A splash of glass, paws hitting the floor, a guttural bark, a human scream. A dull thud that knocked the gunman onto the staircase followed by the clinking of a ball bearing landing on the hardwood floor – rolling into the pool of blood by his side.

"Holy crap!"

The growl of the dog and more thuds as a body hit the floor. An angry dog ripping at flesh.

John opened his eyes, drifting at the edge of consciousness to see a boy in a hoodie and a red cap crawling over the windowsill. There was a scramble of feet as the gunman jerked from the staircase toward his gun, but John saw it out of the corner of his eye and pushed it toward the dog.

The gunman cursed, stalled over John's body, and then ran toward the kitchen's exit.

John's eyes closed. His eyelids felt like lead.

"Kit, stop!"

The growling and tearing ceased, and suddenly the boy and dog were at his side. He could hear their breath over the sounds of the gunmen escaping outside.

"John. John! What do I do? You're shot."

"I know, boy," he muttered. "I know."

"What do I do? Press it?"

He felt the boy's hands press and the pain forced him to groan. "Ugh! Just…just call…911."

Greyson gulped down a breath and kept his hands pressed against the wound. He felt the warm blood oozing against his palms, through his fingers. He had to keep pressure on the wound, to keep the blood inside. If he called the police, he would have to leave John. But he had to, or John would die.

"I – I…okay. Just…here. Kit, come."

John laid his head back as he felt the dog's paw take the place of Greyson's hands on his wound.

"Stay, boy. I'll be right back."

Time passed slowly as he listened to Greyson talk to the 911 operator, felt the boy's hands once again on the numb wound, and heard his reassurances.

"You'll be fine. You've gone through worse, right? And you showed them."

"Who…who were…?"

"They were terrorists. After me. It was my fault. But…I came back. I want to stand for 'Good', too. But I realized too late…"

John's breathing was heavy, but he felt too weak to respond. Too cold.

Several minutes passed before they heard the sirens. Greyson attempted a smile at the man. "I gotta go. Please don't tell them about me – the cops – or anyone."

John nodded.

"You'll be alright. As good as new."

With no response, Greyson's eyes watered, hoping what he had said was true. Then, working up the courage, he put John's hands on his own wound, and bolted away.

Splashing through the wet grass and mud, Greyson swung himself onto the horse, still reeling from the battle. Tire tracks had torn up the dirt in the front where the gunmen had escaped. Now they were gone. But for how long? They had found him here, somehow. They could find him again. Chase him down no matter how fast he ran.

"Yah!"

The horse blasted away, sending the pellets of rain into Greyson's face like marbles. Soon the horse reached the hills, and they slowed during the ascent. Lightning flashed and the thunder rolled over him like a passing train.

Once safe on a flat overlook, he watched the lights from the ambulance and police car as they pulled into John's driveway. His bloody hands were shaking as he wiped them on his hoodie.

He felt safer in the hills, but his mind was far from okay. Fear and worry plagued him. *How did they find me?* An image of the drone, its camera's iris zooming in and out like an eye's pupil was still frozen in his mind – sure to haunt his dreams later.

*Will John survive?*

Looking through the rain at the farmhouse lit with the ambulance's red and blue lights, the guilt scraped at his heart like a dagger, nagging at him – rebuking him for not going back sooner.

He added another notch to his list of demons. Another life might have been taken because of him. Eight thousand, plus Liam, plus John. More than a legion.

When the EMTs carried the stretcher with John's body to the ambulance, Greyson turned, heeled the horse, and disappeared into the forest.

----------------

"My face!" Buzz screamed, touching the glass shards sticking from his fleshy cheeks. Blood dripped from his chin and arm to the SUV's floor. He shook with the shock, crying off and on. If he opened his eyes, he was afraid he wouldn't be able to see. "My face, man!"

"Shut up!" Orion bellowed from the driver's seat, trying to navigate the gravel road with the rain covering the windshield between every slash of the wipers.

"And my arm! That dog! That stupid dog! We have to get to the hospital!"

"No! Shut up! They will be looking for anyone suspicious after that. You're not going to die."

"But Jeremy, man."

Orion gripped the steering wheel until his knuckles turned white. "I know, I know." They had left Lanky's body behind.

Their other brother, Glasses, groaned from the backseat where they had thrown him, unconscious, before speeding away. Despite the log to the forehead, he was still alive.

Orion steered onto the main road and had just gotten up to speed as a police car sped past in the opposite direction. Orion nodded to himself, thinking. Greyson had called 911, just like he had expected. That meant either the cops would find him and take him back to Iowa, or he would run before they got there.

Buzz's painful whines and Glasses' groans soon irritated Orion. They were such pansies. Wimps. But they would only get stronger through this. He would show them how to be strong.

"We're going to kill him. Now."

He turned sharply onto another gravel road, toward the dark hills. That's where he'd be headed. They would cut him off. No escape.

He rolled the window down and released the Hornet. It vanished into the night and rain.

Buzz whined, trying to hold his arm out straight, pressing his torn flesh back over the wide-open gash where the dog's teeth had shaken furiously. He breathed heavily and put his head against the window, muttering something indiscernible.

Orion sneered. "Just shut up."

# Chapter 22

As the hours wore on, Greyson's horse grew more and more tired, huffing and puffing, even staggering at times. Kit, too, was weary, trotting at their side – and they were all soaked to the bone.

"Come on! Yah!"

Greyson heeled the horse over and over.

"Yah!"

He heeled it harder, venting his frustration, and the horse reacted likewise, bucking just as hard.

Before he knew it, Greyson had spun to the ground in a muddy splash.

Kit was at his side, but the pain had jarred his spine, stunning him. For a moment he sat in the puddle, feeling it soak through his shorts. Like the straw that broke the camel's back, his anger broke free.

He slapped at the puddled ground, shaking with the cold and holding off the tears. The rain seemed to find just the right angles to make it through the trees, pestering his face. When Kit tried to comfort, Greyson pushed him away with muddy hands, grumbling. For now, he wanted to stay in the mud with his thoughts and his guilt, like the demon-possessed man who had escaped to the tombs. He deserved it.

He raised his hands to ward off Kit's attempts to comfort, but he froze, staring at them as if they weren't his own.

*Though his Dad had a wide smile on his face, his hands were covered in dried blood. Little Greyson stopped short of a hug, gasped, and ran to his mother.*

*"It's okay, honey," his mother soothed, rubbing his back. "It's not his blood. He's not hurt."*

*"Then…whose blood is it?"*

*"The deer's."*

*His dad held his large hands in front, palms-up. It looked just like his blood.*

*"Why is it on his hands?"*

*His mom gave his dad a smile and then knelt at Greyson's level. "Your dad had to clean it, so he could feed us. But that question you asked was a good one, Greys. If someone has blood on their hands, it's good to know why."*

Greyson stared at his hands.

*Why? Why did I get blood on my hands?*

Though most of the blood had washed away, he still felt it under his fingernails and in the crevices. He rubbed his hands together, smooshed mud through his fingers, and washed them in the puddle water, but nothing could free him from the feeling of blood. And he had only made himself dirtier and more miserable.

*Because I was responsible for his death. I brought them there. I left him.*

A piece of him fought the guilt, arguing that he had done the right thing, despite the risk. After all, he *had* gone back.

He used to be a better person, but he had forced that selfless part of him into surrender at the fair. He'd given up Sam in order to find his dad and now he had left John in a rush to do the same.

John's warning had already come true. *Don't lose yourself in finding him.* He had lost himself and had realized it too late.

But no more.

He wouldn't leave anyone behind ever again. That wasn't who he was. He would be like a new person. He'd put on a new self and make up for it all, pay it back somehow. No matter what it took.

Shaking his head, Greyson rose, dripping from the puddle, and tied the uneasy horse to the tree. The way it was huffing, he knew it was angry.

"Sorry, guy," he whispered before a long sigh. "I didn't mean to hurt you. I'll make it up to you, 'kay? You thirsty?"

But he didn't have any water. He pet the horse, thinking. And then he saw the rainwater fall from his arm.

*Duh.*

Mentally slapping himself, he pulled Kit's bowl from his pack and pulled off his soaking shirt. Ringing it out over the bowl gave nearly an inch of good drinking water, which the horse drank in a few seconds. Greyson finished the shirt's supply with a few more twists over his own mouth and then pulled the shirt back on, already shivering with the cold.

"There. Now we have to keep going, horse. Just keep your chin up and eyes forward…"

*Clunk.*

A car door.

Kit's ears were perked, and Greyson matched his gaze into the dark woods. The first signs of daybreak glistened in the wet grass, and everything looked like a haze. Blinking and wiping his eyes, he focused on something that glimmered through the trees. *Headlights?*

Greyson's heart beat fast as he rose to his feet. In a flash he had smashed the blanket into his backpack and wielded his slingshot. He knew very well who it could be. They had followed him. Trying to cut him off. They would have guns.

"Stay close, boy," he commanded, trekking toward the light, fingers on the ammunition pocket.

He listened for further sounds over the pattering rain. Thunder rumbled in the distance, but when it was gone, he heard the voices. A little frantic. Someone giving commands.

He padded closer and closer, darting from tree to tree. Soon he could make out the headlights and hear the voices more closely.

Putting his back against a thick tree, he exchanged a look with Kit. Greyson's eyes said what his mouth could not. *This may be a losing battle.*

But Kit didn't look afraid. He seemed anxious – like some dogs do when they want to go for a ride.

"Get the roasting sticks!"

He could make out the voices now.

"Anything else?"

"I don't think so! Oh! We left out the hotdog buns."

"You left them out all night?"

"Ah, man! Oh well, just leave 'em. Hurry in! We got to beat the traffic, or we won't make it home 'til Tuesday."

Greyson breathed in deep and long, a smile jerking at his lips. It was a family on a camping trip.

He peeked around the tree. The sun was itching at the horizon, giving just enough light to make out the family's motor home and the tiny campgrounds. A young boy was running around, picking things up while a man, presumably his father, was packing things into the car that was hitched to the back of the RV. They were towing the car with them on vacation.

And then he saw it. He didn't believe his eyes, so he scrambled to another tree even closer to the car. It was true. The license plate had an orange in the middle. Above the letters was his destination written in all capital letters.

*FLORIDA.*

And they were about to head home.

A switch flipped and Greyson bolted from the scene, sending mud into the air behind him. Kit stood undecided for a moment but followed Greyson back to the horse where he grabbed his backpack, untied the horse, and then trekked back to the campground.

Just as the last family member entered the motor home, Greyson emerged from the trees, slunk to the empty car, and opened the back door. Kit jumped in after Greyson, and he quietly closed the door behind. A moment later, the motor home started and pulled away.

It took a full minute of bouncing along in the backseat of the car for him to catch his breath. Even then he didn't have much to say. All he could do was hug Kit with all his might and ruffle his wet fur.

As soon as he felt safe enough, he laughed and let out an awkward squeal; but he didn't care. It had been amazing luck – a miracle. And he didn't even know how lucky he'd been.

As they pulled onto the main road, an SUV passed them, headed to the campgrounds where the Hornet had just spotted a horse. The driver's face glowed with hate. The passenger's face was full of glass and blood.

Greyson sighed and sat in the seat, thinking it must be the softest seat he had ever felt in a car. Maybe ever. He watched the trees whizz by and felt the hope rush into his empty tank.

Kit nosed the window, panting. Greyson laughed.

"That's right, boy. We're going to Florida."

---------------

"Morning, Sam."

*"Morning, Sydney. How are you?"*

"Good. You?"

*"Good, too. Just got into the hotel in D.C. See the room?"*

"Sweet! Looks all fancy! Is that a whirlpool in the corner?"

*"Yeah! Should I try it out?"*

"Ha! By yourself?"

*"I guess. My bodyguard would probably look at me weird if I asked him."*

"Remember the last time you were in a hot tub?"

*"Yeah, with you. Hiding."*

"Right. Not a good memory."

*"Hey! I didn't mind it."*

122

"Right..."

*"Just saying. Wish we could do it again – without the whole being chased part."*

Sydney turned the phone's camera from her face to hide her blushing smile. "That'd be fun."

Sam smiled back on the screen, his perfect winning smile.

Sydney tried to change the subject. "How long you staying again?"

*"A week or so."*

"Cool. Will you be busy?"

*"Well, mostly my dad will be. But I'll make sure to call you every day, if that's what you're worried about."*

"Yeah, I was *real* worried. But it is good to have someone to talk to."

*"Same here. Adults are boring. But I just met a new one who's pretty cool."*

"Who's that?"

*"His name's Calvin. My new tutor."*

"Oh, what happened to the old one?"

*"They told me it was because he couldn't travel – the whole nationwide campaign thing. But I also think it's because he was teaching me stuff that didn't go over too well with my dad or his advisors. I liked him...but whatever. Anyway..."* The camera on Sam's phone wobbled as he seemed to be walking about the room. *"Just a sec."*

Sydney waited until Sam returned to the king-sized bed and the camera focused on his face, which was now serious.

*"He's helping me get you to the Bahamas. But I need your help as well."*

Sydney's eyes brightened. "The *Bahamas*? No way. How?"

*"I'm learning from Calvin. I think he knows what I'm doing – but I don't know. It doesn't matter. Anyway, Calvin said passports are the hardest to forge quickly, but the only way to get to the Bahamas without a passport is through a closed-loop cruise."*

"We're going on a cruise?"

*"Hopefully. Your family and the Aldemans. But you'll be under different names. And we'll have to convince everyone, including the FBI, that it was an ordered gift from my dad – to pay you back for all you've done and to make up for stuff, you know? And the fewer people who know, the better; you never know who might give up the secret on accident. So, this is just you and me."*

Sydney nodded. It would be hard to keep such a big secret from everyone else, but she would give it her best shot.

*"Calvin said we'll use Witness Protection protocols against them or something like that. To prevent bad guys within the FBI from finding out, there will be only one person who knows where you all are – and it will be a fake name. We'll give your parents the emergency*

*contact, but it'll just be Calvin's number in case they ever call it."* He paused before adding, *"I think we can actually do this."*

Sydney was lost in thought, but her hands shook with excitement. "When do we go?" She listened thoughtfully to the answer and replied, "You have to tell the twins."

-------------

*DING-DONG!*

Jarryd cocked his head at the early-morning doorbell, but shrugged it off, rubbing the firming cream on the dark circles under his eyes. He hadn't slept much. Maybe he had jet lag from the time difference. *How many hours difference was it from Iowa to Texas?* He pulled at the dark bags. He would need the cold pack to get rid of those bad boys.

*DING-DONG!*

*Who rings the frickin' doorbell at 7am? Do Texans have manners?*

*DING-DONG!*

His parents would get it. Or Nick.

*DING-DONG!*

"Ugh!" Jarryd swung open the bathroom door and marched to the front door of their new, and very empty, home.

On the doorstep, a boy and a middle-aged woman stood before him with dishes of food in their hands.

"Welcome to Tex-Sucks!" the boy declared.

Jarryd's jaw dropped. "Patrick?" Jarryd recognized the boy. Patrick had been in their Cowboys Gold huddle at Morris All-Sports Camp several months ago, though he had opted out of most of their antics – sneaking into the observatory, stealing the terrorists' keys, and nearly getting incinerated under a gigantic nuclear missile.

"You…" Patrick muttered, recognizing Jarryd. "You're the loud, chipmunkish one."

"You're the one who hates everything."

The boys exchanged sneers before Patrick's mother broke the tension. "You're one of the twins? From camp? That's wonderful!"

"Yeah. Why are *you* here?"

The women remained chipper. "Well, we're your new neighbors. We just moved in a week ago."

124

Patrick shrugged. "This place sucks worse than our last neighborhood. And our old one is radioactive ash."

"Patrick!" his mom scolded. "It is not." She turned to Jarryd. "They just moved us out of precaution – with the radiation. Your family here with the Texas Refugee Housing Program, too?"

"Yeah," he said, scanning the rows of cookie-cutter houses that had been built in a matter of weeks.

Jarryd wiped his wet bangs from his eyes. There was an awkward pause.

Finally, Patrick held out a Ziploc of cookies. "Here. They're called Death by Chocolate." His face drooped in disappointment. "But they don't work."

Jarryd grabbed the bag as Patrick's mom squinted her weaning patience away. "They're fudge mocha chocolate chip."

"They're about the worst cookies you'll ever taste," Patrick added. "Taste like diapers. But if you eat'm and die, I'll be a murderer. And Tex-Sucks has the death penalty." Patrick faked a smile. "Enjoy!"

"Patrick!" Nick ran from behind Jarryd and shook Patrick's limp hand. "You're the smart one."

Nick smiled sheepishly and shook Patrick's mother's hand, too. As Patrick's mother re-explained their appearance at the door, Nick handed his cell phone to Jarryd with a whisper. "You'll want to hear this."

Jarryd was all-too happy to retreat from the doorway as his parents and Sammy joined the excitement at the door. Once a safe distance away, Jarryd raised Nick's cell phone to his ear. "Hello?"

*"Jarryd?"* It was Sam Reckhemmer. *"I was talking with Nick. What's going on?"*

"Hey. An old friend showed up at our door. What's up?"

*"How'd he know where to find you? Jarryd, be careful. You can't trust anyone."*

Jarryd peeked at Patrick and his mother. Nick was already sampling a cookie with bulging cheeks. "This one's harmless. He'd rather be killed than kill. And he brought cookies."

*"Cookies? Geez. You check if they're poisoned?"*

Jarryd watched Nick chew and chew. He didn't fall over.

*"Yeah. I checked."*

*"Good. But still. Don't tell them anything – especially what I'm about to tell you."*

"What? Did Greyson make it?"

He could hear Sam sigh on the other end. *"No. Well, I don't know. But you're going to find out."*

125

As Sam explained, Jarryd's smile grew. Nick nodded from the distance with mutual understanding.

"That's awesome!" Jarryd whispered, keeping his excitement from Patrick. "When? When do we go?"

*"You leave in eight days."*

# PART 3

# Chapter 23

*Eight days later. Northern Georgia.*

Greyson wiped the sweat from his upper lip with the back of his grimy hand, but he didn't feel the streak of dirt he left behind; he was focused. He quietly edged around the corner of one of the dumpsters and peeked through a hole in the wooden fence that had hidden him as he had searched for food in the dumpsters. His hunger had woken him, forcing him from the mountains' pines into the town below.

All he needed was one car. He waited for several minutes, but the traffic at the gas station was still slow.

"Come on...come on..." he muttered, watching a van pull into the lot. Kit watched as well, huffing a silent bark.

His feet ached, his stomach was an empty pit, and his head pounded – but that wasn't the worse of it. The worse part was the layers of sweat and grime on his body and the smell that came with it.

Sure, most of it was his body odor. It seemed like he sweated more and more lately – maybe because his body was changing, growing – but some of the smell came from the dumpsters. He'd been in many of them. The best one had been behind the McDonald's, where he'd found a few fries and slurps of Coke at the bottoms of cups, but he had only emerged craving more.

But this new idea could improve his fortune – if it worked.

Once, when he was very young, his family had been traveling through downtown Des Moines when an old man – probably homeless – had startled them as they stopped at a stoplight. He had sprayed their windshield with cleaner and wiped it down with a rag. Before the light had turned green, his dad had rolled down the window and given him money.

*Money.* He needed money just as bad as that man had needed it.

A van swung around and parked in front of a gas pump.

"Yes. Bingo. Let's go, Kit."

Springing into action, Greyson closed the wooden fence behind him, put on his hood and sunglasses, and jogged toward the woman. When he got close, the woman stopped mid-stroke with the squeegee and her eyes grew wide.

"Hi! I can help you with that! Let me." He held out his hand and strode toward her, smiling. But she didn't respond. She looked inside her van at a child asleep in the front seat.

"Hold on," she said sternly, holding up her hand.

Greyson stopped and Kit paused next to him, confused. "I just want to –"

"I know what ya want, but ya just stay where ya are, ya hear?" the woman shouted, nervously shutting off the pump. "Here! Take this and get some help; but leave us be." She fumbled in her purse, took out a few bills and threw them in his direction. A moment later she was back in her van and speeding off, leaving Greyson in a state of confusion.

The bills drifted to the concrete and began scuttling along with the wind. For a few moments he couldn't move. *What just happened? Why would she…*

And then he felt the hunger pains, a scissors-sharp jab in the gut, and he jumped at the bills one by one. The last one managed to evade him until it reached the front of the gas station. Catching it against the wall, Greyson placed it nicely with all the others and counted. Eight bucks.

Suddenly realizing where he was, he looked up, right into the glass of the station's large picture window. His reflection greeted him poorly. Sunglasses, hood, face covered in dirt, clothes plastered with mud and dried blood. No wonder the woman had been afraid.

His eyes suddenly focused through the window where a cashier was staring at him. The cashier's brow was scrunched in concern.

Greyson couldn't think of anything to do except to wave as he retreated around the side, back to the wooden fence that surrounded the dumpsters, hiding from the cashier and hoping he wouldn't find him suspicious enough to follow.

Putting his back against the dumpster, he looked again at the money. *Happy Birthday to me! Eight bucks!* He could buy several meals – or a tarp! A tarp would be smarter in case it rained again, like it had the hours after he had left John. How long ago was that now? A week? Or longer? Whenever it was, that was when he had been thirteen. Today was different. Now he was fourteen, with eight bucks.

Lost in a daydream, he remembered the first wonderful hours in the Florida-plated car, napping, watching the landscape fly by mile after mile, imagining how hard it would have been to walk them all – especially as the hills turned to mountains in Kentucky and then Tennessee.

At the first stop he and Kit had managed to slip out of the car while the family was busy buying snacks. The next stop had been their undoing. They left the car unnoticed and did their business separately; but something had caught Greyson's attention on the way out. A teenaged boy was arguing with his girlfriend – at least Greyson thought it was his girlfriend. But the boy's hands had been all over her, and she didn't seem to like it.

Greyson had given Kit a look, pleading with him to tell him what to do – but all he had needed was one more of the girl's screams. Something had clicked inside of him, turning off all thoughts except for one. Determined to do good, to inch one step closer to the cure, he had marched up to the boy, jaw set and fists clenched. Before he knew it, his punch had taken the boy down.

The sharp pain from his knuckles had plunged him back into reality. The boy on the ground and his startled girlfriend were staring at him, and so was their driver from Florida.

His cover had been blown. Without a word, he had sprinted away, leaving behind the teenaged boy's screams and the free ride to Florida.

A few miserable nights had followed. He and Kit had wandered through Nashville, watched a night-time protest turn into a riot – complete with tear gas, police with shields, and police drones – including scary robotic ones with four legs – and then mingled with a few other homeless, even taking a meal at a shelter before moving on. It had been hard to navigate the city, with all its cameras and people. It was a whole different world to him, and it seemed to be falling apart. Though the country was more peaceful, food had been even harder to come by.

Greyson shook his head, feeling light-headed. What had he been thinking about? Feeling the bills in his hand, he remembered. The woman's frightened face. Her shouts and shaking hand – like she had to protect her family from him. *From me.*

Trying to ignore the pangs of conscience, he turned to the front cover of his Bible where the Payback List had grown much longer. On top he had hastily scrawled, "8,002 lives." Below that, in an organized list, was everything he had stolen so far, starting with the things he owed John and Eric and Alyssa. There was the horse from John's neighbor (Ol' Steve), the Georgia map he'd taken from inside a car with license plate number A67 BTR, the orchard's apples that had fed him and Kit for two days, the bike that had blown a tire after a day and a half, the lighter that had helped him cook the rabbit he had managed to kill and skin in the forest, and so on.

But as he added the eight dollars to the list, the guilt came trickling back in. He had no idea who she was; there was no way he would be able to pay her back. He had taken her money; he was happy to. He'd have taken more from her if she'd had it. The whole list was full of similar choices.

Now-familiar thoughts tormented him. *You're a thief. A thief! A low-life. You're no better than CheekBones.*

It had only taken a week or two to sink that low.

He felt the familiar signs of crying begin to suck at his lungs, but he fought hard to press it down with deep, conscious breaths. He'd become harder since giving up in that puddle.

*No more crying. Fight it. You'll make it right. You'll pay it all back.*

"Let's hide out here for a bit, boy, then we'll find somewhere to spend it."

Greyson quickly pocketed the cash, laid out his dinosaur blanket, and rested against his backpack. His backpack made a solid pillow, though it had seen better days. He'd made sure to repair the rips as much as possible by stealing used duct tape from someone's thrown-out garden hoe; if something was useful, he'd never throw it out.

Once he saw Greyson settle on the soft blanket, Kit snuggled close as well. He knew the now-familiar routine. Whenever Greyson needed a distraction from the cold, the hunger, or the guilt, he pulled out the tiny book and flipped open to the page where he had left off. He'd read it in many odd, solitary places over the last few days – under a bridge, in a rail car on abandoned railroad tracks, and even inside a playground's covered slide, listening to the pattering rain on the plastic above.

Though his parents had kept a Bible at home somewhere and would open it at Easter and Christmas church services, he had never thought to read it by himself. It was so big and boring. But John's story had interested him, and the other stories so far had been interesting as well. Before he had started reading the book of Luke, he'd always thought of the main character, Jesus, as a kind of hippie who told everyone to love each other, to do good, and to be peaceful – like hippies are supposed to – but he was starting to think Jesus was not just love and flowers. He was actually super-confident and ruffled a lot of feathers.

Still fighting off the guilt, Greyson slipped the Polaroid from its position as bookmark and put it near the back. He started by skimming the first six chapters, reviewing what he'd read already. In six chapters, the teacher, Jesus, had gone around breaking laws, messing with demons, and commanding a group of men he called disciples to do his bidding. He was a man on a mission, and he wouldn't stop for anything or anyone – except to heal someone or drive out evil. Greyson liked that about him.

131

He glanced at Kit, who rested his head on his front legs at the edge of the book's flimsy pages. Kit liked to listen to him, and often Greyson was so confused or surprised by what he read, he just had to share. "So…" Greyson started, pointing at the text as if Kit could understand, "…he's just healed a guy with leopardsy…"

Kit cocked his head and Greyson shrugged. "It's like a skin disease, I think, where you get spots all over. But anyway, he's also raised some kids from the dead, and a mob of people tried to throw him off a cliff, but he went all ninja on them and vanished. He's pretty beast."

Greyson returned to the seventh chapter and read on, holding the book in one hand and stroking Kit's ears with the other. When he had finished the story, he scrunched his brow. "Weird…"

Kit's ears perked up like he wanted to hear. Greyson laughed. "Jesus goes to this rich guy's house and is eating at the table when this lady walks in and like starts *bawling*…" he said, acting out what she did, "…just weeping at his feet. And she gets his feet all wet with her tears…so she wipes them off with her *hair*."

Greyson chuckled as he imagined the scene, and Kit tilted his head in response. "But then she…yeah this is weird…she *kisses* his feet! And to top it all off…she pours perfume on them."

Still laughing, Greyson looked again at the text. "I didn't know Jesus was such a lady's man. Or maybe this chick's just kind of obsessed. Whatcha think?"

Kit didn't answer, so Greyson shrugged. "It's kind of…well, *really*, weird…but I guess if Sydney rubbed her hair on my feet, my feet would smell a whole lot better than they smell like now. Probably like strawberries."

Though he once had a rotation going, he hadn't changed socks for days. He was pretty sure they made a squishing sound when he walked. "But I bet Jesus' feet were even worse than mine, wearing sandals all the time with all those *animals* around pooping on whatever they wanted. No offense."

Kit didn't act offended. He just panted.

"Oh. I should finish. The rich guy gets angry at Jesus for letting her do that because…just a second," he paused as he found the place in the text to quote, "because he should know what kind of woman she is – a sinner."

*Sinner. An evil-doer.* Greyson wasn't sure what the woman had done, but it must have been bad. Not as bad as 8,002 lives worth of bad, though.

"But Jesus says it's cool, because she's done so much bad stuff that she should be even more grateful to him. He says, uh… 'He who has been forgiven much, loves much. He who has been forgiven little, loves little."

Greyson let the words sink in as he thought of how to explain them to the dog. Suddenly he realized that the words – the story – was much like what he was going through. He was like that woman – without the whole foot kissing thing. He was a sinner. He was the one who should love much because he needed so much forgiveness. If he loved much, maybe he could he be forgiven for all the evil he had done.

Getting excited, he returned to the story.

"Finally, Jesus says, 'Your faith has saved you. Go in peace.'" Greyson cocked his head. "That whole hair cleaning thing saved her!" he said, exasperated. "That was it! She just did this like crazy act of kindness and Jesus said she was saved. Maybe it was so good that it outweighed her bad. But all she had to do was…wash…"

*Wash.*

The thought triggered an idea. He knew what he had to do with the money. If he bought food, he'd be hungry again in a few hours. If he bought a tarp, he'd stay dry, but still hungry. If he got a cab, he'd only gain a few miles. He needed to use the money to get *more* money – and he couldn't steal anymore, or he'd never be able to make it up to God.

He put the list away and hurried to peek through a gap in the fence. At first, he shook it off as a bad idea, but the more he looked at it, the more confident he became. He opened the gate to see it clearly.

The carwash. It was beautiful. "Yes…"

133

# Chapter 24

"YES!"

Jarryd bounced up and down on the gangway, the reflection of the gigantic cruise ship filling his aviator sunglasses. It was spectacular. Over three football fields long and twenty stories high, it was almost a floating city, holding nearly 8,000 people at a given time. And their group would account for only eight.

Nick nodded, putting his hands on his hips, just above his red fanny pack. "It has four swimming pools, ten hot tubs, two wave-pools, two rock walls, a miniature golf course, a basketball court, a zip-line, a surfing simulator, a carousel, and a park."

"And no dishes or laundry..." Sydney's mother added.

"And unlimited, delicious food," Sydney's father added, winking at his wife.

"And a spa!" Jarryd concluded. After the long drive and a week of unloading and unpacking, he needed a massage. And female interaction. He hadn't met a single Texan female his own age in their new lame neighborhood. The only friend he'd made was Patrick, but the only thing he had ever wanted to do was nothing.

"But most important..." Sydney exclaimed, still marveling at its size, "...no terrorists." She crossed her fingers. It was weird to be out and free after so many days cooped up. It was also weird knowing they were probably safer now than before. Only a few people knew where they were, and no one in the port city of Galveston, Texas knew who they were. With new names and a vacation ahead of them, Sydney felt as if they had escaped, just like Greyson had. And hopefully his escape was going as well as theirs.

Nick eyed his skinny biceps that were an unflattering white in the Texas sun. "There's also a huge fitness center."

Jarryd shook his head. "We don't need a Greyson replacement, Try-Hard."

"Shut up," Nick said, adjusting his glasses. "What's wrong with wanting to be jacked?"

"Why do you want to get jacked all of a sudden?"

"Why does it matter? Why do you want to go to the spa?"

"To meet the ladies."

"Well, *maybe* that's why *I* want to get jacked."

All eyes turned to him, and he blushed red.

"What? Fine. Don't believe me."

Sammy suddenly burst toward the open door in the hull. "Dibth on the carouthel!"

"Wait!" Mrs. Aldeman shouted. "Uh...what's-your-name!"

Her husband shook his head at her. "Sammy, dear. It's been weeks and you don't remember his name?"

"His *other* name...*dear.* His new one."

The many name changes were getting confusing.

"Oh, right. Chandler! Come back here!"

"Well, I got dibs on the surfing simulator," Jarryd proclaimed.

"You'll have to shower first."

"Really, Mom? I don't want to shower *again,*" Jarryd complained. "That'll take half an hour! I'll have to re-spray!"

---------------

Finally. A shower. It was glorious; but it was also the most difficult one Greyson had ever had. The jets of water blasted into his body, sending waves of caked mud and debris to the car wash's cement floor. He had yelped when the jets had first hit him, they were so cold. And he had to keep pace with the upside-down J-shaped sprayer that hung from the ceiling and swiveled around the shape of a car.

He laughed as he tried to keep up, his bare feet pattering on the wet cement as the cold jets continued to pepper his skin. Kit looked on, fascinated, but unwilling to get wet. Greyson had given up on him quickly, realizing the car wash was only on for limited time. He had to make the most of his four dollars.

*DING!*

The lights on the display panel shifted from 'Pre-soak' to a picture of bubbles, and suddenly another sprayer squirted streams of liquid soap onto his slender body and boxer briefs. It was slimy and made the floor slippery, but he followed it around in a car-shaped lap as if on a skating rink, rubbing the liquid into fresh-smelling suds.

He threw some at Kit, who moved back a few steps and continued to stare.

*DING!*

Greyson peeked through the coat of bubbles he wore to the image of a brush. There was a mechanical whirring sound and a clunk as three giant brushes came from both sides and above, whipping their blue washing pads around like they were upside-down Christmas trees being spun like tops.

For a moment, he froze, but feeling the exhilaration of the cold and the clean, he slid into the path of the pads and took the soft beating. He could hear Kit growling as the pads slapped at him, but he was smiling and laughing. It was like twenty ferocious nurses were sponge-bathing him at once.

*DING!*

The rinse cycle shed the remaining suds and left him time to soak his clothes and hat as well.

*DING!*

*Wax.*

"Aagh!"

He jumped out of the way of the sprayer just in time and let it do its thing. He laughed at the thought of being a giant candle.

*DING!*

The huge tube-dryer hummed to life at the exit, and Greyson skidded over to it, holding his clothes in both outstretched arms like he was about to take a swan dive. The hot air streamed onto his face and arms, blowing away the beads of water, rustling through his damp hair, and tickling his eyelashes. His smile could not be blown away.

"Hey!" The cashier. "What are you doing?"

Greyson jolted and had to run toward him to snatch his backpack, scampering along the sudsy floor with clothes in hand. Then, frightened and ecstatic at the same time, he hurried out the exit with dog in tow.

As he turned the corner, he could hear the cashier one last time. "Are you that kid?"

# Chapter 25

*"Hey! What's your name?"* That's all Jarryd would have to say. Four simple words. Or was it five? *Do contractions count as one word or two?*

He shook his head. He was overthinking things. But, why? Talking to girls was as easy as riding a bike. Why was he treating it like a unicycle?

It was because this girl was different.

He glanced at her again, and this time she made eye contact, followed by a shy smile. Her long hair was wet, draping to her sun-tanned shoulders. Her blue and yellow one-piece swimming suit hugged every curve of her body. And she was right in front of him in line for the surfing simulator.

He'd seen beautiful girls before, but there was something about this one. Like, superstar quality. Her eyelashes were long and dark, accenting her striking eyes. She had freckles, but even those were like a leopard's spots, blending into her face like a perfect mosaic. And then there were her plump, red lips, moving like they were begging to be kissed.

"Done this before?" her lips asked.

Jarryd blubbered to himself, waking from his daydream. "Oh – uh…what?"

"The simulat'ah?"

*Oh. My. Gosh. She's Australian. A velvety-voiced one.*

He stalled by pulling his bangs across his brow. "Nope. You?" He watched a surfer wipe out, falling straight on his back in the jets of water that rocketed him up the slope to where he would retrieve his board and dignity.

"Yeah. It's not as fun as real su'fing, but easi'ah."

He could listen to her talk for hours. And he really didn't want to wipe out in front of her. "You've surfed before? That's cool." *Come on, Jarryd. Get on your game.*

"Yeah. The Box mostly, or Byron Bay."

"Nice. I've surfed, too."

"Oh, yeah? Where?"

"The Internet mostly, or Couch Potato Bay."

She velvety-laughed. "You're a funny dag, aren't you?"

"Thanks. I try." *Dag?*

"I can give you some tips if you'd like. I once was a shark biscuit myself."

*That must've been a lucky shark.* "Sure!"

He might have sounded too enthusiastic, so he glanced around the deck that was rapidly filling with people. It was a party-like atmosphere, with thumping music on the basketball court, smiling putters at the miniature golf, and food and drinks galore in most everyone's hands – and they hadn't even left the port yet.

"First tip, be confident. If you panic, you get all wo'bleh."

He loved how she pronounced 'wobbly'. "Got it. I won't be a wallaby."

She laughed. "Nice one."

"Don't worry. Confidence is my middle name."

"What's y'ah first name?"

Jarryd balked. His fake name was so stupid. "Joey."

"Like a baby 'roo?"

He blushed as they stepped forward in line. They were getting closer to the front. "No. Like the character from that old TV sitcom."

She smirked. "*Friends*?"

"I hope so. Maybe more than that, but let's not rush."

At first, he thought he'd gone too far as she scrunched her eyebrows like Sydney would before hitting him, but then she let her eyes drop over him, inspecting his body. He suddenly wished he hadn't eaten that extra Cinnabon at the airport.

"You look sooky enough. We can be mates. Have some fun."

"*Mates?*"

"Yeah."

He smiled so wide his lips hurt. But he wanted to hide his front teeth, so he forced his lips down.

They took a step closer to the front as the line moved. Only one more kid before it was her turn.

"Next tip: Bend y'ah knees and put most of the weight on your front foot. You've got nice calves, so you'll have a strong foundation."

She'd noticed. "Thanks. You have nice calves, too."

She smirked. "Thanks. Wish I had yours, though. Do you wax them?"

"Nope. Naturally smooth. You?"

"Yeah. Oth'awise they're like sandpap'ah."

He laughed. "Sandpaper, huh? Ouch."

"You'll be fine as long as you don't touch them."

"No promises."

Her cheeks flushed red, and a few kids turned their heads. She ignored them. "You are *something else...*"

"Yup. And you are…?"

"Avery."

"Avery? Is your last name 'PrettyGirl'?"

She giggled. "No, but thanks! But I don't really like the name. You don't like y'ah teeth – I don't like my name."

*She noticed I hid my teeth?*

"Oh. Well, while we're saying what we don't like, I have a twin brother."

"Ah. What's his name?"

"Ross."

"Ross? Like the other charact'ah from *Friends?*"

"Yup."

"Your parents must have liked that show."

*Why'd they let my parents choose the names?* "Yeah. I have an adopted brother I'm ashamed of, too."

"Chandler?"

"You got it."

She laughed just as a kid on the surfboard biffed hard; the water pounded into his back as his body skidded up the rounded blue hill.

Avery was next in line. After the kid had safely exited, the instructor grabbed another board for her. Before she stepped out, she turned back to Jarryd. "I'll meet you after."

She deftly stepped on the board and surfed for a full minute, earning the applause from all who watched her – except from him. He couldn't move and couldn't take his eyes off her. Bent knees, tense thighs, toned arms, focused eyes. She was beautiful.

And he was in love.

-----------

The unlit room still managed to glow with the yellowing light of sunset shining through the balcony's sliding glass door. Sydney's video call with Sam had started outside as soon as her parents had unpacked, but as soon as they had left to explore the ship, she had moved the conversation inside.

"Goooood afternoon, sailors!"

The chipper voice from the ship-wide intercom startled Sydney.

"Just a sec, Sam," she whispered to the phone. Sam smiled on the video screen, listening as well.

"This is your Captain, Chip, welcoming you to the American Dream Ocean Liner. We are now departing Galveston. Say good-bye to the loved ones you left behind, but also say goodbye to stress, worry, and anxiety!"

"Aren't those the same thing?" Sam whispered with a laugh.

"Shh!"

"And get ready to say hello to amusement, enjoyment, and fun!"

Sam snickered again.

Captain Chip continued, "Please use this time to unpack or to acquaint yourself with the ship. Be sure to read our Dream Guide or watch the video playing on Channel 9 for all the information you need about on-deck entertainment, dining, and room service. Also – get ready for an exciting presentation on emergency procedures! In just a few minutes, we will ask you to find your assigned muster station that is written in big red letters on your door. Reference your map, the arrows in the hallway, or any of our kind staff to help you get where you need to be. This is mandatory – but don't worry – the fun gets better tonight with the All-Hands-On-Deck Departure Party at the AquaTheatre Stage at 7pm. Until then, this is Captain Chip signing out! Enjoy the ride."

"He sounds...chipper."

Sydney laughed.

"But didn't he say American Dream? I thought you were on the American Spirit."

She shrugged. "Guess they changed it. It's going to Nassau, so that's all that matters." She looked out the balcony window as the ship began to pull away from the port. "And I don't know how much longer I'll have reception."

Sam nodded solemnly in her phone's screen. "Too bad we won't be able to call or text for a while."

"Yeah. My parents are paranoid. Even though we don't really use them anymore, they're still holding our phones hostage as soon as we leave port."

"Right. But it's probably for the best. Every call or text or email will be filtered through the ship's satellite dishes. I wouldn't know how to bypass...well...nevermind. I'm paranoid, too."

"Yeah, you are."

He laughed. "Anyway, you've still got my letters. Those are like, ancient texts."

She smiled, thinking of the package he'd sent her before she had left. The package had seven envelopes in it, each labeled with the date it was be opened. "Yeah. But it's not fair. I didn't get you anything."

"Just come back safely. No matter what."

She knew what he meant. He wanted her to come back whether or not she found Greyson. It was a long shot to find him, she knew, but she had to try.

"I will." Sydney let the silence drift in afterward. But silences weren't always awkward when talking to Sam. Over the last eight days, there had been plenty of opportunity to work through the awkwardness to the point where they were now. They'd video-called while doing chores, brushing their teeth, and even while just sitting and being bored together. He'd given her what she had needed – a friend who listened and cared when Greyson couldn't.

Lying down on the bed, Sydney sighed and just smiled at the screen meekly. Sam smiled back, but he descended into contemplative mode – when Sydney noticed his eyebrows would clench and his mouth moved as if arguing with himself.

"What?" she asked. "What is it?"

"This sucks. I've gotten used to talking to you more. I've liked it."

The words were flattering, but they cut at her defenses. It made her uncomfortable, and sad. But it felt good to be missed.

"Thanks," she said, trying not to think too hard about it. "I've liked it, too."

"Read that first letter."

"Okay."

"And just for fun…" he pressed his cheek to the phone's camera.

Sydney laughed, but hesitated, looking at the close up of Sam's cheek on the screen. It would just be an innocent peck. And she wouldn't actually be kissing him. A friendly peck. *Friends can kiss whenever they want…*

But she couldn't do it.

"Sorry. My phone's been in my pocket, and…it's kind of nasty."

Sam tried not to look hurt. "No worries," he said. "I'll wait for the real thing in a week. Better find your mustard station."

"Ha…ha. I will."

"Goodbye."

"Bye."

She stared at the screen until his face flickered and vanished. Even as twinges of guilt weighed her down, she hurried to her suitcase and pulled Sam's first envelope out of a side compartment.

After a cautious glance at the door and a deep sigh, she removed the

141

contents. It was a small picture of Sam. She turned it and read the pristine handwriting. "My favorite picture of myself. Make sure to bring it back to me."

Smiling to herself, she gazed at his picture. He hadn't wanted her to forget about him. He was so thoughtful. She wished she had thought to give him a picture of herself – at least the Polaroid one, even though her smile had been messed up. But it had gotten lost in the hasty move. She'd found the broken frame and the picture of her and Melinda, but the Polaroid hadn't been in the trash bag. It had gone missing, or someone had...

And then she realized. *Someone* hadn't wanted to forget about *her*.

---------------

Sydney's image smiled at Greyson through the Polaroid. He had almost memorized her face by now. He liked the gentle slope of her nose with the perfectly round bulb at the end. Her blue eyes were even more sparkly than usual, like the laughter she had been caught in was genuine. And her smile. He was often mesmerized by her lips. He'd remember the time they half-kissed. The shock had sent shivers through his body. And then the time she'd fallen on him at the fair. She had been about to kiss him then, too. Maybe it had been out of relief – like a thank-you for the rescue. But there had been nothing in the weeks afterwards. Maybe Jarryd's joke about him loving her had scared her off. Or maybe she'd been thinking more about Sam and how he'd stolen a kiss from her. And maybe she had liked Sam's kiss more than his half-one.

No. Nope to all of those. Well, maybe not the love one. He wasn't sure what to think about that. Did he love her? How was he supposed to know? And did it even matter anymore?

He shook off the thought and wiped his hand over his freshly cut hair, feeling the tug at his scalp.

"Like it, Syd?"

Sydney's smile meant she liked his haircut – thought it was even cuter than before. Greyson smiled back.

The cut-hair lay in brown clumps around his log-seat and would provide good nesting materials for the birds. His knife had worked really well, he thought, and he hadn't even cut himself.

And now, he would be harder for people like the gas station cashier to recognize him. Though the change of hair length probably wouldn't make too much difference, at least it wouldn't get as dirty as it had before.

He felt so much better, like he was a new person. Maybe it had been the cold water or the brand of soap, but more likely it was how he felt about himself. Knowing he could talk to people without scaring them off made him feel normal again. Sure, since he'd been spotted, he would have to abandon the idea of cleaning people's windshields, but he could come back to the idea after he put a few more miles between them.

Greyson slid the Polaroid back into the Bible and stored it in his fanny pack. The picture of his father had made its way to his backpack to keep his place in his mother's research papers – though he'd abandoned reading those for his Bible long ago.

Standing up and turning the fanny pack to his back, he adjusted the new holster for his slingshot. It was simple, but effective. Using a ripped coat he'd found in a dumpster, he had torn strips of material with button snaps on each end. With a few cuts and knots, he now had a simple holster that gave him access to his slingshot with a quick snap, and without fumbling through his fanny pack.

Encouraged by his success, he'd used the same material to make two other useful creations that attached to his fanny pack's waistband. He'd made another snap to secure his hat for when he worried he might lose it to wind or water, and he'd crafted a small cloth pouch to hold three ball bearings for quick access. The fanny pack was becoming quite the utility belt, and he wore it proudly, like a soldier.

After making the final preparation – cinching his dinosaur blanket to the bottom of his backpack with twine – he pumped his eyebrows at Kit. "Ready, boy?"

Kit gave a sharp bark and wagged his tail.

Laughing, Greyson swung his backpack on and fit his cap over his chopped hair as he took a last glimpse of his surroundings. They were on the edge of a forested mountain, covered in maple trees, whose leaves looked like little flames, red and orange and yellow, wisping toward the sky. And there were thousands all around, like a forest fire frozen in time.

From this vantage, he could see the town tucked in the valley below, and even the roof of the car wash and gas station far off in the distance. Taller mountains lay in the direction he was headed, but he felt more confident to tackle them now. Though his clothes were still damp, he felt lighter now, cleaner. And thanks to four dollars' worth of trail mix and jerky, he felt a new vigor. Every day he was closer to finding his dad. Mile after mile, despite setbacks, brought him nearer. And now that the map he'd taken told him he was in Georgia, he knew he was only a state away from Florida.

"Come on, boy."

They trekked all day on winding forested slopes, stopping for drinks and to rest their feet and paws, but their pace was strong and their attitudes positive. Greyson was happy – motivated with a new brand of confidence. He was on a mission. He had purpose. His dad was his goal, and the only thing he could do was take one step after the other.

On top of all that, there was the beaming sun and the glory of nature. At times their path would grant them a beauty he had never seen before. During the afternoon they stopped to admire the green peaks battling with brilliant white clouds in the crisp blue air. Though the wildlife was adept at avoiding them, and Kit was no good at catching them, every so often Greyson would stop and hush Kit, kneel low, and point them out – a river otter, a skittering shrew, two white-tailed deer watching from afar.

A few hours later they ran across a rushing stream babbling its way through the rocks. They drank from its frigid water, and Greyson managed to splash Kit – as close as he could get to a bath.

All afternoon they trekked along the stream, until the sound of the water changed. It grew louder as it meandered to the distance beyond.

Greyson turned to Kit and then rushed along the shore, bounding over fallen branches. Kit followed closely and then ran ahead as they got closer. The dog stopped suddenly, and Greyson skidded next to him. His eyes lit up with fascination. It was unlike anything he'd seen in Iowa. The stream ended in a shimmering waterfall, plummeting thirty or forty feet to a blue pool below.

After marveling at its beauty, it took Greyson only a few seconds to shed most of his clothes and do what every daring boy would do. He slapped the fear away and dove from the cliff into the best bath he'd ever taken. Though he had just had a fantastic shower, this was glorious. He let the fall's water smash into his scalp and his shoulders – a powerful massage. He swam and dove to the bottom, testing its depth, and then kicked to the top.

GRRRRRRR...

He emerged to Kit's growls. And then he heard voices.

# Chapter 26

*It's them! Orion tracked me all the way here!*

Startled, Greyson thrashed around uselessly, suddenly seized by memories of the night he'd searched for Sydney and Liam in the river. His arms felt like lead as the panic fought him. He felt as if Liam and Sydney's weight were pulling him under. His fingers pulled at Liam's, setting him free.

"Wow! Look at it!"

The voices were getting closer. But it wasn't Orion and his brothers. They were tourists, marveling at the waterfall from afar.

He'd forgotten he was in a state park. Of course, this would be a point of interest. *Stupid!*

Though it wasn't Plurbs, tourists could be just as dangerous to his mission. He snapped from the nightmare and into action, racing out of the pool and up to his clothes just as the hikers came into view below. He hid and dried off, unseen.

As soon as he and Kit were able to sneak away, they left the waterfall behind, keeping their distance from the stream and the tourists.

He didn't tell Kit why he had gotten so scared. The nightmares were already ruining his dreams; he couldn't let them ruin his waking life as well. He had to forget them – put them away – far away, where they should be. To talk about them would let them invade even further.

"That was fun. We'll have to come back someday."

He smiled at Kit and took in a deep breath as they continued in silence. Slowly, the distant sound of the stream and the chirping birds calmed him again. After a few hours, he'd forgotten all about the scare.

But then, just before sunset, while crossing over a grassy ridge, he dropped to his knees. Across the ridge, on the alternate mountain, was a hulk of black fur bobbing around the trees.

"Black bear," he told Kit.

Kit growled low, and the hair rose along the spine of his back. Greyson put his hand on his back, keeping him put. "Stay. Don't provoke him."

But Kit kept growling, louder and louder.

"What, boy? Calm down. It's okay; he's far off. And he's probably more scared of us than we are of –"

And then the bear turned suddenly, staring straight at them. Greyson startled, realizing how exposed they were on the ridge.

He stood up to run when it happened.

*WHUPWHUPWHUPWHUPWHUP!*

They had come upon them like a swarm of locusts, and the sound of their blades, once hidden behind trees, blanketed them with beats that rattled their insides. Helicopters, the type with long bodies and two separate blades, zipped across the sky in numbers he'd never seen.

His head craned upward to watch them soaring above in perfect formation. Dozens in a flock, heading to the west, not far above the trees, one after another, after another, after another.

"Whooooaaa. Cooool!"

Amazed, Greyson watched the swarm fly on without moving a muscle, though the beats of the blades rattled his chest. To them he was hopefully just another hiker. Besides, they were obviously not looking for him. They had somewhere else they needed to be – and fast.

After the last beat of their blades had faded into the distance, Greyson patted Kit on the head.

He growled one last time as if he had scared them away.

"You scared 'em off. Well done." He looked over his shoulder. "And the bear, too. You're a scary animal."

At least he thought the bear was gone. He hadn't seen which direction he went. There was something scarier than seeing a bear – it was knowing one was close, but not seeing it. A chill went through his body, but he shook it off.

Kit was panting at his side, still proud of himself.

"Thirsty? I guess we should stop soon anyway. Find a good place to camp and hunt a little, maybe."

He unzipped the backpack, retrieved his handy bark-bowl and poured Kit a good amount of stream water.

A rumble – deep and guttural – interrupted Kit's drink and shook their bones. Tiny stones vibrated at his feet and a sound came from the trees just below the ridge.

Something else was coming.

------------------

"WAAAAAAAAHHH!" Seven-year-old Asher gave his loudest roar,

clawed with his T-Rex claws, and snapped with his T-Rex jaws. He was vicious, powerful – the King of All Beasts – and very hungry.

"No-oooo!"

His victim fell before him, helpless to do anything but squirm. Asher's claws tore at the man's belly and went for his ribs – his favorite food.

"Not my ribs! But there's no barbeque sauce! They'll be so dry!"

"Wibs not dwy! Bloooood saaaauce," Asher growled, never caring about his inability to pronounce 'r's. "Nom, nom!"

"Nom, nom? Does T-Rex say nom nom?"

His victim laughed and so did the T-Rex. And then the man fought back with his secret weapon.

"T-Rex is T-icklish!"

The man grabbed at Asher's sides and lifted him in the air, only to throw him onto his bed. The T-Rex tried to fight back, but his growls were snorts and his roars were of laughter. Soon it was all over. The T-Rex was buried under the heap of covers.

"Ah haha! T-Rex is defeated!"

"Nuh, uh! T-Wex died, yeah. But T-Wex comes back as…T-Wex the zombie!"

Asher pushed his jaw to the side, moaned, and waved his T-Rex claws side to side as he rose from the covers. "Bwwwwaaaains."

His dad, Dan, laughed, but pushed him back down. "Sleeeeep."

"Ah, man. It's like 8 o'clock."

"Ah, boy. That's because I know you'll be reading for another half hour."

Asher smiled and reached under his bed, where dozens of books had once been stacked but were now toppled like a deck of cards. He came out with a book about pirates, looked at it and then put it back. Going down again, he came up with a book about Star Wars.

"Now we'ah talkin'."

As Dan handed Asher his book light, his cell phone buzzed.

"Good night, buddy."

"Night, Dad!"

"Sleep tight." He flicked off the lights as he left and answered the phone. "What is it?"

The man on the phone got straight to the point. "The team's mobilizing. The kid we've been looking for was spotted in Allenworth."

"Allenworth? Here in Georgia?"

"Yes. In your backyard."

"How do you know it's not like all the other sightings?"

"Red backpack and a German Shepherd."

"I see."

"Dan…" came a softer tone. But coming from such a large, deep-chested man, it still rumbled in his ear.

"I know."

"This is a sign. It's time to get back in. This halfway stuff isn't enough."

"We've talked about this," Dan said stiffly. "I'm doing what I can from here. Asher…" he peaked at the door and took a few more steps away lest Asher was eavesdropping. "Asher likes it here."

"Grover might not admit it, but we need you. In the field or in support. And by the looks of it, you may not have a choice. We're coming to you."

Dan wanted to argue, but he knew the man on the phone wouldn't be deterred. He hadn't been deterred for months – ever since the botched nuke attack in Morris. The whole team wanted Dan back and regularly called.

"I'll keep my eye out for the boy." Dan hung up and looked through the crack in the door, imagining his own son out on his own for nearly two weeks, off the grid. How had Greyson made it thus far? And where was he so determined to go?

Concern plagued his grim face as he watched his son read. The book light illuminated the large picture book, his big eyes, and his moving lips as he read to himself about battles and weapons and war.

Perhaps tomorrow he would find him another book. One about survival.

--------------------

Emory read the report. The kid had made it to Georgia. Survived. Hid.

He'd survived bombs. Gunfire. A plummet from a moving vehicle into a river. A nuclear blast. And Orion's clumsy attacks.

It seemed Fate wanted the boy to live.

But Emory also knew of others who wanted the boy alive. But for what? What did they want him for? Why, even after the boy had forced them into back-up plans, twice, would they still see a need for him?

Emory had his guesses, but that's all they were. He needed answers. And to get them, he needed to find the boy.

There was no doubt they would be trying to track him down as well.

If it came down to it, Emory would rather the boy be dead than have him fall into their hands. Greyson was plucking at a nerve, and it was about time his distractions stop.

That's why he'd sent the Fisherman to Nassau.

Orion was upset, but he'd had his chance.

Emory leaned back on his lawn chair and thought to himself, rubbing the beard that grew red despite his brown hair. He liked the beard, but he couldn't get used to it. His look would change in a day or two. New clothes, new wig, new facial hair – and always a hat or roof above his head to ward off pesky satellite or drone pictures. They would never find him.

They were trying. Every resource the government had at its disposal was being used. All its money, all its technology. They were in crisis mode. He was the most wanted man in United States history – more than Lee Harvey Oswald, John Wilkes Booth, or Osama bin Laden. But their armies, their drones, their hackers wouldn't find him. Not him, the Eye of Eyes, because *he* was watching *them*. One step ahead, two steps ahead. And this wasn't the tortoise and the hare. This was David and Goliath. For all their armor and all their strength, he had speed, agility, an endless supply of prosthetic faces, and a plan. Every step they took he had foreseen, taking them deeper and deeper into a trap of their own making.

Though he hadn't foreseen Greyson.

Maybe he shouldn't underestimate him.

Emory turned to one of the six men stationed around the lake's dock. A dozen more were in the lake house; a small army wore civilian clothes and were posted about the town and the resort, sniffing out any suspicious activity. His personal army had fended off attacks from small countries before, but never from within the American Beast. Here, it was best to keep a lower profile – to blend in until ready to strike. And even then, it was best to let expendable men do the striking.

"Give word to the loyal militias in Georgia and Florida," he ordered. "Don't let the boy get to Nassau. Bring him back to me alive, preferably. If the Feds get to him first, take him back at all costs. That's all."

"Yes, sir."

The messenger left in a hurry, and Emory turned back to the lake. He contemplated going without any prosthetics for just a few minutes, but he knew he could never let his guard down. One insect drone, one satellite picture was all it took to end it all. No, he kept his head in the game, face and all. His masks had become part of him anyway. They kept him alive just as his right arm had. He couldn't more go without the masks than he could his gun hand.

Instead, he surrendered to the moment of blissful freedom. The floating dock rolled with the calm waves, a comforting flow, as if it were being rocked and consoled by a loving mother. He closed his eyes and let his head sway with the movement.

# Chapter 27

"Ugh…" Jarryd moaned, holding his stomach. "How can you guys eat with all this rocking?"

Nick, Sammy, Sydney, and both sets of parents sat around the banquet table in the exquisite dining room decorated with pristine white linens, gold banisters and crystal chandeliers as waiters in customary black and white uniforms bustled around with hand towels and trays of beautifully plated dishes. Before their food arrived, many guests would wander to the south wall, which was made entirely of glass, and marvel at the view of the park running through the ship's valley-like interior below.

"I don't know how you *can't* eat, with all this good food," Nick said, sawing at a piece of juicy steak. Since he hadn't been able to decide which type of potato he wanted with the steak, he'd ordered mashed, tator tots, and baked. But it wasn't as big as Sammy's food pile.

Jarryd watched Sammy chew on a crab's leg and slurp at the small bowl of butter. "Ugh…"

"You know what?" his stepdad began, holding a roll in one hand and a forked chicken breast in the other, "I heard that humming to yourself cures motion sickness."

"I already took a pill and I'm wearing six motion-sick patches…"

"Well, have they worked?"

Jarryd shot his stepdad a skeptical look but began humming to himself as the rest of the table snickered. Soon, he was feeling better, rocking with the music and gesturing with bold arm reaches.

"Is that the song from *Titanic*?" Sydney asked. "'My Heart Will Go On?'"

Jarryd shrugged, still humming. He pulled at Sydney's arm during a swell in the music, and for once she didn't hit him or push him away. She even acted along, grabbing his hand and humming along, faking a romance.

"You know the Titanic was a giant ship that sunk, right?" Nick asked, still eating. "And we're *on* a giant ship."

Jarryd stopped with a smirk. "Oh. My bad."

The table laughed, quickly returning to their food. But as their waiter filled their drinks, Nick glanced at his nametag, which had his home country engraved beneath.

*Pham. Vietnam.*

The cruise workers' nationalities had fascinated Nick. He'd seen nine different countries represented already, though most had been from the Pacific islands or southeastern Asia.

But Nick took a double take at Pham and froze in fear. *He can't be…*

Pham was refilling Mr. Hansen's water now, giving Nick a closer view of his face. Nick wrestled with his thoughts, convincing himself it was just a coincidence, but re-convincing himself that it couldn't be.

On Pham's left eyebrow was a diagonal cut, like a scar that prevented hair from growing. Just like the scar Nick had received after initiation. From Pluribus.

"Nice watch!" Jarryd exclaimed, noticing the screen on Pham's wrist that displayed the time digitally. It also displayed the date, temperature, and a background picture – which looked like some sort of flower.

"T'ank you," he said with a heavy accent and without a smile.

"Is that the new…?" Jarryd asked. But Pham had already left. He shrugged and turned to his friends. "Did you see that watch? It's one of those new satellite ones that you can surf the Internet or even do video calls from anywhere in the world – no matter what. It syncs with your phone and pretty much does everything."

"Doeth it cut your food for you?" Sammy inquired, holding up a lobster tail with his fork.

"I'll cut your face for you."

"Jarryd!" his mother scolded.

"What? He was making fun of me."

"No, I wathn't," Sammy complained, trying to get his lazy eye to glare at Jarryd. "I want to know for real."

"If it cuts your food?"

"Yeah."

"No, Sammy. A watch doesn't cut food. That's what knives are –"

"Then it doethn't do everything."

Jarryd raised his knife in the air in a threatening gesture.

His stepdad put up his hand to stop him but gave a concerned look to Nick. "Nick, you okay?"

Nick was staring at his plate of half-eaten steak, the blood still pooling around it. "M-maybe I'm a little motion sick, too."

He wanted to tell them, but now wasn't the time. And there was still that

152

off chance that it was a coincidental scar.

He glanced around, looking for other waiters and guests with the scar, but instead noticed something else. Two...no, three more waiters wore the same watch.

"Humming worked for me, bro."

"I heard sticking French fries up your nose works, too," his stepdad joked.

"Or jutht puke. Workth for me," Sammy suggested.

"No, no. I'll be fine."

Ignoring the suggestions, Nick scanned the room, examining each waiter. Some waiters didn't have a smart watch. But the three who did suddenly stopped – all at the same moment, as if they were programmed robots. If he hadn't been watching each of them, he wouldn't have noticed. They stopped what they were doing, looked down at their watches, and then moved on.

Nick's stomach bubbled in fear. It could be nothing – just a coincidence. Besides, he had the mark, too, and he wasn't a terrorist. Not all Plurbs are the bad ones.

*But some are. And if there are more than one on this cruise...*

Nick wrapped his arms over his stomach and couldn't stop looking at his plate. Did Greyson get sick with fear when he thought something was wrong? Probably not. But Greyson wouldn't go around telling everybody there were terrorists on the cruise...yet. Greyson would seek more information, find out what they were up to, then stop them in heroic fashion. He'd be busy right now, thinking of plans – ways to take them down no matter how dangerous it was. The more daring the better.

But all Nick could do was stare at his bleeding steak.

---------------

Greyson stared at the can of cat vomit. Though it really wasn't cat vomit, it was just as yellow, chunky, and pungent as the stuff cats deposit on the carpet.

*Creamed corn.* It even sounded nasty. But it was all he had left. And his stomach, his weakness, and his head told him now was the time. It was an emergency.

After the helicopters and then the jets had roared overhead, scaring the wits out of him, he'd given up on the hunting idea. Instead, he had searched for a good place to camp for the night, out of view of any more airborne vehicles. It hadn't taken long to find a rocky outcropping that formed a nice ceiling overhead. He didn't know for sure but thought the rock would provide good cover in case anything overhead was using infrared to search for him.

"Want to try it first?" he asked Kit, holding out the can. Kit whined and took a few steps backward.

Laughing, Greyson took two fingers and dipped them in the corny mix. It had taken several minutes using his multi-tool's tiny can opener to get the can open, and he'd carried it halfway across the country. He had to make it worth it. "Here goes nothing." He slurped it from his fingers, cringed, and gagged, but kept it down.

"That *is* nasty!" he exclaimed to the curious dog. "But not as nasty as I thought."

He took another dip and then another. Soon Kit scooted closer, showing interest. Greyson ignored him, slurping faster and faster with his two-fingered spoon, until Kit let out a sharp bark.

"Geez, dude! Quiet." He glanced around the dark woods, thankful at least for the full moon, which gave a gray hue to everything that its light touched. Though he could have made a fire, he had been afraid it would give away their position. "Here."

He poured some in Kit's bowl and watched him sniff it, back away, and then come in full bore until it was all gone.

"You can thank Sydney when…if you ever meet her."

Once he and Kit had finished all but a few remains inside the can, he hiked back to the trap he'd been working on. Though he couldn't quite make a few designs work, he was satisfied with this one. In theory, once the critter pulled at the bait, it would release the bend in a live branch, snapping it forward, knocking out the thick stick that once held the rock up above the critter.

After placing the bait, he stepped back to admire his work. *What animal will go for creamed corn?* He didn't know, but it was worth a shot.

Returning to camp, Greyson sat beneath his rock ceiling, staring out at the bluish green valley between the two mountain ridges. The stars above were bright, set out vividly against the blackest of black skies, and the moon was the brightest light of all, a white disc so big that each of its craters was easily discernable from the others.

"It's almost like a giant cookie. Like an Oreo without one of its sides."

He held out his hand as if to pluck it from the sky. Squinting, he imagined holding it between his fingers – the entire delicious moon cookie in his grasp.

Sensing motion, he looked over to see Kit pawing at the sky, mimicking him. He tried over and over again, but he could only lift his paw so far. He looked disappointed.

Greyson laughed at the clever dog and then paused with a sudden thought. "What else do you know?"

Kit cocked his head as if he wanted to understand.

*He knows "speak", "sic", and "stand". What else?* "Roll over."

Kit rolled over and stared at him excitedly.

Greyson laughed. "Beg."

Kit sat on his hind legs and whimpered. Greyson cheered.

"Play dead."

Like he had been shot, Kit rolled onto his back, his four legs bent above him as if he were jumping over a fence. Greyson laughed and pet his furry stomach. "Might have to work on that – make it more realistic looking. But what else..." he started, thinking. He pointed toward a tree in the distance. "Go over..." he trailed off – Kit was already headed toward the tree at a trot.

Astounded, Greyson stood up. Kit responded to hand motions, too? Making sure not to make a sound, he motioned for Kit to come to him. Sure enough, Kit trotted back, panting in anticipation of the next command.

"Geez. What *don't* you know? How about...?" He pressed his hands together and then separated them quickly, like a tiny explosion. "Teleport!"

Kit cocked his head.

"Teleport! To the Bahamas!"

The dog smacked its lips, letting out a frustrated little bark.

"Oh well. We'll work on that one." Greyson laughed and scratched Kit behind his ears. The dog was amazing. He would have to experiment more to see all that he knew. Maybe he could even teach him some more tricks.

He found himself looking at Kit – his glassy eyes and slobbering mouth. Man's best friend. Loving protector. Guardian. A random thought popped into his mind. There were angels in the Bible as well as demons. Were angels real? Could they take the form of people? Could they take other forms?

Kit panted at Greyson but didn't give him any more evidence. But he supposed it didn't matter. Greyson had enough evidence already. Plus, if it were true, dog's mortal enemies – cats – would be demons.

*Totally makes sense.*

He smiled at Kit, and together they turned back to the moon.

# Chapter 28

The moon hovered over the dark ocean like a single light bulb, reflected in the rolling waves. The moon was beautiful, but Sydney couldn't take her eyes off the ocean. It was mesmerizing, but it was also frightening. It was as big as the sky and felt even more powerful. She could feel its mass underneath the gigantic ship, tossing it to and fro like it was a toy in a bathtub. And while she could see into the sky, millions of miles to the stars, she couldn't see even a foot beneath the ocean's dark waters. A whole other powerful world existed underneath her, around her, and beyond the horizon.

Nick leaned onto the railing next to Sydney on the top deck. "I once convinced Jarryd that the moon was the sun after it switched to night light."

Sydney laughed, but kept her gaze on the undulating waves.

"Worried about him?" he asked.

Sydney pursed her lips. "Who?"

"Uh, who else?" Nick gave her a look.

"Greyson? Yeah. Some. You?"

Nick nodded with a sigh. "A little."

They stared out to sea until Nick turned back toward the ship's interior. They were near the middle of the ship, just a few yards from where their parents relaxed in a hot tub. After dinner they had danced at the Departure Party. After a few thumping dances, a slow song had come on and Nick and Sydney had danced. But only for a minute. She had thought about Greyson – how he hated to dance – and she'd grown sad. So, instead they had explored the ship, navigating with the Dream Guide's map.

The map showed that the ship was shaped almost like a hotdog bun, with a deep valley in the center encircled by rooms with balconies overlooking a central park that ran through the bottom of the valley. Toward the bow of the ship there were deck chairs situated around lush vegetation meant for more private relaxation, while the stern of the ship had the basketball courts, surfing simulators, and mini-golf course. Just below the stern's top deck was the spectacular Aqua Theatre. Its hundreds of auditorium seats faced a winding pool where performances would be held with the ocean as a backdrop, even as climbers scaled the two rock walls behind the audience.

As they had walked the halls, they couldn't help thinking that it was like a massive hotel had blended with a city's downtown. Though the ship would travel to tourist destinations for its passengers to explore, Sydney could understand why some passengers never even left the ship. Every day there were new shows in multiple theatres, tons of restaurants, dance clubs, contests, and of course, the zip line that ran across the interior valley. She couldn't imagine a better vacation opportunity.

But she wasn't happy. Maybe if Greyson were there. Or Sam.

"Want to come back to the hot tub?" Nick asked. "Might as well enjoy it, you know?"

She smiled at him. "Alright."

Together she and Nick made their way to the hot tub where their families were laughing and smiling. As soon as they slipped into the bubbly water, Nick caught a glimpse of something astonishing. "No. Frickin'. Way."

Sydney turned to Nick and then followed his gaze. Jarryd was strutting, towel over his shoulder, chin in a permanent pump upward. To his right was a girl no one recognized, but Sydney instantly disliked. The girl was the type of girl that made girls like Sydney feel self-conscious about their bodies.

Even their parents' mouths had dropped open, exhaling little gasps of exclamation as Jarryd and Avery came closer.

"Hey, peeps!" Jarryd shouted, his strut turning into a pose as he stood over their hot tub. "Got room for two more?"

"Uh…who's this?" Sydney's mom asked as welcoming as she could.

"Oh, uh, sorry," he said gesturing to the girl. "This is Avery."

"G'day," Avery said, revealing her Australian accent.

"She's my *mate*," Jarryd said with a smirk and a pump of his chin.

Jarryd's stepdad smiled as the rest found themselves at a loss for words.

"Good day," Sydney replied, breaking the silence. "Come on in." *By all means, hide your body under the water.*

"Thank you," she said, stepping in and taking a seat next to Sydney.

"I'm Rachel," Sydney said.

Avery reacted as if she knew some hidden meaning behind her name.

Before Avery could ask, the Aldemans gave their names as Al and Peggy and the Hansens as Tim and Jill. For a while they interrogated her, in a nice way, and found out that her parents were business owners – one in robotics and one in aerospace. *Rich.* Her hobbies were surfing and tennis. *Athletic.* And she was thinking of graduating high school a few years early to attend a university in the states. *Smart.*

Jealousy rose in Sydney's heart, but she fought to keep it at bay. She seemed nice. But she had to have flaws. Why else would she want to hang with Jarryd?

"This hot tub is nice," Jarryd's stepdad exclaimed, "but it doesn't have as good of service as the one in Serenity with that bar. No kids there either." He winked at Jarryd and then saw something out of the corner of his eye. "Hey! Waiter!"

The waiter stopped and, just visible in the deck lights, rolled his eyes. But he approached with a smile. "What can I get you, sir?"

"A Hairy Navel, please."

"Dave – er – Al!" his wife chastised, forgetting his fake name in a rush to rebuke.

"What? That's what the drink's called, right?" he said with a grin.

Nick's eyes were examining the waiter's face and this his wrist.

Sydney gave Nick a look. She could tell he was fighting to say something, but something else was fighting back. Finally, he blurted, "Hey! Where'd you get the watch?"

The waiter, Adrian from the Philippines, gave him a hard look. "It was a gift." And then he walked away, leaving their hot tub with puzzled expressions.

Sydney gave Nick an even more puzzled look that said *what'd you ask that for?*

He replied with a sideways glance that said *I'll tell you later.*

"Did Joey tell you he su'fed earliah today?" Avery asked the group. "He was a bonz'ah, doing amazing until –"

"Until my knees got all wallaby."

They laughed together and Jarryd slapped his hand at the water to show what happened to him.

"He hit so ha'd, I thought he carked it, but he's as tough as woodpeck'ah lips."

"But no worries. I'm uncarked."

Avery laughed. Even her laugh was pleasant. "Sorry for some of the lingo. This is my first vacation with Americans. You'll have to teach me some of yours."

As the group chimed in, teaching her American lingo, Sydney turned to look again at the moon. She was tired already and wanted to retreat to the room, but that would mean standing up in her bathing suit in front of everyone – and Avery. Though she was sure they had all made the comparison in their minds, she didn't want to help them out.

Maybe she should go to the fitness center with Nick tomorrow morning – to hear what's up and to work out. It couldn't hurt. Well, it might hurt, since she hadn't really worked out since the fair attack and resulting move had eliminated her dance practices.

Suddenly Nick was getting out of the tub and drying off. "I'm going to call it a night," he said, nonchalantly. "I've got a room key."

The others tried to persuade him to stay, but he kindly brushed them off, donned his t-shirt, and walked away.

"I'm going, too. Ross, wait up!" Sydney burst from the water, slipping a little on the edge and almost putting her butt in Avery's face, but gaining control and sprinting to Nick. She came back for her towel. "I'm tired, too. Catch you later!" She turned to Avery. "G'night."

Nick waited for her around the corner.

"You okay?" he asked.

"Are *you* okay?" she asked back.

He scoffed and shrugged, turning in the direction of their rooms. "I'm just…I guess I'm scared…well, not *scared*…"

Sydney walked alongside him, still drying off. "Of what?"

"It's weird being here. Having fun. Pretending like everything is normal."

She nodded, agreeing with him. Eight hours ago, they were in Texas. Not long before that they were under FBI protection.

"I feel like…we're running away…or running right into something worse." Nick opened the door for her, descended a few floors, and followed her into Miko Deck's lobby, where plush red carpet greeted their toes. The high-pitched plinks and clings of the casino played at their ears, and the flashing lights took their attention as they walked by. They admired the off-limits place like they were at a zoo, admiring the various games, the excited players, and a grand-prize waverunner elevated above the slot machines, like it was riding on a wave of dollar bills.

Nick stopped and stared. "That would be sweet."

Sydney stopped briefly next to him, but then continued on, giving it a passing glance. "Sure, buddy."

"No, really," he said, catching up to her. "Jarryd and I rode them a couple summers ago at the Lake of the Ozarks. I'm horrible, but Jarryd's a natural with things like that. It was pretty fun."

"I'm sure it was. Everything was fun back then."

There was already a line waiting for the elevators, so they headed for the stairway that wound down from one deck's lobby to the next, all the way down to their deck – the Seriano Deck.

"Do you feel the same?" Nick asked with a whisper to not be overheard by the passersby. "That we're running away, or running into something worse?"

They passed the golden sign reading *Empress Deck*.

Sydney sighed, thinking to herself as they descended. "I guess it seems like whenever things are going well…then that's when it happens. It's like we're just in the peaceful eye of the storm, just waiting for…"

Nick gave her a sympathetic smile. "…it to go all crazy again?"

"Yeah." She smiled back, glancing at the mural on the staircase wall of an underwater castle, complete with a drawbridge, a keep, and watchtowers. Tiny little flags blew in the water's current and colorful fish darted within the gates.

Suddenly Nick's face turned grave, and he stopped on the landing, pulling Sydney's arm. Making sure they were alone, he removed his glasses and rubbed the scar on his eyebrow. His voice turned to a whisper. "See this mark?"

She nodded.

"It was given to me by Pluribus." He let that sink in. "And now I've seen that same mark, two times. On this ship."

Sydney drew back with dismay. Nick put his glasses back on and leveled his eyes with hers. "I think we're heading straight into it again."

Though she was scared, a determination broke her frown. She gave Nick a look. "And you want to check it out, don't you?"

He shrugged. "We have to."

She rocked on her heels and gave a surrendered nod. "You're just like him."

He blushed, trying not to put his hands on his fanny pack. "Not really. Am I?"

"Sure you are," she said with a shrug. "What's your plan? I know you're thinking of something – just like he would."

A surge of confidence swelled into Nick's smile. Suddenly he pulled her around a corner and glanced both ways to make sure the coast was clear. Then, feeding off of her excitement, he whispered the plan.

# Chapter 29

The bowels of the American Dream were as much dark and musty as the exterior was bright and welcoming. The corridors were narrow, the lights dim and blue, and the air stifling. Workers shuffled about robotically, with barely a word exchanged among them. Those that wore the watches were more aware – shifty-eyed and quick on their feet – while those without went about their business carrying laundry and trash like they had done it a thousand times. And many had.

Nick's plan had gone smoothly so far, if one could call it a plan. The plan had called for them to follow a Plurb-marked worker in order to gather more information. Once they had found one, Sydney had distracted him with a spilled drink just as he had opened a security door. Nick had caught the security door before it closed and slipped past, hiding in a janitor cart's pile of laundry. After Nick let Sydney in the security zone, they had followed the workers for several minutes, finally darting to a hiding place behind a mound of sheets as big as an igloo.

The gigantic laundry machine's tiny circular window glowed ahead of them, twirling the clothes in ghostly shapes as it jerked and jostled the laundry as if chewing a rubbery steak. Watching it made Nick dizzy, and his stomach already ached. His grand plan had only gotten them deep into enemy territory – and soiled sheets.

"There," Sydney whispered, pointing toward the corner of the massive room, past several more machines that were chewing towels. "They stopped in the corner."

Nick spotted them as well. They were talking with each other, glancing around nervously, but without enough suspicion to spot the kids' faces amongst the piles.

"What are they doing?" Sydney asked.

"I don't know. Looks like they're just waiting."

"For what?"

Nick rolled his eyes. "How am I supposed to know?"

"Well," Sydney said, glancing at the mark cut from his brow. "...you *are* one of them."

"No, I'm not. Just because I was with them for a week or two..."

"Shh!"

A worker passed by with a cart of striped bath towels. Once he had gone an adequate distance, Nick continued. "I'm not one of them."

She stared blankly. "I know."

Nick wasn't convinced in her response. But all he could do was sigh and continue watching the men. It was another two minutes before their watches lit up. Like they were programmed, the two men gave each other a look and left the room.

"They're going!"

Nick and Sydney snuck around the edge of the laundry piles, passing behind one grinding machine after another. The noise was louder than their thoughts, and when they finally reached the door, their ears welcomed the silence with relief.

"They keep going further in," Nick mentioned. "Maybe we should head back…"

Sydney caught a glimpse of one of the men's shoes disappearing down the hall. "That way!"

Nick followed with a sigh, light on his feet and crouching low. One passage led to another until a dark stairwell loomed at the end of the hall. After waiting for the Plurbs to descend first, Nick and Sydney followed on the cramped staircase with deliberate steps, the metal creaking beneath their weight no matter how careful they were.

Nick had to remind himself to breathe. He'd spent hours in visualization and preparation, but now it was real – and his plan had already run its course. The panic was nipping at his heart – sending spurts of adrenaline washing through his veins. This wasn't what he was supposed to be doing, and he knew it. He was supposed to be the one who stayed behind with the binoculars and maps – the one who warned the adventurous ones when trouble was coming. He wasn't the adventurous one. Or at least he wasn't supposed to be.

Finally reaching the bottom of the staircase, he scooted past Sydney, made a gesture to hold up, and peeked around the corner. Only twenty yards down, the men had stopped at a door labeled "Authorized Personnel Only." Just as the men were closing the door behind them, Nick glanced away.

Whether or not he was adventurous or not, he didn't have a choice now. There wasn't any more time to pretend. There had to come a time when the pretending would run out. And this was it. "I think they've reached their destination."

"We're not going to find out anything by staying here," Sydney complained. "What are we waiting for?"

Nick put his back to the wall and took in deep breaths, fighting the panic.

Sydney arched her brow. "Want me to go first?"

*Yes, please!* "No way! I'm just thinking."

"Why? Let's go."

Sydney started around the corner, but Nick stopped her with a stiff hand. "I'm going first. No questions."

He stared her down, gave her a stern nod, and then wrapped around the corner mouthing 'stupid' over and over again as the door loomed nearer. They were near the bottom of the ship, and they could sense the pressure of the ocean on all sides, as if it were crushing the hull. Nick tried hard not to imagine the dark depths of water just below his feet.

His hand reached for the door's lever and rubbed over the cold steel. A loud mechanical churning reverberated through the door, rattling the handle and Nick's hand. Breathing out and closing his eyes, he pushed the lever down, feeling the mechanism unlatch.

"Easy," Sydney whispered, just behind his ear.

The door cracked open, and the scene inside slowly came into view. Nick and Sydney pressed their eyes up to it, taking it in.

It was a long and narrow room with large rectangular doors that could be opened to the outside but were now latched securely shut. Just inside the docks were bright orange plastic crates that would require two men to carry. Several of the containers were open, but the lids were still blocking the contents from view.

The two men they had followed were kneeling over the contents of a crate and talking with two others, but the mechanical churning was loud and clunking, like the ship's engine was only a room or two away. Only phrases were audible above the din.

"...won't be suspicious...doing their jobs...won't see it coming."

Nick's eyes grew wider and his mouth was agape.

It was true. Really true. His suspicions had been correct. Something was going to happen *right here* on this ship. A lump gripped his throat tight.

163

Sydney squinted and leaned in closer over Nick's crouched body, yearning to hear more.

"Leave early…panic…muster stations…down with the ship…"

Nick begged himself to calm down, but every instinct was telling him to run. These were dangerous men – terrorists. They wouldn't hesitate to kill him if discovered. But he couldn't run. Not yet. He had to know more. What were they planning?

The men's hands appeared around the edge of the crate's lid and then disappeared into it, as if they were arranging the contents. A strap flung into view and then something orange. Nick struggled to see anything that would tell him what they were doing.

And then he saw it. Just enough of it to know what it was.

"Life vests."

Sydney sneered with disappointment. "Life vests?"

The crate slammed shut, revealing the four men's faces. One was looking directly at the door.

*SHOOT!*

Nick and Sydney froze, eyes like marbles.

"Who left the door open?"

Without a word, Sydney bolted first, rocketing down the corridor and up the stairs. Nick started close on her tail, but he stopped, turned back, and emptied the ball bearings from his fanny pack into the hallway just as footsteps stomped to the doorway.

Nick let out an embarrassing whimper but bolted after her. He tripped on the stairs. He banged his shin but scampered on. He flew around corners and caught Sydney. He followed her left and right, through doors and past a few workers – thankfully only those without watches.

But they were lost.

"Now where?" Sydney shouted.

A mental picture of the ship's interior snapped into Nick's mind. "This way!"

They zipped into an expansive kitchen that was plunged into darkness. Counters and carts filled the middle, but rows and rows of ovens and mixers and other appliances surrounded the edges. Amongst the electric hums filling the room, one small person sat on a counter with his back to them, silhouetted by the light from an open refrigerator. His hands reached down to the platters in front of him, grabbing at the food and carrying it to his face. Wild hair bounced around his scalp as he chewed.

When the door closed behind Sydney, the person sat up rigid and turned slowly, a piece of cheesecake halfway in his mouth.

"Sammy?" Nick asked, his heart pounding up to his throat.

"Ugh?" Sammy asked, mouth full enough to overflow with each attempt at words. "Udda uh unt?"

Sydney shook her head in confusion. "What are you doing here?"

"Eh-eh. Ooo?"

"We're being chased! We got to -"

"Oh!" Sammy spat out the half-finished cheesecake into one hand and patted a spot next to him on the counter with the other. "In that caith, join me.":

Nick glanced back at the door, his heart still racing – imagining the men giving chase through the corridor. "No. Umm…we got to go."

Sammy waved his head back and forth. "Fine. More food for me."

The two gave the boy a confused look.

"Quick!" Sydney commanded. "Is there another way out of here, Sammy?"

He put the half-finished blob of cheesecake back in his mouth and pointed toward another door on the opposite side. "Ub-bye!"

Just as Nick and Sydney escaped through the opposite door, two men burst through the other door. One limped and gritted his teeth, still cursing the ball bearings under his breath.

"Were you just running from us, kid?" they asked Sammy.

Sammy spat out his cheesecake again. "No, you're not."

The men looked at each other in confusion. "What? We're not what?"

"You're not that thtupid. Do I *look* like I've been running…ever? Or maybe you *are* that thtupid."

The man in front shrugged again, eyeing the kid's pot belly. "Have you seen anybody else come through here?"

"I heard thomeone run patht." He pointed at the door they'd come through and then slammed the cheesecake back in his mouth. The men, getting nowhere, bolted out the way they had come.

Sydney slowly withdrew her eye from the kitchen window. "They're gone. What now?"

Doubled over and still catching his breath, Nick gave her a thumbs up. "Now...we go to bed...and wake up...alive." He stood up, panting. "And then we go about our business...."

"But you heard them..."

"...until we find out how to steal one of those watches. And we got to do it before we reach Nassau." He looked at his own watch and did the math in his head. We have 80 hours."

# Chapter 30

*48 hours later…*

With a satisfied smile on his face, Greyson wiped the last dried blood off the bolt-arrow using the flickering light from the dying fire. After a successful hunt and a cooked meal, his stomach was full, really *full*, for the first time in a long while, and he couldn't help smiling. The fire had been worth the risk. Added to his list of favorite foods, right along bacon and Dr. Pepper, was cooked rabbit and crabapple mash.

Ever since the creamed corn trap had worked two mornings ago, he had been desperately hungry. Kit had stirred awake first at the sound of the rabbit's squeal, but the deadfall hadn't been heavy enough. It had been more of a paralysis-fall. He had felt sorry for the little bunny, but Kit had put it out of its misery in quick fashion. Greyson had then spent the next hour skinning and deboning the thing for Kit to eat raw, too afraid to start a fire.

Greyson rose from his log-seat and walked to his practice tree, where his other bolt arrow stuck halfway inside the trunk. He tied the bag of crabapples tight and hung it on the bolt to keep the night critters away. Raw, the things tasted like stale grapefruit. But the fire had done wonders on them as well.

Putting out the fire and surveying the darkness one more time, he crawled into his crude shelter, curled into his blanket, and turned on his flashlight to scout his route on the map. When he saw their progress, he let out a frustrated sigh. If he calculated their current location correctly, they would come across a town in the morning called Meyer's Crossing. And if that were true, they had only traveled 18 miles in three days.

On one hand he knew he should be thankful for the miles he *had* gone. On the other hand, at this pace, it would take weeks to get to Florida.

He had to do something different. Maybe he'd cut toward the coast and hope to find a ship to the Bahamas from there. Or maybe he'd ask someone where the nearest trains heading south were. Or, he thought, he could try to make money in Meyer's Crossing tomorrow – enough for a taxi to get out of the mountains, and maybe even around Atlanta.

Still undecided and frustrated with the uncertainty, he put the map away and switched to his nighttime reading. The last two nights he had stayed up late reading Luke by flashlight until his eyelids couldn't stay open any longer.

Most of the time he loved what Jesus said. He even drew a star by a few verses he especially liked. One said, *"Don't be afraid of those who kill the body and after that can do no more, rather fear him who after the killing of the body, has power to throw you into hell."*

Greyson loved that thought. *Don't fear those who kill the body.* It meant he shouldn't fear the terrorists, because even if they did kill him, they'd just be killing his body. So, he must be more than a body. He was a soul. He thought that was cool. And it comforted him to think that his mother and Liam were still out there. It had only been their bodies that had died.

But that also scared him. *What did God do with their souls? What will he do with mine? Does he throw them into hell or heaven — or just destroy them or something?* Greyson didn't like thinking about that. But he knew what God should do with the terrorists' souls. If they even had them.

On top of certain verses, he was rarely bored with the stories and already had plans to reread them. But for now, though, he just wanted to see what happened in the end; so he read faster and faster, chapter after chapter.

Soon, though, his eyes grew weary and his flashlight flickered off, leaving the text unreadable. The flashlight was running out of juice, so he shook it until it shone again. Quickening his pace, he read on.

He read of a short man named Zacchaeus and sped through a summary to Kit. "This guy named Zacchaeus — let's call him Zach — is so short he has to climb a tree to see Jesus over the crowd. Jesus sees him and then invites himself over to Zach's house; but the crowd complains that Zach is a sinner."

There was that *sinner* word again. And poor Zach. Everyone knew he was a sinner. *At least there aren't as many people who know how much I've sinned.* The flashlight flickered and once again he had to shake it back on. In the flickers he caught the last exchange between Jesus and Zach.

"Zach yells, 'Look, Lord! Here and now I give half my wealth to the poor, and if I have cheated anybody out of anything, I will pay back four times the amount.'"

Greyson glanced at Kit. *Four times?* Kit cocked his head. Greyson mimicked him with his own confusion. "Anyway, Jesus says, 'Today, salvation has come to his house, for the Son of Man came...'"

The flashlight blinked its last. Giving a frustrated sigh, Greyson rolled his eyes and tried to fight back his anger. Suddenly he slammed the tiny book as hard as he could and turned over on his back, staring into the night sky through a gap in his shelter's roof.

*Four times as much.*

"That's stupid, Kit. There's no way! How am I supposed to pay back four times as much as I've taken? How am I supposed to repay Liam's family for letting him die? It's not possible."

Kit nuzzled closer into his armpit like he wanted a hug, so Greyson massaged his ears, grateful for the distraction. For several minutes he fought both his hopelessness and his tiredness. He didn't want to sleep; he knew the nightmares would come back. But he didn't want to stay awake with his frustration either.

Turning onto his side, he put his arm around Kit and closed his eyes, listening to the sounds of the night and making his decision. Zach had earned enough money to pay off his sins. *The least I can do is make enough money to get a cab.*

# Chapter 31

*24 hours until Nassau*

Sydney woke up slowly, her eyes fluttering and adjusting to the sun coming in from the sliding glass doors. After nuzzling her face on the cool side of the pillow, she stretched, curling her toes around the silky sheets. The bed was too comfortable to leave easily, but the sunrise was calling her.

Careful not to wake her parents in the bed next to her, she made her way to the balcony and lay in the deck chair with a towel as her pillow. The ocean greeted her with brilliant, cascading sunlight glistening off its waves.

It was the perfect setting to read Sam's next note. She unfolded it and read it with a smile.

*Hi. I hope this note finds you enjoying the American Spirit and the sun. Don't suntan too much and get Melanoma. I think you're pretty just the shade you are. Me, I'm half Asian, so I don't know whether to try to tan or try to be white. You can tell me what I should do when I see you next. PS – My mole's not cancerous in case you were wondering. Just looks like it.*

"Morning."

Sydney jolted. She hadn't heard Nick open the door from the adjacent balcony.

He yawned and sleepily sauntered to his own deck chair.

"Morning," she replied, yawning and hiding the note in her shorts. "Mind if we skip the fitness center this morning?" They had worked out together the past two mornings – though the morning after their adventure in the bowels of the ship hadn't been very productive. They'd been so paranoid, they'd spent most of the time looking over their shoulders rather than working out.

Besides working out, it had been a long and eventful two days. They had made port in Key West, Florida, where Jarryd had shown off his waverunner prowess and Sydney had fallen asleep on the beach. When not at port, they'd tried all the ship had to offer, even the zip-line.

But beyond all the fun, Sydney and Nick had been scouting the men with smart watches, readying the next phase of their plan. They'd documented nearly a dozen already – all employees. Again, they caught two of them

170

receiving some sort of message on their watches at the exact same time. And as Nick had feared, all of them had the Pluribus mark.

Nick scanned the horizon through his red-framed glasses.

For the first time, Sydney realized how much more attractive he was than Jarryd, without the pudge on his cheekbones, and with leaner arms. The way the breeze blew through his short hair, glowing a bright yellow in the sun's rays, made Sydney imagine him as an actor in some seafarer movie.

"Let's go down," he said. "We'll go easy on the legs. Just in case we need them in top shape tonight."

"Getting one of those watches better be worth it."

"We need a watch. You heard them. They're up to something." He descended into thought, staring at the deck below his feet. "It doesn't make sense, though. Why would we want to sink a ship? How does that help the cause?"

Staring at him, Sydney cocked her head. Finally, she gave him a scoff so that he would notice her staring. When he looked, she raised her eyebrows. "We? You said 'we'."

Caught, Nick shook it off. "Sorry. Whatever. I didn't mean it."

"Sure, you didn't. But you're right. It doesn't make sense. Why kill a bunch of innocent people? But that's terrorists. They don't make sense."

"Oh, come on," Nick said, frustrated. "Lumping all terrorists together is what the government does. Anyone who is willing to stand up to tyranny is…" he stopped himself and let out a sigh. After a breather he started again, more in control. "It could be nothing. They could have been talking about life vests preventing people from going down with the ship."

He leaned his elbows on his knees, making gestures with his hands but staring straight ahead as if speaking to a camera. "But if it is something, we know how they work. They'll have security on their side. If we report to them, they kill us. Plus, they're probably listening to every method of communication on this ship. If we try warning someone on the outside, they kill us. We tell our parents – our parents tell someone *else* – the Plurbs kill us *and* them."

Sydney nodded along, agreeing with everything he said. "So…we steal the watch, get more evidence, and…stop them ourselves."

Nick finally turned to her. "Yeah. At least until we get to Nassau tomorrow. Then we can find a way to get the word out without them knowing."

"Sounds good." Sydney started to lean her head back to relax, but stopped short with a thought. "But, about tonight. I want to scout a few more people.

I'm just not sure…there's gotta be an easier way. It's too hard to get to the workers' rooms. And I don't want to go that deep into the ship again."

"We can try," he said finally. "But the only time we're able to get their watches without them noticing is when they take them off. Employees don't swim, so…"

"Showers, I know. But maybe…I don't know."

"It's the only way."

"And why Jarryd?"

"I think I'm meant to be the one behind the scenes," he said, remembering the fear he'd felt in the ship's belly. "And he's sneakier. One time he snuck into our parent's room – before the divorce – and wiped chocolate on our Dad's underwear," his eyes sparkled as he tried to contain his smile. "He actually didn't notice, but Mom did when doing laundry!" He laughed under his breath. "She thought he had some digestion issues – wanted him to go to the doctor!"

Sydney laughed politely, shaking her head. Together they let the sound of the waves gradually replace the silence. Nick's smile faded with the memory.

Debating whether to ask, Sydney finally blurted, "What do you think of him and Avery?"

After a pause, Nick shrugged. "They seem happy together. They got up early for a *spa* treatment."

"Together?"

"Yeah."

"Your parents were okay with that?"

"Yup. Well, at least my stepdad was. And that's who he asked."

"He's not going to tell Avery about tonight, is he?"

"He promised not to."

She sighed. "You should have *dared* him not to."

-----------------

Jarryd groaned with pleasure. The masseuse's hands were like angel hands. "Angel hands made of pure warmth," he said, nearly drooling as the masseuse pushed at the muscles on his back. "You're like the Greek goddess of massage – Massage-a-phone or something."

Avery laughed through her squished cheeks at the table next to him where another masseuse gave tiny karate chops to the sides of her spine. "This is awe-uh-uh-uh-uh-uh-uh-uh-some," she moaned with the chops.

172

"Can you get my calves next, please?" Jarryd asked the masseuse. She nodded, put a warm towel over his back, and lathered oil on his calves. "Ah, yeah. That's the stuff."

"I still like y'ah calves," Avery said, catching a glimpse of them being oiled.

"I still like your face."

"I like y'ah mum's face."

His squished face smiled. "You Aussies are like boomerangs. You always have a comeback."

She laughed.

"Jutht tho you know," Sammy said from his massage table. "Both your faceth thuck. Thtrawth."

Avery and Jarryd rolled their eyes. They'd almost forgotten that he was there. His presence was the one condition her parents had set for the spa privilege.

"Thank you, Chandler," Jarryd muttered with sarcasm. "Now, be quiet or I'll massage your brain, with my fist."

"To mathage my brain, you'd have to get through my thkull firtht. But nothing getth through *my* thkull – rockth, the thtreet, wallth, a football, a tack hammer. Tho good luck."

Avery laughed, defusing Jarryd's anger with her smile. He soon laughed, too, until the masseuse made her way to his calves with a rolling rubdown. He groaned in delight

"This...should never end."

But it did. Just in time for the mud bath. Fully immersed in the mud with their swimsuits, they sat in separate tubs with mud caked on their faces and cucumbers over their eyes. Incense candles burned around them, and oils were dripped into the bath for aromatherapy. The mixture was pungent, but heavenly.

"What do we didgeri-do now?" he asked with a muddy smirk.

"Just relax," Avery whispered. "Let it take away the toxins or whatev'ah."

Jarryd started reaching around the edge of the tub, blindly. His fingers could barely reach the ground. "Where is...?" His fingers found the can of Dr. Pepper. "There it is. Come to papa."

"You're supposed to be gettin' *rid* of toxins," she noted.

"Dr. Pepper knows what's good for me. And listen. She speaks to me." He opened the can. *PSSSSST.* "Hear that? Every time I open her she says, 'Pssst. I love you.'"

173

Avery laughed, trying to imagine his face though she couldn't see him through her cucumbers.

"Then we open mouth kiss and I feel all bubbly inside."

She laughed again, listening to him gulp the fizzy drink. "You two take it easy ov'ah the'ah."

"Ahhh!" He set the can back down. "She's good for a few swigs, but I'd spend time with you over her any day. *Kangaryou* go to the sauna with me after this?" he asked with a muddy smirk.

"Sure thing. Get 'ahr sweat on?"

"Or off. So, we'll sauna it up, *dingo* to the buffet after."

"Sounds good."

"Then we can go *outback* to the water park."

"How about we sunbake first?"

"Sure! That's what I *aboriginally* wanted to do."

"I'll need to check in with my oldies around noon for lunch."

"Me, too. *Rugby* there by noon-thirty?"

"Wow, Joey. Just wow."

She took off a cucumber and glared at him with the free eye.

His smile was cracking the mud on his cheeks.

"You're almost a genuine Aussie now with all that lingo."

"*Wallaby* darned. Thanks."

Suddenly Sammy's hand was reaching into Jarryd's tub.

"WHOA!" He sat up, dropping the cucumbers to the mud. "Watch your hand! What are you doing?"

Sammy had exited his tub. He stood and smiled wide, chewing on one of his cucumbers with his teeth protruding in all directions. "Thtealing your mud."

"Why?" He pointed to Sammy's tub. "You have a whole tub of your own."

He shrugged. "I farted in mine. Kinda ruined the aroma therapy."

"Oh...my." Avery laughed again, covering her mouth with a muddy hand.

Jarryd shook his head at her and scooped out two handfuls of mud into Sammy's hands. "There. Plenty of my aroma for you."

"Thank you very much!" Sammy rubbed the mud over his chest and face and hair.

Trying to ignore him, Jarryd turned again to Avery with a plastered-on smile. "SO...what were we talking about?"

Avery shrugged. "I forget. But do you want to go to the dance club tonight?

174

Tonight's just for teens."

Jarryd's smile faded. He had been recruited for an important mission tonight. And she couldn't know. How to get out this?

"I'm actually not a teen – I'm only thirteen."

She took off her other cucumber to better examine him. "Thirteen is a teenage'ah. Thir-*teen*."

"Not in America."

She raised a brow, onto his game. "We're not *in* America."

He sighed, beaten by her logic. "Sorry. I just can't."

"Why?"

"Uh…"

"No, that's okay. You don't have to tell me. I should hang with my oldies anyway. Or find anoth'ah date."

He glanced at Sammy, who knew exactly what his plans were. Sammy shrugged, winked, then made his way toward the door. "I'm going to athk for more mud."

They watched Sammy leave.

Jarryd turned back. "Sorry, I want to go with you. I just can't."

"We could go whenev'ah your oth'ah thing ends. The club's open late."

"Um…"

"What time does your oth'ah thing end?"

"It uh…well." He started to sweat, but the mud was constricting his skin.

"Can I watch?" she asked.

"No, I don't think so. I'll be in someone else's room."

"Really? That sounds interesting."

He'd said too much. "Nope. Nope. Not really."

"Whose room?"

"Some guy."

"You're going to be in another guy's room?"

He panicked. "No! Well, yes, but just while he's shower – uh, just to get something."

"Get what?" She was leaning over the edge of her tub, dripping mud from her chin. Her muddy arms were draped over the side, slender and elegant.

"Just to borrow it," he said, putting his cucumbers back over his eyes, but peeking through the side.

Her arm reached over him and gently removed one of the cucumber slices. "Borrow *what?*"

175

His wide eye stared at her as he gulped. "The thing that tells time." He hadn't really told her anything.

"Oh," she said softly taking a bite of his cucumber. "A little cat burglary?"

"Who would steal a cat? We're just checking something out."

"Ah. A little reconnaissance?"

"I don't even know what that is." He was being honest.

Her face hovered over him, her eyes feisty. She had never looked hotter. "I can help."

"I promised Ross it would just be us."

"He doesn't like me?"

"No. It's Sydney…"

"Who's Sydney? Like the city?"

*Ah, crap.* He messed up again. "Yeah. Is it warm there this time of year?"

She eyed him and then jerked away his other cucumber slice. "Is that Rachel's real name?"

He shifted in the mud bath, making it slosh over the side. "Well…"

She smiled – a playful, devilish smile. "You're hiding something…"

Jarryd's heart slapped his ribs and his fingers gripped the edge of the tub. He couldn't tell if he wanted to run or to grab her and hold her close.

"…and I *like* it." She bit her lower lip and examined his face, that same playful smile drawing closer across the gap.

Jarryd gulped long and hard. "I'm hiding *a lot.*"

# Chapter 32

"Stay in the truck, buddy," Dan said. "Want anything?"

Asher bit his lip, in deep thought. "A slushie! Stwawbewwy."

"Gotcha." Dan clicked his tongue and jogged toward the gas station, leaving Asher by the pump.

Asher immediately took out his e-reader and pulled up the book he was reading. It was a survival book his dad had told him to read. There were tons of interesting tips – like how to hunt, which berries were edible, first aid, and how to make traps. He was just reading about a trap called a deadfall when someone waved at him from the front of the car.

It was a boy with large sunglasses, wearing a red hat underneath a shabby hoodie. He looked friendly, though, with a big smile. He held a dripping squeegee in his hand.

Asher rolled down the passenger window, and the boy approached cautiously.

"Hey," the boy said. "Can I clean your windows for you?"

Asher shot a glance to the gas station. His dad was inside. But he wouldn't mind.

"Okay. Why?"

"Just to be nice. And if your mom or dad wants to give a donation, that's cool, too."

Asher smiled. He didn't get to talk to big kids much. "My name's Ash'uh. A'w you in high school?"

"Nope. Not yet. I would be in eighth grade, but I'm...uh...not in school."

The boy began wiping the wet squeegee back and forth on the windshield, removing a layer of dirt Asher hadn't realized had been there before.

"Wha'ah you fwom?"

The boy hesitated. "Pretty far away."

Asher turned his e-reader off, excited about the idea that popped into his head. His dad would be so proud. "You should come to ou'ah place tonight."

The boy laughed. "Thanks for the offer, but I got to get going soon. I've still got a long way to go."

Disappointed, Asher didn't give up easily. "My dad has a plane. He can take you anywhe'ah."

The boy stopped suddenly and returned to the passenger window. "Really? His own plane?"

"Yeah-yeah! I bet he could take you after Fellowship tonight!"

The boy was so excited. But then he flinched. "Fellowship? Like a church thing?"

Asher laughed. "No. Chu'ch is on Sunday. They changed the name from Plu'ibus after the bomb. I like Plu'ibus bett'ah though. Wolled wight off yah tongue. Fellowship sounds bo'wing even though it's not."

But the boy must have thought Asher was boring. He left in a hurry, leaving the windshield half done and the squeegee lying on the cement. Asher caught sight of him as he ran to where a dog sat next to a backpack.

"Cool dog!" he yelled out the window, hoping the boy would come back. But he was gone.

Breathing a deep sigh, Asher pouted. What had he done? The boy would have been a cool friend. None of his friends at school had an eighth grader with sweet sunglasses and a police dog as their friend.

The driver's door opened. "One strawberry slushie for…" Dan stopped mid-sentence, gawking at the half-washed windshield with streaks of blue cleaner running down to the wipers. "Did you try to clean the windshield?"

Asher shook his head. "No. Someone else."

"Who?" his dad asked craning his neck to scan the area.

"A boy. Eighth gwad'ah."

His dad's eyes lit up. "Eighth grader? You talked to him?"

"Yeah. He was nice. Not f'om around he'ah. Says he's going fa'w away."

"Which way did he go?"

His dad's voice was tense. Asher could tell he was serious. "That way. With his dog."

Dan turned on the truck, punched it into gear, and sped in the direction Asher directed. "Don't ever talk to strangers like that again, okay?"

Asher gulped, and his lip started to quiver. The anger and panic in his dad's voice was frightening. It hadn't been directed toward him in years.

"Okay?"

"Okay."

"Did he say anything else? Did you tell him anything?"

Asher looked at his feet, trying to hold back his tears as the truck swung around the corner. "No."

---------------

"Is that Jarryd and Avery?" Sydney asked Nick. Together they had spotted the two love birds hiding behind a post and pointing toward a bald sunbather laying out on a deck chair. They were snickering, up to no good it seemed.

"Hey, guys!" Sydney said loudly.

"Shhh!" Jarryd shushed, motioning for them to join him behind the post.

"What are you up to?"

"Just wait for it. Here comes the waiter."

The waiter weaved around deck chairs with a platter on his hand, carrying several cold drinks complete with straws, little umbrellas, and lemon slices. They looked delicious.

The man took a clear liquid from the waiter and leaned on his side for a drink. Jarryd and Avery tried to contain their laughter with snorts and gasps instead.

"What?" Nick asked. "Did you spit in his drink?"

"Noooo. We collected our drips in the sauna."

The bald man sipped at the straw and then recoiled with a blasting spit that left a mist in the air as he tumbled over the side of the chair. The drink fell to the deck but didn't break, sloshing the drink to the ground with a loud crack.

After Jarryd and Avery had laughed hysterically for several seconds, the waiter returned, frantically helping the man up and apologizing. But the man wouldn't have it. He was up in the waiter's face, yelling obscenities at him.

The kids pressed themselves against the post, barely peeking out.

After a few moments, the bald man had cooled and adjusted the waiter's collar, which he had grabbed in the heat of the moment. And that's when Sydney saw it.

"He has a watch, too! They both do."

And she was right. Both the bald man and the waiter had the same smart watch. This was the first non-worker they had seen with the watch. Sydney's face lit up. And then the watches did too – at the same time.

The bald man looked at his and so did the waiter. With a knowing look, they nodded to each other and went their separate ways.

When they were a safe distance away, Jarryd and Avery shared the same look of confusion. But Nick was satisfied. "That's the third time. The watches are not a coincidence. They are being used for coordinated communication, like we thought," he looked at Sydney. "And we have to get one."

179

Sydney elbowed Nick and gave a sideways glance to Avery. He grimaced, but only until Avery interrupted.

"I know already," she said. "I'm in."

"What? You know?" Sydney asked, perturbed.

Jarryd squirmed, backing away from Sydney.

"Yeah. You're going to take one of their watches."

"Do you know why?" Sydney asked.

"It doesn't matter," Nick said, putting his hand on Sydney's arm as she began to lean toward Jarryd – most likely for a pummeling.

Avery arched her brow. "For fun? Why else?"

Nick gave Sydney a look and shrugged. At least she didn't know *everything*. "Yeah. Why else? We might need, you, Avery. Ross has been MIA all day. Yesterday he vomited off the zip-line after eating too many shrimp."

"He's better now. We saw him doing Karaoke on the stage after lunch," Jarryd said. "He was actually pretty good. Did 'What Does the Fox Say?' all by himself. He's got pipes!"

Nick sighed. "He's still unreliable. Avery can help."

Sydney's eyes burned a hole through Nick's glasses, but he just gave her a tiny shrug. Avery caught the look and put up her hands as if to surrender. "Sounds like fun."

"Whatever," Sydney said. "But I've got to go follow him. We have better odds getting into a guest's room than a worker's."

"I'll go with," Nick asserted. "You two, meet us in Central Park at seven. It's going down tonight."

---------------

The town of Meyer's Crossing was quaint. Greyson guessed only a thousand or so people lived there. There was a small main street with one stoplight and several shops; and radiating from its center was avenue after avenue of homes. There weren't many apartment buildings, and the only two buildings tall enough to stick out above the rest had steeples. Churches. If he'd understood the young boy correctly, at one of the churches would be a Pluribus meeting.

Greyson eyed them from his perch on the foothills east of town, where he had retreated after meeting the boy with the Plurb-pilot for a father. The run from the gas station had been filled with panic, but also exhilaration. There had been many places to hide, and his backpack was much lighter now, so escape had been easier. What had made his heart race, though, was what the boy had said.

*A plane.* The dad had his own plane. The thought of it still made him giddy. If he could somehow convince the man to give him a ride, he could be in the Bahamas in a matter of hours instead of weeks. *Hours!*

His multi-tool's knife may be the answer. He twisted it around with his fingers, examining the blade.

Nick had told him everything he knew from his week or two with Pluribus after the bomb. And he could use that knowledge to get closer to the man who could take him where he needed to go. It would be very risky – almost foolish – but not entirely. It was one of those things right on the edge of stupid, but still barely in the sane range. It walked the line between crazy and courageous.

It would be daring.

He held the knife blade against his eyebrow, guiding it with his other hand. Kit watched with concern, stopping in mid-pant to stare.

"It's okay, boy. It doesn't mean anything."

Kit let out a whimper.

"I mean it. It'll grow back."

He turned the blade and pressed the sharp edge against his brow. He would have to get all of the hair in a clean streak, right down to the skin.

Kit buried his face in his paws.

# Chapter 33

*12 hours until Nassau*

"Target's about a three-minute walk away," Sydney reported into her walkie-talkie, judging how long it would take him to get back to his room. The ship was as busy as ever, with people finding supper, attending shows, or, like their bald target, starting their night at the bar. "Good position."

The bald man was sitting down in a little piano lounge nearby. The balcony a floor above provided the perfect surveillance point. If there was a good time to make their move, it was now.

"Ten-four. Cleaners are still two rooms down," Nick reported through the walkie.

Sydney nodded to herself. "Everyone else in position?"

---------------

Nick eyed Jarryd, Avery, and Sammy next to him in the elevator lobby. They were all in position and they knew what to do. Sammy – the distraction. Jarryd – the thief. Nick – the overseer. And Avery monitored the elevators, making sure one would be available at just the right time.

"Yeah, we're all ready," he replied to Sydney.

Nick peeked down the hallway again, watching the cleaning man exchanging old towels for new, taking out trash, and doing whatever else he did in the guests' rooms as they were away. The next door down had a 'Do Not Disturb' sign hanging from its doorknob, so he knew the cleaners would pass that one. Then, two doors further down was room 1303, the room they had followed the bald man to after his sweat-drink incident. Judging from the time the cleaners took on the last three rooms, it would be another fifteen minutes.

"Fifteen minutes," he informed Sydney via walkie talkie.

"Roger that. Let's hope he's thirsty."

"Just a quick question," Jarryd whispered to Nick. "What if he doesn't take a shower? What if he goes to bed while I'm in the room?"

"Find a comfortable place to hide. And take a pillow."

Jarryd scowled.

"Don't worry," Avery joined in. "Sydney will make sure he wants to shower. She said she'd handle it."

"Well, I'm still frickin' worried. What if he doesn't take off his watch? What if it's water-proof?"

"Then you'll just get out, and we'll think of something else," she said, trying her calmest, motherly voice.

"But what if he catches me, and he's a creeper and he kills me and stuff?"

Avery grimaced. "Just stop worrying; we'll be right outside."

"While I'm being creepered to death?"

Impatient with all the questions, Nick stepped in. "I could go in instead."

Jarryd was offended. "Are you kidding me? Are you *kidding* me? I can run circles around you. Like five. Maybe seven before throwing up. But you – you'd chicken out at the first whiff of trouble. No – at the first whiff of a whiff of trouble. Not me! I don't smell trouble. Trouble smells me and trembles. Watch me."

Nick gave Avery a look that said, *"That's how it's done."*

------------------

"How do we do this, Kit?"

Kit licked at Greyson's chin, but Greyson retreated.

"Like that, huh? Straight for it?"

Safely hidden behind a bush and anticipating the darkness coming with the setting sun, he scanned the church from across the block. Ten long stairs led to the church's massive front doors. Stained glass windows, tall oak trees, and even the steeple seemed to stretch toward the sky in a sort of yearning.

Just as the church was dark and showed signs of abandonment, the neighborhood followed suit. While some houses were well-kept – with small gardens, clean cars, and decorated mailboxes – others were abandoned, bearing plywood signs nailed over the door that read 'FOSTER HOME' in spray-painted letters with a drawing of an upside-down pyramid underneath. Greyson guessed it had to do with President Foster. And while American flags hung outside most of the houses, except for the 'Foster Homes', there were a few that were oddly hung upside down.

Greyson would have taken them down and rehung them the correct way as a favor to them, but he didn't have the time. The meeting was supposed to start in fifteen minutes, but he hadn't seen anyone go in yet.

Perhaps Kit was right. He should just go straight through the front door that was covered with a sign reading "FOSTER CHURCH" and see if anyone was home. Be confident. Pretend he was one of them. He had the shaved gash in the eyebrow to prove it, too. Or perhaps he should try to sneak in and avoid any confrontation at all.

*Sapere Aude. Dare to be wise,* he told himself. *Dare to be wise.*

Finding a good hiding place in the bush, he stored his backpack.

"Kit. Stay. Protect the bag until I get back. Okay?"

Kit sat obediently.

"Good boy."

Kicking himself in gear, he bolted across the street to the alley beside the church and began the search for an alternative way in. It didn't take long. Hanging over a backdoor was a piece of plywood with an upside-down pyramid sketched on it. When he examined it, it swung loosely, revealing a gaping hole in the back door. Looking over his shoulder, he stepped through the hole, letting the plywood swing back into place.

# Chapter 34

"Going in. Radio silence," Jarryd uttered into the walkie just before he put it away. A voice from his pocket replied, "Roger that," just as he approached the cleaner's cart outside room 1303's open door. The cleaner was emptying a small trashcan into a larger one attached to the front of his cart. He smiled at Jarryd as he approached.

"Hey."

"Hey," the cleaner replied with a wide smile.

He looked very friendly. His nametag said his name was Sal from the Philippines. This one didn't have a smart watch or a Plurb mark. But Jarryd didn't stop; he kept walking, as if his room were further down the narrow hall.

On cue, Sammy came stumbling around the corner, clutching his stomach. "OOOHHHHHHhhhhh," he groaned, his face a mask of anguish, his eyes rolling about as if they were bobbing in water.

The cleaner looked up and froze.

"I'M GONNA BARF UP A BUFFET!"

Jumping to action to spare the cleanup, the cleaner grabbed a fresh garbage bag and ran to the nauseous boy. Jarryd was inside room 1303 with ease.

*But now what?*

He probed the room. It was gently used, with a few clothing items around – but nothing too suspicious. No guns, knives, counterfeit money, or anything. A little disappointing, but also quite a relief. But he'd have more time to search later.

"IT FEELS LIKE I THWALLOWED A FOUNTAIN!"

Jarryd had to find his place before Sammy drew even more attention. The closet was an option and so was the balcony, but underneath the bed was clearly the best if he happened to have an extended stay.

He slid under the bed and fingered the 'talk' button on the walkie. "The stud has reached the stable."

"Roger that."

Nick's voice rose in the hallway. "Ross! Come on, bro. Thanks for getting him the bag, sir. I'll take care of him now."

The cleaner responded kindly, offering more assistance, but Nick declined. After the footsteps had faded, Jarryd listened to the crinkling of a garbage bag and the jostling of bottles on the cart.

And then he saw the cleaner's feet coming straight for him.

---------------

Greyson stepped inside the hole and didn't even have a chance to see his captor. The hulking man snapped his hand over Greyson's arm and pulled him into a bulging belly that hung over his belt like a sideways cupcake.

His heart racing, Greyson blinked rapidly to adjust to the darkness. The man's face came into view. It was drooping and tan, with a goofy smile that revealed a few missing teeth. His greasy hair swept over his bald spot, stains plagued his massive polo shirt and cloth shorts, and he smelled like he hadn't bathed in days. Bathed in sweat, maybe – but not water.

"Hey," the man said gruffly. "Who are you?"

Greyson tried to remain calm. *Confidence. You are one of them*, he told himself. *If he knows me, I'm already dead.* "Who are *you*?"

The man's folded cheeks jiggled as he scoffed. "Terry Humphry. People calls me Humpy."

Greyson didn't laugh, though he nearly let one burst out. "I'm Jarryd," he lied. He would have to change it every time lest they catch on. "People call me lots of things."

Humpy sneered. "Is that right?" His eyes settled on Greyson's – or maybe they were examining the mark on his brow. "Who are you with?"

"Just me."

Doubtful, Humpy scrunched his forehead. "Who told you to come?"

"The cops, who do ya think?"

"Oh, yeah? You's a smart guy, huh? But really? Who?"

*This is stupid. This is stupid!* "Asher."

"Asher? Dan's boy?"

"Yeah. Dan was talking about taking me up in the plane sometime. Know him?"

Humpy didn't respond. He was too busy trying to intimidate him with his stare. He must have not thought fondly of Dan.

Greyson shrugged him off. "Now, where's this meeting?"

"You's first one here. It'll be down the hall. To the right. But I gots to check you first."

"Check me?"

"That's right." The smile on Humpy's face frightened Greyson. "Against the wall. Spread your legs and arms up."

*No.* Part of him told him to run. He'd have a chance against the man, though his massive body took up most of the hallway.

But Greyson did as he was told, trying to think of how a Plurb would respond. "I thought this is what the *government* does."

Humpy laughed off the argument and began searching Greyson for something – weapons, cameras, or whatever else he might have as a spy. He cringed as Humpy's rough hands followed the curve of his hips and found his fanny pack under his shirt. The man's fingers pulled his shirt up and unzipped the pack. He could hear him rustling through all of his goods.

*Don't take the slingshot. Don't take the slingshot.*

Humpy pulled at the slingshot and felt the makeshift holster and the ammo pouch. Greyson cringed, anticipating some angry reaction, but Humpy just grunted and zipped the pack back up. "Hunting squirrels?"

Greyson took a deep breath. "Uh, yeah. And other stuff."

"Me, too. But I gots a pellet gun back home – just as good as any .22 out there and you's don't got no Feds breathing down your neck. My baby girl, she has problems with men, you know? Has to fight them off with a stun gun sometimes. I gots to tell her 'bout your pack there. Pritty fancy."

Greyson kept facing the wall, legs spread, listening awkwardly. "It gets the job done. Can I turn around now?"

"Oh, yeah. My bad, Squirt."

Greyson turned and attempted a smile. The man smiled back, not as intimidating as before, but just as unappealing. Humpy looked as if he wanted to talk more, but Greyson was already stepping toward the hall. He could hear more voices outside, and the last thing he needed was more inspection.

"Down the hall, to the right?"

"Yeah," Humpy took a few lumbering steps toward him, like an obese penguin, but Greyson was moving too fast. "See you in there."

"See you," he said, disappointment in his voice.

*I hope not.*

Greyson slipped down the hall. When Humpy wasn't looking, he turned to the left.

------------------

Asher held his dad's hand and waved at the two men on the other side of the street, walking toward the church. It was Mr. Brandt and Mr. Halverson. They waved back.

"Bringing Ash along again, huh, Critter?" Mr. Halverson hollered across the street.

Asher's dad smiled and winked at his son. "Yup! Couldn't convince Lucas to come?"

"Nah. Can't drag him away from that stupid computer. Teenagers."

They laughed and that was the end of their cross-street conversation. As the church came into view, Asher's ever-present curiosity began to bubble over.

"Think people will call me Cwitt'ah, too, someday?"

"Maybe. Would you like that?"

Asher had never really thought about whether or not he liked his last name. Critterdon. There was nothing special about it. But then again, he'd never change it for the world.

"Yeah. But it might get confusing if we'ah both a'wound."

"We'll just ask them to call me Mr. Critter."

"And why doesn't Mr. Halverson make Lucas come if he wants him to?"

His dad shrugged. "A boy becomes a teenager, most parents start letting them make more and more decisions on their own. Even important ones. And Lucas doesn't feel the same way as his dad on this. But the Halversons aren't the only ones with a divided house, so don't be looking down on them. There's good people on both sides – just like Lucas and his dad."

Asher tried to imagine a time when he would disagree with his dad on something super important. It was hard. Actually, it was hard to imagine anyone disagreeing with his dad. He was the smartest one in Meyer's Crossing and probably all of Georgia. Most people knew it, too. His teacher had even said that he would have won the Senate race if he hadn't dropped out. That was when he was born. And when his mother had died.

Now, even though he wasn't a soldier anymore or a Senator, he was still an awesome dad.

"What are you thinking, Ash?"

Asher sighed, thinking of what he was thinking. Then he noticed the flags stretching down the avenue. "Why do some people put the flag on upside-down?"

Long pauses were typical with his father, and he took an extra-long one. *Quick to listen, slow to speak* he would say.

"Well, they've given up, I think."

"On what?"

"On America."

"Why?"

Together they examined the nearest upside-down flag, trying to peer through closed window drapes as if trying to understand the inhabitants' motives by looking inside their homes.

"If you ask ten people, you might get ten different reasons. Some say we've stopped following the Constitution – what our first founding fathers wanted us to do. Others, they want any excuse to shoot their guns. They get excited thinking of war."

"Why?"

Dan tried not to smile at his son's incessant curiosity. "Well, they've never been in a war I imagine. Or something's wrong in their heads."

"Wa'h was w'eally that bad?"

"It was bad."

"How bad?"

"Remember when you broke your arm?"

"Yeah."

"Remember how scared you were? How much it hurt?"

"Yeah."

"Increase that by a million. War brings that much pain, and that much fear."

"Then why do they want it?"

"I guess they don't have any idea of what it's like. They think it's like the movies or the video games that end when and how you want them to."

There was movement behind the Andersons' curtains. Critter imagined them to be shaking their heads – perhaps calling the police again. Fiercely patriotic, Mr. Anderson often yelled at those walking to meetings, shaming them. Critter had avoided getting into shouting matches with him, but others had nearly struck the elderly man. Critter admired the man's conviction, and secretly thought him to be right, but he could never reveal his true thoughts while attending the Fellowship meetings.

They reached the alleyway, now following the two men ahead of them. Asher whispered to not be overheard. "Do the men in Fellowship want wa'h?"

"Some do."

"They've given up?"

189

"Some. But most are just hoping for change. They want to give it another year."

"'Til the elections?"

"That's right."

"So, who do we want to win?"

Dan took another long pause, shaking his head and laughing to himself. "I don't know."

They stopped in front of the back-door's plywood, a sense of foreboding passing from father to son. The breeze that had come with the dark nipped at Asher's arms, but the church offered a wave of warmth from within. It was almost as if they could feel the body heat from the men inside. They could hear the shouting, the crude language, and the call to order.

The meeting had begun.

# Chapter 35

"Nickel," Jarryd whispered into the walkie. "I'm scared."

The cleaner had made the bed, taken out the trash, and replaced used glasses, and he was now working in the bathroom. Several times Jarryd had decided to abandon the plan and make a run for it, but each time Nick had talked him out of it.

"I know, but you're doing good. Any time now he'll be done, and you'll be alone."

Jarryd watched the bathroom door from under the bed. He heard a flush. "But I got to go to the bathroom. Like now."

"No, hold it, dude."

"No, no. You know when I get nervous man…I gotta go now. I gotta bail."

"A pail? Geez, dude, just wait and use the toilet."

"Not a *pail*, moron. I need to *bail*. With a 'b'."

"A 'b' as in 'bladder' or a 'p' as in 'pee'?"

Jarryd cringed. "Jerk, how about a 'B' as in *be quiet*."

"Good one."

"Thanks."

"Now just keep your cool. Hold on."

Jarryd gripped the walkie and surveyed the dust by his nose while he waited. "Jer-bear. Baldy is on the move. Sydy-Cat is about to pounce."

--------------------

Sydney hurried to her place on the mezzanine, directly above her target's path to the elevators. She'd only have one shot to hit the shiny, bald mark.

Gripping the glass of broccoli-cheese soup mixed with clear soda, bits of shrimp, and garlic sauce she had made at the buffet, she watched him walk, analyzing his pace. No obstacles were in his way. He wasn't looking up. Wind was not a factor. She could do this.

Making her final judgment, she dumped the glass over the mezzanine rail as she made her best vocal impression of a seasick vomit-launcher.

The mess hit its mark with a splash as she clutched at her stomach and stumbled away. As she radioed in, she could hear the gasps from below as people rushed to help.

"He's going to be headed to the shower, boys. And he's going to be mad."

------------------

Greyson inched closer, crawling on his stomach to the edge of the balcony overlooking the church's sanctuary. He was alone up here, but dozens of men were below, scattered around the pews facing goateed man who stood at the podium. Though the goateed man held a gavel and had a commanding voice, he seemed amused when the audience blurted out. To the man's left was an organ in the corner, with gold-painted pipes towering toward the ceiling. To his right was an old television on a mobile cart, which another man tinkered with. Behind the podium and against the wall, a giant cross rose tall and proud, big enough to crucify the jolly green giant and gold enough to capture anyone's attention.

But Greyson's attention was on the evil men below. They were surprisingly diverse. Some wore overalls, others wore suits. Some looked to be in their twenties, while there were several with white hair. Though many didn't sound as if they had been well educated, there were a few whose eloquence seemed out of place.

Greyson hadn't imagined that terrorists would be so diverse, yet he knew that they all wanted to tear the nation apart and were willing to kill innocent people to do so. Maybe some of the ones below had already killed. Or was this the meeting where they planned who to kill next?

Someone said his name.

"...but he will most likely go by a fake name. Possibly Nolan. But keep your eye out. He is wanted alive, if possible. So, shoot for non-violent organs."

The men laughed at the joke – except for Humpy, who shifted in his seat, uncomfortably glancing around the room. Greyson's heart raced. They'd heard about him? They knew he was close? And Humpy...would he say anything? At least for now he was keeping quiet – probably too ashamed to speak up.

"Next item. There's another train headed to the interior. Passing by tonight in fact. Destination's probably Fort Leavenworth. It's the third one this month. We're nearing what we've been planning for. There is no doubt they are gearing up for raids and martial law."

Humpy jumped up from his pew and addressed the crowd. "And the FEMA camps popping up with them huge fences and guards armed to the

192

teeth. They says they're for displaced peoples or whatever, but yous can bet that's where they's take us when they's label us all terrorists."

"Right on, Humpy. As soon as they label Pluribus a terrorist organization, they will be filled with our friends and neighbors, brothers and sons."

There was murmuring in the crowd. Another man stood up. Greyson reached the end of the railing and squinted into the dark sanctuary. *Is it Dan, Asher's father? How am I supposed to tell?*

The man, wearing a denim hat, spoke up. "Why don't we hijack one of these trains, Wayne? Show them they can't move weapons past our town without giving us a say in it?"

Many of the men gave shouts of approval, but Wayne waved them down. "Not yet, boys. Not yet. We have teams monitoring it as we speak, but those are not our orders."

"Screw orders! We never should'a joined Pluribus in the first place!"

Others joined in and the shouts grew louder, making Greyson uncomfortable. The men's anger sent a buzz in the air, as if it were a beehive ready to erupt. He took a moment to collect his fading courage. Yes, he was in the lions' den. But no, they didn't know he was here. Plus, he had an escape plan. A window to his left, leading to the roof. Just in case.

But all he needed was to find Asher and his pilot father. Then, if he could manage to talk with them alone, he would have his chance to either convince them or to steal the plane keys.

"Calm down, all of you! We can't win a war if we're off doing what we want in Georgia, and Texas is doing what Texas wants to do and so on. We follow orders here. If you don't like them, just shut up and do them anyway. If you don't do them, well, you can go and join the Camden militia."

This time there were laughs, and those who had been angry cooled down.

"Speaking of orders, we have new communication if Marv here can get it working."

The man still tinkered with the television and his laptop while making an obscene gesture toward Wayne. As the crowd laughed and watched the television, Greyson leaned his head past the bottom of the railing into open space. Craning his neck, he could just see the last pew in the back of the sanctuary. A stoic man sat with elbows on his knees. Next to him was the small boy Greyson recognized as Asher. *He's here!* The man was the pilot. The man that would take him to his father.

There were cheers and claps from the crowd, so Greyson pushed himself back from the edge and watched the television flicker. There were more moans of impatience, but eventually Marv got it working, adjusted the volume, and sat back to watch.

The black screen flickered again, and this time there was a man's face. It was a face set for war – horrible, yet handsome – appealing and frightening at the same time. Silence struck the crowd in anticipation, but no one was more silent than Greyson. His breath had stalled in his throat and his fingernails scraped at the stiff carpet, sending fragments of dirt in little hops toward the edge of the balcony. He couldn't take his eyes from the man's, though they were a different color than before.

"To the men and women of this once-great country. To the men and women meeting together, who may be scared, who may fear for their future, but who brave the opposition and risk to hear from me today, I want to thank you. Though I can't see you now, and most of you I've never met, I feel like I still know you."

Greyson's face burned with hatred and fear. *Oh, he knows me alright.* And Greyson knew *him*. The Eye of Eyes. The world's most wanted terrorist. Everett Oliver Emory.

# Chapter 36

Jarryd's silent inhales and exhales pulled and pushed at the dust balls under the bed. His eyes were bigger and whiter than his large front teeth, and his fingers were tense with anticipation. His lips mouthed *please, please, please.*

Baldy was sitting on the bed, right above him. The springs creaked in his ears, and he could sense the man's weight almost sagging into his shoulders. *Don't fart. Don't fart.* If the man did, it would seep straight through the mattress into Jarryd's face.

But another kind of stink came from the man's socks as he slipped his shoes off. Jarryd eyed the man's feet with disgust, just inches in front of him.

And then his socks came off. And then his fake-barf-covered shirt plopped onto the carpet.

*Oh…my…frickin'…goodness.*

A small panic came over him, and he shifted, trying to stifle a groan that fought hard to escape. It escaped instead through the hideous grimace on his face.

Next came the man's pants. Jarryd covered his eyes, though all he could see were the man's ankles. But those were hairy enough; he could only imagine how nasty the rest of his body was.

When he heard the man's underpants hit the carpet, he peeked out, watching the feet tread to the bathroom.

*Whew.*

"Nickel. This is Jer-Bear. Baldy's about to get wet. Should I go?"

"Wait. Make sure he doesn't come back. Can you hear the water?"

He listened.

"No. But I hear other noises. I think he's dropping the kids off at the pool if you know what I mean."

"Yeah, gross. But wait. Once the shower starts, you go."

"Got it. I'll just wait and listen," he said, dripping with annoyance. "Just what I like to do on my evenings, Nick. Listen to other guys poop."

"Dude. Use code."

"Fine. Listen to him build a log cabin. Coil a rope. Release the chocolate hostage. Take the Browns to the Super Bowl."

"That's enough."

"I have more."

"Please no."

---------------

"They have gone too far," Emory said through the video recording. "Lying is their second language. They tell you they are looking out for you, the people, but really, they are lining their own pockets with money and setting themselves up in positions of power. They say they want equality for all, freedom for all. But what about those freedoms guaranteed in our Bill of Rights? Where went our freedom to worship as we please? Churches are closing all over this country because they call out sin for what it is and refuse to kneel down to the Almighty Government. If churches don't conform to Big Brother's changing morality, then they are forced to close through ridiculous tax laws and litigation."

Greyson was seething. This man was setting himself up as some holy preacher, telling his followers how immoral the government was. *Oh, yeah? Look who's talking! Who is the immoral one? Why are they listening to this guy?*

"Freedom to bear arms? Not anymore. You cannot protect yourself. Nanny Government will do it for you. Don't want to work? Nanny Government will give you other hard-working people's money, all while ignoring the trillions of dollars of debt that our creditors are now calling to the table. You've lost your freedom to do what you want with your money, and your children and all the children that follow are already in debt to China as well. In chains."

Greyson could sense the crowd's grumbles. They were tracking with Emory, following his every passionate syllable – sipping at the truth he was filtering to them through a straw. But Greyson wasn't fooled. He knew the true Emory, the liar - the one who set off a nuclear bomb in Des Moines – the one who didn't care one iota about these people in Georgia.

"But as they lock your wrists in chains, they do so with a smile, telling you that the chains are meant to give you security – like you are some patient in a psych ward who may hurt himself. But many believe it. And you know why? Because of fear. Fear is their first and most powerful tool."

---------------

When he heard the shower start, Jarryd crawled out from underneath the bed, narrowly avoiding the man's undies, and stretched his aching back. After a few toe touches and a crack of his neck, he jumped to work, searching the man's things for the watch.

He hadn't set it on the end table or kept it in his pocket. It wasn't on the bed, and Jarryd hadn't heard him open the room safe. The more he searched, the faster he realized that his fear had been realized.

Baldy had kept the watch on.

"Bad news," he reported in the walkie with a whisper.

There was a pause on the other side. "You have to check the bathroom."

Jarryd's head collapsed to his chest. "Come on…"

"You have to. He might have taken it off and put it on the counter."

"How do you expect me to get in there without him noticing?"

Another long pause. Jarryd grew fidgety, glancing from the bathroom door to the balcony door where he would escape if the man suddenly came barreling out. Finally, a response came.

"I dare you."

"Oh, come on."

"Your mate dares you, too. She wants to see what you can do."

"Don't use her like that."

"I just *did.*"

------------------

Anger simmered in Greyson's eyes, so hot that he almost cried. He hated the man so much. If Emory was actually in the sanctuary, he would have put a bolt-arrow in his knee minutes ago. But he still contemplated blasting the TV screen to pieces.

"If you are afraid, you allow them to grow stronger. They convince you that more of *them* is what you need. More security, more supervision, more government. But what we need is more *truth.*"

*Truth?*

"If you knew them for what they really are – liars, frauds, want-to-be-kings, then you would not be afraid. You would be angry. But they are deceitful beyond our imagination. And they have grown far too good at it. So, I tell you, if you want to survive, if you want to prevent our little American heaven from becoming an American hell, then you must listen to me. Don't trust the politicians. Don't trust those who claim that a 'miracle compromise' or some great new states' convention will bring peace. We don't compromise our principles or our freedom. It is mere talk, more lies, more manipulation and delays – don't trust any of it. Do not be deceived!"

*Amen to that! But he was the deceiver. He was the greatest threat to America.*

"So, let me tell you the truth."

---------------------

Jarryd's fingers pressed against the wooden door and pushed ever so slowly. Hot steam swirled through the open crack, and the volume of splashing water increased above the sound of Jarryd's crashing heart. Breathing in the steam in short gasps, it was harder and harder to keep his cool.

As the door opened wider, he saw more and more of the room. The foggy mirror, the porcelain sink counter, the toilet. He paused, letting out a deep breath, listening for signs he'd been discovered, but there were only off-tune hums that Jarryd hoped would not transform into off-tune lyrics.

He stood for a long moment in the doorway, letting the steam join the beads of sweat on his forehead. Gulping, he fought the fear by convincing himself that it would earn him at least a hug from Avery. Perhaps even a kiss on the cheek.

His foot wavered in the air before finally setting down on the tile. Pause. No change. Another step. Pause. No change. Again and again, until he finally found it. He was standing in the middle of the bathroom, but he saw it – just above the towel rack on a little shelf. The smart watch.

-----------------

"The truth may sound crazy, but that is what they want you to think. They put labels on it. Conspiracy theories are mocked, discarded. Fake conspiracies are promoted in hopes of diluting the truthful ones. Deceit. It's all their deceit. But know this. We did not nuke Des Moines."

The shock set a burning sensation through Greyson's lungs. It tickled his eyes and pricked his heart.

"The government has no proof, only speculation. Their witnesses are children who have never been interviewed by the public – who have been hidden from cross-examination. For all we know, they are fictional. Just like their fantastic story about the governor who shoots a missile at his own kid in a valiant effort to save the city."

Greyson's anger grew too large - he couldn't bear it. His fingers tore at the edges of the hard carpet, and his teeth ground against one another. *I have to say something. I can't let him get away with this. Lies! LIES!*

"On the one hand, they say that those of Pluribus are backwoods, bitter people who are clinging to their guns and their religion. On the other hand, they say we are sophisticated enough to steal a nuclear weapon and hateful enough to destroy a Midwestern city – something very anti-religious. They can't have it both ways. But we make a very convenient enemy. A very convenient tool to increase fear."

Emory paused for effect, and it worked. The sanctuary was quiet. But Greyson was steaming, like a teakettle about to scream. His breath came out like it did before a great sob. The veins on his neck bulged, his cheeks glowed as red as his hat, and tears pooled in his eyes. He had to say something, but he couldn't.

"Watch this video. A missile comes in, shot from an American F-16. A moment later – a nuclear explosion. This is the evidence they have been withholding. *They* nuked Des Moines. *They* killed 8,000 of their own citizens, to give themselves an excuse for more power. *That* is the truth."

"Liiiii----EEEEES!"

His scream had come out in the worst way possible. A squeaky pubescent voice-crack the likes of which no one had ever heard. Like deer suddenly sensing a hunter, heads turned and latched onto him with steeled focus. One of the men stopped the video, but the rest were frozen, still trying to make sense of the boy who stood in the balcony.

Greyson wanted to crawl back under the pew, or just run through the window, but he had gone this far. He cleared his throat and tried to sense if it would crack again.

"Lies," he said timidly. "He is lying!"

The men began murmuring to one another, some frantic, others jovial – laughing at the absurdity of it all. But Wayne, the leader at the front, slowly reached for his cell phone.

"I…I was there. At the fair…and in the truck…with the bomb…"

*This is a mistake. This is a mistake.*

The men grew restless and began shouting at him. "Who are you?" "What's your name?" "How'd you get in here?"

But he held firm, hands gripping the railing like it was the only thing keeping him from falling into the abyss.

"My name is Greyson Gray. And I'm telling the truth. *He* is not. *He* killed 8,000 people. *He* killed my friend. *He* killed my mom."

Down below, the room reached a fever pitch. Some shouted obscenities; others began yelling commands at Wayne, who ignored them, waving them off with one hand as he held a phone to his ear.

But the pilot, Dan, remained calm, though his son, Asher, tugged at his jacket, whispering, "That's him! That's the kid!" After a few seconds of letting the situation sink in, Dan spoke succinctly, face to face with his son. "Go home and get the bug-out bag. Know where it is?"

"Yes, but…"

"Take it to the truck and wait in the passenger seat for me. I'll be right there."

"But…"

"You will not stop for anyone but me. You understand?"

Asher wanted to question him again, but he knew better. "Yes, sir."

"Now go."

Just as Asher scrambled out the side door, Dan pounded out a text.

Found kid. Need extract ASAP.

"EVERYONE SHUT UP!" Wayne's booming voice shut them up in an instant. "Now looky here, boy. What you are saying is very interesting, but it also happens to be the very thing we would expect a government agent to say." He eyed the two men he had sent to the doors behind the stage. They'd be making their way around to the balcony in no time.

"And sneaking into one of our meetings here is also something a government agent might do." Wayne smugly stroked his goatee. The other men nodded to themselves.

Greyson shook his head, confused. "But I'm not…"

"I'm not saying you are, boy. I'm saying we don't know. So why don't you come on down here, and we can talk it out, and you can give us some more evidence."

Dan took a few steps toward Wayne so that he could see up to the balcony. Greyson noticed him and they shared a look.

"I-I can't," Greyson told Wayne. "I'm not staying. I just wanted you to

200

know that Emory is bad. He's a liar!"

Wayne smiled condescendingly and put his hands on his waist – near the holstered pistol he kept at his side. He shook his head and prepared to say something, but someone cut him off.

"Thank you," Dan said to the surprise of the audience. Even Wayne cocked his head. "Thanks for having the courage to speak up."

Greyson nodded slowly, feeling the warmth of Dan's gaze. It was oddly comforting to have the praise of a stranger. At least it was someone. "You're welcome."

"Now you're going to have to run for your life, Greyson."

The room was tethered together, tense and ready to snap. Greyson held his breath, his mind moving faster than his legs. *Had he…? Did he…?*

"RUN!"

He heard the footsteps on the stairs behind, sprinted toward the window and braced for the jump.

# Chapter 37

Greyson judged the wooden grate covering the window. It was old – the slats were thin. *They'll break, right?*

*Only one way to find out!* He leveled his shoulder and smashed into it. The wood bent and broke around him, flying in dozens of directions as his body flew through the opening and into the night air. His feet hit the roof's shingles, and suddenly the edge was only a few feet away. He dug in, stopping his momentum. Wood debris bounced from the roof and fell to the alley two-stories below as Greyson tiptoed to the edge, swinging his arms behind him.

He took a cautious step back. The voices coming through the window were loud and angry.

An idea sprang to his mind, and he quickly removed from his pack the device he had made for just this type of occasion using a Ziploc, aluminum foil, and drain cleaner. The memories of his father's experiments with the homemade bomb sprang into mind. The goofy way they looked in goggles and gloves as they shook the device, mixing the drain cleaner with the aluminum. Running from the device, laughing. Watching from behind the kitchen window. His mother's scowl. The explosion.

It had taken ten seconds.

He darted to his left along the edge of the roof, glancing behind for any followers and shaking the explosive.

*Six, five…*

A man was stepping through the broken window. They caught eyes.

He pulled back and pitched the device toward the man like they were playing catch.

And the man caught it, stopping in bewilderment.

*One second.*

*POOOOOOSHHH!*

The bottle burst, sending out a plume of caustic chemicals.

"AAAGGGH!" The man jerked back and dropped to his knees on the angled roof, his face and hands distorted as the acid burned his flesh. His body tumbled down the shingles and over the side.

Grimacing, Greyson turned back to find his target – the dumpster below. Half of it was open, revealing the trash bags that would soften his fall. The other half was covered with a hard, plastic lid. He'd have to be accurate.

"Stop! Don't do it!"

Another man had joined him on the roof. More were streaming around the back of the alley entrance. Greyson hovered at the edge, eyeing his chasers and the opening below. He'd just cliff-dived from a further distance into a waterfall not long ago. He could do this.

He stepped off and plummeted.

---

Jarryd gulped and wiped at the sweat on his forehead. He could see the faint outline of the man behind the shower curtain and hear his hands working at the shampoo on his bald scalp. Maybe it was Rogaine. Either way, without much hair, the shower would be over soon. He had to make his move.

Reaching toward the little shelf, he grabbed the smart watch's band and slowly drew it to himself. Finally, it was his.

And then it beeped.

The man's humming stopped, and the top of the curtain drew back. Suddenly Baldy was looking straight at Jarryd – a look of utter surprise etched on his face. Jarryd was frozen – the watch in his hand.

"Sorry?" Jarryd mumbled.

Baldie's face turned from surprise to anger in an instant. The curtain ripped from the shower rod as he launched toward Jarryd. But Jarryd was gone, screaming as he bounced off the walls, pulled open the door, and scampered into the hall.

---

Greyson hit the trash bags and crumpled into them. The smell splashed in his face, thick and pungent. He reacted fast, before his senses could settle. Pulling himself out, he jumped to the alley and burst toward the street. Men yelled at him from behind and from the roof. Some shouted orders, others obscenities. He anticipated gunshots, but there were none. They wanted him alive.

The street was empty, but someone was pounding at the front door of the church, breaking through the plywood. Whoever it was called for him. "Greyson!"

203

He ignored it and ran toward Kit. He was barking now, angry but wagging his tail. Greyson snatched his backpack and sped past.

"Come!"

Together they circled around the house's backyard, weaved around a sandbox and a birdfeeder, and cut across several more yards. Motion-sensing lights flicked on, but as far as he knew, they weren't spotted. The shouts grew fainter in the background, but the sounds of truck engines churned by on each side of the block. They would be trying to box him in.

But he only had to break one side of the box to get out.

"Over here!" He waved Kit toward him, cutting behind a fence and heading toward the hills in the distance. He unsnapped his slingshot and fished a ball out of his ammo pouch. As tempting as it was to use the arrow ammunition, he didn't want to waste the few arrows he had.

Breathing hard, he eyed his surroundings. Decks, lawn furniture, gardens – but no men, yet. But he couldn't stop. A few more blocks and he could take a break.

Rounding a corner and approaching a road, he put his back to the wall of a shed and listened. A truck squealed around the street and buzzed past, lighting the side of the shed and the houses with its blazing headlights. When it had passed, he snuck a peak. Red Toyota. Three men standing in the bed – armed with rifles.

"Frick." Maybe they *were* going to kill him. Fear pricked him, and he felt the familiar jolt of adrenaline that swirled through his veins. He'd need it.

He waited another beat and then turned toward the street.

"There you are."

A slender man with a cut-off, plaid shirt took a step toward him adjusting his denim hat. A handgun jutted from the waist of his jeans, and his other hand lingered close to it.

Kit growled at his side, waiting for the command to sic, but it never came.

Before Greyson could even raise his slingshot, a well-built man quietly curled around the corner with his jaw set. The well-built man didn't waste time. He kicked the back of the slender man's knee, grabbed him by his collar, and flung him against the side of the shed like a doll. The man watched his victim's limp body for a moment, making sure he didn't get up, and then looked to Greyson.

It was Dan. "Are you telling the truth?" he snapped.

Kit growled as Greyson struggled to answer.

"Are you telling the truth?" he asked again, with urgency. "About Emory? Pluribus did the nuke?"

Greyson put his hand behind Kit's ears as if to hold him back, for now. "Y-yeah. They did. All of it. I was —"

"Then follow me."

----------------

Jarryd ran, looking over his shoulder, expecting to see Baldy giving chase, but he was alone. His walkie-talkie chirped at him, Nick's voice frantic, but he ignored it. He turned down one hall and then another, flew up a flight of stairs, until he had to catch his breath in a lobby. Still no followers.

He'd done it.

"You went the wrong way!" the walkie screamed.

Jarryd looked around. *Oh, yeah.*

In his panic, he'd forgotten the plan. He was supposed to have handed the watch off to Nick. He was supposed to have gone to the elevator where Avery was waiting.

"I thought this way was better! Is he chasing?"

"No. Not yet. But get to our room. Hurry!"

Jarryd breathed hard and put his hands on his knees. He was way out of shape. He wasn't cut out for this adventure stuff. This was Greyson's domain. *I'm good for moral support, not this James Bond crap.*

He took in another deep breath and began his run again but stopped as soon as he started. A Korean cruise officer was glaring at him, dressed in full white with a black tie and ranking displayed on each of his shoulder's epaulettes. His nametag read: Suk Toh.

Suk's eyes latched on to the watch in Jarryd's hand. And then the officer reached for his own watch and spoke into it. "A boy has stolen a watch. Chubby, buck-toothed. Long, girl hair. Empress Deck."

Jarryd glared back and raised his walkie. "A man named 'Suck' has discovered us. Uni-browed, twig-armed mouth-breather. Empress Deck."

The man sneered and then pounced.

# Chapter 38

*Huff. Puff. Huff. Puff. Huff. Puff.*

Greyson was growing weary and the backpack was rubbing his shoulders raw, but he ignored the pain. He couldn't show any weakness to Dan, because he was the one doing all the hard work.

"Hold here. Wait for it."

As he had for the last several blocks, he followed exactly what Dan said. So far, they had outmaneuvered the Plurbs several times. It was as if Dan knew exactly what their enemies would do, where they would go, and how fast they would do it.

From across the street, Greyson watched three well-armed Plurbs peer inside windows, run around the side of the house, and disappear behind.

"Quick."

They kept low and shuffled across the street, careful to avoid the streetlights. Dan had only given commands since his first question: *"Are you telling the truth?"* He was focused now with steeled eyes and stiff reflexes. It was as if he saw more than Greyson did. Heard more. Had more confidence. He had to have done this before.

They zigzagged through more yards until finally they rested behind a hedge of bushes.

"Your dog. He's a police dog?"

Greyson looked at Kit. "Uh…no. Well, I don't know."

Dan didn't flinch. "He's trained. I'm going to need him here."

He hadn't really thought too much about who had trained Kit before, but Dan seemed to know what he was talking about. "Okay."

"We're going for my truck – outside the bookstore. Then we'll see if we can avoid the roadblocks."

Greyson nodded, trying to fight off the panic. This had gotten out of hand faster than he imagined. Roadblocks? Just for him? It was like a whole army was after him.

"We're getting my son, and then we're getting you out of here."

"On your plane?"

Dan finally flinched, the folds on his large forehead scrunching together. "No. The airfield is miles away. You're getting out on the train."

Jarryd felt Suk gaining on him. The man had longer legs, longer arms, and made a very annoying wheezing sound when he ran. The wheezing grew louder and louder as they pounded through the guest room halls.

*Run faster! Faster! Stupid muscular calves!*

A T-intersection was just ahead. Maybe he could fake him out. He edged to the left, and just as he felt the wheezing on his neck, he turned right. Suk's arm whisked past Jarryd's shoulders as he went careening into the wall face-first. The bang was astounding, and the uni-browed man crumpled to the blue carpet.

He had faked him out big time! *Must have broken the guy's ankles! I'm a baller, a scholar, and a...*

"You're welcome."

Sydney was staring at him with her hands on her hips.

Suddenly it all came together. She had tripped him as he came around the corner. If only he had planned it that way...

"I led him right to you. All you had to do was put your foot out."

She kept glaring at him until the man groaned and shifted at their feet.

"Quick. Give me the watch! Split up!"

Jarryd didn't debate. He threw her the watch, and she instantly darted the opposite way. He stood still for a moment and then looked behind. Another worker stood at the far end of the hall. He didn't look happy.

Jarryd jumped over Suk and pushed off his back down the opposite hall. He was not only running for his life – he still had to go to the bathroom.

---

"Stay. Watch. Zo-ston. Po-zar."

Dan looked straight into Kit's eyes as he gave the odd commands, and Kit looked like he understood. He sat on his haunches on the sidewalk, ears alert like little satellite dishes. Greyson flashed him the stay command just in case.

When Dan gave the signal, they left Kit and made their way across the street to the beginnings of a main street with businesses lined up for blocks on both sides. There was a neon sign with a coffee cup, a small movie theatre, and a barbershop. It was quaint and quiet. It seemed like a place Greyson would

207

like to live – where the neighbors knew one another and cared for each other. A place to raise kids.

But it wasn't any place for kids right now. Trucks raced about town with men hollering his name and waking the neighborhood. Roadblocks were being set up on the roads out of town, guarded by armed sentries. And drapes were being pulled, lights turned off. At most, a camera could be seen in the corner of a window, hoping to catch something worthy to be put on online – to feed the hype on the national news.

When they made it to the bookstore, Dan ran to the truck parked at the curb in front. Asher rolled down the window from inside.

"Got the bag?"

"Yeah," the boy said, scared.

"Good. Greyson, get in."

Greyson shot to the door and Asher scooted over. He smiled at him, clutching his backpack as Greyson did his.

Dan swung around to the driver's door but stopped suddenly. It was Kit's bark that stopped him. A warning bark.

Greyson examined Dan's face as it descended into rapid thought. His eyes darted back and forth, from Asher, to Kit, and back to Asher. Greyson didn't envy his position. For once, he wasn't the one making the decisions.

The Plurbs' truck came peeling around the corner, past Kit, who still stood sentry, barking mad and fast. But he stood his ground.

And then the nightmare came flooding in. Instead of Dan, it was Kip, Greyson's old bodyguard standing at the driver's door. Two cops pulled up, and Kip trusted them. They fired into his chest, three, four, five times. Over and over. His body fell…

"Greyson! Get down on the floor. Asher, stay where you are."

Greyson did as he was told, lying at Asher's feet. Asher's young face was frozen in fear, and he clutched at the bug-out bag like a giant stuffed animal. Fear was etched on his forehead, and his lip trembled.

"And don't watch, Ash. Greyson, make sure he doesn't watch."

"Yes, sir."

Dan leaned in through the door. "Don't be afraid," he whispered, staring straight at Asher. "Remember who's with you."

Asher and Greyson shared a look as Dan walked toward the oncoming truck.

Sydney sprinted through Central Park, ignoring the winding path; instead, she jumped over bushes and weaved around the pedestrians who were on their way to the various stores and restaurants on either side. Above and around them were hundreds of balconies, all the way up to the top deck of the ship, where cruisers sat and talked about the beautiful scenery of the park in the valley below.

But Sydney wasn't taking in the beauty. If she stopped to smell the roses, they would catch her. Her plan was to find a more public place where she could lose them. Though there were many people in the park, there were even more at the Aqua Theatre at the end of the ship. She burst through a set of thick doors and into the sound of the show's music. Beyond the amphitheater she could see the giant projector screens with the ocean just beyond.

She had almost made it to the first seats when one of the ushers turned toward the park as if scanning for someone. And the usher's eyes found her. She stopped dead in her tracks.

She could outmaneuver the usher – or kick his groin. But he seemed more athletic than the other ones. What if it didn't work? Maybe she should scream? Make a scene and hope the guests stop him?

"Sydney."

It was an Australian voice. When she turned, Sydney saw the Australian it belonged to.

"Give me the watch!" Avery was strapping herself into climber's gear. Rising above her was one of two giant climbing walls, towering beside the rows of balconies. "Hurry!"

The usher took a step forward, speaking into his watch. Another usher rushed from the side, joining him. Together they advanced.

Sydney eyed Avery and then the ushers. Choices ran through her mind, but she knew better than to make decisions based on petty dislike. She threw the watch to Avery who immediately jumped to the wall, latching on to the fake-rock handholds. In a matter of seconds, she was out of reach of the ushers who had raced to her, jumping to grab her feet. One of them tried to climb after her but was obviously not up to the challenge. Avery was like a monkey on the wall.

Was there anything she was not good at?

But then the ushers headed to the woman who was holding Avery's rope, giving her slack while keeping a good grip in case she fell. The rope was tied to Avery's back. It could keep her safe – it could also pull her off the wall.

"Avery! The rope!"

Avery heard the warning just in time. The usher reached for the rope and tugged it hard, but to no avail. Avery had clicked it free from the carabineer. The rope swung free and loose, jangling all the way to the top deck, some twelve stories higher.

But Avery was now climbing without any safety rope, digging into the handholds with her fingers and pushing off footholds with the toes of her sneakers.

Disappearing into the gathering crowd, Sydney made her way to a side door and watched from afar as Avery made it to the side of the wall. With a mighty leap and a collective gasp from the crowd, she flew to the closest balcony, latching onto the railing. She pulled herself up with great upper-body strength and swung her legs up and over the side. When her feet struck the balcony's floor, she turned with a big smile on her face. With bright eyes and a winning smile, she waved to the crowd and winked at the ushers. As the audience applauded, she vanished into the room.

Sydney wanted to be sick.

-----------------

Asher looked sick with fear, but Greyson reached up from the floor and grabbed his hand. He didn't know what to say – he'd never had a younger brother or spent much time with younger kids – but he had to do something.

"Just keep your eyes on me," he whispered. "Okay?"

Asher nodded.

"No matter what you hear. I'm here. Like your dad said."

The boy whispered back. "He wasn't talking about you."

Greyson perked up as he heard a truck pull to a stop next to theirs.

"Hey there, Critter! Whatcha doing?"

"We don't want any part of this," Dan responded. "Chasing a kid with guns, waking the whole neighborhood..."

"What's your problem? Huh? Kid's a liar. A government plant."

"This is not what we're about. We don't silence people who disagree with us – we hear them out."

"Is that right?" A car door opened, and a few footsteps hit the pavement.

The others were jumping down from the bed. "Sounded to me like you told the boy to run. Is that what you call hearing him out?"

There was a pause, and a new edge came to the Plurb's voice. "Are you hiding him, Critter? You find him?"

Asher was shaking. Greyson squeezed his hand and mouthed, *"It's okay. Eyes on me. Eyes on me."*

"No. It's just me and Ash."

"Where you headed?"

The voices got closer. They were walking toward the truck. Greyson breathed hard, but silent. Every instinct told him to run or fight. His free hand pulled at his slingshot's snap.

"My brother's place. Like I said, we don't want anything to do with this, so if you'll…"

"Then you wouldn't mind if we check your truck. Just to check—"

But the man didn't finish his sentence. A crack interrupted it, and then a fury of sounds followed. Surprised shouts – shuffling feet on asphalt – more cracks – a thud – a gun hitting the street – a body hitting the side of the truck – a groan.

Greyson suddenly bolted up and pushed Asher to the floor. "Sic 'em boy!"

But Kit was already on his way; a blurry flash of brown leaped through the air and pounded the back of one of the men with all four paws. He went down and the dog followed, ripping at his arm, growling fierce and loud.

Greyson pulled up his slingshot, but there was no need. Dan walked to the man being mauled on the ground, called the dog off, pulled the man up, and put him out with a hard-right fist. The other three men were already down.

Suddenly, there were no more sounds. The silence sunk in deeply. Only Asher was making a sound, his thin gasps on the edge of crying. Sensing the violence was over, Greyson turned to him and put a hand on his back.

"It's okay. It's over."

Dan opened the door and Kit jumped in after, crowding the space even further. "You guys okay?"

"Yeah. You?"

Dan nodded grimly. He was barely breathing hard. But Greyson knew that violence left more marks than the visible ones. Still, though, he really looked ok. And he'd just put down three men in ten seconds. *Who is this guy?*

"I'm fine. But we gotta go. Buckle in."

Greyson did as he was told.

211

# Chapter 39

Avery ran through the random guestroom, smiling at the couple watching a movie on their bed, and exited with a little wave. The hall was clear and so was the elevator lobby. She pushed the down button but second-guessed herself. With the elevator, she didn't have control. If it happened to open on a floor with a Plurb, she was toast. Stairs, though, at least gave her a chance for escape.

She jogged to the staircase, and sure enough, hurried footsteps were bounding up from below. The ushers were coming for her. *Up it is.*

-------------

The truck blasted through the streets and zipped past house after house.

"Whe'ah we goin'?" Asher asked, still clutching the bag.

"To the hills west of town, where the train tracks cut through," Dan answered, checking his mirrors.

Worry slipped into Greyson's mind. "Which way does the train go?"

"It goes away from here."

"No. Which way does it go? Direction."

Dan gave him a glance. "West. Why does it matter?"

"I'm going south. I can't go west. Can't we get to your plane?"

Dan jerked the wheel, buzzing around the corner, heading toward a factory with all kinds of storage bins and piping piled high outside. Streetlights flashed overhead, one after another, yet sparser and sparser as they neared the outskirts of town.

"Why south? Where are you going?"

"To my dad. He's in the Bahamas. Nassau."

Dan's eyes narrowed as he looked in the rear-view mirror. They were being followed. "Hold on."

Dan hit the accelerator, but the car caught up quickly, flashing its brights. "Heads down!"

The warning came just in time. Bullets blasted through the back window and smacked the truck's bed with loud clangs. Greyson ducked, but kept his eyes open and his hands busy with the slingshot. In the shaking side mirror, he caught a glimpse of the gunman leaning out from the backseat with a hunting rifle.

*BANG BANG!*

Two more bullets hit on Greyson's side as the car pulled alongside them. Suddenly Dan punched the brakes and swung into the car with a resounding smack and metallic screech. From his window, Greyson could see the driver sneering. The man in the back leveled his rifle.

"Aagh!"

Greyson's window burst apart, sending shards inside, dancing at their feet.

"Get my gun from the bag!" Dan ordered.

But Asher clutched at Greyson's arm, digging into his flesh. Greyson pulled free, watching the Plurb car drift a distance away, and made his own decision.

"I got it!"

He had been trading out the bands and loading the steel arrow. Waiting for the car to come back around, he pulled it back as far as he could, turned in his seat and aimed out the broken window.

When it all lined up, Greyson let the bolt-arrow fly.

*WHIIIZZZ! BANG!*

The Plurb's front wheel burst into shreds, flopping on the road as the driver yanked on the wheel. The car flung left and then right, turned on its side and then rolled in a spectacular spin, whipping dirt into the sky as it barreled into the ditch with a cloud of dust and debris.

Asher's face was a mix of fright and amazement, but a smile crept in as he turned to watch the aftermath. "Cool!"

Greyson settled back into his seat, catching his breath and smiling to himself. Asher caught his attention, and they shared the smile. Even Dan gave him a look.

But Dan spotted more headlights ahead. Roadblock. "Not out yet."

He swerved to the right and busted through a chain-linked gate, sending it spiraling through the dirt.

Asher watched it, and again he smiled. "Geez, Dad!"

Dan buzzed around stacks of pipes, clearly taking a detour. "Sometimes you have to go west to go south."

Greyson thought hard for a moment, eyeing the dark, rolling slopes ahead. He had gotten his hopes up. The images of a plane flying high above, where he could watch the mountains slide by his window, were now crumbling with every squeak of the truck's shocks.

---------------

Wayne watched the tiny headlights in the distance veer to the left and bounce through the factory yard. It was them.

"Critter, you piece of..." he muttered to himself, turning to his men. "After them!" He slung his large rifle over his shoulder and jumped in the passenger seat. Their truck took the lead, headed toward the hills.

His phone rang, a flurry of banjo strums in the tune of *America the Beautiful*, and he cleared his throat. "Yes?"

"Has the FBI plant been captured?"

"Not yet. He has help. One of our own, a lousy turncoat –"

"He wants him captured. At all costs."

"Yes, sir."

"At...all...costs."

The man hung up.

Wayne thought long and hard, stroking his goatee. He knew where Critter was headed. He knew the costs of stopping them. The boy must be worth the costs. The cost of war is high.

He dialed Humpy. "How many people do we got in Camden? Thirty-six? Get'em all. We're going to need them. This is going to be big."

------------

Nighttime had fallen on the ship's top deck, but the stars were out in full force, keeping the night bright. Adding their own flair to the stars were the blazing spotlights bouncing around the open-aired dance floor with music's beat. The bass was pounding, and the cruisers who hadn't poked a hornet's nest of terrorists were letting loose under the stars.

Avery cut through the thickest mob of dancers, swinging her arms and twirling with a laugh. She was enjoying this. To her, those giving chase were only cruise workers – not terrorists. If she got caught, she would be chastised and probably grounded, but that would be the extent of it. Or so she thought.

The two ushers pushed through the mob as well, but she was skinnier – much faster through the crowd. She emerged first and checked her surroundings. Sensing their approach from behind, she leapt over a deck chair and bounced on several more, using them as miniature trampolines as the ushers gave chase. They were getting tired and slow, which made the chase

214

almost too easy.

She stopped for a drink, sipping at someone's soda and thanking them with a smile, but bolted just before the ushers caught up. Another waiter joined them in the hunt, but she spun around him and taunted him for good measure. The cruisers watching were entertained. She liked to please them.

Exiting the food area, Avery slid through the water park, pulling the rope that dumped an over-sized bucket full of water on top of one of their heads. She laughed as he lost his sense of direction and fell into the kiddie pool. The kids liked that one.

The other Plurb almost nabbed her, but she ducked under a slide and headed back to the center of the ship. *That was too close.*

She couldn't keep up the chase forever, and she knew exactly how to end it.

----------------

Dan slammed on the brakes and exited in a hurry. Greyson opened his door, but hesitated, looking at the trees all around. *Here? Where is the train?*

"Let's go!" Dan ordered.

Greyson unbuckled and pulled his backpack on as he jumped to the grass. Kit followed. But as the man and his son ran off, hand in hand, Greyson paused.

Now was his chance.

He could outrun them. Maybe he should. Sure, he would be right back where he started – alone; but at least he wouldn't be blindly following someone he didn't trust to some invisible train. There wasn't any train out here. And even if there were, it would be heading west. Dad was south. He'd always been headed south. Why should he be misled now? Why should he trust this guy?

Dan had stopped, holding Asher's hand. He looked back at Greyson but didn't bark any orders. He paused, as if he understood. Greyson shifted on his feet, still unsure. He wanted to be alone, but then again, he really didn't. It had been nice talking with someone who talked back. He'd forgotten how long he had gone without human interaction.

"You'll be free of us soon enough. I have friends who will meet you in Camden and take you where you need to go."

"I need to go to Nassau."

"You need to get to safety, first."

"Why aren't *you* going with?"

215

The man paused, still holding Asher's hand. Greyson tightened his chin to keep it from trembling.

"Because he can't make the jump," Dan explained stoically, looking at Asher. "And I'm staying to protect him."

*The jump? What jump?* But whatever he meant by that, there was something worse. He was leaving.

It was happening again. They always left. They'd be with him for a while, but then they'd be gone. And Dan was no different.

Headlights flashed through the woods, lighting the sides of the trees. Someone was chasing them.

"Greyson. I'll come back and help you. But for now, you have to trust me."

"You will?" His voice was doing that thing again. Breaking. "You'll come back?"

"Yes. I promise."

Greyson fought the lump in his throat and blinked away the moisture in his eyes as he made his decision. He jerked into a jog after them, distracted by the headlights that bounced all around, casting weird shadows in the night. The sounds of tires digging through the terrain below grew louder, but Greyson heard another sound.

*Clackclackclackclackclack.*

There *was* a train.

"Hurry!"

He put on speed, ignoring the pain in his side and the chafing of the bag on his shoulders. There was no stopping. Running. Running. Trees whipping by like rungs of a ladder. And the sound of the train's engine began to thump at his chest. It was close.

A clearing of the trees was up ahead; they'd reached the opposite side of the ridge. Dan stopped first at the edge of a precipice and looked back at Greyson. The look on Dan's face made Greyson slow to a walk as he approached.

*CLACKCLACKCLACKCLACK!*

The next cautious step allowed Greyson to peek over the edge. Train cars rumbled underneath. The vibrations jostled his ribs and teeth. The train was huge and heavy and rushing past only a few feet below, hugging the ridge as it weaved through the mountains.

Greyson took a step back.

"You'll have to get a running start."

Greyson could read the regret in Dan's voice. He knew it was near impossible. He knew that Greyson could die.

"But…"

"You have to do it. Now. There's not much train left."

The fear formed a hard pit in his gut, pressing against his intestines like a bowling ball. He had to take deep breaths just to keep it down.

There was daring, but then there was stupid.

"This is stupid!" Greyson shouted over the sound of the train. "I'm staying with you. We…we can get out together."

"I don't know if we'll make it. But *you* have to. You're too important." He stared Greyson down.

"What will you do? Will you get away? I can help…"

"They're after you; I can evade them. Now go!"

After a moment's deliberation, Greyson pointed at him. "Promise me!" he demanded. "Promise me you'll fly me to my dad!"

Dan scanned the trees. Faint shouts and flashlights were pursuing them. He turned back. "Yes, I promise!"

"And Kit?"

"We'll take care of him!"

Greyson eyed the train. There were maybe ten cars left. He quickly snapped his hat to his fanny pack, knelt to Kit's level, and grabbed his face.

"Be a good boy. Sic the bad ones. Lick the good ones."

Kit licked his face – a goodbye – and Greyson bolted through the trees alongside the train. He ran through the grass and almost slipped off the side, sending a small dirt avalanche onto the train. Regaining his balance, he gained speed. But the train was faster. The third to last car pulled ahead.

Greyson eyed the best portion of the cliff for takeoff. No trees, no overhanging branches, solid ground. It was twenty feet away. And then ten.

He held his breath, planted his foot, and leapt.

In a blur, the train car appeared under him – a green metal grating zipping by, threatening to tear his legs out from underneath. His feet hit and he fell forward, banging his knees and hands on the grating; and suddenly he had lost control. He lashed out at anything and everything. His fingernails scraped metal, but he couldn't find a grip. The train swept up his momentum and knocked him to the side; he saw the trees swoosh overhead, the stars in white streaking lines. His body flung over the side and headed for the rocks below.

*UGH!* Something jerked his backpack; his arms slipped through, but he snagged the strap and held on to it for dear life. As his mind reeled to figure

217

out what had happened, he hung over the side, grasping the backpack's strap and flailing to get control.

The train chugged on and twisted around each turn, jostling Greyson's body from side to side, banging his feet against the metal plating. The ground rushed below, but the backpack held strong with one of the straps wrapped over the corner of the top grating.

As Greyson's body swung less and less, he finally beat the panic. He had screamed when he fell, but now he could only make anguished groans, like an animal begging for its life. And then he heard another animal sound. Sniffing.

Swinging his body around to face the side of the car, he pressed his feet against the wall and grabbed higher on the strap.

Sure enough, Kit was above him, wagging his tail and sniffing at his backpack. He had followed him?

"Little help?"

Kit scratched at the metal grating, as if he were telling him what to do. And he knew it. He had to climb, or his strength would run out.

Placing his feet against the side, he took his first step higher. Another step upward against the side and another grab took him a few inches closer to the top. His forearms were burning and shaking, but he had reached the edge. Kit bit his shirt and tugged, pulling him far enough up to press his elbows on the grating for leverage; then, with one big push, he rolled onto the top and latched on.

*CLACKCLACKCLACKCLACK!*

*I did it. I'm okay. I'm alive. Somehow.*

Kit was already licking him with his thick tongue, forcing Greyson's lips and cheeks around his face, but he just let it happen. He was too tired.

He breathed in deep and long, closing his eyes as he felt the vibrations of the train on his back. It was horribly uncomfortable, but he didn't want to move. He was safe.

Eventually tiring of Kit's licks, he sat up and opened his eyes. The stars were beautiful – as was typical in the mountains – but even more so after a near-death experience. And he hadn't realized how near death it had been. He was on top of the last car.

# Chapter 40

Sydney burst through the door. "Nick! Jarryd!" And then she stopped. They were both sitting on the bed. They had been in the heat of an argument but were now very happy to see Sydney.

"Do you still have the watch?" Nick asked.

Jarryd threw in his own question. "Have you seen Avery?"

"Avery has it."

She turned to check the hall one more time and began to close the door, but Jarryd was suddenly at her side, halfway out the door. "She's still out there! We've got to help!"

Nick shook his head. "No, they've already seen you too much. They'll be looking for you both now. It's only a matter of time before they track us down. It wasn't supposed to happen this way."

"I can't leave her out there." Jarryd held the doorknob with one hand, waiting for the go-ahead.

But Sydney and Nick were dumbfounded. Had he really said that?

"No…" Nick began, still sorting through all the options, "…we have to tell our parents. Don't worry; they're not going to kill her – not on the ship in front of everyone."

"How do you know that?" Jarryd sneered, closing the door.

"They won't kill her yet. They wouldn't risk messing up their plan."

"Oh, yeah? Just because it's not Wednesday yet? How do you know what Daryl is going to do?"

The sound seemed to be vacuumed out of the room. Nick and Sydney were speechless for a few good seconds, racking their brains to make sense of Jarryd's questions.

"Uh…what?" Sydney asked.

Jarryd still held the doorknob, but his grip loosened as he thought. "What *what?*"

"What the heck are you talking about? Who is Daryl?"

"I don't know."

"Then *why'd* you say his name – whoever he is?"

"That's what the message on the watch said. 'Daryl is expected to arrive Wednesday night. Disembark Wednesday at 4 pm.'"

"Ohhhhh." Sydney and Nick shared a sigh and a look of wonder. Finally, they understood. Jarryd had intercepted a message on the watch.

Though they were both thinking the same thing, Sydney spoke first. "Is that enough information?"

"I think it is," Nick whispered, still thinking. "It'll have to do."

Nodding, as if he understood the other two, Jarryd twisted the doorknob. "Enough talking? Can I go rescue my girl now?"

Nick stood up victoriously. "Yes. Before she does anything stupid, we have to give them their watch back."

--------------

Sam typed vigorously, the code flying across the screen. Calvin watched, chiming in when necessary to correct or to guide him. Though he was odd and annoyingly paranoid, Sam considered him the perfect tutor. He never pushed him beyond his limits, he gave almost no homework, and he chose what they studied based on his interests.

"Perfect, Samster. Save that program to my thumb drive and pop it over."

Sam did as he was told and gave the thumb drive back to Calvin.

"Now – I'll play the unwitting Iranian nuclear scientist. When I get home, I'll plug it in – the program will run automatically. Check in tonight after your fundraiser thingy – if it works, you'll be able to access all my stuff from your laptop. My desktop, my files, my webcam...but not after 10. My girlfriend's coming over and if I forget to close it..."

Sam laughed and gave him a wink. "I didn't sign up for a make-out lesson."

Calvin laughed so hard he had to cough to stop. "Oh, man! Too much. Too much."

Sam watched him until he calmed down. "Now what?"

Still shaking off his laughter, Calvin fought hard with his memory. "Math. I need to check your algorithms. How much time do we have?"

"'Til my piano lesson?"

"Yeah."

Sam began digging for his homework thumb drive. "About twenty minutes." Still digging in his pocket, he came out with two of them and a few quarters from the vending machine in the hotel's hallway.

Calvin pointed at the thumb drives. "What's that black one? Your personal one?"

Sam put the blue one for his homework in the laptop and then held the black one in his fingers. A long while ago it had been in the Pluribus headquarters at the State Fair, then it had been in Jarryd's underwear, then Jarryd had given it to him. After a thorough disinfectant job, he had kept it.

"Yeah, it's mine now, I guess."

"Where you keep your secret stuff, huh?"

Sam gave him a fake glare. "No. It was one of Pluribus', from before the bomb."

Calvin's eyebrows arched halfway up his forehead. "For real?"

"Yeah, but I showed them to my dad already. He said they found nothing in them they could use. It was all old news."

Calvin leaned in across the table, awkwardly close. He spoke succinctly. "And you still have them?"

Sam nodded, unsure of what the big deal was. "Yeah. I gave them the files on a different drive. This is the original. So?"

Calvin and Sam exchanged a long look until Calvin's demeanor finally softened. "Why? Why'd you give them copies instead of the original?"

There was a hint of the adult tone that told Sam he was in trouble. "I...I don't know. I guess I'm just in the habit of backing up all my files."

Calvin watched him for a few moments beyond awkward, as if he were studying him – searching for any lies that lay underneath. Uncomfortable, Sam shrugged. "What? Don't believe me?"

"Of course I don't. I don't trust anyone. No offense."

"None taken."

"I don't think you trust anyone either. And that's good, because that's hard to teach."

Sam thought hard about what he meant. "Wait. Are you saying I did it because I don't trust my dad?"

Calvin shrugged.

"That's stupid. He's my dad. He's like the biggest Plurb-hater in the world. He even tried to kill me to stop the Plurbs. Why would he lie about it?"

Calvin shrugged again. "I don't know. Didn't say he did. But it's a possibility. It's also a possibility that someone told him a lie, and he believed it."

"Okay?"

"Mind if I check it out for you?"

Sam held the thumb drive loosely, fighting a battle in his head as he traced its outline with his eyes. What if Calvin found something out about his dad's friends or the computer guys who reviewed it? Would it make his dad look bad? Should he ask his dad about it? But what if Dad got mad? Would that mean…?

"Okay. But…"

"It won't be traceable to you. I know just what to do little man. Make a quick copy to your homework drive."

Sam squinted at him and then did what he was told. In a few seconds, the files were on both the black Plurb thumb drive and his blue homework one.

"No more copies," Calvin said solemnly, holding out his hand. "You can trust me." Calvin smiled his wide, goofy smile.

Sam handed him the blue thumb drive and said what his tutor wanted to hear. "I don't trust anyone."

--------------

Though Greyson's body was moving at great speed on top of the train, the stars seemed unmoving above him – little specks suspended millions of miles away.

*ZOOOOOM!*

Another tunnel flashed over Greyson's head, replacing the stars with streaks of artificial light. The train's sound echoed inside the tunnel, waking Greyson from his trance and prompting him to grasp even tighter to the metal grating and to Kit's fur.

When the train emerged from the tunnel, Greyson eyed the new surroundings. The moonlight lay blue over the tops of the rolling trees, like the giant waves of a green ocean. A town glowed with a yellow hue on the distant horizon, and it looked like the train would head straight through its center.

Was this Camden, where he would meet Dan's friends? Would there be a train station, with people waiting to get on the train? If so, he'd have to hide himself well.

But where could he hide? After the first few minutes on the train, he'd tried to walk from one car to the other, but he'd grown tipsy as the train curved through the hills. It had been dangerous for Kit, as well. After a few jumps, he had decided that it wasn't worth the risk when he had a free trip to Nassau waiting for him – that is, if Dan was telling the truth.

What if Dan wasn't telling the truth?

Greyson suddenly sat up in a panic, looking toward the town.

*Is this a deadfall?*

Would Dan's friends promise him one thing, but actually turn him in? Greyson didn't trust adults, especially ones he'd just met.

The panic pushed him to his feet. The wind blasted at his clothes, whipping them to his sides, but he pushed forward, making sure his hat was pulled tightly down to his ears.

He had to be ready for anything – to get off the train at a moment's notice, or to fight his way off. But first, he had to know more about this train. Nothing stupid – he'd just explore.

They jumped the first gap without any problem and then gained confidence, clanging across a dozen more roofs before he realized that it would take him half an hour to get to the front of the train. Besides, he was more curious about what was inside than out.

Looking near his feet, he discovered a square hatch underneath the grating. He wrapped his fingers around the edge of the grating and pulled the heavy hatch over to one side with a painfully sharp squeak.

He looked down. The hole was nearly pitch black and perfectly quiet. Maybe the car was empty.

Shrugging at Kit, Greyson kneeled over the hole and dipped his head into the darkness. In an instant he jerked up from the hole, his eyes wide and confused. He didn't realize he had triggered an alarm, but he was just as scared. He knew what he'd seen, and his heart began pumping as the realization hit him. The military train the Plurbs had been talking about. He was on it.

Military meant government, and the government would end his adventure.

All at once, a metallic bang erupted, Kit growled, and Greyson jerked up.

He jolted – startled at the sight.

A soldier in uniform stood aside a hatch on the car in front of him. His automatic rifle aimed at Greyson's chest.

"Don't...move."

# Chapter 41

Kit growled lower and deeper but awaited a command. The soldier seemed hesitant as well, staring the boy and his dog down, skeptical of what he was seeing.

Greyson was frozen, except for his eyes, which were busy searching for options. As far as he knew, there were three – stay, jump, or dive inside the hole. If he stayed, they would try to take him back to Iowa. If he dove in the hole, they might treat him like an enemy – or a train-hijacker or something. If he jumped...

As he tried to decide, the soldier's gun was captivating him. He couldn't stop looking at the end of the barrel. If he made a wrong move, it might be the last thing he saw. His fingers rested close to his slingshot's snap, but the temptation to draw was dispersed by a glance at the soldier's trigger finger. There was no way he could even raise the slingshot before being torn down by gunfire.

"It's just a boy, sir. And a dog." The soldier nodded his head, like he was receiving a reply through his earpiece; then he pulled a tiny band with a quarter-sized glass piece over his eye. Greyson wondered at its purpose. *A fancy binocular? Infrared? A video camera?*

"There are terrorists – Plurbs – lots of them!" Greyson yelled through the wind. "Back at Meyer's Crossing in a church! They're chasing me!"

The soldier seemed to ignore him, listening instead to a voice in his ear. "You also reading positive ID?"

*That didn't work.* Greyson took the opportunity to slide his feet closer to the hole. He felt his toe reach the gap. All he had to do was take one step and let gravity do the rest.

"What's your name?" the soldier barked. "How'd you get here?"

The debate started in his mind. He swallowed hard. "Liam. Liam Swank. And they were right behind –"

"Are you Greyson Gray?"

Greyson's heart leapt to his throat. "No."

*OOOOOOOT – OOOOOOT!*

The train's whistle blew as it entered the town, cutting behind rows of backyards – but it didn't slow. There was no station.

The soldier paused, listening. A few long moments passed until his eyebrows arched and his eyes registered surprise. Something he was hearing didn't sit well with him. Finally, he nodded, and his focus turned from his ear to the boy in front of him. "You're a fugitive. Guilty of treason against your country and supplying terrorists with sensitive information."

"*What?*"

The surprise nearly knocked him into the hole. *They think what? Why? Now what?* They wouldn't just send a traitor home.

Greyson looked to Kit and then the town beyond. *Where is Dan's friend? Is he in the town?*

Along the train, more and more soldiers had peeked up through hatches, their guns leveled in his direction. Trying to count them, he eyed a silver truck rapidly approaching the train far ahead.

"Affirmative." The soldier took a deep breath and pushed the eye band back into his helmet. His posture and his voice changed suddenly, but his gun remained leveled. "I'm sorry."

Greyson's heart skipped a beat. And another.

*He's going to kill me!* "No. Don't!"

The soldier shook his head and flicked the safety.

Greyson's toe dipped into the hole as the soldier raised the gun and aimed down the scope.

*What's that?* Greyson's attention snapped past the soldier's gun to the truck in the distance as it darted into the railroad barriers. The wood posts splintered, and the truck crumpled into the train.

The explosion's flash came first, the blasting sound second, and the rippling shake third. Like a horizontal wave, train cars swayed one by one ahead of them.

The soldier turned to see the disturbance, and Greyson jerked to action. This time there was only one option.

Two steps and he leapt off, aiming for a leafy tree, and the world seemed to stop in mid-flight. The train screamed metallically as it rocked off the rails – the soldier was jerked from his feet – and Greyson sailed forward, skydiving horizontally, carrying the same speed as the train cars that toppled into the ditch like giant Legos.

As he approached the tree, he caught a glimpse of the train cars far ahead bouncing and spinning into the neighborhood – knocking down trees, piercing roofs and blasting through houses like out-of-control battering rams on a warpath. Dirt and wood flung from the impacts – but his impact would be worse. He wasn't made of steel, but of flesh and bone.

His body snapped through thin branches, slowing his descent considerably, but the grass came on fast; he hit hard. He was like an unconscious downhill skier, flailing and bouncing. His body hit a bush and then a fence, but the fence was already breaking as a train car dashed it to pieces just to his left. The car toppled end over end, swiping a blast of air over his hair as it rolled past.

The ground punched his body – his shoulders, his legs – until he finally rolled to rest, the starry sky spinning above. Eyes still open and on his back, he couldn't move. The metallic noise had been punched out of his eardrums – replaced with an eerie ringing – but the train cars kept coming.

Not far ahead of him, cars smashed the ground. One seemed to dance, knocking into another container and twirling onward, thumping the ground with a graceful landing. A few others had ripped open, spilling guns and Bradley Fighting Vehicles into back yards and living rooms.

The ringing buzzed louder and louder as the chaos surrounded him, small explosions sending orange flashes over his sensitive eyes, but he lay still, taking deep breaths. He was afraid – afraid that if he tried to move, he wouldn't be able to.

As one last car slammed into the grass next to him, he felt his body lift a few inches in the air before jarring the ground again. Then he just lay there, trying to make sense of it all.

He crinked his neck to the side, finding the cargo container that spun in his vision. Its back end was stuck on top of another container, but the front end had crumpled open in front of him, exposing the Bradley Fighting Vehicle inside, only feet from his body.

His vision was still shaky, and the pain made him nauseous, but he could swear it moved. And then it moved again, and he saw the strap that had broken loose. There was one more strap over the front of its treads, and it was vibrating.

It would crush him.

Pushing himself up to his elbows, he crawled a few feet, but collapsed. His head was swooning – it felt like a balloon about to pop. But he pulled at the grass and pushed with his feet again and again.

The Bradley's barrel pointed at him, the front grille meant for smashing through barriers inching forward.

As his hearing slowly returned, he could hear the strap creaking with its weight. And then it snapped.

Finding his last ounce of energy, he pushed at the grass and rolled to the side as the Bradley invaded the yard as if it had landed on a foreign shore, crushing the grass where he had lain.

As he lost consciousness, he stared through the glass doors of the home whose yard he had trespassed. A boy about his age was gaping at him, holding an old shotgun at his side.

# Chapter 42

Nightmares beat at Greyson's eyes. His eyelids fluttered; his breath sucked in and gasped out like the air was too thin.

The boy leaned down and poked him with the shotgun's barrel. "Hey. Hey, kid. Wake up." The boy rolled his eyes, which had dark circles underneath, and blinked through the smoke at the destruction all around. Fires had erupted in several houses, sending smoke over the starry sky, and the jagged train cars stuck from ground and houses like stalagmites in a cave.

Though the destruction had nearly taken the boy's house, a smile attempted to break the boy's steeled frown. "They's actually done it." Then he saw the Bradley Fighting Vehicle. "Dang…" After admiring its turret and missile launcher, he prodded Greyson in the side. "Git'up!"

Greyson jerked from his sleep, though his eyes still rolled in the back of his head. With another prod from the boy's gun he was fully awake. "Stop!" Greyson yelled, trying to push himself up.

"Can ya walk? Which militia ya in?"

Rolling to his back, Greyson took in deep breaths, trying to assess his pain and the longhaired boy at the same time. Though he felt like he'd fallen down a mountain, there weren't any visible breaks. Blood trickled down his leg and he felt the warm ooziness behind his ear, but he was afraid of what he'd find if he touched it.

"Git up and tell me who you is!"

Greyson gave him a hard look. A dirty brown mullet hung over his ears and neck and down to his eyes – but it wasn't well groomed like Jarryd's. A streak of black hung from each of his grumpy eyes, his cut-off shirt looked nearly as stained as Greyson's, and his slumped shoulders were spindly, but strong. Though the kid held the double-barreled shotgun, Greyson doubted that he would use it. "I…have…have you seen my dog?" His voice was hoarse and weak.

"Nah. If I had, I'd wanna know who he is, too."

The boy seemed unfazed by the destruction around him. It was almost as if he was amused, rather than afraid.

Greyson's head swam as he tried to sort through the boy's odd behavior, the smoky darkness, and the fatigue swooning in his head. "My hat." He hadn't snapped it on his belt. "My backpack. Have you seen my backpack? It's red. My hat, too." Greyson staggered to his feet, almost fell, and balanced himself against the armored fighting machine.

"Yeah. I's seen it. But roadblock's just down the road; they's gonna be here 'fore long an' ya best not be if you's militia. Now that we've done start the fight, they have their excuse to end it."

"Roadblock? The military…" Greyson muttered darkly. His memory kicked in, and another shot of adrenaline shot through his veins. The soldier had been about to kill him. He had no idea why, but for now it didn't matter. He had to get out of there. "I need my backpack. And my dog. Kit! Kiii-it!"

The mulleted boy had had enough. "Don't be bringing 'em to us!" He marched to Greyson, grabbed him by the shirt collar and pulled him across the debris-ridden yard. Greyson complained and groaned, the bruises and scrapes making their voices heard, but the boy marched on. Greyson didn't like being thrown around. They made it to a toppled picket fence when Greyson made his move.

Grabbing the boy's gun arm, Greyson yanked it backwards and shoved him onto the fallen fence. Just as the boy rose to his feet with the gun aimed, Greyson drew his own weapon, pulled back to its full and loaded. He almost grinned, happy with himself for the holster's work. It had been fast. And he had needed it to be.

The two boys glared at each other as the sound of car alarms continued to blare down the street. Men's shouts were faint over the din and a few screams peeked out over the rustling fires.

"I need my backpack. And a place to hide – quick! They'll be looking for me."

The boy gave a disdainful curl of his lip. "So, you *is* militia." He cursed. "Why didn't ya tell me in the first place?"

Greyson cringed at the boy's language and let him believe he was militia. There was too little time to explain. "I don't advertise it." He sheathed his slingshot and its ammo. "We need to hurry. They'll be…"

A new rumbling sound drowned out all the rest as a winged drone suddenly streaked overhead, not far above the smoke. The boys followed its flight as it disappeared over the roof. Finally, the sounds of squealing tires spurred them both to action.

Mullet surged past Greyson and came out from behind the Bradley with his worn, red backpack. Without a word, he dropped it at Greyson's feet and marched to the glass doors with a sort of strut.

Still trying to figure him out, Greyson picked up the bag and hurried in – whether he was invited or not.

Though the boy's house had been mostly spared from the disaster, the inside was a disaster in and of itself.

*No wonder he isn't afraid of the train wreck in his backyard. He already lives in one.* There was little room on the floor; it was being used by trash and broken furniture. A few nails stuck from the walls where picture frames may have been knocked loose, but it was hard to tell. The walls were bare, a bland white color streaked with liquid stains waist high and below. The only thing that appeared to have had attention paid to it was the recliner in the corner and the TV propped up by two-by-fours and cement blocks. Beer cans surrounded it with crumpled wrappers in between.

Limping quickly on his bloodied leg, Greyson maneuvered through the maze of trash to the front door. He opened it and peeked out to the street. Lights had turned on throughout Mullet's neighborhood and a few of his neighbors had wandered outside, dressed in pajamas and robes, sleepily staring at the train wreck across the street. Others began running toward one fire or the next to lend a hand. No sign of Plurbs or soldiers yet.

"I need like a car or something," he asked, in a hurry. "Do you have one? Can I borrow it?"

"Naw. Pa took it. 'S'pose he's part'a this."

*His father's a Plurb.*

Greyson peeked out the window's drapes. He closed the drapes and turned back to Mullet. "Aren't you going to go find him?"

"*Heck* no!" Mullet declared; but he didn't say *heck.* He checked the window as well. "He bites it, the world's better off."

Greyson bit his lip. He'd never met someone like this kid before. Who would want his dad dead? "But he's your dad…"

"But the truck – I's worried 'bout her. Silver F150 – 365 horsepower, V8…"

Greyson remembered seeing it hit the train. He cast his eyes downward. Now wasn't the time. "The truck. Is that your only one?"

Squinting his disgust, the boy put his finger against Greyson's chest. "You's one of those spoiled pansies from Atlanta, a'int ya? Two cars, big frickin' house, bigwig ma and pa."

"No. I'm not."

The boy scoffed. "Sure ya is – go find y'self someone else's truck ta steal."

Greyson nodded and tried to steady himself from an onslaught of wooziness. The pain reverberated in every muscle. "How about water?"

Mullet gave him a look and locked the front door. "What 'bout it?"

"You got any?"

He laughed. "Is that what ya thinks o' us? We's so poor we ain't got no water?"

"I—I was just…"

"You's just bein' all prejudicial. Beer?"

Greyson sighed and peeked through the sliding glass doors in the back. An orange and red glow flickered through, casting flowing shapes on the dark walls, but there was still no sign of the military or the Plurbs.

"Sure. I'll take anything. Just hurry."

The boy strutted to the kitchen. Greyson followed, eyeing the caked dishes, molded chunks of leftovers, and greasy pizza boxes. There was some crust left in one box that didn't look too bad. Suddenly his stomach felt painfully deflated. Before he could make a move for the crust, Mullet handed him a glass and motioned for the sink.

"Pa'd beat ya brain-dead if ya jacked his beer."

"Water's great. Thank you!" Hands shaking, Greyson filled the glass at the tap and drank it greedily. He instantly felt better, a wave of clarity clearing his head.

"Slow down, Gulpy," the boy joked. "It a'int goin' nowhere."

Greyson took a few more gulps despite the look Mullet gave him.

"Your militia still do their fancy mark, huh?"

Breathing hard from the excessive drinking, Greyson set down the glass. "Yeah. You don't got a Plurb mark."

The boy stared at him with narrowed eyes. "Ya's still call it Pluribus? Ain't no'un calls it Pluribus anymore. Name's gittin' heat."

Greyson shrugged and glanced around, trying not to wince from the pain in his shoulder and hip. "Thanks for the water – and for taking me in. But we got to go – now."

"You're all kinds of crazy – acting all polite one second n'telling me what to do the next. You want to get kill't on the street, that's your choice. This is my home. I'll defend it 'til I die."

Greyson's eyes bounced around the room, thinking of what to do. The longer he stayed, the more likely it was that the Mullet's death wish would

231

come true. He had to go.

But then they heard it. Like a child's fireworks, popping outside. He recognized the sound of gunfire instantly. Greyson quick-limped to the front window, pulled back the drapes an inch, and drew back with shock.

A truck full of Plurbs – or militia – or whatever they were called – raced by. Another one followed.

"I need to hide!"

The boy opened the drapes and then gave him a look. "This place is as good as any 'nother. Pa and his buddies will be back an'..."

"You don't understand! They're all after me! All of them!"

But it was too late. A sound came from the glass doors.

# Chapter 43

The sound came again, but this time Greyson recognized it. It was the scrape of a dog's paw.

He rushed to the glass doors, pulled them open, and knelt to Kit's level.

"Kit!" To his surprise, Kit held his red hat in his jaws. Greyson was speechless.

But when Kit dropped the hat at Greyson's feet and held his paw in the air, Greyson gasped. "Geez, Kit!" His leg was covered in dark blood.

Kit licked at Greyson as he reached for the paw, examining the leg. Mullet eyed the dog over Greyson's shoulder.

"I'll git some wrappings."

Greyson turned back and they shared a look. "Thank you."

Mullet nodded and sped through the living room to a narrow hall that led to the bathroom. Greyson put his hat on and stayed by Kit, holding the paw and petting his shaking body. The wound was a pretty nasty gash and it was still dripping on the linoleum. Greyson's own leg wound had already begun to dry, but not before the streak of blood had reached his sock.

As Greyson poked at the fur around the wound, Kit nipped at Greyson's hand. But he stopped his nipping with a sudden jerk, and his ears perking up.

Greyson followed suit. He sensed movement outside the glass doors. Someone else was coming.

Thinking fast, he motioned Kit to the kitchen and hid him behind the counter with the 'stay' hand command. Kit obeyed, and his gaze followed Greyson expectantly for the next command as he scurried to the kitchen window.

Greyson tried to calm himself. *Sapere Aude. Nothing stupid, Greyson.*

His fingers found the edge of the greyed drapes and pulled it just an inch.

A single soldier, the same one who had confronted him on the train. But he was badly injured, hunched over and dragging one leg. His rifle was slung over his shoulder, swinging like a pendulum with each of his steps. He approached the Bradley and swept his eyes over it, checking its condition.

A moment later, tires squealed out front.

Greyson dropped the drapes and swung around.

*Plurbs.*

He was surrounded.

------------

Sam inserted his keycard and pulled the hotel door open. With an extended sigh, he threw off his suit jacket and dress shoes and plopped himself on the fresh sheets.

*Alone at last.*

The event had been an enormous fundraiser dinner. Fancy food, fancy chandeliers, fancy everything. He had been forced to smile pretty much the entire time, and even though he'd had to go to the bathroom, his bodyguards hadn't let him. It would have offended everyone if he had left during one speech or another. It would have offended others if he hadn't laughed at their jokes or shaken the hands of hundreds of people he didn't know. At least they hadn't made him stay for the after party.

Suddenly remembering his last lesson with Calvin, he took out his laptop and opened to the program that would allow him to eavesdrop on Calvin's screen.

A little nighttime entertainment. If it would work.

After only a few seconds loading time with code scrolling across his screen, the window opened. It was another screen. Sam laughed at Calvin's computer desktop which had a background picture of a mother Husky pawing one of her puppies with a caption underneath saying, "You're not fat. You're just a little husky."

Sam moved his mouse around and, to his joy, found that his mouse was now acting as Calvin's mouse. Could Calvin see it move? Sam did spirals and made the cursor pick the dogs' noses – but there was no response. Calvin must not be around his computer.

Deciding to take it a step further, he clicked on a word-processing document and typed in a message.

I'm here. Whatcha doing?

He gave it a minute, but again there was no response. Shrugging, he bit his lip and maneuvered the mouse to the icon for the webcam. Remembering that Calvin mentioned he might be with his girlfriend tonight, Sam crossed his fingers and clicked.

The camera popped to life, and the inside of Calvin's room came into focus. Trying to make sense of it, Sam figured there was a piece of clothing covering most of the camera, but not all. He could see half of a frame and make out Calvin's bed, art pieces on the wall, and someone sitting on a chair.

And then he realized it was Calvin. He leaned in and gasped. He was tied to the chair. Something covered his mouth. And someone else was in the room.

Panic swelled inside his chest, but as fast as it came, Sam forced it away.

*It's a joke! Of course!* Calvin knew that he would be peeking in. This was a pretty cruel set-up. He would have to let him have it the next time he saw –

The other man stepped up to Calvin and put a gun to his chest. The shots were muffled, but Sam watched in shock as his body shook with the blasts. Calvin's head slumped down and a dark, red stain formed where the gun had been.

Sam's lungs had stopped working. And then it all came out at once in panicked breaths. *This can't be happening. It can't!*

His eyes shot around the room, hoping Calvin would jump out, but no one came. He glanced back at the video to see a blurred figure walking to and fro in the room. It was a bulking figure – male, wearing gloves. He checked under the bed, in the dresser, throwing drawers around.

And then he turned and saw Calvin's computer. The man rushed toward the camera and peered at it, within inches of the screen.

Suddenly, the mouse cursor on Sam's laptop moved and the word-processing document reappeared. The letters appeared as the man typed.

Who is here?

Sam pounded a few buttons to close the programs and slammed the laptop shut.

-------------------

Greyson dropped to his hands and knees and skidded through a pile of beers cans behind the recliner just before the front door burst open; three armed men kicked open the door, watching their backs and shutting the broken door like they were shutting out a pursuing animal.

"Frick!" one of the men cursed. "How'd they get here so fast? Cael! Get your..."

235

"I'm here!" Cael came rushing into the room.

"We gots to go – now!"

"I'm not goin' nowhere. Where's my pa?"

Greyson gingerly lowered himself to the carpet, careful to avoid the beer cans. Once low enough, he peeked underneath the recliner at the men's feet; he could just make out a faint reflection on the dark TV screen as a man's figure approached Cael and stood square with him, putting his hands on the boy's shoulders. There was a period of silence when only faint gunshots and the crackling of fire could be heard. Greyson glanced at Kit, who stared at him from around the kitchen corner, out of the men's view. He gave him another 'stay' motion just in case.

"Your pa's a hero," the man spoke softly. "A frickin' hero. But he's not comin' back."

"He's a martyr," another one added. "Should be proud."

Cael shook his head. "No, he's not. Don't tell me lies."

Greyson watched the boy's reflection. His jaw was firm, and his knuckles clenched on his shorts. He knew the signs. Cael was fighting the emotion. Fighting hard.

"They're here!" one of the men's walkie talkies erupted. "Juniper and Oak!"

"Frick!" The man released Cael's shoulders with a push. "He is now. And now you best act like one, too. Got yer gun?"

Cael nodded.

"We's lookin' for a boy. Or judgin' from the wreck – a boy's body. About your age. Find'm before theys do."

Greyson gulped a lump in his throat. *Please, Cael. Don't do it.* His hand reached around his slingshot's grip and the other removed two ball bearings from the pouch.

Cael was struck silent. He glanced at the recliner. "What we want a boy for?"

"It don't matter. Them's the orders. Now come with us."

"Wait."

*No…*

The men stopped in the doorway and looked to Cael. His eyes went to the recliner.

*Don't! Don't do it!*

"I think I seen him out back."

"Out back?"

"Yeah."

"Then what we waitin' for? Truck's running outside, Cael. Go git in. Won't take us long."

The men jogged to the sliding glass door and Greyson breathed out a slow sigh of relief. He didn't know why, but Cael had saved him.

When he heard the sliding glass door open, he peeked over the armrest; Cael had stopped. He gave Greyson a sly look, still holding the bandages for the dog.

Greyson motioned Kit over as he watched the militiamen make their way into the backyard with guns raised. They were encircling the Bradley.

Cael knelt and bandaged Kit's leg.

"Why?" Greyson asked in a whisper.

The boy held his frown. "I like ya more than them. Ain't saying much, though."

Greyson paused, watching him wrap. "Thanks. I'll pay you back somehow."

"I don't want your money."

"What do you want?"

He stared at Greyson, his hands still wrapping. "Nothin', no more – now that he's dead." He tore the tape and secured it. "I'm free now."

Greyson eyed the bandages. It was well done, and Kit seemed pleased as well. He didn't quite know how to respond to Cael, so he shrugged it off. "Thanks again."

Shouts erupted outside and they both jerked their necks toward the noise. Gunshots banged in the backyard, and bullets ricocheted off the Bradley's armor with firefly sparks. The light from the house reflected off the four-foot-high treads as they began to churn, tearing up the grass and dirt.

The injured soldier had managed to start the thing.

Cael jumped to action first, racing toward the backyard.

"Wait!" Greyson yelled.

Cael stopped and turned.

"Come with me."

Cael shook his head. "When everybody's tryin' to kill ya? I ain't stupid. You're on your own, pretty boy."

With that, Cael darted into the backyard with his shotgun drawn. Greyson took in a deep breath and darted the other way – toward the running truck. He had bounded all the way to the curb when he suddenly remembered he had left without his backpack. He looked back at Cael's front door. It was inside.

He had to get it. Everything he had was in it.

But headlights flashed on the house's siding, bouncing hard as if the vehicles were traveling at high speeds.

*Leave it!* Greyson ducked behind the running truck just as two trucks came flying around the corner from his left, squealing and honking. Another two approached further down the street to the right, full of ragtag men, armed and angry.

*Two left. Two right.*

A few of the neighbors who had wandered outside to view the mayhem panicked and ran back inside, slamming and locking the doors. Lights behind windows went out.

Desperate, Greyson fought with himself, opening the passenger door of the running truck, but deciding against it. He'd never make it that way. He'd have to cut through the alleys and yards to escape – like Dan had done in Meyer's Crossing.

But he never got the chance to run.

He heard the trucks on the left squeal to a stop two houses down. He heard the men's shouts and the click of guns. Somehow, they spotted him.

"There he is!"

He knew the next thing he'd hear would be the shots, but they never came. Instead, he heard Kit's low growl. But Kit wasn't growling at the men – his nose was pointed toward the sky, his lips drawn back in a snarl.

Greyson had seen that look before.

It was a drone.

# Chapter 44

Greyson followed Kit's gaze, squinting at the tiny fire in the sky. But before he could cover his ears, a screaming sound came from heaven.

Eeeeeeeeee*EEEEEOOOOOOO!*

And then he heard nothing, like his ears were jammed with tuning forks ringing in a soprano's note. Like a strike of lightning, the drone's missile had hit the second truck on the left, disintegrating it from within and blasting shrapnel outward with a thunderous explosion that rippled and burst the block's windows as it ripped the other truck into the air, men and all. Greyson was swallowed by the shockwave and flung into Cael's yard as the burning men were tossed like dolls, crashing to the asphalt and skidding in all directions.

Greyson came to rest with a flop. The grass poked as his face. His lips pressed against the soft blades as he sucked in smoky air.

Again, the ringing. Again, the disorientation.

He lay in the grass and squeezed the earth as the world churned behind his eyes. He coughed and rolled to his stomach as debris rained down around him, heat still fresh against his skin and the explosion's cloud flowing upward like a black fountain.

Rubbing at his ears, he worked away the ringing and fought against the swirling haze in his head. He looked for the militiamen, still afraid. But they were gone. The portion of street where they had been was now a cobbled crater.

Finally getting his senses back, he pushed himself up and staggered aimlessly toward Cael's neighbor's house even as debris continued to rain onto the grass and roofs. Kit was still limping behind him – he'd almost forgotten about him.

The other two Plurb trucks at an intersection down the street unloaded quickly – the militiamen suddenly afraid to be close to the vehicles. Greyson glimpsed Humpy in one of the driver seats as he drove off, disappearing around the corner.

And just when he thought the worst was over, the rumble of engines grew louder until a camouflaged Humvee parted the smoke, weaving around debris by the crater. Another followed it and several soldiers jumped out, guns raised, staying clear of the fiery crater. One soldier spotted the Plurbs on the other end of the street. Angry shouts followed. One of the leaders motioned the soldiers to cover and another typed at a keyboard attached to his wrist. Suddenly, two disc-shaped drones zipped overhead, swerving over the roofs as if surfing on air.

Greyson stalled in the alley between houses, watching the two opposing sides take up positions. It was surreal. Was it really about to happen? Could he stop it? He wanted to yell, to break up the fight, to warn them both, but he didn't. He was too late.

The shots rang out, one and then two more – then a furious volley like he had never heard before. One of the drones crashed to a lawn, its rotors still churning like a tipped lawn mower.

Covering his ears, Greyson staggered between Cael's house and his neighbor's. Looking back, he saw another group of men, flowing through the backyards of the street across, dressed in hunter's camouflage. One was celebrating the drone kill.

*Definitely more militia.* A few he recognized. These were Meyer's Crossing's. They'd chased him all the way here, and they were just joining the fight.

*This is crazy! Too crazy!* His mind swirled, lost in panic. He had to hide, somewhere, get out of the sudden warzone.

But before he could move from the alley, the ground shook beneath Greyson's feet, and the shards of glass in the street clattered and clanged together. Greyson looked right and left, but it felt like the sound was coming from all sides, like a roller coaster pulling up its first peak.

And then he heard Kit whimper. Not wanting to look, Greyson turned and followed Kit's nose toward Cael's backyard. There was a scream, an eruption of gunfire, and a blast from a larger gun. A man's body flew across the alley, crashing through a wooden fence. And then the whole fence toppled, cracking and splintering. As soon as the treads came into view, Greyson's heart plummeted to his feet.

The Bradley Fight Vehicle churned the dirt as it entered the alley; its turret turned toward him.

*RUN!*

------------------

Silence enveloped him, but Sam didn't feel alone. It felt like Calvin's killer was with him. Watching him.

But the worst thing was, Sam had recognized him.

The man had been at a different fundraiser, part of the event's security team. Sam could remember walking past him on the way to the bathroom. He'd had a security badge with *StoneWater* etched on it, but he couldn't remember the name on his tag.

*Why had he killed Calvin?*

Suddenly he snapped to his senses and ran to the door. He had to tell someone.

"Help!" he yelled into the hallway.

The guard down the hall raced to him, hand on his holster. "What? What is it?"

"He shot him! Someone killed my friend!"

---------------

Greyson darted to the right and dove through the neighbor's side window just as the Bradley opened fire.

*DOOOOOT-DOOOOOT-DOOOOOT!*

Kit followed just behind, landing on Greyson's back and collapsing with a whimper. Once the Bradley rolled past, Greyson gingerly picked himself off the floor, grimacing as the glass tore at his forearms. Once he had managed to kneel, he pulled Kit close and peeked out the window.

The Bradley flew through the alley, as fast as a car, shooting its gun liberally at hostile targets.

*DOOOOOT-DOOOOOT-DOOOOOT!*

Each bullet took chunks out of the ground, a house, or a man. Whatever was targeted was shredded to pulp. The militiamen across the street dispersed, and those lucky enough to survive the first barrage took refuge inside houses. The Bradley darted down the street shooting left and then right, taking bullets like nothing, stopping on a dime and reversing just as fast.

Suddenly another Pluribus truck swerved around the corner and a few of the men in the back caught sight of the Bradley as its turret swiveled toward them. A few of them stumbled out, and the driver started to drive off before they were all out safely.

*DOOOOOT-DOOOOOT-DOOOOOT!*

Bodies flung to the curb, helpless to do anything. The bullets tore the back end off the truck as it ran over a fire hydrant, sending water blasting into its

241

undercarriage and spewing into the street.

Sensing it had a deathblow to deal, a mechanical whirring sound accompanied the box-like missile launcher that lowered from the side of the Bradley's turret.

Greyson wanted to scream. *Get out! Get out!*

The driver fell from the open door, slipping on the hydrant's gushing water.

The missile launched with a fantastic whoosh of smoke and fire. Greyson winced. Almost instantaneously, a great thunderclap shook the block and the vehicle blew sky high, smashing against a front porch with a roar of fire.

Seemingly wanting more, two more militiamen opened fire from the second floor across the street. The remaining drone swerved in their direction and the soldiers returned fire, peppering the outside of the house with bullet-holes. The Bradley's turret was already turning that way.

Greyson ducked back inside. He'd seen enough. It was a massacre. And somehow it was real. War. Actual war. It scared the wits out of him.

Then he heard soldiers' shouts and the crackle of radios toward the front of the house, out of view. Humvee engines passed by. Maybe they were leaving. Maybe. He had to check.

But when he did, he saw them – two soldiers with their backs to a Humvee, watching the flanks. They had been looking directly at his window.

*Frick!*

He ducked.

------------

The soldier kept his eye on the dark window and tapped the bulletproof glass band that extended from his helmet to his right eye. The tactical reticle displayed the information he needed in a firefight right before his eye – like a transparent computer screen. He could see the drones' targeting cameras, his text objectives, and all of the friendlies' tracker positions spread about on a map layout of the town.

"Rewind ten seconds."

The soldier's tactical reticle rewound his own sight-video.

"Stop. Analyze." A green box zoomed in on the boy's face. It only took a second to process. The box's color turned from green to red and the text gave him all the information he needed to know.

The boy was a high-value target and wanted dead.

242

His conscience prickled, but the orders were clear.

He turned to the other soldier. "The boy's a hostile. On me."

----------------

Greyson peeked out the window. They were coming straight for him!

"Kit, come!"

Greyson jumped to his feet and zipped to the hallway, but shapes ran by the side window. Startled, he jolted back just as two soldiers crashed through the front door.

"U.S. Marines! Surrender!"

Greyson glanced back as he sprinted into the kitchen but dug to a stop as soon as his feet hit tile. He froze in place, startled and in awe – a Bradley had fallen through the second floor, crushing the kitchen table before nestling at a jagged angle. The countertops lay in pieces about the room, and water sprayed from underneath the sink, cascading off its brilliant armor.

Brushing the surprise off, he realized it had blocked the back doors, trapping them inside. But before he could panic, Kit was way ahead of him, crawling underneath the mechanical beast.

"Go, boy!"

Greyson slid through the watery tile and followed Kit, crawling underneath the tipping treads. The metal creaked and groaned above him, its weight playing with gravity, begging to crush him.

But he made it through just as the soldier's gloved hands reached in after him. He jerked his shoe away and bound to his feet.

Breathing heavy, he surveyed the new set of dark halls in the back of the house. A stairway rose to the second floor and a backdoor showed an unlit patio. He thought of sneaking away, but he spotted a motion-sensing light just under the awning.

Heavy footsteps. Radio crackle.

The soldiers had found a way around. Flashlights were also bouncing outside. The only way out was up, and he had an idea.

He motioned for Kit to be quiet, jerked open the backdoor, triggered the motion light with a well-placed ball bearing, and padded stealthily up the stairs, leaving the back door wide open. As quiet as possible, they made their way up the stairs where the cargo container had pierced the roof before dumping the Bradley into the kitchen. Just beyond the container, a man huddled with his

243

wife and children in the bathtub, wearing their pajamas.

"Shh!" Greyson whispered to them with his finger to his lips as he tiptoed up the last step.

The soldiers' voices came from below as they spotted the back door. "Through here!"

*They took the bait.*

The soldiers had just stepped outside when the smallest child waved at Kit. "Doggy!"

Greyson cursed under his breath. The soldiers halted on the patio and turned quickly. Their flashlights lit the bottom of the staircase.

Changing plans, Greyson put his back to the landing's wall and motioned Kit to a spot at the top of the stairs. "Play dead," he whispered. Kit obediently rolled to his side and lay still with the more realistic death they had practiced. A moment later the soldiers bounded up, their equipment rattling on their backs. They were heavy. That would be their downfall.

Greyson locked eyes with Kit – and waited. The soldiers approached. He could hear their breaths.

"Is it dead?" one of them asked.

"Just leave it…"

Greyson held up his hand to Kit, and just as the front soldier hit the last step, he gave Kit the talking motion.

In a dark, confined place, a dog's bark can be a frightening weapon.

*RrrUUUUUFFF!*

The soldier visibly jerked and yelped at the top of the stairs, stiffening his back and holding his weapon in front of him just as Greyson shouted, "Sic 'em!" and rounded the corner. Dog and boy pushed with all their might.

The soldier wavered at the top, lashed out, grabbing for something, but came up with nothing as he toppled backward into his friend. Their bodies tangled as they fell stair after stair.

Not waiting to watch, Greyson jolted back into escape mode.

Using the back end of the Bradley as a foothold, he grabbed the empty container's lip and pulled himself inside. Making sure Kit followed, he caught the voice of the pursuing soldier, talking into his radio. "High-value target on the run. Back-up at my position!"

Greyson eyed his escape. The container served as a ramp upward through the roof, hanging out the side of the house. It was just close enough to the neighboring roof for an escape – he hoped.

"We gotta jump!"

Kit whimpered and circled in the slippery container, holding his bandaged leg in the air. His leg was too weak.

"Come on, boy!"

The soldiers rattled up the stairs.

Greyson couldn't wait any longer. "Follow me!" He burst up the metal ramp as Kit surprised the pursuing soldier coming from behind.

*Clang-clang-clang-clang-CLANG!*

Greyson leapt over the alleyway between the houses and pounded onto the neighbor's shingles. Gaining his balance, he turned for Kit.

But he wasn't there.

In his place was the soldier, gearing for the jump.

*Clang-clang-clang-clang-CLANG!*

With a snap, Greyson's ball-bearing struck him just before he leapt, throwing him off. The soldier awkwardly flew toward the shingles but came up short. He hit the sidewall hard and collapsed to the alley below.

Greyson only had time to let out a guilty sigh before another soldier pulled himself into the container; he drew his rifle.

Greyson bolted across the roof and slid down the opposite side as the bullets rang out behind him. Finally, with the crest of the roof at his back he took a frantic moment to breathe – to think of his next step – but his mind was hijacked by one thought. Kit.

*He'll make it out. He will. He has to.*

*But will I? How?*

His breathing slowed as his eyes opened to the world around his rooftop vantage point. Suddenly the entire battle was in his periphery, the lights and sounds producing a haunting show. Fires pockmarked the black night, the gunfire ringing like fireworks. An attack helicopter's guns flashed red with yellow tracer fire, bolting into the mountains like surges of electricity on wire. Soldiers weaved through the broken train like a playground. The winged-drone zipped overhead, taking spirals of smoke with it through the air. A transport copter hovered, blowing the grass into a perfect circle as soldiers roped to its center. And amongst it all, Bradleys danced between alleys and roads, with white headlights for eyes, fishing for men.

War was frightening and beautiful at the same time.

--------------

Sydney and Jarryd gaped in amazement. The show was spectacular. Though they had been frantically looking for Avery, they had arrived just in time for the Aqua Theater's performance.

Soaring orchestra music and resounding drums thumped the air with the National Anthem, all as red, white, and blue lights swirled in the pools and on the giant projector screens. Images of firemen, soldiers, and Red Cross workers made a patriotic collage, paying homage to the heroes of the August attacks.

Though Sydney was still scouring the standing crowd for any signs of Avery or her pursuers, Jarryd covered his heart with his hand and sung along with sparkling eyes.

"...and the rockets red glaaaaaa-re..."

Fireworks blasted overheard, shooting reds and whites and blues in beautiful circles behind the massive ship, sending the flashes onto the heads of the "ooo"ing and "awe"ing spectators.

Sydney and Jarryd were looking up, watching the display just at the right time. Streaking across the night sky was a girl, churning her legs as if running in mid-air.

"What...?"

"It's her," Sydney said, disappointed.

Sure enough, Avery zipped across the gap above, holding tightly to the zip-line's handlebars.

Jarryd was lost in admiration. "Wallaby darned. Isn't she awesome?"

The spectators seemed to agree as the fireworks finished with a bang.

--------------

Greyson watched the battle like a movie happening all around him. He was in awe and terrified at the same time. He had to give up. This was beyond him. He couldn't run from this.

And what came next only confirmed his surrender.

A haunting, disc-shaped drone rose from behind the house with a sickening mechanical hum. It was larger than the other drones, sleek and shiny. It rose slowly, straight up, until it was eye level with Greyson, two little red dots gleaming through a tinted black ring circling its perimeter. It was watching him, and a thick gun hung from its underside, pointed at his chest.

Already frozen, Greyson stared at it in horror. There was nothing he could do. He was dead.

"Greyson!"

He jerked.

"Here!"

It was a man's voice from below. He followed the sound but couldn't see anything. Until someone waved. It was a figure in all black, hidden in the night's shadows behind a shed, half destroyed by the train. The figure had no face – only a mask with glowing green lenses for eyes.

And then, faster than Greyson could react, the drone swiveled and fired its gun. The sound and muzzle flash popped like a firecracker, Greyson gritted his teeth, but it hadn't been aimed at him. Another drone that had risen behind Greyson burst apart like plastic struck with a hammer. Its remains bounced down the roof to the grass below.

Greyson didn't know how to react – so he didn't. He couldn't anymore.

The disc drone, his savior, suddenly buzzed away, over the black figure's head.

"Hurry!" the figure yelled at Greyson.

When the Bradley began unleashing its fury on the house, he didn't need to be asked twice.

*DOOOOOT-DOOOOOT-DOOOOOT-DOOOOOT!*

Holes ripped into the roof as he ran. Suddenly the shingles wavered under his weight, and Greyson fell through, falling to a bed below. Regaining his senses and rolling to the side, he darted down the hall and flew down the stairs as the house was devoured around him. Wood and plaster sprayed his body; flashes from the Bradley's gun filtered in through the holes, lighting the inside with polka dots.

But Greyson ran on. Stairs. Turn. Hall. Fall. Get up. Kitchen. Dining room. Hole in the wall. Dive. Backyard. Man in black. Run.

The man in black grabbed him and tagged him with an infrared locator, explaining that it'd keep the drones off him. Another man in black joined them. They zigged and zagged through wrecked train cars. Their guns shot in short bursts. Soldiers fell. A sniper covered them from the hills, knocking men down as if God had reached out to stop their hearts. Trees. Four-wheelers! He hopped on.

"Hold on!"

They bumped along, further and further from the gunfire and chaos, skidding around trees and making rough paths, but he was numb. The safety only made him feel worse. He didn't feel the pain anymore. He wasn't even scared. Wasn't relieved. Maybe he was in shock. Or maybe he was just too wired to feel anything. Except for one thing. Despite the Georgia heat, he felt cold – as if the soldier's back was air-conditioned.

"It's cold. Your back," Greyson muttered.

The soldier hollered back gruffly. "Confuses heat sensors."

Greyson's numb mind scattered for a meaning but suddenly latched like an anchor on one thought.

"Kit! Do you have him? My dog?"

Silence. Their three four-wheelers swerved through the trees.

"My dog! We have to go back!"

Silence.

There was only one thing he could do to make them stop.

"I'll get off this thing. I'll – I'll jump! Watch me – I'll – I'll do it." He pushed at the man's back and began to squirm.

The goggled man driving for Greyson shook his head and cursed. "Forge, go back and see about the dog!"

One of the other masked drivers, Forge, turned and gave them a long look between passing trees. Greyson stared at him.

"Ah heck, why not?" Forge veered away, bouncing through the woods.

Greyson hugged his driver's cold back a little tighter and closed his eyes. The ringing in his ears still sung, like Kit's whimper on replay. Even with the rushing wind, it was always there. He could hear him crying.

# Chapter 45

Avery ran and ran, finally tiring of the chase. She slid down the stair railing, burst toward a hall where a pair of couches looked out to sea, and hid. After a few tense moments, her last pursuers bounded past. She gave it another few seconds until she felt safe enough to emerge. When she did, her friends were just across the hall.

"Hold on!" Sydney shouted, running up to her and grabbing her arm.

"What? Why?" Avery shook free and frantically scanned for pursuers. "We're almost there; let's go!"

"No, change of plan," Sydney commanded. "Give me the watch."

"Why? I got it. Joey, what's going on?"

Jarryd shrugged, and Nick stepped in before she could say anything. "We've got to give it back. Say it was for fun."

Avery grasped the watch tightly, but it suddenly buzzed. She held it up as another message lit the screen.

Enraptured by the watch's sudden life, the kids scrambled around her to read the message.

"Militia attack
on military in GA.
Anticipate highest security.
Plan still a go."

"Wow," Jarryd exclaimed.

The others nodded their heads in agreement.

"The screen is so bright! You could use it as a flashlight if you were stuck in a cave."

The others shook their heads.

Before Avery could retain her grasp, Nick took the watch from her and waved it at them. "You know what this means?"

Jarryd cocked his head at his brother's waving hand. "Hello?"

Nick sighed. "No, moron. It means we were right that this is a Plurb watch; but now they know who took it. We're in a huge mess."

"Wait, what?" Avery exclaimed. "A *Plurb* watch?" Her eyes wondered into the past, her face a picture of confusion. "There are Plurbs on the ship?"

Jarryd nodded. "Yup."

"You really *have* been hiding things. What else don't I know?"

"My real name's Jarryd."

Her concern turned to fascination. "Jarryd, huh? I like it. It fits you."

"So do you."

Avery blushed, and Nick rolled his eyes. "No time to explain everything now," Nick said, already heading for the stairs. "But they will catch us eventually, so our only hope is to turn ourselves in. We've got to apologize and act like we were playing a prank. Like we never knew a thing. You know? Play dumb."

Sydney smirked at Avery. *Shouldn't be hard for her*, she thought.

------------------

President Foster lowered his signature brown glasses from his nose so that he could rub his eyes. He let out an audible sigh meant more to signal his frustration than anything else. It was late for a sixty-six-year-old man with bright grey hair and bad knees. And to be interrupted because of yet another terrorist attack irked him as much as it enraged him.

Both the President and Governor Reckhemmer had attended the fundraiser dinner's after-party when the secret service had whispered in the President's ear, and, to the Governor's surprise, the President had requested his company on the drive to the Situation Room. And no one said no to President Foster.

"I have many voices in my ear as you know, Joshua," Foster said, still rubbing his eyes inside the luxurious interior of the Presidential SUV. "Some urge patience while others call for severe action on these Pluribus fools. You have been one of the loudest voices calling for more robust action."

Foster pushed his glasses back into place and looked him straight in the eye. "You have my ear. After all, you'll inherit this mess of mine come a year, if all goes as planned."

The Governor nodded, trying not to show too much enthusiasm. He *did* want to inherit his mess – with a fiery passion. He wanted to fix it. He lived to get his hands inside of problems and fix them. And the country had a deep problem. But he didn't say anything. He would let the President take the lead.

The President explained what he had been told. An attack on a military transport train in Georgia. Dozens of militia, soldiers, and citizens dead. A town on fire. Another nightmare that the President had promised to stop after the wave of attacks just months ago.

When the President had finished, he took a sip of his drink and leaned his head against the headrest with eyes closed. "So, how would you react if you were me?"

The Governor gathered his thoughts, watching the D.C. traffic out the window. He knew what he wanted to say, but he also knew what he had to say. "We've had enough patience, Mr. President."

"Is that so?" The President's eyes registered no surprise.

"Yes, Mr. President. American soldiers have been killed on our own soil. They rightfully responded with just self-defense. Our immediate reaction should be one of utmost sorrow for the victims, but it should be followed with swift and complete justice along with a resolve to do everything in our power to see that it never happens again."

"The Vigilant Shepherd Act?"

"Absolutely. It's time. Label Pluribus a terrorist organization and root this cancer out before it spreads."

President Foster sighed. "I want Pluribus gone more than anyone, but this attack was perpetrated by a Georgia militia, one not going by the name Pluribus. This is more than Pluribus – and it could be said that we have pushed our security measures too hard, too fast, driving people to this violence. And to then double-down could only make it worse."

"When fighting cancer, you take it out where you see it. No good doctor waits to see if it will go away on its own if we spare the scalpel."

Foster peered out the window and didn't lose a beat. "But a good doctor uses a scalpel – not an axe."

Reckhemmer had to agree. Inside, he knew it to be true. "I understand. By enacting even more security measures, we'll be playing into their hand. They'll keep pumping this ARC nonsense, feeding their followers paranoia."

"That's right," Foster said, eying the streets. "The people's fear is growing, but it's fear of the government just as much as it is of terrorism. It's real, and no longer just the most radical of the radical. When we regulated assault weapons, fought religious bigotry, a small minority felt attacked. If the VSA passes, Americans will see thousands of government agents breaking down doors, extinguishing bank accounts, and playing the very part of an oppressive government that Pluribus wants them to."

"If the Cancer points out the sharp scalpel to the patient…"

251

Foster chuckled. "So, what are you suggesting? We hide the scalpel?"

"Yes," Reckhemmer said bluntly. "If video gets out showing the amount of military hardware you're moving to the country's interior for example..."

President Foster's brow was frozen in a perplexing fold. Joshua ignored it, going on.

"So, we do what the good doctor does. Convince the patient that the scalpel is necessary. Remind the people that America is beautiful, her soldiers are heroes, and the militias and the Plurbs are those that are to be hated. Not us. Make the secessionists and the terrorists out to be the same and then isolate them both. Win the war for our country's hearts and minds."

"Ah, propaganda."

"It's convincing the patient. Make sure the information coming out of Meyer's Crossing is in our favor. Use the media, buy bloggers, CEOs. And *then*, quietly, with no fanfare, discredit every Plurb you can." A spurt of anger sneaked through his restraint. "Find a reason to arrest them. Humiliate them. Pass the VSA in small, less noticeable portions if needed. If anybody in the press wants to make it public, they'll look like they're one of them." He stiffened his lips. "You swore to protect this nation as its Commander in Chief; there's no reason you can't do it in the dark."

Taking another sip of his drink, President Foster let out a satisfied sigh and licked his lips. "You're sly, Joshua. More devious than I imagined."

"I will do what it takes to protect this country, Mr. President."

The SUV came to a guarded gate and passed through, pulling into the White House's back drive.

"Now, one last thing. Just a few minutes before I was informed about the attack, I received another call. They informed me a soldier on that very train had caught a boy trying to sneak into one of the train cars. They confirmed that it was one of the child witnesses from the fair. And apparently a standing order had been given for his termination."

"Yes," the Governor answered solemnly, a plague of guilt threatening to betray his confident demeanor. "The Plurbs helped him to escape from FBI protection. An agent was shot in cold blood. He's been on the run since."

"I was unaware. I don't like being unaware."

"That was my failure to inform you. I've been supervising the case."

The President lowered his brow, bottling his annoyance. "You...knew of this order?"

The Governor nodded. "It's unfortunate."

Foster examined his eyes, searching for deceit, but sensing only regret. Finally, his stare relented. "Well, somehow he made it out. He was spotted after the wreck. What's worse, he had help. Paramilitaries. We don't know whose; we're still looking. It's getting messy."

Joshua nodded. "May I suggest StoneWater?"

"Fight paramilitaries with mercenaries?"

"*Security contractors*. They'll clean up messes, get dirty so our boys stay clean. To keep this country alive, we must rid it of its cancer, in whatever way possible."

A secret service agent knocked on the President's window, a reminder he was needed in the situation room. The nation was in another crisis that needed his attention. The President opened the door and took one last look at the governor. "One last thing. I know your reach is growing, Joshua, and I like you – but know your *boundaries*. This isn't your office yet." The President examined his face again, nodded, and shut the door.

---------------

"It was a computer program," Sam muttered, red-faced and annoyed. "He helped me write it, we installed it on the thumb drive, and then it implanted itself on his laptop when he put it in."

The secret-service agent stared at him. "And he wanted you to do this?"

Sam eyed the security monitors that provided the only light in the hotel's security room. "Yes. It was a lesson. He was teaching me. Because he's my *tutor*."

He knew it wouldn't help to be sassy, but they'd kept him in the security room for twenty minutes already; and, as far as he knew, they hadn't done anything to find the killer.

"Did he expect you to access his laptop tonight? Was there a time frame?"

"Kind of, yes. He said his girlfriend would be coming over after 10."

For the first time, the agent seemed interested. He scribbled furiously in his notepad and underlined it. "Do you know anything about this girlfriend of his?"

"No, but it wasn't her. I told you; it was a guy – a big guy with…"

"Did he mention anything to you that would lead you to think someone may try to kill him? Was he paranoid? Was he hiding anything?"

It struck Sam hard. The thumb drive. Not the one with the program virus on it, but the one he'd given him with the Pluribus documents. His mind reeled, thinking it through.

"What are you thinking?" the man inquired, noticing his face.

Sam grew restless. The room became stifling and small. The heat seemed to radiate from the security monitors. And the man's gaze bore a hole through him. He felt horrible about hiding anything from them. All they wanted was to help, and the fact that he could have led to the murder sent shivers down his back.

"When will my dad get back?"

"He's on his way." The man cleared his throat and leaned closer. "What was he hiding?"

He had to tell him. "My homework drive," he said at last. "It had the documents taken from the Pluribus headquarters in Des Moines – before the attack on the fair."

"The same ones you showed your father?"

This man already knew exactly what he wanted.

"Yes."

"Were there any other copies of these documents that you are aware of?"

The breath halted midway up Sam's throat. His conscience battled within him. He'd already given them what they needed. They didn't need to know about the copies.

*I don't trust anyone,* Calvin had said. *And I don't think you do either.*

He didn't know exactly why he didn't trust the man in front of him, but he didn't, and that's all that mattered. He put on his best politician face – even with a hint of a smile. "Those were my only copies. You guys said they weren't important. So why would someone kill…?"

"We'll need to make sure. Pat you down, double check your laptop. I'm sure you understand. It's not that we don't trust you – it's a matter of national security."

"I understand completely," Sam said with a smile, standing up and holding out his arms.

The agent smiled back, patted Sam down, pulled out his pockets, and made him take off his shoes. They only found a few quarters.

"Sorry about that. We'll get to the bottom of this, Sam. For now, we need you to stay in your room."

"Can I go now?"

"Sure. Just leave the laptop with us."

Sam left in a hurry, rushed to his room and removed the thumb drive from his underwear.

---------------

Sammy, Sydney, Avery, and the twins eyed the security monitors in the stuffy security room. They sat across from the youthful Captain Chip, Suk, and Baldy. Even their parents had joined them after Suk had tracked down enough chairs. Avery's parents were tall, tanned, and a little loopy. Sydney couldn't stand the smell of alcohol on their clothes.

Jarryd had been the first to share the story: "So we saw one of those awesome watches while we were at dinner and I was like 'I have to have that fine piece of bling', but the one guy – what was his name – Shis-Ka-Bob or something – he wouldn't let me even see it. Then we saw how many of the employees had one and we were like…interested or whatever. And I know you don't know us, but we like to pretend we're daring or whatever and do stupid things pretending we're all super ninjas on an adventure or something." He gave a dismissive laugh. "So, I followed Baldy…you, I mean…to your room one day, and we made a plan. I snuck in while the guy was cleaning, to look for your watch, and then you came in and scared me, so I hid. Then I went to grab your watch and we ran. True story."

"And we're very sorry," Nick added.

"Oh, yeah. Yes. Very." Jarryd nodded with enthusiasm.

Suk continued to ask questions, but the kids stuck to the story. Eventually he turned to Baldy and gave him a hard look. "Do you have any questions for them?"

Baldy's eyes glazed over each kid with a little fire, but when he glanced at the humiliated parents, they dimmed. A hint of compassion came over him. "I have my watch back. And you can assure me that you didn't mess with any of the settings or snoop at any of the messages?"

The kids all turned to each other with nods and shrugs. "No, sir. We didn't get a chance."

He laughed a little and leaned back.

Avery's dad took the break in conversation as an opportunity. "I would like to apologize personally for Avery's behav'ah in all this. It is unacceptable and she will be punished appropriately. And we owe you an apology, too. She is ah'r responsibility and we w'ah having a night out on ah'r own."

255

Jarryd gazed at Avery. She had her head down and her eyes closed.

Her dad took a small card from his shirt pocket. "Take this and let me know if th'ahs anything we c'ahn to do to repay you. But we would like to put this night behind us."

Baldy took a moment to respond, letting Avery's father hold the card outstretched over the middle of the table. Finally, he reached forward and snagged it with a smirk. "Thank you, Mr. Redmond. I'll keep that in mind."

Captain Chip rose from his chair abruptly. "If you'd please just give us one moment."

Baldy and Suk joined him in a corner of the room in hushed conversation.

"Are all of them here?" Captain Chip asked in a whisper. "No one would miss them?"

"This is all of their group," Suk said, re-examining the documents in his hand. "They wouldn't be missed."

"Can you do it discreetly? Dispose of the bodies?" Captain Chip glanced at the somber kids. Sydney was eyeing him. He gave her a reassuring smile.

"All of them?"

Chip gave Suk a condescending stare as if he were a student caught daydreaming. "You don't touch *him*. He's worth more than a hundred of you. None of the Redmonds."

Suk jutted his chin out and his hand rested near the gun at his hip. "The others won't be a problem."

"Then we must. Just to be sure. We're too close."

Baldy sighed, shaking his head. "But what if they *are* missed? What if someone is expecting contact from them and reports them missing?"

"Excuse me." The group turned to Avery's dad, who had risen from his seat, holding out his phone. "If you don't mind, I have an important meeting in a few minutes – a video conference."

Suk, Chip, and Baldy gave each other a long look. Their eyes spoke of a confirmation of their fears. It would be too risky to act so rashly, this close to the end goal.

Chip was the first to break through his apprehension. "Of *course*. Too bad for your vacation to be interrupted by work, though."

Mr. Redmond laughed. "The world's too small to get f'ah enough away."

"True, true. You all must have things to get to – a vacation to enjoy." Assured of their change in plan, Baldy stepped forward. "I accept your apology."

The parents were the first to shake hands with him, followed by the kids. They exchanged pleasantries and parted ways.

When the room was emptied of the guests, Baldy walked to a corner, turned on the watch, and pored over the settings. "Even if they had seen the messages before they self-deleted, they would mean nothing to them. It's just gibberish to a kid."

Chip sneered. "You better hope so."

"So should you. We're all in the same boat here."

They shared a nervous smile at the pun, but Chip broke it first. "Word of this does not leave this ship."

"The great CEO of Redmond Aerospace Defense can't even keep track of his own kid," Baldy complained.

"You'll get your chance to mention it to him." Chip glanced at his watch. "Ten hours until we port."

"And Daryl?"

"Eighteen." Chip scoffed to himself, thinking with a smirk. "Better keep the guests calm. Do nothing with the kids or their parents until Nassau. Then we kill them."

# Chapter 46

"Sam, you awake?"

Turning over on his bed, Sam squinted through the dark to the open door where his father peeked in. "Yeah," he said sleepily, pushing the covers off.

"No, no. Don't get up." The Governor slipped inside and turned on the hotel room's bathroom light so that he could make his way to Sam's bed. He pulled Sam's covers back over him.

"You doing okay?"

Sam nodded, rubbing his eyes and glancing at the clock. And then the memories he had gladly let slip away into sleep came rushing back. The man with the gun – shooting Calvin. The interrogation.

He shoved one hand under his pillow, clutching the thumb drive. "I guess. You?"

His father smiled and sat on the bed. "I've been better." He paused, and after a long sigh, placed a hand on Sam's shoulder. "There's been another attack, Sam."

Sam's eyes grew wide and searched his dad's face for clues to its severity. *Another nuclear bomb?*

"A radical militia derailed a military transport train in Georgia and then attacked the survivors. Soldiers from a nearby checkpoint came to their aid. They called in a drone strike. It was bloody, but they fought bravely."

"Did we win?"

His father swallowed hard, choking down his emotion, and squeezed Sam's hand. "We did. But at a cost. Civilians, too. It was in the middle of a town. But that didn't matter to the terrorists."

The hatred swelled in Sam's chest. He wanted to fight them, right in the bed if he had to. His cheeks swelled with heat. "Now what? What does it mean?"

"It means a lot of things. But it's Foster's problem to deal with. Not mine yet."

"But…what can we do?"

"We can do our part. Whatever Foster asks us to do."

Sam's eyes searched the dark room as he thought. "We have to wait? Why?" He sat up, rigid. "Why do we have to do what he tells us to do? Can't we do

258

something on our own? And with Calvin. I told them. I told them who did it. Can't we…"

"Hold on, buckaroo. I know, I know." The Governor pushed him slowly back to his pillow and scooted closer to him. "You know what? You and me. We're a lot alike. We look alike. We think alike."

Sam nodded, though his mind still raced.

"And we like to fix things. Make them work right, the way we want them to. The way they're supposed to."

The way his father gazed at the ceiling and then at the lamp, finding things to look at, reminded Sam of the day his father told him his mother had died. He had that same sad look on his face that wavered between a forced smile and genuine despair.

A memory clicked for the governor and he smiled. "You remember when we set up that elaborate, really cool domino chain?"

"Yeah."

"It started on your cabinet, down the drawers, under your bed, through the living room, across the piano keys, and ended in the bathroom?"

"In the toilet."

They laughed together. Sam still remembered the 'plunk' sound it made when the final domino dropped in.

"What'd you call it?"

"The domino dump."

They laughed again until the governor retreated into the memory. "But…you remember when we were almost done – and me, being clumsy, accidentally bumped one of the first ones? They all started toppling, one after another – just like they were supposed to – but too soon."

"Oh, yeah!"

He leaned in, a serious gleam in his eye. "But you remember what I did?"

Sam searched his memory but shook his head 'no.'

"I reached out and…" The governor reached into mid-air and pulled at an imaginary domino like it was his prize, "… *plucked* two dominoes from the chain, further down." He turned with them still in his hand. "And viola! The domino effect stopped at the gap. The crisis was averted, and we returned those that had gone off to their proper positions."

"Then we set it off when we were ready."

"Just the way they were supposed to." He took Sam's hand again and put his other hand on the side of his head. "Sometimes, Sam, we have to reach out

259

in life, and pluck things that are in the way. Even if they're good. Even if we knew they once had a great purpose, sometimes they become obstacles to a greater success. And if we have the privilege to see the big picture – the end goal – it is our duty to do what needs to be done. And sometimes, it just takes…" He reached out and plucked another imaginary domino. "Pluck."

Suddenly a wave blindsided Sam – a wave of understanding and nausea. The 'pluck' repeated itself in his mind, but in a new way. Something that had to be removed. An obstacle. What if it were a person? What if Calvin had been an obstacle?

"Calvin…" Sam whispered.

The Governor's eyes gave Sam his answer.

"Did you…?"

"No." The Governor said as if he were taking an oath. "But someone had to."

Sam couldn't believe it, and he couldn't breathe. He was scared – scared of his own father. He tried to wrap his mind around it – to make it seem like the right thing to do, but he couldn't see it. He knew Calvin. He was a good man. He didn't deserve to be 'plucked.' Couldn't there have been another way? Who had set off the chain, anyway? Whose fault was it that Calvin had to be…

"He had Pluribus files on his computer, Sam. Files with important government secrets that he intended to leak to the press. He was working with them – the terrorists."

Sam swallowed hard, and his hand, still under the covers, grasped hard at the black thumb drive. It had the same files that had gotten Calvin killed. The same ones that had made him out to be a traitor. *If I'm found with the same files – will I be plucked, too?*

The governor pinched Sam's chin. "But don't you feel guilty in any of this, okay? It's not your fault."

"He got the files from me."

"We know. But you didn't know they were bad. We told you they were harmless so as not to scare you. And as long as there are no more files, you're clear."

A spurt of anger vibrated on Sam's chin. It was an accusation – subtle, political. "They took my laptop. They searched me – patted me down. I don't have any more!"

His father read his anger. "I know, I know. Buddy, I know. But they were just doing their jobs. It's their job not to trust anyone."

"Like Calvin?"

The governor sighed with a slow blink for acknowledgment. Sam remembered what Calvin had said about trust. *Trust no one.*

"What were the secrets?"

The question hung in the air as his father blinked, examining Sam's eyes like he was trying to figure him out. He was the first to look away. "Sam...I love this country. You know that. So do you. It's exceptional in many ways, beautiful, free. But that freedom is not free. There's a steep cost to secure our freedom. And sometimes..." he sighed with regret, "...sometimes that cost is doing something that no one wants to do but has to be done. Something that looks really bad, but in the end, works for the good."

Sam stared at the American flag pin on his father's suit, thinking over the words. The words sounded familiar.

"But if everyone knew all those things that look bad, they wouldn't understand the bigger picture. They might want to rebel, like the terrorists. They would want to bite the hand that feeds them. Everyone has secrets, for whatever reason. But we keep secrets...for the good of our country and its people."

Sam turned over on the pillow and acted like he was about to sleep. Underneath the pillow, his fingers wrapped neatly around the thumb drive. "He was a *good person.*"

His dad stood up from the bed and walked to the door. He shut off the light. "They always seem that way."

# Chapter 47

Greyson's eyes were heavy – swollen with tears and tiredness. It hurt even to breathe, so he did so slowly, staring ahead at the brush. The train tracks he sat on cut through the woods and curved away to the east and the west, leaving him alone with his thoughts. On the other side of the trees, where columns of smoke still rose in the distance, the rising sun was finally cracking the darkness with orange and red light, but it only made Greyson more aware of how tired he was, and how alone.

*Kit.*

*Dead.*

His breath staggered, and he didn't have to mask his crying anymore. Another friend had left him. And he had left another friend to die.

Memories of Kit ran through his mind, making him cry even harder. The times he had saved him. The time spent cuddling in the cold. The time he pawed at the moon. His whimper. His soft fur and wet nose. His licks.

Suddenly angry, Greyson kicked at the gravel. He picked up a fistful and threw it. He gritted his teeth and unclipped his slingshot. He loaded it with a rock and pelted the nearest tree. He did it again and again, harder and harder. If he had a punching bag, he would have punched it over and over and over until his knuckles bled.

He drew back another rock but stopped. He held the band back, stretched to its max, his hand and arm shaking with the tension. But he didn't release. His eye had caught a cat slinking from the underbrush onto the railroad.

Sleek and white, it pawed silently along the gravel as graceful as a snake and oblivious to Greyson.

He twisted and put the cat between his crosshairs. He hated cats. He always had. Something about them – their selfish aloofness, their lack of obedience, their claws – just made them evil. And now, this one had come to mock him after his dog had died.

His shoulder ached with pain, sharper and sharper as he held the band. Sweat began to bead on his lip as the cat slinked in his direction twenty yards away. Now ten.

It stopped.

And he saw its collar. It belonged to someone.

Everything inside him wanted to take out his aggression on the cat, but something inside him had changed. The cat had an owner, somewhere, probably missing it as much as he missed Kit.

With a giant breath, he let the slingshot down, dropping the rock to the gravel. The cat meowed and walked up to him without any hesitation. Greyson tensed and put his hands up awkwardly as the cat pressed its flank against his knee and purred.

His eyes were wide as the last tears dripped away. Soon, his shy hands lowered, setting the slingshot down. Then, timidly, he put a hand on the cat's head and pet it down its back. It purred louder and arched its back into his hand as if it liked it.

A smile worked its way onto his face as the cat continued pressing him for more. *You'll need a new self,* John had said. *Well, this is a big first step.*

After a few more pets, he grasped the collar and took a look at its nametag.

"Pawl"

374 Damascus Avenue

Camden, GA

706-342-3532

"Pawl?" Greyson whispered, sniffing. The cat meowed, and Greyson picked it up. "You lived in Camden, huh?" His eyes glazed over, and he stared into the brush, remembering the panic there. Families had been sleeping, only to awaken to a train wreck and a battle in their neighborhood – and for some, inside their home. And Pawl had been one of them. Some little girl or boy could be missing him right now, like he was missing Kit.

And then the emotions came back to him again. He hugged Pawl close and laid his head on the cat's back, choking back the sobs. He had loved Kit. He needed him. He was his guardian angel. Angels weren't supposed to die.

He cried until his head hurt too much and then cried a little more. He was too tired to overcome them.

But soon Pawl squirmed, slithered from his arms, and slunk down the railroad toward another figure approaching from the east. Greyson looked up through blurry eyes.

The figure was dressed in all black, with a rifle slung over his shoulder. Though he was far away, Greyson could tell that he was carrying something.

263

The breath caught in his throat.

He wiped away his tears.

And like he was in slow motion, he stood up, shaking with fatigue and a rushing sensation surging in his veins.

"Kit?"

It started as curiosity, bloomed into hope and then burst into unquenchable joy. He surged forward at a sprint, scaring Pawl and shouting at the top of his lungs.

"KIT! KIT!"

Kit barked in reply, feeble, but unmistakably Kit.

Greyson ran until Kit was in his arms, but the man held him close. Kit's entire chest was wrapped in white gauze, but he was panting – alive.

"He's alive! He's ALIVE!"

He buried his face into Kit's fur and let him lick anywhere he wanted. He wanted to pet him everywhere at once, to love him as much as possible, but he could only do so much.

The soldier spoke with a slight Hispanic accent. "He's going to need more attention."

For the first time, Greyson acknowledged Kit's rescuer. The other soldier had referred to him as Forge. "What happened?" Greyson asked Forge. "Will he be okay?"

The man showed no emotion. The sweat had beaded on his brown skin, but the mask pulled over his wavy hair kept most of it from his piercing eyes. "They had left him there."

Greyson's energy dimmed for just a second as he thought about what could have happened to Kit. "Thank you, sir. So much. Thank you."

"I had a combat dog once. He was a great soldier…and friend." He squinted at Greyson. "Yours was brave. But I had to hurt more of our own. It's…it's not right – just not right at all."

Greyson let him pass on his way to the camp, taking in what he'd said. It *wasn't* right. It was hard to believe that their own would try to kill him, but they had. How could American soldiers be enemies? They were defenders of freedom around the globe, standing up for good when others couldn't. Greyson had looked up to them since he was young enough to stand.

But now they were trying to kill him. *Am I on the right side?*

Though it made him pause, he shook it off, catching up to Forge and Kit.

Before long they entered a clearing and met the bearded Grover, who seemed to Greyson to be in charge. Still dressed in full gear, he was putting away the cameras that had recorded Greyson's testimony.

After bandaging Greyson's wounds, it had been the first thing they'd had him do when they had reached the clearing on the four-wheelers. He'd been distracted, depressed, and bruised, but he had told his whole story, sparing nothing – even the stuff about betraying Sam and searching for his father. Grover had listened from behind the camera, stroking his beard with only a flicker in his eyes signaling his comprehension. The third soldier, the sniper, never said a word. He had only listened from afar, his long rifle stretched across his back like a sword.

"Forge found Kit!" Greyson shouted to Grover, too ecstatic to hide it.

Grover looked up and stared. And then he went back to work. Greyson wasn't affected by his lack of enthusiasm. He nearly danced around Forge as he laid Kit on the bed of a pickup truck and tended again to the bandages. And he couldn't help smiling – a goofy kind of smile that made the soldiers give him looks – but it wasn't all for Kit. He knew what was coming.

"When will they get here, sir?"

"Soon," Grover said brusquely.

"He said he'd fly me to the Bahamas."

Grover gave him a look and shook his head, intent on arranging the items in the back of a van with an American Renovation logo on its side. His tattooed arms bulged as he picked up a box of ammunition.

Still bouncing on his toes and petting Kit, Greyson kept the questions coming. "Sir, how'd he get his own plane? Is he rich?"

"No."

"Well, how'd he get it?"

"If I tell you, will you shut up?"

Scrunching his brow, Greyson drew back. "Sorry, sir. Just a question."

Grover turned to him and squared his broad shoulders. "He was our pilot. He earned it. And stop being so frickin' polite – calling me sir like some Nancy-boy."

Greyson froze at the callous words, but his stubbornness rose against the insult. "Sorry. Should I be rude?"

Grover turned back to his work. "Better than your sissy talk."

Thinking to himself, Greyson turned away, shrugged to himself, and then turned back. "So, tell me…was he your pilot in the army, Jerk?"

Eavesdropping, Forge stifled a laugh as he opened the truck's passenger

265

door. He hid his face with his hand. Grover turned toward Greyson again, even slower, not a hint of a smile on his worn face. For a moment Greyson thought he was going to hit him – or throw him somewhere hard.

"*Jerk* is the best you can do?"

"Well…"

"You afraid your mom's gonna wash your mouth out with soap?"

Greyson's expression dropped into frustration. "My mom was killed at the fair."

The man seemed annoyed. "I heard the story. You're an orphan."

Greyson shrugged. "For now."

Grover leaned down with a jerk, giving Greyson a close-up of each one of his scars. One cut across his right cheek. Another jetted diagonally from his eye to his left ear. His skin had the leathery, open-pore texture of someone who'd been in the sun too many years. But he wasn't ugly. And he wasn't as scary as he thought he was.

"A lot of parents died in Des Moines, Orphan… and in Chicago, New Orleans, Dallas. More victims than I care to think about. Quit your complaining. Don't be another one."

The soldier leaned back, still glaring at Greyson as he contemplated the words. *He's calling me a victim? For complaining?*

The anger bubbled up and spouted from Greyson's lips. "You're a *butthole*."

Grover let the surprise register in his brow, but he chuckled, deep and quiet in this throat. "That's better. Now shut up and hand me that bag over there. Be useful."

After a pathetic glare, Greyson shuffled to the duffel bag, kicking at the dirt. He grabbed the bag that was nearly as large as he was and lugged it to the van like a forklift. Grover took it with one hand, without a thank you.

Avoiding Grover, Greyson circled to the other side of the van to where Forge was loading more gear. Greyson looked for other things he could help with, but he didn't know the first thing about the equipment. Instead, he eyed the computer pad attached to the man's wrist. He'd seen Forge type on it as soon as he had returned to the clearing; the drone had buzzed over their heads, off to some other mission, obedient to Forge's silent commands.

Every now and then the same drone would buzz overhead, always from a different direction.

"Is the drone watching around us? For Plurbs – or soldiers?"

Forge nodded to the sky. "It's on overwatch. Random sweeps so no one tracks it to us. And Diablo's keeping watch as well."

"Diablo?"

Forge nodded to the tree line where the third soldier was nearly invisible in his ghillie suit of leaves and brush.

"Why you call him that?"

"Long story – and don't ask him. Diablo...he doesn't talk much; just be glad he's on your side."

"Is this all of you?"

"Smokestack didn't make it to the fight in time. He'll be here before too long."

"Smokestack? How'd he get *his* name?"

Forge smirked and tied a complicated knot over a container like he'd done it a thousand times. "You ask too many questions."

"But you guys saved me. And...and I don't even know who you are."

Forge pulled a strap tight. "We like it that way."

"You guys in the Army? Like, Navy Seals or something?"

"Only a few men in the world know who we are. Think you can just *ask*?"

He shrugged. "Worth a try."

Suddenly, Forge's wrist pad beeped, and he glanced at it. "That's the drone speaking. You're so curious 'bout names. The drone needs a name. All I can think of is 714 Dash M because that's its model number. Got any other ideas?"

Greyson shrugged. There weren't many names cooler than Diablo. "I don't know. Can I see him again?"

Forge thought for a moment, glanced toward Grover and then made up his mind. "Sure." He typed a few keys on his wrist pad and then craned his neck toward the sky.

Greyson matched his gaze until the drone appeared. It dropped altitude fast and banked toward them. Moments later it hovered in front of them with the hum of an air conditioner. It was ten times the size of the drone John had destroyed, twice as big as the police drone he'd seen in Nashville, and twice as intimidating. As Forge pulled it closer and explained its features, Greyson admired its sleek metal with a fearful knot in his throat.

It was shaped like a tire, with a silver panel of armor covering the entire exterior except for a black-tinted strip of material that Forge explained was a window for the six cameras contained inside. Sticking out from the underside was a single gun barrel. "It has 144 armor piercing rounds inside and can reload itself if you use the right ammunition canisters. It ejects the old and lands on the new. Clicks right in."

Forge brought it down and showed the four whirling rotors inside, like those on a helicopter. "Each works independently. But the cool thing about this particular drone is its extendable wings…"

"Cool!"

But the drone's wings didn't extend. Forge sighed. "…if I could figure them out. It's a prototype – didn't come with an instruction manual."

"Where'd you get it?" Greyson asked, rubbing the *714-M* stenciled on its side.

"You have to know the right person who has the right set of skills – who can get things." Forge smirked. "It's me."

Greyson gave him a look of admiration, but it dissolved into contemplation. These men were professionals. The type of heroes he saw in movies. He hadn't really thought that they actually existed. To see them here was surreal.

Forge released the drone, watching it buzz back into the sky. "So," he said, looking back to Greyson. "Get any name inspiration?"

"No, but can I get a name?" He started cycling through all of the coolest options. "How about *Grey*ve Stone? Or *Grey*zy Horse?"

Forge shook his head. "First of all, you suck at coming up with names. Second, names are given, not chosen. Besides. I think you already have one."

Greyson arched his brow, but Forge interrupted his thoughts, peering at his wristpad. "The nameless drone says a truck's approaching. Should be your ride."

The same joy he'd had at seeing Kit returned with the same intensity. Dan and Asher pulled up in their truck, and he met Asher with a hug. When the boy asked for another one, Greyson obliged, picking him up and swinging him in the kind of hug his father had given him when he'd been as small as Asher.

"Kit's alive! And we're going to the Bahamas!" Greyson turned to Dan, but he was already talking in whispers with Grover. They seemed to be good friends, exchanging a flurry of words, with intermittent glances in Greyson's direction. Forge joined the other soldiers, shaking his hand and giving a nod of relief. It was an adult conversation.

Growing impatient, Greyson eventually tapped Dan on the arm. "Excuse me."

Grover's glare nearly made him topple backwards. But he continued, "You're taking me, now, right? You promised."

Dan apologized to Grover, dropped his chin to his chest, and stepped up to

Greyson. He grabbed his shoulders. "I'm needed here..."

"But you promised!"

"Let me finish."

"Sorry, sir."

Dan sighed and knelt to Greyson's level. "You have to understand – you can't see it all. All the links in the chain. The consequences of today's attack. Congress is in emergency session, militias are arming, the media's raising the war banner. But it won't happen. It can't. Not yet. And I've got to help see that it doesn't."

"But..."

"Everyone has their own war to fight. You have yours and each of us has our own as well – just as complicated, just as difficult. You can't imagine all the hands at play here. The stakes are higher than they have ever been."

Downcast and beaten, Greyson lowered his head and kicked at the gravel. Anger fought for control, but he kept biting it down and biting it down.

"But a promise is a promise."

Greyson's eyes lit up, and Asher's next to him.

"So, I'll take you, but I can't stay."

"You'll take me? On the plane?"

"Yes."

"Right now?"

"Soon."

The way Greyson jumped and shouted for joy startled the soldiers, but Asher joined in with just as much enthusiasm.

The wait flew by. After Forge decided to keep Kit with him to recover, Greyson and Asher gave the dog a long hug. Before parting, Asher whispered in Kit's ear. "Sic the bad ones. Lick the good ones."

From their hideout in the woods, it only took a few stressful hours to make it to the small airport. Greyson spent the time hidden in a giant toolbox in the truck bed, sleeping as if it were his coffin. He even slept through the military checkpoint. But they made it safely and boarded the twin-engine Cessna without incident.

After fueling and pre-flight preparations, the plane finally barreled down the runway – its engines humming louder and louder as the g-force dragged at Greyson's face. He watched out the window in fascination as the landscape rushed by faster than he had ever seen.

"This is awesome!"

269

Asher looked at him from the adjacent seat, holding his armrests like they were the only things keeping him from falling. "Yah! Totally!"

"We're flying! Look!" He pointed out the window, watching the trees shrink and the roads dwindle to lines. Soon the forest melted away into farmland and small towns passed one by one. Asher handed him a set of headphones and they pointed out the landmarks to one another.

When the plane leveled out above the clouds, he leaned back in his chair with a deep sigh, the adrenaline and the joy still flowing through his tired body.

*Finally.* He was on his way. He'd be there in a few hours. And there were no more obstacles in the way. At least not until Nassau.

He smiled at Asher and then at Dan in the cockpit ahead. As he drifted toward sleep, images of his journey ran before his eyelids. The couple he hitchhiked with, the horse he rode through the storm, the car behind the RV, the rioters' faces and protest signs, the bike he left behind with a flat tire, the wrecked train, and now the plane. He'd gone a long way.

But the last thing he thought about before he fell asleep was the cat, Pawl. Perhaps he could have brought him along for a pillow. Plus, he could have tested to see if cats land on their feet when dropped from an airplane.

He smiled to himself as he dozed off.

*New self? Maybe not yet. Not entirely.*

*Besides. If I change too much, Dad might not recognize me.*

*He will recognize me, won't he?*

# PART 4

# Chapter 48

*Thirty minutes until Nassau*

Sydney hadn't been able to sleep very well. There were too many things to think about. First on her mind was how to actually find Greyson once they ported in Nassau. With their parents now dedicated to never letting them out of sight, they were stuck. Unless they ran away.

And then her mind wandered to the Plurbs on their ship. She replayed the messages they had intercepted over and over. Nick had thought it was enough…but was it? All they knew was that the Plurbs planned to depart at four o'clock before a man named Daryl arrived, and that there had been another attack in the USA that would cause security to be tighter. Putting those two together, Nick had reasoned that they were planning some other attack revolving around Daryl's arrival. But how to find out who Daryl is?

With so much on her mind she had taken to the balcony to read Sam's note just as the sun peeked over the lip of the ocean's horizon.

*Good morning! Are you reading these in the morning? I hope so. Mornings are good times to hear something to set the heart and mind right for the rest of the day. Mom used to do yoga in the mornings, I hear. Dad reads. Me? I watch cartoons. Haha! But anyway, here's something to set you right. I admire you. Tomorrow you'll be arriving at Nassau (if I did the math right). You traveled halfway across the nation and across the sea to help your friend. That's devotion and loyalty. Keep it up! I hope you find him. - Sam*

Sydney wrapped the note in her arms with a deep sigh. He was so good with words, even though he must have gotten the math wrong. They were arriving today. Still, it made her giddy just thinking about him writing the note, with that dimpled smile on his face.

"Gooooood morning, American Dreamers!"

Sydney jumped, nearly losing the note to the ocean breeze. But it was just the cruise's intercom.

"This is your Captain, Chip. I trust you all had a glooo-rious rest after a goooo-rgeous night of festivities, and you are now feeling *ship*-shape for an excursion to the beautiful port city of Nassau. Located on the island of New Providence, Nassau was once known as a stronghold for pirates, but is now known for its luxurious resorts and pristine beaches."

The first outlines of the island came into view as the ship made a turn. The ship bellowed its massive horn as it pulled closer to harbor.

"Make sure to stop by our excursion counter to make your stay a memorable one. You can take a guided island tour on a plucky scooter or a Segway. You can swim with stingrays or learn how to jet ski. Or, my personal favorite – you can get a day pass to the legendary Atlantis Resort Waterpark! Finally, for those of you leaving the ship, make sure to be back by 6pm. You'll have plenty of time to avoid Daryl, so don't you worry! Unless of course you get left behind. Haha!"

*Daryl?*

Had she heard him right? Or had she drifted off to sleep?

"He said Daryl, right?"

She snapped to her right. Nick was on the adjacent balcony again, his pajamas and bedhead blowing in the breeze.

"Yeah," she replied, hastily hiding Sam's note in her drawstring bag. "Weird."

Nick's stare caught her attention. He was transfixed on some point past the sea, past the island and beyond. Glancing at her puzzled look, he pointed to where he was looking.

She followed his finger, squinting to see something worth staring at. There were deep blue clouds out to sea to the east. They weren't much to look at, being so far away, but the breeze had already picked up since she had been outside. On the island, the palm trees were swaying with regularity and the waves were coming in at a good pace.

"I think I know who Daryl is. Or *what* he is."

Sydney nodded, putting it all together. And suddenly, when it all made sense, a chill ran over her arms.

They had been right. They *were* headed back into the storm. A storm so big they gave it a name.

"Hurricane Daryl."

# Chapter 49

Nassau brimmed with life, enthusiasm, and tourists. The gusty wind may have dampened some of the passengers' moods, but to others it raised the level of excitement. They were the last ship to dock and would be the last to leave. Honeymooning couples and families flowed from the ship onto the wooden dock, stopping to get their picture taken next to a fake anchor and a costumed pirate.

When Sammy put the pirate's hook in his mouth, Jarryd rolled his eyes. But where his eyes landed happened to be their future destination. Across the channel, giant pink towers rose above the palm trees like a portion of a medieval castle had been cut and pasted onto the small island. It was the majestic Atlantis Resort. Jarryd's eyes grew wide, and he prodded Nick and Sydney to look as well. Soon, both of their families were gawking – until the other passengers complained, urging them on.

Jarryd nearly salivated. "I can't believe we're going there."

Sydney's mom turned to him as they followed the crowd down the dock and toward the welcome center. "Too bad our stay is cut short. We'll only have a few hours in the waterpark after the tour."

Mr. Hansen eyed the horizon. "Well, it does look bad."

"Dibth on the water park," Sammy exclaimed.

"You can't dib the whole park," Jarryd whined.

"Then dibth on the water thlideth."

"You can't do that either."

"I jutht did. And the beacheth." His saliva bubbled on his lips. "And the girlth."

"I'll dib your face with my fist," Jarryd threatened.

"Boys! Knock it off," Mrs. Hansen chided. "We're on Paradise Island and you're arguing?"

"Yeah, Sammy. Going to dib paradise, too?"

"I may."

"Boys!" Mrs. Hansen repeated, gently shoving them toward the welcome center at the end of the dock. Sammy stuck his tongue out at Jarryd and Jarryd returned a sneer.

As the families passed through the welcome center entrance, one man stood at a distance, watching, smoking a cigar and blowing out the smoke in small puffs. He wore a pair of dark sunglasses, so large they nearly covered his cheeks. He wore them casually, near the tip of his bulky nose. His skin was brown and dark, like one who had been under the sun for most of his life, and indeed he had. Before he had become a bounty hunter, hunting men, he had been a fisherman, hunting fish and sharks.

It had been an easy transition. Both needed the necessary bait and the proper hook. If anything, fishing for prey above water was easier. And it paid a whole lot better.

Pluribus was a relatively new entrant into the game of mercenaries, but it was proving to be one of the most lucrative. The Fisherman had already successfully rendered three transactions with them in a matter of months. None of them yet had been children, so today would be a new experience. His conscience pestered him every now and then, but it had never pestered him when he had caught baby sharks. He'd even killed a pregnant shark before.

And this time there were eight sharks, four of them babies. When the bald man from the cruise had instructed him to take care of them quietly and quickly, he had almost killed the man on the spot. No one told him how to do his job except the one who paid. But he had restrained himself, blaming his impatience on his other assignment. He had been waiting for another one of his targets, an orphan boy, to show up on the island.

He'd keep his eyes open for that one, but at least now he had something to entertain him during the wait.

He followed the targets through the welcome center where store vendors hocked their cheap tourist wares — mementos, hats, baskets, dolls, bottled water, and sunscreen amongst others. His targets didn't buy anything — they looked to be in a rush — failing to enjoy their last precious hours of life. Instead, they rushed by the local shop selling conch burgers; they skipped the face painting and the scooter rental; and they didn't stop to breathe in the fresh ocean air.

And then they had to wait in line for a tour vehicle, along with hundreds of other anxious tourists talking nervously to one another, pointing to the shop that had already boarded up with plywood sign reading, *Nassau Welcomes Everyone (Except Darryl)!*

The Fisherman crushed his cigar under his shoe and lugged his rusty green tackle box toward a row of mopeds. He'd wait in line to rent one, as patient as a fisherman.

---------------

Greyson woke with a start, short of breath and terrified. His hands reached for his holster and instinctively found the snap.

"Good mo'ning," Asher said, smiling wide. "Dad says we 'ah almost the'ah."

He was still on the plane. Greyson eyed Asher and tried to take deep breaths to calm down. He glanced outside and saw that the sun had come up in force. There was nothing but blue sky and blue ocean. How long had he slept?

"You w'ah having a nightma'ah."

*He was watching me sleep?* He reached for a water bottle. "Was I?"

"I have them, too. Monst'ahs and zombies mostly. You d'weamin' of zombies?"

"Uh, no."

"Then what?"

"I don't remember."

"Well, what are you af'aid of?"

He thought to himself, still shaking off the sleep. He was afraid of lots of things. Not finding his father – or finding him dead. Plurbs. Drones. Being tortured. Losing Sydney. Oh, and one of the worst…

"Snakes," he said. "I hate snakes."

"Me, too. Is your mom okay?"

Greyson stopped in the middle of rubbing his face awake. "What?"

Asher scrunched his forehead. "Your mom. You were saying somethin' 'bout her in your d'weam."

Greyson's eyes fell to his shoes. "No. She's…she's dead."

"Mine, too."

"Asher." Dan spoke from the open cockpit. He'd been listening in.

"So'wwy, Dad." He leaned in to whisper to Greyson. "Not supposed to talk about it."

"Okay. I'm sorry. I'm sure you miss her a lot."

Asher glanced at his dad and whispered quieter. "I nev'ah knew her. She died having me, but it's not my fault."

Trying not to show it, Greyson felt the tug at his heart. He turned from the boy and watched the clouds pass by. At least he had been able to have twelve years with both of his parents. Asher hadn't had a single day with his mother.

"You okay?" Asher was leaning over him, trying to see his face.

Greyson faked a smile. "Yeah. It's just soaking in, you know?"

"What? You wet yourself?"

Greyson laughed and then caught the kid's serious face. Maybe wetting himself was a real issue for him. "Uh…no. All good. I just can't believe we're on our way. You guys are the best."

Asher smiled. "Anytime! Maybe we could go to the pool lat'uh! Or I could show you a'wound the bookshop! Dad owns it."

"That sounds great. Maybe if you give me your phone number, I can get hold of you after I find my dad."

"Sh'uwa! I know Dad's cell phone."

Greyson searched in his fanny pack and pulled out the Bible and pencil. "Here. Write it down."

Asher grabbed the Bible and pencil and went to work, his tongue flicking left and right as he made the numbers just right. His letters were large, and he moved at a snail's pace; and just when Greyson thought he was done, he flicked through the pages, circled something, and then finally pressed the Bible and the pencil back into Greyson's hands. "I also circled my favorite ve'wse. You'll have to find it. Like a scaveng'ah hunt."

Greyson shrugged. "Sounds fun."

Asher bit his lip as if he were debating with himself. Then his curiosity got the best of him. "What's a 'Payback List'?"

*He'd snuck a peek.*

"It's just what I owe people. I'll pay them back someday. I should put you guys on it for sure." He started adding their names to the list.

Asher was still curious. "So…it's like an IOU…or debt?"

*Smart kid.* "Um…sure. I guess."

"Debt's bad. Our gove'ment has lots of it," the boy said, glancing at his dad. "Dad says they're making us slaves to China 'cuz we can nev'ah pay it all back. And that's why all the businesses are closing and people are getting ang'wy – cuz the gove'ment's trying to make us pay it back for them."

Greyson smirked. *He has a good memory.*

"Asher…" his dad chided from the cockpit.

Asher huffed, unsure of what he did wrong. "But you don't have as much debt as the gove'ment. You can pay it all back, yeah?"

"Maybe. I'll try."

"You need more money? I've got like fifteen doll'ahs and fo'wty th'wee cents."

He laughed. "Whoa! Loaded. But no – most of it's not money."

"Then how do you pay it back?"

Greyson scrunched his brow and played with a scratch on the seatback in front of him. He thought of the 8,002 lives.

"Um…well, I guess if I owe someone something because I did something wrong…I'll have to do something just as good to make up for it."

"Oh." Asher scrunched his brow just like Greyson had and rubbed a different scratch on the seat ahead of him. "But how will you know if it's good enough?"

Greyson shifted uncomfortably in his seat. "I don't know. I guess I don't."

"That sucks."

"Asher!"

Asher bowed his head. "So'wwy. Bad wo'd. Maybe I should say something *good* to make up for it." He winked at Greyson.

Greyson smiled back, though the weight of what Asher had said still weighed on him. How would he know when his debt was paid? And if debt made the government a slave to China, who was he a slave to?

"What's something good to say…?" Asher thought to himself, rubbing again at the scratch.

As he was thinking, everything changed.

The radio burst on. Nassau's airport controller started barking orders. Dan replied calmly over and over again, but he couldn't argue his way through it. The man was speaking so fast it was hard to catch what he said, but there was one word he caught, despite the man's heavy accent.

*Hurricane.*

His eyes shot to the horizon where dark clouds loomed ominously across the sea. His heart dropped as Dan put the plane on autopilot and turned to them.

"Listen. There is heightened security because of the attack. When we land, they will check the entire plane – every passenger."

Greyson gulped. The plane shook with increasing turbulence.

"We're going to have to turn around."

Asher and Greyson shared a look; Greyson's face had gone pale.

"No! We can't go back! We're here! He's down there!"

"If you stay, they'll find you. There's nowhere to hide on this little plane."

"There's got to be something – another way!"

The hum of the plane was the only sound for several seconds as Dan thought to himself. Finally, he spoke. "You could jump."

"Jump?"

"No. Nevermind. I'll take you back, we can regroup, wait out the hurricane, let security calm…"

"No! I'm done waiting. I'll jump," Greyson declared. Then he thought. "Wait. Do you have a parachute?"

Dan's sigh was long and deep, his conscience drawing lines on his forehead.

When he looked into Greyson's eyes, Dan knew what he had to do. The boy deserved a chance. "Hurry. Asher, help him put on the chute. I'll talk you through it."

Greyson was in a haze, caught up with the sound of wind, the image of the dark clouds, and the word *jump*. Asher grabbed the parachute from its place, helped him fit it over his arms, and clipped it on. It felt just like the rappelling straps at camp – or the chains that had saved him when he'd fallen from the moving truck. He shuddered at the memory.

With a flurry of words, Dan instructed him how to work it; his fingers found the 'drogue' handle in the back he was supposed to pull to release the chute. Dan told him how to steer the chute, how to land, and how to detach it. Greyson tried to envision all the instructions – forcing the words into his memory.

"Asher, buckle in!" Dan yelled, turning from the cockpit. "Then, Greyson, open the side door!"

Greyson found the latch and pulled it with all his might until it finally budged; the sound that struck him was like a thousand shrieking ghosts released from a vault.

The sun poured in with the sound, blazing into Greyson's face. One hand shielded his eyes, the other held the door latch, keeping him from falling into the portal ahead.

"We're almost over the island!" Dan yelled. "We'll have a short jump window! Grab some money from our bug-out bag!"

Greyson found the red bag and shuffled through the belongings. He stopped when the butt of a pistol poked through, but only hesitated for a moment. Quickly he found a wad of cash.

"How much?"

"One bundle. A thousand. Don't be afraid to bribe someone if you need to!

It's my gift to you – all of this. You deserve a chance."

Greyson thumbed through the cash with a blank expression. If he'd had that type of money a few weeks ago…

"Thank you!"

"And make sure to hide the chute as soon as you land!"

Greyson took one last look at the bag's contents before he zipped it up. Passports. Several of them. "Okay!"

He returned the bag to its place and looked out the portal to the clouds wisping by. He imagined his body plummeting to the earth and the sound it would make hitting the ground.

Asher waved at him. "Bye Gray's son! Hope you find Mr. Gray!"

Greyson blinked, still holding the latch with white knuckles. *Gray's son? Greyson.* He repeated it to himself several times. Of all the years he'd been called by that name, he'd never heard it that way before.

*Dad must have sucked at coming up with names as much as I do.*

"Thank you," Greyson said, giving the boy a fist pound.

Dan leaned back. "Call if you need anything! I hope your testimony changes a lot of minds about Pluribus. Now you've got to go!"

They shared a look. He nodded, and Dan nodded back. Then, grasping the sides of the plane, he bent his knees and readied himself.

"Greyson!"

He turned to Asher.

"Your hat."

Greyson smiled a 'thank you' and snapped his hat to his belt. Satisfied, he turned back to the opening and took a deep breath.

*I dare you.*

Giving the clouds one more look, he flung himself into them.

# Chapter 50

Greyson had fallen before. He'd fallen from a bridge into a river. He'd fallen from a crashing train into a backyard. And he'd fallen for a girl who fell for someone better. Each time hurt.

But this was like all three put together – an unending free fall with a sinking desperation, a frightening loss of control, and the wind smacking his every sense. Even so, there was a time of exhilaration when he forgot his fear and told himself it would be okay. He assured himself the chute would open, he would land safely, and he would be where his dad was. He loved those few precious seconds, just floating, like he was surfing on a pillow of air, smiling and dreaming.

As the last clouds vanished around him, the island lay open below like an unwrapped package. Tiny buildings speckled the green landscape, all lining the vein-like streets that tangled their way with little organization. Greyson tried to take it all in through the tears streaming from his eyes, but it was difficult to concentrate. The sound strapped at his ears, and the wind pushed his cheeks against the back of his jaws. His clothes felt like they'd rip from his skin or become a part of him. And worst of all, the hat felt like it was pulling the snap from his belt. He reached for it, but sent himself into a tailspin, tumbling through the air like he had when he'd first jumped from the plane.

Eventually he pressed the snap in stronger and turned back, spreading his legs and arms to ride the wave of air. The houses had gotten much larger. The earth seemed to rocket toward him.

Panicking, he grasped at the chute's straps, searching for the tiny drogue handle he was supposed to pull. And then he remembered. It was in the back.

His hands swiped behind him and he lost control again. *Stupid!*

He spun around twice…three times before spreading his arms again and regaining control. Now he could see the colors of vehicles. The shingles on houses.

*Calm down. Calm down.*

This time he reached back slowly with one hand. His fingers played along the pack, searching and searching until finally they found the handle. He grasped it and pulled it with a rush of relief.

But nothing happened. He had felt it pull away. Something had come out, but...

*WHOOOOSH!*

The straps yanked at his body, pulling him toward the sky above like the chute had caught on a cloud. Greyson's breath was crushed from his lungs; his eyes spun; his limbs flopped down like gravity had suddenly taken hold, and he no longer floated – he dangled.

It took a few seconds for the world to make sense again. He looked about, blinking away the tears and feeling the blood rush back to his face. He gulped in air but only once before he panicked.

*Water tower!*

He was heading straight for it.

He kicked at the air out of impulse, as if he could run; his hands pulled at the straps. Still nothing.

The wooden tower barreled toward him.

Suddenly he remembered Dan's instruction. He found the handles that dangled above each of his shoulders.

He let out a yelp and yanked on the right handle. The chute dipped to the right and he took a hard turn. His feet whipped by the tower, leaving a shadow on the splintered wood.

He was still falling fast and gliding forward even faster; houses' roofs slid underneath like a treadmill. Palm trees and electric lines threatened on nearly every side.

Banking left and then right, he gained control of the massive chute that canopied above. The wind was powerful from the oncoming storm, pushing him hard through the air. He had no time to think. Only to react.

*Frick!*

He narrowly avoided a tree, skimming the leaves on the left and then nearly pummeling a rocky bank on the right.

Yanking on both handles at once, the chute jerked him back like he had hit the brakes. A rush of wind erupted from a narrow canyon below and hit him like a wave, sending him higher into the air, just above another set of trees.

Finally, he saw a landing spot just past the market below, busy with people he could now see and hear, boarding up their shops and racing around – too distracted to see him – until he swooped over their heads like a giant bird of prey.

He pulled again and again at both straps, pounding the brakes. Keeping his sneakers out in front of him, he guided them toward the landing like they were his crosshairs. The wind pushed him to the side and another wave of panic hit him. His landing was a rocky fort overlooking a cliff. If he missed the landing, he'd fall off the cliff, toward the busy city where the best landing would be the highway.

He gave the left handle a pull with all his strength. The ground prepared to swallow him. He found the chute's release.

*Ground!*

His feet hit the concrete and he tried to run with the chute, but the wind jerked him headlong. His shoulder hit next and he toppled toward the cliff, the parachute's lines tangling with themselves and dragging him along. Somehow through the chaos his hand found the release.

The chute floated off the cliff and Greyson rolled after it. His body scraped at the cement; his fingernails pulled at anything – but there was nothing he could do. He closed his eyes as he flopped one last time toward the cliff.

And then he felt as if he were falling again – over the edge. His eyes swam, swirling behind his eyelids. His hands shook and his stomach reeled, but he wasn't actually falling. He'd stopped. He felt the cement under his knees, on his fingers, on his stomach, on his cheek. He hugged it tight, still fearful that it might let him go. Opening his eyes, the cement's pockmarks swiped across his vision like the moon was a bowling ball spinning inches from his eyes.

*Stop. Stop.*

He mouthed the words with forced breaths, his fingers stinging raw, still pulling at the rough cement.

*I'm stopped. I'm stopped.*

After several more deep breaths, he pushed himself up and blinked out over the city. His chute drifted lazily hundreds of feet above the buildings below, carrying its tangled lines below like a jellyfish in water.

Brushing himself off and assessing the scrapes on his body, he glanced at the old, abandoned fortress he had landed on. He'd made the only flat section, an odd triangular shape jutting toward the city, like it was a pirate's ship protecting the harbor. Below was a deck with cannons set to bombard those who threatened to invade – like he had just done.

When he glanced behind, he saw that he had gathered a small audience of the natives – and a few tourists. At least he assumed so - judging by their clothing. One tourist even had a fanny pack. But they all looked just as surprised.

He gave them a brief wave but turned back to the city. It was so beautiful.

283

Lush with vegetation. Pink and orange paint, abundant and lively. A giant resort rose from a small island across the channel. And the massive cruise ship, just as large as the resort towering from the harbor, sat on the water, majestic and breathtaking.

Suddenly the realization hit him.

He had arrived.

The thought took the breath from him again, and he felt the tears of joy pull at his cheeks. After so long. After so much.

*Dad, I'm here.*

*I'll find you. I'll give you your hat back.*

*My hat!*

The wind played with his hair; the snap on his belt was undone; the ground around him was bare. It was gone!

He desperately looked around and down the cliff.

And then it landed behind him. It bounced on the cement and tumbled with the wind – on its top and then on its side.

Greyson put his foot down to block its progress and grabbed it by its bill. With a sigh of relief and a smile to match, he held it in front of him, gazing at the white 'G' that had gotten less and less white over time. Soon it would be completely...gray.

The big 'G'. He'd always assumed it stood for 'Gray', but it hadn't really mattered to him until John mentioned it. No matter what letter had been on it before, it had always reminded him of Dad. But now it would also remind him to pursue both Good and his dad. That's what the hat stood for now. That's what he stood for. He just decided.

Narrowing his eyes at the darkening skies, he fit the hat on his head.

# Chapter 51

Sydney peered through the tour van's window at the giant kite floating over the city. It looked like it had been lost and tangled in the vicious wind that was getting worse by the minute. Trash blew through the streets and palm fronds that had been knocked loose from the trees scuttled along with tourists who held their hats to their heads.

But the coming hurricane didn't have Sydney nervous. She was nervous instead about the phone call her father was making.

Realizing that the relative sanctuary of the tour van was the safest place away from the Plurbs' ears, the kids had finally told their parents the entire story near the end of their tour. The four adults had reacted with a mix of doubts and extreme concern. Their mothers had been angry with them, but it was Sydney's father who calmed them down, setting them thinking more about what to do next rather than blaming them for past mistakes.

It was his decision to call their FBI contact.

Sydney eyed the phone that her dad held to his ear remembering what Sam had said about the contact's fake name – and whose number it really was.

Her dad gave her a sideways glance of concern as they all listened. Above the hum of the road they could hear the faintest ring.

*Riiiiiing…riiiiiiing…riiiiiiing.*

--------------------

"It's incoming from the Bahamas, sir. Nassau."

A suited man furrowed his brow and pushed his face closer to the computer screen to double-check. "We need to answer it. Give it to me."

Another man reached among the rest of Calvin's belongings and handed him the buzzing phone; the agent put it to his ear. "Yes?"

*"Hello? Is this Agent Lee?"*

The man on the phone eyed his friend, confused. He could play the part. "Yes, it is."

*"Then we need you – the whole FBI…"*

As Sydney's father began to explain himself on the other line, the suited man gave a knowing nod, beginning to understand the call. The man at the

285

computer listened as well through his own earphones, a slight smile creasing his lips.

"Are you in danger?" the man asked, playing the part. He nodded as the father unveiled his suspicions of an impending terrorist attack on the cruise ship, giving details and assuring them that his children could be trusted.

"I understand," the fake agent said, pacing to the window. "We will be sending a team immediately. Where are you now?" He listened to the reply. "Get somewhere safe as soon as you can – a hotel room – and stay there. The Atlantis? We can get you a room there. I'll notify their security as well."

*"What about the embassy?"* Sydney's father asked.

"No, no. If they are planning an attack, they may have a mole in the embassy."

The man at the computer nodded with a smile, satisfied with the suited man's deception.

Peering out the window, the agent continued, "And don't contact anyone else; throw away the phone you are using as soon as you are finished with this call. We will handle it from here. Understand?" The fake agent blinked slowly, happy with the response.

Sydney's father described the hurricane.

"Hunker down. We will find you."

The man at the computer laughed silently.

"We will be in touch."

As Sydney's father thanked him, the fake agent stared outside the hotel at the Washington Monument standing as tall and proud as he was.

------------

As he guided his motorized scooter through the bumper-to-bumper traffic, the Fisherman pressed the receiver in his ear and listened to his instructions. They came from Washington, DC.

Still listening, he eyed the top of the Atlantis Resort, just visible over the traffic. "Sí."

He pressed the receiver again and hit the accelerator.

--------------

Sydney's father updated the rest of those in the crammed tour van on what the agent had said, just in case they hadn't overheard. A sudden pallor swept the group. There would be no more vacation. No more water slides, spa treatments, or sunny beaches. It was over. Instead, they'd hunker down somewhere in the hotel and ride out the storm.

"This sucks," Jarryd said finally, speaking for the rest of them.

Nodding, Sydney sighed and watched the cars across from them as their van crawled forward. Suddenly a motorized scooter buzzed past their window, down the narrow alley between the rows of cars. The driver's tackle box attached to the back seat nearly clunked into the side-view mirrors, but he deftly maneuvered, inches from an impact on both sides. He was in a hurry.

--------------

The initial excitement Greyson had felt after the landing was already fading. Nassau was big. And he had no idea where to look.

All he knew from the research he'd done at the Hansen's home were the most popular landmarks. After he had left his landing pad, he'd realized that he'd landed on Fort Fincastle, a fort originally built by the British on the highest point of the island to look out for pirates.

Then, once he'd escaped from the curious onlookers with bribes and pleas for their silence, he'd found the narrow canyon that he'd glided over. A huge, limestone staircase descended through its middle, with a cascading waterfall on one side and crawling vines draping down its rock walls. As he'd buzzed past tourists marveling at its beauty, he'd realized it was the Queen's Staircase, named after Queen Victoria. Just as the staircase had once provided British soldiers a protected route from the city to Fort Fincastle, it had provided him a route to the city.

He'd gawked at the natural beauty of the limestone valley, but after a slow, painful run, he stopped at an intersection jam-packed with taxis, with a bright pink bar on the corner blaring music and advertising for piña coladas. Some shops had their doors wide open, still hocking their island dresses or hair-braiding services, but others were being boarded up. Nail guns plunked just down the street. Cars and buses honked incessantly, and car radios blasted reggae music to compete with the bar's music. The few tourists walking by looked to be in a hurry to their ships or hotel for shelter.

Greyson glanced at the wall of clouds, still darkening in the distance. If those were only the storms preceding the hurricane, he didn't want to see the hurricane itself.

When he turned back to the cars, he had an idea.

*I can show people my dad's picture and...oh no.*

He didn't have his dad's picture anymore.

He'd left it in his backpack, which he'd left at Cael's house with the Plurbs and the soldiers. *No...it's gone.*

It had been the only picture of him, and now it was gone forever – along with all his mother's research. He shuddered in anger. What if he never found his dad? Would he forget what he looked like?

Another honk jerked him from his frustration, and he eyed the traffic that wound its way to the bridge to Paradise Island, where the Atlantis Resort dominated the landscape.

"Excuse me," he said, catching up to a tourist. "Have you seen a man that looks like me, but like, older and taller?"

He stammered out a few more descriptions, but the elderly man shook his head and held on to his flimsy hat, moving on.

Greyson sighed, spun around, and entered a bar through a pair of swinging doors. He nearly gagged on the smell, it was so thick. Alcohol. It was sharp and seemed to rise from the sticky floor. But there were other smells, too. Fried food, burgers, nachos. He could nearly taste them, and the saliva began to pool in his mouth as his stomach gurgled, suddenly aware of its emptiness.

He was so hungry. Too hungry. And tired. It hit him like another train wreck. But he didn't have time to eat. He had to find him before the storm struck.

"Ay, Mon! Ar'nt you a little 'ung to be in a seedy place like d'is?"

"I'm looking for someone," he said. "American. Dark brown hair, green eyes – six foot somethin'. Seen'm?"

The Bahamian threw his long dreadlocks over his shoulder and flashed his white teeth. They were so white compared to his dark skin. Greyson was enthralled with them.

"No, Mon. Haven't seen'm. But we'll keep a real eye out for 'em."

"Thanks," he mumbled, disappointed.

"Peace, 'Lil Mon."

"Peace...Mon."

He ran to the next store and then another. He crossed the block and tried every person he ran across, but every response was the same mix of confusion and pity. They knew it before he did. It was a helpless endeavor.

288

After another failed attempt in a dress shop, he pushed his way outside. The sun hit his eyes again and he squinted, blocking out the sun with his hand until he threw it down, muttering incoherent curses.

*This is stupid!* This was no strategy. It was the desperate, maniacal whims of a boy on his last leg. He had to get to his senses. He was too hungry, too pained to think clearly. For now, he didn't need a strategy. He needed a burger. And for the first time in weeks, he had money – and plenty of it.

He eyed the bar across the street – the one that had smelled of fried food. The street's traffic was moving now, a slow and steady stream to the resort. He would have to wait to cross, but as he did, he scanned the faces as they passed by. Each one started as a possibility; but he disregarded them just as fast.

A woman. Another woman. Too old. Too fat. A woman. A dog with its head out the window. A black man. A close one, but too skinny. A boy with his mouth against the window, blowing his cheeks out like a puffer fish – who looks a lot like Sammy – who drools just like Sammy. Who wipes off the saliva-window with his arm just like Sammy would?

*It is Sammy.*

His heart skipped a beat and his feet danced in place.

*How? Could it really be?*

His mind and feet found traction and he hopped to the right, following the van as it made its way through traffic.

"Sammy? SAMMY!" He cried out and jogged down the sidewalk, trying to keep up. The van sped up and made a turn onto the bridge.

"STOP! SAM-my!" His voice did that thing again, but he didn't care. Running into a tourist, he yelled an apology but kept running.

------------

Sammy blew as hard as he could against the window. His cheeks vibrated and his lips flapped at the glass, but he knew he could get his cheeks bigger. He gasped in air and then went back at it. His eyes watched the skin from his cheeks peek into his peripheral vision – until his vision grew blurry.

"Sammy! Knock it off!" Sydney yelled. "Or Chandler – whatever. That's gross."

"Yeah," Jarryd agreed as Sammy's head swooned with the lack of air. "You don't know how many other people's lips have been on that…never mind. And dude! Now both your eyes are crazy!"

The kids watched as his eyes lolled about. Sammy tried to smile, but he couldn't. His cheeks had gone numb.

"Er curnt merv mer cherkth."

The kids laughed. Jarryd made a face. "What is your stupid face saying?"

"Erth nert furner," Sammy mumbled, trying to rub life back into his cheeks. "Mer cherkth er derd."

They laughed again as their taxi sped up. Their parents also let out a sigh of relief. Mr. Aldeman patted his wife's knee. "Finally. I don't know what the holdup was."

She didn't notice policemen examining the parachute stuck in the power lines across the street.

"We should get a room on the bottom floor, in case the top ones blow off," Jarryd suggested.

"We'll get whatever room they give us," Mrs. Hansen said.

"I don't know 'bout y'all, but I'm headed to the bar," the twins' stepdad replied.

His wife elbowed him.

"Well, someone's got to enjoy this vacation."

Jarryd piped up. "I'll go to the bar with you!"

Jarryd's mom glared at her husband, and then at Jarryd. "We're staying *together.*"

"Erverwon to the ber! It'th a perty!"

Mr. Hansen had had enough. "Stop it! Everyone quiet!"

The cab went silent. Even the tour guide had given up long ago.

"Look. This is serious. No one is going to the bar. If you do, you'll be putting us all in danger." He gave an awkward look to Mr. Aldeman. "The only safe place for us is in the room."

---------------

The Fisherman sauntered to the front desk, slowly and deliberately, his tackle box forcing him to walk off kilter. "Hola, senorita. You will tell me where Mr. Tim Allen is staying tonight."

"Welcome to Atlantis, sir. Unfortunately, we are unable to..."

He put an envelope on the desk with his large, dry hand. The clerk gave it a concerned look.

"I'd like to leave them a welcome present in their room."

The woman reached timidly for the envelope. "That's…very nice of you, sir…perhaps I could have one of our attendants bring it to their room…"

The Fishermen withdrew the envelope from her fingers. "The package is very…important. I will go with the attendant."

He pushed the envelope across the desk. Glancing around, the woman peeked at the cash inside. Her eyes grew wide, and she quickly put the envelope in her pocket.

"I think we can arrange that."

"Now."

"Just one moment."

"Gracias."

--------------

Greyson's instincts took over as he maneuvered through traffic, bounding from car to car, clunking their trunks and hoods with his sneakers. The honking blared beneath him, but it was background noise to him; he was too focused on the van ahead, now speeding toward the resort.

*I have to go faster.*

Jetting to the sidewalk, Greyson began to sprint along the bridge railing, eyeing the ferry passing underneath and the gigantic cruise ship still towering in the harbor.

He huffed and puffed, his arms pumping like pistons, but he still couldn't catch the van. He could barely make out the van as it turned into the resort's roundabout. In a few minutes they would be checking into their room and he would lose them in the web of hundreds of rooms spread across the resort's many buildings.

*Faster!*

His second wind kicked in, letting the cars blur past him to his right. The pains he felt soon numbed and he felt looser, faster, and ready for anything.

He imagined the twins would be with Sammy and their parents. Would they have brought Sydney with them?

He smiled at the thought.

Looking both ways, he crossed the street and wound through an avenue of shops. Finally, he could see the van unloading beyond several docks jam-packed with sailboats and yachts swaying in the wind. He saw her get out.

*Sydney.*

"SYDNEY!"

But she was too far away.

------------

The lobby was beautiful and golden – a sanctuary from the wind that had almost knocked them down on the way in. But there was tension inside. Busboys were urgently lugging suitcases about, guests were lingering in clumps, anxiously talking amongst themselves, and a crowd had gathered around a lone television in the carpeted area past the massive fountain. Sydney could make out the familiar image of a weather radar screen – this one with a sizable red circle jerkily moving across the screen. One of the guests pointed at it, following the movement across the blue water to a little green speck. She guessed it was their island.

"Wercurm tur Paradie!" Sammy exclaimed, his arms in the air triumphantly.

"Sammy – come on," Sydney pulled him with the family as they bypassed a few guests at the front desk. Her mother was leading the charge to get them checked in.

The kids hung back a little, but Sydney's father leaned down to them. "Stay close, now. You guys like to find trouble – but not today. You've had enough. We're letting the pros handle it this time."

It was like her dad could read her mind. Sydney eyed the crowd, pulling on the drawstring bag she had packed for running off on her own.

If they were going to find Greyson, it wasn't going to be from their hotel room. He would be out looking for his dad. Maybe he had found him already – but there was no way of knowing. Either way, she had to look for him. She hadn't led them this far to hole up in a room and hide. She'd been looking for the right opportunity, and this could be it.

"Erm hurngry!" Sammy complained, breaking her train of thought.

Mrs. Hansen looked in her purse. "Well, I think I put some snacks in here. Cheaper than the tourist trap stuff. Five dollars for bottled water! Can you believe it? Oh, yeah. Here are some pop tarts."

Sammy's eyes lit up and the non-lazy one landed on the shiny silver wrapping. "Ermigerd. A perp tert!"

--------------------

Greyson's eyes searched the channel of water blocking his way, full of yachts and sailboats tied to narrow docks. The wind picked up again, shaking the boats, and the sun went behind the first of the storm clouds, cloaking the once bright-white sails in shadow.

He could go around – but the shortcut would save him precious time. *Here goes nothing.*

He leapt for the first boat and smacked the deck with both feet. The deck wobbled underneath him like a waterbed, but it was secure. *This will work.*

Deck, deck, railing, jump! Deck, duck under the mast, railing, jump! He ran a length of the dock and then bounded from one ship to another, sending them bouncing up and down in the water with the weight of his jumps.

Finally, he landed safely on the last dock, jetted up the stairs to the roundabout and sprinted through the cars to the front doors. A well-dressed busboy made a motion to stop him and a mother yelped, tugging her child away, but he made it inside, heaving for air and sweating profusely.

He put his hands on his knees, scanning the area. He barely noticed how beautiful it was – the ornate sculptors and furniture, the lush red carpet, the magnificent pillars and archways – he only noticed it was empty of the ones he loved.

"SYDNEY?"

No response.

He ran to the front desk, budging past a line of concerned guests.

"How long will we have to stay in our rooms?" An anxious guest whined. "I'm claustrophobic and my asthma…"

"Excuse me!" Greyson interrupted. "My parents! They just checked in. The Hansens. Had a girl with them…Sydney."

The hotel clerk raised an eyebrow and apologized to the claustrophobic asthmatic as she turned to Greyson. "Let me see if I can help you, sir. You said your parents just checked in?"

*Or they had already checked in days ago. How long had they been here?*

"Uh…well. They just got back. I forgot the room number. Hansens. Last name."

The clerk typed away as Greyson glanced nervously around the large room.

"No one by the name Hansen is checked in, sir. Maybe you're at the wrong hotel?" She turned back to the man. "Sir, if you'd rather, we have plenty of room in our underground aquarium. I'd suggest heading there now to avoid the rush…"

Annoyed, Greyson bolted from the desk and ran across the lobby to another hallway. It stretched past several shops on both sides, filled with fancy clothes and jewelry. He darted to the other side, around the fountain – ignoring the crowd at the television and stopped in the middle of the hall.

He heard their voices. Sammy's squeal. Parents – the twins' parents – yelling. Jarryd's pleas for justice. They were all here!

He blasted down the hall and turned into the elevator lobby, prepared to see their faces – but the last doors shut with a clunk. They had gotten on the elevator!

He ran to it and pounded on the doors with his fists.

"Sydney! Nick!"

*No!*

*Now what?*

He stepped back with a sigh and saw it.

*Five…six…seven…eight…nine…*

With each new number that lit up, Greyson grew more and more excited. He knew where they were.

His feet danced, and he pounded the up-arrow to follow.

*Eleven…twelve…*

"Hey!" A suited man stood down the hall, approaching him with his hand out. "Are you a guest here?"

The security man must have seen him running through the lobby.

"Do you have a room key on you?"

*Fifteen…sixteen…*

Greyson took glances in each direction and found the door for the stairs. His eyes rested on the numbers as the security man drew closer.

*Eighteen…still eighteen.*

"Hey! Stop!"

----------

"Oh my gosh!"

Sydney gasped as she took in the size of the presidential suite. It was breathtaking in luxury, like a palace of gold and blue.

"It's bigger than our house!" Nick exclaimed. "Amazing."

It truly was. There was a massive living room with two couches decorated in coral blue, sparkling drapes hanging on the sides of the largest balcony they'd ever seen, a golden dining room table with matching chairs, and a beautiful chandelier – all decorated with shells and blue colors that made them feel as if they were the kings and queens of a mermaid kingdom.

The parents found their way to the bedrooms to stake their claims, but the children plopped on the couches – all except Sammy, who was scouring the refrigerator for food.

"These are nice," Nick said, bouncing on the cushion next to Sydney.

Sydney bounced to her feet and walked to the sliding glass door. The sun had entirely disappeared, and rain had begun to fall, spattering along the glass. Still the scenery was beautiful. The lush green trees – almost like a jungle below them – covered the entire waterpark except for a few slides poking above. More resort towers rose around the jungle, but their room was near the top of them all, looking down. She could even see the pristine white-sand beach past the waterpark. A few workers were lugging a waverunner from the water toward a storage shed, and they weren't the only ones evacuating the park. It was a bummer to have such weather on vacation, but at least they had an amazing room. Sam and Calvin had gone all out with the reservations.

But for now, she wasn't thinking about Sam. Greyson was out there somewhere – back on the main island – not at Paradise, in a fancy resort gazing at the ocean. Guilt came down with the rain, and she clutched the drawstrings on her bag.

Her breath caught in her throat as she contemplated it. Looking over her shoulder, she saw the parents in their rooms, taking the mints from their pillows and commenting on how tasty they were. Sammy was stalking a plate full of extra mints, and the twins were curling into the soft couch pillows – readying for an afternoon nap.

She could leave now. It was her opportunity.

*Don't chicken out now, Syd.*

She slipped around the edge of the room, pretending to look at the artwork.

"Hey! You're eating all our mints!" Jarryd cried, suddenly noticing Sammy as he dumped the plate of mints into his mouth.

Sammy laughed as he chomped. "Ahahaha! Yumm – OW!"

He dropped the plate with a crash, its pieces clattering on the hardwood floor. His hand grabbed at his mouth like he was pulling at his teeth.

The kids were frozen. "You okay?" Sydney said at last.

"Ow-ah-ow!"

And then they saw it as he pulled it from his mouth. A drop of blood dripped from the end of the shiny gold fishing hook. Sammy held it in his trembling fingers and then threw it in the sink, working his mouth and tongue, full of chocolate and blood.

"You ate the decoration?" Jarryd asked callously.

Sydney rushed to him, ushering him to the kitchen sink, "Mom! Dad! Sammy's hurt!"

She grabbed a paper towel and pushed it at Sammy's mouth. "Press it against it. No, no. Spit first. Don't swallow!"

*Gulp.*

Sammy shared a startled look with Sydney as he suddenly appeared weary. Her eyes latched on him as his good eye joined his lazy one in the back of his head. Before she knew what had happened, he had hit the floor, out cold.

"Mom!"

Kneeling at Sammy's side in a panic, she glanced at her parents' room. Her mother's arm stretched across the floor, just visible in the doorway.

The twins ran to Sydney, a look of fear wiping across their faces as chocolate drooled from the corner of Sammy's mouth.

"Sammy! Sammy!"

"What's wrong with him?"

"I don't know!"

Nick dashed to his parents' room and stalled in the doorway. "Mom!" He disappeared, running to his parents' aid.

Trying not to panic, Sydney gulped at the lump in her throat, pushing Sammy's head to the side so that he didn't choke. "Jarryd, stay with them. Make sure they keep breathing! I'll go get help!" She sprinted across the living room but stopped short at the door. Someone was knocking.

"Security," came the husky voice from the other side of the door. "I heard screaming. Need help, niña?"

Letting out a sigh of relief, she went to let him in.

# Chapter 52

Greyson sweat through his shirt, and his heart drummed against his ribs. He desperately wanted to stop, but the security man was still close on his heels. Just when he thought his hamstrings would snap, he finally reached floor 18. With a glance backward at the huffing security guard, he swung open the stairwell door.

What he saw froze the air inside his lungs. He took it in slowly, like a horrible piece of art. A large, ugly man with a fisherman's hat and vest took a stance outside a room, leaning into his weapon – a five-barreled Gatling gun loaded with arrow-sized harpoons. The Fisherman's finger was on the trigger, but he was waiting for something – waiting for a room door to open.

But the Fisherman had seen the stairwell door open out of the corner of his eye. Greyson reacted before the shot, dodging left as the harpoon seared past his shoulder and burrowed into the stairwell's cement wall. The second harpoon hit the security guard in the neck as he reached for Greyson. His body crumpled at Greyson's feet.

The horror struck Greyson like a hammer to the skull. For a moment he couldn't think or feel. In a daze, he watched the dead man's body twitch.

But he could hear the Fisherman's steps approaching and he knew he had to run – and his legs seemed to know it before he did.

It was a blur from then on. Back down the steps – bounding, tripping, stumbling – sliding down the rails and listening for the Fisherman trailing behind. *He's after me.*

"Heeeee-re fishy, fishy," came his voice from above.

Greyson burst through the door to the first floor. The lobby. A sharp pain in his side – gasping for air. Guests giving him looks. "Help!" he cried out, but the Fisherman pushed anyone who stood in his way aside and waved his gun.

The Fisherman was slower than Greyson, but with fresh legs. He would outlast him. Let the boy tire out.

Greyson staggered through the rich hallway, circled around a fountain with a golden dolphin squirting spurts of water from its mouth. Past the movie theater and into the casino.

He stopped for a second inside, surrounded by bright lights and happy sounds, like a million video games rewarding him at once, begging to be played. The guests were too busy to notice the boy with a sweat-drenched shirt and fanny pack searching for a way out.

"Help!" he cried again. A few heads turned just in time to see a harpoon crash into a slot machine, setting off its jackpot light with flashes and loud music. Thinking fast, Greyson jerked the bundle of money from his pack and threw it in the air. The cloud of bills sent the place mad. The crowd swarmed just as Greyson slipped past, making his way to a side door.

As he reached the door, he looked back to see the Fisherman jostling with the crowd. He was slowed, but not for long. He jabbed the tip of the harpoon left and right, stuck it in a security guard's chest.

Fear shot through Greyson's veins as he turned and ran into the storm. Wind whipped at the water park's palm trees and loose leaves slapped at his skin before being blown away. The sidewalk led him on a winding path through the artificial jungle; he passed by an empty pool with beach chairs piled in stacks in the corner.

He glanced back. The Fisherman was leveling his gun.

Darting to the side, he ducked onto another path; a waterfall flowed over a rocky outcropping into a large pool where stingrays swarmed underneath the water; he crossed over a loping wooden bridge to a food area where the bar was shuttered, no longer selling fried food and drinks. The rain pelted the picnic tables' and the wind rippled the food hut's straw roof. The place had been evacuated. He was alone out here.

*Think, Greyson. You can't run forever!*

The rain pouring over his face seemed to finally wake him from panic mode.

*Turn and fight! You have an arrow of your own!*

But he couldn't. He was outmatched.

*Sapere Aude. Dare to be wise.*

He needed a game-changer – he'd just have to find one.

His feet stung inside his shoes as they pounded the cement up a winding slope, higher and higher until he stopped at a T-intersection. A wooden sign. 'Beach' on the right, 'Mayan Temple' to the left.

If he chose the beach, there would be nowhere to run except the ocean. And that's where a psycho with a harpoon gun would want him to go.

He jogged toward the temple and gawked at its size and beauty. Like a pyramid with steps, it looked to be made entirely of brown bricks. He couldn't remember much about the Mayans from history classes, but perhaps the temple would give him sanctuary like it had given the Mayans for centuries – before they went extinct at the hands of the Spanish.

Shaking off the thought, he disappeared inside a cavern cut out of its center. The darkness wrapped around him and sent a shiver down his spine. When his eyes adjusted, the velvety blue hue that waved throughout the room came into focus. The color was coming from both sides where the walls had been replaced by glass. Behind the glass was a view beneath a large pool, full of fish, stone statues, and…

*A shark!*

Goosebumps rose on his arms, and he kept his distance from the glass as more and more sharks slithered through the water, their rubbery bodies winding back and forth like engorged snakes. Their saw-like teeth showed at their gums, jagged and disgusting. Their gills flapped open and closed; their fins cut above like little warning flags.

He couldn't take his eyes off them. They were nasty – but hypnotizing. And as he followed one through the water, he saw it pass underneath a long, clear, plastic tube, big enough for a human to pass through. Big enough to be…a water slide.

*Who would put sharks in a water park?*

But he had stalled too long. He could hear the Fisherman's footsteps outside. He had to think. Fast.

Finding only one option, he burst up the stairs that wound higher and higher. On a normal day most kids would have been excited to climb the staircase without a line, but this wasn't a normal day. And Greyson didn't want the thrill of a slide.

He passed the blue inner tubes that had been stored behind a cage and churned up more and more stairs. Finally, when he reached the top, he managed to read the name of the slide.

Serpent's Slide.

*No way!*

"Heeeeee-re fishy, fishy, fishy."

Greyson gulped in air, wincing at the pain in his side and listening to the man's voice echo up from the staircase below.

"You run harder…hook goes deeeee-per."

The wind howled through the top of the temple and Greyson could see how dark the sky had grown over the waving palm trees. He was scared, but confident in his plan.

He leaned over the staircase railing and bellowed down. "Go away!" He added an extra-high screech to his voice and a sly smile. "Please!"

But then he stared at the black hole where the Serpent Slide began, a pair of serpent's fangs hanging above like a snake's gaping mouth. His smile vanished. The Serpent would suck him in and digest him through its winding belly, corkscrewing down and down until it pooped him into the shark-infested waters below.

He knew what he had to do.

*I dare you.*

Taking a deep breath, he planted his feet and plunged face-first into the snake's mouth.

The water splashed his face and rushed into his nostrils as he careened down the slide in utter darkness. It jostled him to the side – threw him to the other slide – banged his elbows on the other side – and finally plunged him straight into deeper water. *Was that it?*

He rose up from the water with his knees on the bottom of a slippery surface, disoriented. Though the slide's water hit his back from behind, the current slowed here. But it wasn't the end. Using the shuddering blue light, he found that he was in the transparent underwater section of the slide he had seen earlier. This was supposed to be the time in the ride where tube-riders 'ooo'ed and 'ahh'ed about the sharks.

Surrounded by glass and water, it was as if the sharks and the human had switched places in the aquarium. Now he was the one trapped – and they were the ones moving about, watching him.

One sent a shadow drifting over his head, but he was too busy unclipping his holster and unzipping his pack to notice.

His wet hands fumbled with the slingshot. He changed the strap. He loaded it with his last arrow. He placed it against the glass, drew it back as far as he could, closed his eyes, and let it go.

*SHMACK!*

He opened his eyes. The bolt-arrow had pierced the glass, but it had stuck halfway through.

A sudden vibration shook the slide. Another body had entered.

He was almost out of time.

Holstering his slingshot, he grabbed the arrow and pulled at it. He jerked it to the right and left and twisted it – but it barely budged. Tiny cracks had formed around the edges of the hole, but it wasn't enough for his plan.

300

Splashing in the water, he dunked himself under and kicked at the arrow. The cracks split wider and wider. Water began dribbling around the shaft. And then it began spurting inside. Suddenly the cracks made a crunching sound.

*Time to go.*

He half-swam, half-crawled through the last section, eyeing a lurking shark below him but giving backward glances over his shoulder for the greater danger.

He turned just in time to see the Fisherman splash into the shark section. But as the Fisherman rose up with the harpoon gun leveled, his forehead struck the back of the sling-arrow that jutted from the top of the glass. His harpoon fired past Greyson's shoulder, scraping the glass and disappearing through the slide's last plunge into the pool below.

Greyson stalled just before the drop to see the Fisherman grasp at his forehead, blood seeping through his fingers and into the water around him. And his forehead seemed to do the trick on the arrow. The cracks spread like a spider-web. Water gushed through the opening, and with a magnificent crash, an implosion of water followed like a torrent. The entire tube collapsed inward; the tidal wave of water blasted into Greyson and swallowed him as it spat him into the pool.

He toppled head over heels underwater; the water stirred him like he'd fallen into a raging waterfall. Holding his breath, he fought for control; he couldn't tell up from down. The current was too strong.

And then it happened. A large body hit against his, but it wasn't the Fisherman's. Its powerful grey shape loomed over him as he flailed about. Greyson's skin crawled and he let out a muffled scream. Suddenly the grey shape thrashed about; its fin scraped against his arm; the water gurgled and bubbled; he saw its jaws flash by, and red water mixed with blue.

His head felt like it would explode, and his heart thumped with panic; the red water burned his eyes as he searched and kicked until finally, his body hit a wall; he scraped at it until he felt his body lifting higher. He saw the light above; with desperate kicks and a lunge, he burst out of the water, grabbing at the side of the pool.

Just as he pulled himself out, expecting to have his legs ripped from his body, he saw the red dripping over his eyes. And when he rolled to the ground, he realized he was covered in it from head to toe.

*Blood.*

It covered him.

Still gasping for air, he rubbed his hands over his body, searching for bite marks – but there were none. As his heart continued to thrash in his chest, he rolled to his side on the cement and investigated the pool. The current had slowed from the slide opening, but the water that came stirred the red water, diluting it. The grey fin rose above the surface, jerking about like a sail.

The shark lunged above the water and snapped a harpoon in two, submerging again to continue feeding.

*There fishy, fishy, fishy…*

Before he turned away from the grotesque scene, a red hat lolled toward him on the pool's surface. He snagged it, hugged it close, and rolled to his back, staring into the rain clouds, letting the rain wash the blood from his face as he tried to breathe slower and slower. He was almost too tired to move. Too sore. Too scared. It had been right next to him. He could still feel its rough skin on his. He shuddered.

As he closed his eyes, his head still swirled as if underwater. He wanted to drift to sleep, listening to the wind and the pattering rain. He was one with the cement – he was a stone, letting the gravity pull him in, forcing him to rest. A hurricane couldn't make him get up.

"Greyson?"

# Chapter 53

Two figures stood looking at Greyson, the pouring rain bouncing off their shoulders.

Greyson pushed himself off the cement, feeling every sore muscle. He stared at them for a long moment, his mind blank, and the twins stared back – their mouths hanging open. They gawked at the blood twisting down his clothes. His buzzed hair and the scar on his brow. They didn't have the words.

Greyson wanted to greet them but couldn't. Maybe it was the shock or the dizziness from the pool. He just stood there, tottering and trying not to let the wind blow him over.

And then someone came running, shoving her way between the twins and lunging for Greyson. Before he knew what had happened, Sydney had wrapped him in a wet hug, burying her face in his shoulder.

"Greyson!" she cried with a scratch in her voice. "Thank, God. You're alive!"

Grimacing from the painful hug, he wrapped her in his arms as well, holding her close in the rain. He'd been imagining the moment for weeks, and now that it was here, it was so much better. To hug a friend after so long, to smell her hair, to know she had been longing to hug him back made all the days of suffering seem dim in comparison.

Finally, she pulled back and looked at him fully. She was beautiful.

"Hi," he said sheepishly.

She half-smiled, half-frowned as she stroked his eyebrow, examining the mark. "Are you okay?"

"Yeah. It's not my blood."

He donned his hat while watching the shark still thrashing in the pool.

"You look different," she said, matter-of-fact. Her eyes examined his features.

*Different? Is that a good thing?* "I cut my hair."

"Not just your hair…"

Nick took a step forward and cocked his head. "You a Plurb now?" His tone wasn't accusing; it was curious – almost a little hopeful.

"No," he replied. "Just a mark."

Nick nodded.

"You're so tan. And your voice is deeper," Jarryd added, still keeping his distance.

Greyson shrugged.

"You got pit-hair now, too?"

He nodded with a tired smile. "A little."

"Sweet."

Sydney shook her head with a disgusted wince. "Annnny-way...you made it."

"Yeah."

"Your dad?"

He shook his head. "Not yet. Just got here today."

She flashed him a sympathetic look. "Us too. Paradise, huh?"

He gave a short laugh, but an urgency crept into his voice. "I think that guy was after you guys before he went after me."

Sydney recalled walking out of the room to see the Fisherman running toward the staircase. They had followed at a distance. "It's because of what we did on the ship."

The rain began to pick up, and distant voices drifted through the palm trees, prompting Greyson to rush forward. He grabbed her hand. "Come on, boy!" Realizing his mistake, he shook his head, "I mean...come on!" Pulling the confused Sydney past the twins, he urged them onward. "We've got to hide. Fill me in."

Sydney whispered hard over the wind and rain. "They poisoned our parents...and Sammy."

He trodded along as the twins caught up. "What? Poisoned?"

"Yeah," she answered. "The mints at the hotel."

"Are they okay?"

Jarryd blurted, "We don't know. Didn't get to taste them. Sammy ate 'em before –"

"They're still breathing," Sydney interjected. "It must have been like a tranquilizer or something."

They splashed through the wet ground, cutting through the food area and winding along the path. As they made their way to an artificial cave, Greyson stopped and scanned the corners for any more Plurbs. "Wait. Stop here. We have to think."

Nick smiled at Greyson, anxious to hear what he had to say.

"You have to tell me everything," he commanded. It was much quieter, and his voice echoed. "What happened on the ship?"

Sydney and Nick explained everything, and Jarryd added details about Avery. When Sydney told of their discovery of the Plurbs on the cruise, Greyson's eyes were lost in a daydream, visualizing each event. They told him about the text messages they had received while in possession of the watch, the interview with Baldy afterwards, and their eventual discovery of Daryl's identity. Greyson thoughts were making connections every which way.

"…and then we followed you out here."

Greyson nodded, returning from his daydream. For a moment he wrestled with the options. There were so many things to consider, and each one demanded him. The parents inside the hotel, the terrorists on the cruise…his dad. Each one would be good to pursue. Each would be daring.

It was never easy.

*Recruit your friends and find Dad*, part of him urged. *What else did you come here for?*

"What do we do now, Greyson?"

"I…don't know. We could go to your parents…or we could find my dad and he could help."

They were nodding. They were willing.

But he recalled his vow to never again leave anyone behind. If he left the terrorists to do what they want, it would be as if he were leaving all the passengers behind. He couldn't. There was good to do. It would require every ounce of daring he had, but he knew he had to do it.

*Don't lose yourself while finding him.* If he did ever find his dad, he wanted to be the boy his dad had left. A boy who stood for good, no matter how hard it was. A boy, who, like Jesus, was on a mission – but who would still stop to save people or to fight evil.

"Or we could try to save the people on the ship," he whispered.

"All 8,000 of them," Nick added.

Greyson met eyes with each of his friends. They didn't know about the Payback List. They didn't know the significance of the number 8,000. But he did. It confirmed his decision. He had found a stiff resolve, realizing what he had to do. The burden eased from his conscience, and he almost smiled.

But first, he had forgotten something. He took Nick into a hug and patted his back. "Thanks for coming after me. I like your fanny pack."

Surprised, Nick hugged him back with a pat of his own. "Thanks."

Jarryd was next, though he was squeamish about the blood on his clothes.

"You have to meet Avery. She's Australian, so you *know* she's hot."

Nick scoffed. "You're so racist."

"What? How?"

"You prefer one race over another."

Jarryd laughed and pointed at his chest. "You're the one who like the Kentucky Derby but says Nascar is for hicks. Who's racist now?"

"Not that kind of races…"

"Guys." Greyson interrupted.

The twins turned to him. "Sorry."

"Anyway. Thank you guys – for coming all the way here…to help me."

The three of them nodded and smiled.

"You guys are the best friends I could ask for."

"Ah shucks," Jarryd chimed.

"But I need your help again. And we can't go back to the hotel."

"But what about our parents?" Sydney complained, trying not to show her fear. "And Sammy?"

"We got one of them, but who knows how many more are after you…waiting for you to come back? And if we told security, they would contact someone in the US government, who for some reason is trying to kill me."

Nick drew back, concerned. He shared a look with Sydney as Greyson went on.

"Plus, we just don't have time. You said the Plurb text said they would depart at 4 p.m.?"

"Yeah," Nick answered, "that's two hours before Captain Chip said we should be back! They must want to leave some people behind."

Greyson eyed his watch. *3:45.* "Then we have fifteen minutes to get back on the ship."

"What?" the three kids eyed Greyson like he was crazy.

"We have to stop them."

"But…"

"Look. They're going to keep coming after us. We run. We hide – but they find us. And they won't stop until we're all dead."

They stared at him. A confident, almost sinister look formed on his face, the mark on his brow more visible in the cave's hard light.

"I'm tired of running."

Sydney shook her head in frustration. "What about your dad? He's in

Nassau, right? And you want to leave?"

The thought nipped at him once more, but there was a new clarity he hadn't had before. He set his jaw and looked to each one of them. "I don't know where he is, but I know my dad. He finds trouble or it finds him. If the Plurbs have been planning something on Nassau, getting ready for it – maybe he'll be on that ship trying to stop it."

The twins and Sydney gave him skeptical looks, and he was beyond skeptical himself.

"But if he's not – I want him to be proud of me when I find him. I want him to know that we always did what was right – no matter how hard it was."

The rest of the kids felt his passion. Sydney gave him an agreeing nod. "I'm with you."

Her comment gave wind to his sails. She had always been his main supporter. She had urged him to do what was right from the very start. If only she had been with him when he had made the wrong decision at the fair...

"We're in, too," Jarryd declared. "Sucks for you after coming all this way."

"Yeah. But sometimes you have to go west to go south." After his friends gave him confused looks, he went on. "Anyway, have you guys told anyone else about the Plurbs?"

Nick nodded. "Sydney's Dad – he called the FBI."

"No," Sydney sighed, disappointed with herself. "He didn't."

"What?" Nick huffed. "You heard the call..."

She shook her head. "No. He called Sam's tutor. He's like a computer genius or something and he tricked the FBI and set it all up for us to be here. Sam gave our parents his tutor's phone number as the FBI contact when he set it all up."

"Really?" Nick grew angry. He hadn't realized he'd been left out of so much. "So, the FBI doesn't know we're here?"

She shook her head. "Why does it matter? Sam's tutor got us here and now he'll send help."

"Will he? Do you even know him?"

"No, but I know Sam..."

After more arguing, Greyson had enough. "Okay, okay. Cool it. How many minutes do we have now, Nick?"

Nick glanced at his watch and rolled his eyes. "Thirteen."

"How do we get back to the dock in thirteen minutes or less? Think!"

Jarryd pumped his chin. "Find a horse."

"Think harder."

"A steel horse?"

Greyson rolled his eyes. "Think smarter."

"A nerd horse?"

A memory flashed in Sydney's mind and she leaned in. "Waverunners."

Greyson's eyes lit up. "Where?"

"They were putting them away in a shed on the beach."

"Does anyone know how to drive one?"

Jarryd laughed.

---------------

Sam's fingers rested on the piano keys, but his heart was not in the music; his mind was elsewhere. The piano was oddly placed at the end of a wide hallway, placed by two giant ferns and leather chairs meant for casual listeners. The Grand Hotel had wealthy guests who were accustomed to having a grand piano placed in one of their many rooms, so Sam guessed it was placed there to make them feel at home. But for his purposes, it allowed him to get his daily thirty minutes in, even while stuck in Washington D.C.

He glanced down the hall where two men in suits watched the lobby. One of the men sensed Sam's look and turned. Sam took his secret service agent's gaze as a *keep playing*-type of look.

Taking a deep sigh, he tried to slow his rapid thoughts while playing a slow, methodic tune.

He couldn't wrap his head around what had happened to Calvin – and the fact that his dad approved of it. One moment his mind would rush to his dad's defense. *Calvin was helping the terrorists! He was going to share the nation's secrets like a traitor!* But the next moment he'd remember Calvin drinking Mountain Dew, talking about his girlfriend, helping him send his friends to the Bahamas and giving him ideas for his notes to Sydney.

The tune grew lighter, and the tempo picked up. His fingers danced on the keys.

*Secrets.*

The word popped in his mind, and he wrestled with it. The nation had them – kept them from its people. That had been hard to hear, but his dad had made sense. The secrets may look bad but actually be good. And by keeping the secret, the government was actually doing the nation a favor – keeping it together.

*Everyone has secrets.*

He hit a wrong key but didn't flinch. He continued as if it hadn't happened. His piano teacher had taught him the art of covering mistakes – don't acknowledge them. Most in the audience wouldn't even notice one wrong note when it was covered by five right ones, but if he made a face or acted flustered – that's when they'd discover his secret.

*I have a secret.*

It was true. He'd stolen his dad's signature, helped Calvin forge documents, and lied to FBI agents.

His breath caught in his throat, and the rhythm of the song suffered. The guilt pressed at his lungs. He'd lied to the government – just like Calvin. He'd lied to his dad. He'd meant good, but he'd had to do those bad things to do so.

He hated himself as he plucked erratically at the keys. How could he have judged his dad when he was just like him? *At least Dad had been honest – and I am still hiding things from him!*

Playing one last chord, his jaw shook, and a tear streaked down his cheek as he hung his head. He cried onto his tie, keeping his sobs to a whimper.

Suddenly the bench creaked, and his dad scooted next to him. Sam looked at him through blurry eyes.

"Play with me, son. Schubert Serenade."

His father began the song, beating out its slow, but happy melody. Uncertain, Sam took in deep breaths and wiped at his tears – ashamed. As Sam's entrance to the song approached, his father gave him a sideways glance and a nod.

Sam's fingers found their place and he joined in, tentatively at first, but soon matching his father's grace and tempo. The song was one of his favorites – fairly simple, but beautiful – captivating, but somehow somber, too.

Taken with the song, he almost forgot why he was crying. But when he did, he had to say something.

"Dad?"

The governor kept playing, not missing a beat. "Yeah?"

"I…I have to tell you something."

"Go ahead. You can always tell me anything."

Sam cleared his throat and gulped down the lump. He had to share. No matter the consequences, he just had to. "I…have a secret."

"I know."

His response sent a shudder through Sam's body. "Y-you know?"

His father smiled. "Of course. It was a clever idea, and well executed. And they did need the vacation."

It took a few more measures for Sam to process the thought. *He knew the whole time? He let me use his signature? And he was okay with it?* "You're not mad?"

The Governor kept playing. He would tell his son only what he needed to know. He didn't need to know that he had discovered his son's plot early enough to change the families' ship itinerary. They had been slotted for The American Spirit, but having the witnesses on the Spirit wouldn't have given him the perfect opportunity to tie up loose ends like having them on the American Dream would.

"Nah. You made a tough choice out of love for your friends. And you used everything at your disposal to do it – including me."

Sam missed a note but recomposed himself. "But...I..."

"I suppose it's because we share the same blood."

"What?"

His father kept playing, speaking as if to the keys. "When I ordered the attack on the terrorists' moving truck in Des Moines, I thought you were still in it. It was the worst night of my life. I couldn't imagine you in pain, with the terrorists." He seethed with anger for a moment, replacing his sadness, but the gloom returned with the next measure. "And when they made their demands, I made the hardest possible decision any father would have to make – and I made it for the 200,000 citizens of Des Moines. I did what was good for the many...at your expense...just like you did what was good for *your* friends at *my* expense." He gave Sam a sideways look.

"I love you so much, Sam. More than anything! And I know you feel the same. But we also love our country and its people. And I've sworn to protect them. If I had the same choice today, I'd have to make it."

The song built toward the end as Sam furrowed his brow. There was something he had to ask. "But what if it wasn't 200,000 this time? Would you make the same decision to save a hundred, or five?"

The governor gave him a sly smile. "You're worth many more than that, Sam. Millions. Billions. But think about this. If I had chosen to save you, and let the truck go into the heart of the city, how would you have felt afterward, when tens of thousands died so that I could save you?"

Sam suddenly thought of Greyson's story about the bridge and how he'd abandoned the moving truck to rescue Sydney from the river. Did she feel responsible for the deaths because she was the reason Greyson failed to stop the bomb? Or did she feel loved by Greyson beyond all measure? Or both?

"I don't know. Guilty? But also kind of special…loved."

"Well, if you'd like, I can kill 8,000 people for you."

Sam scoffed at the joke. "No, thanks."

His dad laughed as they finished the song with a flurried crescendo. After the final chords had echoed down the hall, leaving a ringing silence, he turned to his son. "Sam – you are special – I love you very much. And I'm going to do everything I can to make it so that I am never faced with that kind of decision again. You're everything to me. Your mom would be proud of you."

They embraced hard. Sam buried his face in his dad's suit and felt his heart beating strong.

"And I forgive you," his father whispered down.

Sam held back his tears. "I forgive you, too."

Finally releasing the hug, his father held him by the shoulders and looked down on him. "No more secrets. We're a team. And I love you…more than like *five* people."

"Five *billion*!"

"That's what I meant."

They laughed as Sam shifted in his seat just to make sure he felt the thumb drive was still there – hidden in his back pocket. He almost told his dad about it, but something stopped him. He needed to know why Calvin had died. He *needed* to know what secrets the government was keeping. He loved his dad more than anything in the world, but like his dad had shown – sometimes people have to hurt the ones they love to do what they think is right. So, he'd check into it himself, find out the government's secrets, and then destroy the evidence. His dad would never know and would never be hurt.

And *then* there would be no more secrets.

311

# Chapter 54

"UGHHH!"

With one last tug, the second waverunner slid down the trailer's ramp and plowed into the ocean water. While it had been easy for Sydney to pick the lock and find the waverunner keys hanging inside the shed, it had been treacherous pulling the trailer through the beach in torrential rain and gusting wind. It had taken all four of them.

The tide washed in and out, pushing the waverunners further onto the sand and then pulling them toward the dark, open sea.

"Ready?" Jarryd yelled, a wide smile dripping with the downpour.

Greyson didn't wait to respond. He rushed through the ankle-high waves and pushed one of the waverunners further out by the handlebars. When the tide came in, the heavy vehicle moved forward several feet until it rested again in the sand. As he was waiting for the next wave, Sydney joined him, pushing on the other side. Together they pushed it out, smashing into a waist-high wave and tasting the saltwater that smacked their faces.

"Now!" Sydney jumped on first as the waverunner free floated, but Greyson was close behind. Her legs just beat his to the seat and she jostled with him for the front position.

"I'm driving," she demanded.

The waverunner rocked back and forth as Greyson's feet nearly slipped from the footrest. He grasped at the seat and held on for dear life. But he wouldn't sit behind her. "No way! I'm driving!"

She scoffed. "What? The fate of the world resting on a first-time jet-skier? Just hold on tight!"

"Where?" He looked for handholds on the side of the long seat, but there were none.

"On my waist – it's got plenty to hold on to."

He looked at her thin waist, which appeared extra thin with the wet t-shirt clinging to it. She was calling herself fat?

"Hurry up. Just act like you like me and sit your *buns* down."

The other waverunner roared to life and Jarryd came alongside, with Nick holding his brother's waist and pressing against his back.

"Like this!" Nick yelled.

Greyson gave them an awkward look before turning to Sydney, who had a death grip on the handlebars. She motioned him over with her eyes.

Another wave sent them rolling upward and Greyson toppled toward the seat. Grunting out of frustration, he flung his leg over. Despite his efforts, his body slid on the seat until it pressed against her back. His hands awkwardly hovered close to her waist before she grabbed them and pressed them on with a huff of frustration. A chill ran up his arms.

"It's okay," she whispered, turning to him. "Friends can hug."

She smiled at him and time froze. He smiled back, suddenly looking at her like he had looked at her picture. The same sparkle in her blue eyes. The wet, blonde strands blowing over her ears. The drops of rain dripping from her long eyelashes and washing down the ski-slope of her nose. The picture had been only a reflection, a captured memory, but now she was here – the imagined now real and warm. She was no longer something beautiful to look at – now she was someone beautiful to hold. A new spark lit inside of him; he had never longed for her in this way.

Maybe this is what love felt like.

Sydney swung her head back around as Jarryd blasted off, bouncing over the waves and screaming manically. And then she twisted the handlebar, accelerating with a jerk. The momentum pushed Greyson backward and a salty wave slapped his face, so he grabbed her shirt and pulled even closer to her on the seat.

The waverunner bounced hard left and right, spraying water from their underside and cutting through swelling waves. The ocean water bit at their exposed skin and burned their eyes, but the exhilaration was real. Sydney kept Jarryd in sight as they buzzed along with the beach on their left.

The ride was frightening for Greyson. He had no control. Sydney jostled with the handlebars, going way too fast, ramping off the bigger and bigger waves, landing with thuds each time before accelerating and skimming over the choppy waters, all while the wind whipped at their clothes. As a passenger, he didn't have the handlebars to break his impact. His body slid upwards with each jump and slammed into the seat with each landing. The friction bit at his wet skin and the drops to the seat made him wince.

But despite the pain, the hug was worth it. He felt guilty liking it, but he couldn't help it.

"It's great, isn't it?" Sydney yelled breathily.

"What?" Greyson's cheek had been nestled in a crook in her back.

"This is fun!"

"Yeah...ugh...just great!"

"There it is!"

Greyson blinked rapidly, trying to shake off the water's mist as they circled around Paradise Island. Though he had to squint through stinging eyes, peeking between the wet locks of Sydney's hair, he saw what she had seen – the gigantic ocean liner, still hugging the narrow dock. "Geez...it's huge. Go around," Greyson yelled, "so they can't see us from the dock!"

"I know, I know!"

Sydney cranked the accelerator to its max and skipped over the waves, passing Jarryd and Nick to show them the way around. Though Jarryd probably didn't like being passed, he caught the hint and followed her in a wide loop, coming in on the side of the ship. They cut the engines at the same time and drifted toward the towering white hull.

Craning their necks upward, they could barely see the top deck. There was nothing but rows and rows of windows, a few rows of balconies, and a line of large, orange lifeboats at the top. No doors, no ramps, and no ropes meant there was no way on the ship.

"Now what?" Jarryd asked as his waverunner sided up to Sydney's.

"We have to find a way in."

"Why not just go in the other side like everyone else?" Jarryd asked.

Nick hit his shoulder from behind. "Cuz they just tried to kill us, dimwit. If we go through their security with our cruise IDs, they'll know they didn't succeed – and they'll try again."

Jarryd nodded slowly as their waverunners lolled on the waves. He flipped his wet hair to the side and then suddenly sat up straight with a look of victory. "Anybody got a phone?"

Nick and Greyson shook their heads.

"Why?" Sydney asked.

Jarryd breathed heavy with excitement. "You got one?"

"Yeah. Stole it back from the parents. Who you gonna call?"

Jarryd pumped his chin. "My beautimus maximus."

"Uh...what?" Sydney asked.

"Avery. She's beatiumus to the maximus."

"Just a tip – don't call her that. But why are you calling her? What's *she* going to do?"

Greyson butted in. "She's on the ship? This girl?"

314

Jarryd smiled wide. "Wait 'til you meet her. Her legs are like longer than…"

"Shut up, Jarryd," Sydney hissed. "Greyson, the phone's in my bag."

Greyson leaned back, pulled her bag's opening wide enough for his hand to fit through, and ruffled through the contents.

"So, you know her number already?" Sydney asked.

"Of course. Even her country code. Sixty-one!"

"Didn't know you could count that high."

"You don't know a lot of things about me."

"Oh, yeah? Neither does she."

"Yeah she does. 'Cuz we talk. You should try it – talking to her. You might like her instead of just being all stuck up and jealous."

Sydney's eyes narrowed. Nick had kept to himself as the two fought, still holding onto Jarryd's back, but he jabbed a finger into his brother's side to let him know that he had gone too far.

"So what if I'm jealous?" Sydney asked with a fighting tone.

"Of course you are," Jarryd shrugged. "Who wouldn't be jealous of her?"

Nick shook his head. "Doesn't help, Jarryd. Doesn't help."

Jarryd bit his lip. "You know what I mean…"

"Oh, I do!" she exclaimed, turning away and watching the waves lick at the sides of the ship. "You mean I should be jealous of her body – and maybe I am – but I shouldn't be. Not all boys are as shallow as you – and some might think I'm perfect just the way I am."

"Like Sam?" Greyson asked. Sydney whipped around and dropped her jaw in despair. Greyson was giving her an accusing look, holding Sam's picture in one hand, his note in the other.

"You read it?" Sydney asked.

A long moment passed as he nodded, letting the wind and the rain do the only talking. He was wrestling with what to say and how to say it. Anger and jealousy battled with disappointment and defeat. *'What the heck?'* he wanted to shout. *Why would you let him give you this? Why would you keep it in your fanny bag? Was it really that important to you?* He also wanted to know for sure. *Are you dating him now? Is this how you dump me? Or were we even dating?*

But he just stared at her, taking deep breaths through his nose to keep calm. She reached out for the note, but he drew it back and held it over the waves. Her eyes widened, and she gulped as she stared at the note, considering what to say. "Fine. Do it," she said at last.

He raised his eyebrows. "Don't you want to keep it safe so you can read it over and over?"

"It's not like that, Greyson."

"Oh, yeah?"

Nick reached across the gap and tapped Greyson. "Give me the phone. I'll call while you guys work this out."

Greyson handed him the phone, keeping his eye on Sydney and the note held over the water. "Then what's it like?"

She sighed. "I…it's just a nice note."

"It says there are other notes."

"It also says he hopes I find you."

"And that he *admires* you."

She flinched. "Is that so bad? Couldn't hurt *you* to say it every once and awhile."

"*Admires?* Who *says* that?"

Suddenly Jarryd swiped the note from Greyson's hand. "This sounds juicy!"

"Hey!"

He hastily read the note.

Sydney almost jumped the gap to tackle the note from Jarryd's stupid hands, but she sat back down in defeat. "Who cares? He's a nice guy. He got us here didn't he? To help us find you, Greyson."

That's what Greyson hated most about him. He was too dang nice. He not only hated him, he felt guilty for hating him.

"Here," he said, handing over the picture. "Maybe we should all go see him after this so I can thank him face to face." *Fist to face.*

"Good," Sydney said, ignoring Greyson's true intentions all while stuffing the picture in her pocket. "Or we can try calling him next."

"Got his number in your phone?"

"Yeah, so? He might be able to help us from D.C."

"Oh, D.C.? He *must* be special."

"Stop being dumb."

A burning anger wrinkled his chin and he nearly surrendered to it. He *almost* said, "Can't you see he's trying to *steal* you? He's helping you, giving his picture, writing you notes, calling you, *admiring* you! He wants you to

316

himself! And then what? They've stolen my mom, my dad, *and* you? What do I have left then? Huh? What do I have left?"

But he didn't. He said, "You stop being dumb!"

Still, though, his friends must have understood. Maybe they could read it in his eyes, his voice, his body language. Whatever it was, the argument was over.

Nick hung up the phone and joined the awkward pause. They watched Greyson turn away to hide his trembling lips. The other three shared a collective desire to comfort him, but none wanted to initiate it. The storm continued to rage on, whipping the palm trees on the shore and whistling over the top deck far above. The storm swells lifted them higher and rocked them over and over.

Finally, Sydney spun on her seat to face Greyson. She put her hand on his shoulder. "I'm sorry, Greyson."

He huffed and puffed, trying to slow his breathing. "Whatever. We need to get on this ship. Maybe look for another way – or we can find a rope..."

"Greyson, hold on." She pressed him down in his seat, but he sneered, trying to ignore her.

"Give me the note," she demanded Jarryd.

Jarryd handed it over and she promptly ripped it and dropped it in the waves. Greyson watched the pieces float away.

"We were both being dumb, alright?" she asked, not waiting for an answer. "You left us, and I let him...well, whatever. But it doesn't matter anymore. We've got each other now and a mission to do."

"That's right, G-Man!" Jarryd shouted over his shoulder. "We stick together. The whole squad. And Avery."

Sydney ignored him. "I think we're all just tired and...scared."

"And I got to go to the bathroom," Jarryd added. "I get cranky when I need to go. Mind if I go off the side?"

"Yes, we mind," Sydney chided.

"Fine." He jumped in the water, grabbing on to the footrest. He smiled at them with his head above water. "Mind all you want. Keep talking."

"You're going right now, aren't you?"

"Ahhhh..."

Greyson cracked a smile. He'd missed Jarryd. He'd missed all of them.

"You're disgusting," Sydney said, turning back to Greyson. "Anyway, what were we saying?"

Greyson made intermittent eye contact with her. "I'm...I'm sorry, too. Just...jealous, I guess."

Sydney looked inward. "You and me both."

"Me, too," said Nick.

Jarryd climbed back up, arching his brow at Nick. "Huh?"

Nick shrugged, holding the phone back to Sydney. "Yeah. Jealous you have a girl who will totally save us! Look!"

Nick pointed into the rain toward the top of the white, mountainous hull. Something large dangled in the sky, drifting toward them, growing larger and larger. The kids' eyes followed it, but only Nick knew what it was – for he had given Avery the instructions.

"It's a lifeboat!"

The orange boat was bigger than a van, with a covered roof that made it look more like a spaceship than a boat. As it lowered closer to them, Jarryd Sydney turned their engines back on.

"Back up!"

The waverunners kicked into reverse and steered clear of the boat as it smacked the water. When Greyson saw that the two ropes still hooked to the top of the boat trailed all the way to cranes on the top deck, the plan fit together.

"Get on the boat!" he commanded. And he gave Nick a nod of acknowledgment for the brilliant idea.

Far above, Avery waved down at them, though the storm and the sudden roar of the ship's engines drowned her voice out. A loud blasting air horn signaled the cruise's departure, and the hull began a slow churn through the water.

It was leaving without them and pulling their lifeboat with it.

"Jump on!"

Sydney made the jump, grabbing one of the hooks and squirming over the slippery top to a sitting position. Nick and then Jarryd followed suit, just barely grabbing the rope as it floated further away.

The lifeboat drifted in front of Greyson's waverunner, pushing it away with its wake. The waves swelled, splashing warm water on his clothes as he balanced on the rocking seat. Finally working up the courage, he took one step and launched from the front panel.

His arms reached out for Nick's hands. Jarryd's mouth hung agape as he watched Greyson fall short.

# Chapter 55

Greyson was still catching his breath as the cranes finally cranked them to the top deck. It had been another close call. He'd just caught the top edge of the lifeboat long enough for Nick and Jarryd to pull him up.

The lifeboat jerked to a stop at the top.

"'Ello, mates!"

Greyson turned and took in the sight of Avery with a white beach dress that flowed in the wind. She smiled at him brilliantly, but he averted his eyes – especially knowing that Sydney was probably watching his reaction.

Avery helped Jarryd over the railing first, and he veered into her arms. He hugged her and looked back to Greyson with a chin pump, but Greyson had already started scanning the boat for terrorists.

Avery reached next for Sydney, but she was already helping herself from the boat to the deck. Instead, she grabbed Greyson's arm and helped him.

As soon as he found his sea legs, he was able to take a closer look at their rescuer. Jarryd had been right about her beauty. He couldn't help but take a second look. She smiled, still taking glances at him as she helped Nick.

"Thanks," Greyson managed to say, turning his hat and tipping it at her.

"Any time."

Greyson felt Sydney's eyes on him.

"I'm Avery."

Greyson nodded at her but furrowed his brow with determination. "Greyson," he noted as he rushed past her. Much to Sydney's surprise, he was rushing to her. He looked straight at her eyes. "We need to hide. Know a place?"

Sydney stumbled with her words as she noticed Avery arch her brow. She probably wasn't used to getting brushed off. "Uh…actually, the best place will probably be the top deck. No one will be up here in the storm."

"How about the waterpark?" Nick suggested.

Greyson drew back. "They have a waterpark?"

"Dude, you missed out," Jarryd exclaimed, patting him on the back.

Sydney smiled. "We'll take you with us next time."

Abruptly, Greyson's face changed, and he pulled Sydney down to the wooden floor. "Down!" he whispered.

The rest followed suit and peered across the darkened deck that shone with a glaze of rainwater. They heard footsteps and masculine voices.

"Quick." Greyson led them along the wall to a corner. At their backs were stacks of rooms where the cockpit would be. Guests weren't allowed up, but they could see the crew walkway that led to the communications tower and satellite dishes. It was on that walkway that two men dressed in full white sailor gear and long, black raincoats were making their way to the top. A spiral staircase led them to the tower.

"It's Suk!" Jarryd whispered with a rasp. "He's a Plurb, and he's got a wicked uni-brow…"

"His name isn't 'Suck'," Nick scolded.

"Yeah it is. S-U-K. Last name's 'Toe'. Haha!"

Nick shook his head. "It's probably pronounced 'Sook', but I don't think that matters to you."

"You're right."

"Well, it should. He's probably just as sensitive about his name as you are about your teeth. How would you like it if Jarryd meant Buck-Toothed in Korean?"

"I'd avoid all Koreans…wait…maybe that's why he wants to kill us? 'Cuz a bunch of Americans keep making fun of his sucky name."

Nick raised his eyebrows. "Makes you think."

Greyson hushed them and they listened closely; but the men were no longer talking.

"What are they doing?" Jarryd asked.

"They're cleaning the satellite dishes," Nick responded.

"Really?"

"Yeah. They don't fit in the dishwasher." Nick rolled his eyes.

Greyson hushed them again. "Remember the fair? When that van raised that antenna and our cell phones didn't work? This could be the same thing."

"They're shutting down the cell tower," Nick agreed.

Sydney suddenly whipped her drawstring bag around and removed the phone. "I know they might intercept this, but I don't care."

---------------

Sam felt the phone buzz in his pocket but didn't let his face register it. He knew who was calling, and desperately wanted to answer, but his dad was in the middle of another speech. He glanced at the people at his table, and then across the room to the guard with the StoneWater emblem on his suit. The guard was already watching him. He let the phone buzz its last.

--------------

Greyson watched the two men open the control hatch and insert some sort of tool. He turned to Sydney as she hung up.

"No answer," she whispered. "He must not be able to…"

Greyson reached for the phone, but Sydney pulled it away. "Wait," she said, "I have to try our parents."

-----------------

Sydney's mother's phone rang in her purse, a ringtone of "The Sun Will Come Out Tomorrow" from the musical Annie. It had always cheered her up, but not today. Her body was lifeless.

A gloved hand reached into her purse and answered the phone. "Hello?"

*"Dad – is that you?"*

In the hotel suite, the gloved man smiled and eyed the girl's dad. His limp hands were being tied by another gloved man, preparing to move the unconscious body. "No, Deary. We are emergency responders. Is this your mother's phone I'm talking on?"

*"Yes, it is. Are they okay?"*

"Yes, they'll be just fine in a few hours. What about you? Where are you? Do you need help?"

There was a long pause on the other line.

The man tried again. "I hear the wind. You must be outside. Awful dangerous out there. Can you make it back here?"

After another long pause and hushed voices, a boy came on the phone.

*"We killed the fisherman guy you sent after us, and we called the FBI. They'll be there to kill you shortly."*

The gloved man gave his partner a look and a shrug. He dropped his nice voice. "If you called the FBI, we'd know about it, kid. Now come back to the hotel or you'll never see your parents and brother again."

*"We would come back to kill you, too, but we can't right now. We can call you back in a*

321

*day or two, maybe. What's your name?"*

"Listen kid, you don't…"

*Click.*

----------------

Greyson swallowed hard and nodded at Sydney and then the twins. "They're alive. We'll go back to get'em, okay?"

They nodded their approval, still watching the men work at the communication tower. Sparks blasted from the pane, but the men continued working. Greyson looked at Sydney's phone. It still had a connection.

Excited with an idea, he whipped out his Bible to find the number he needed. Sydney watched. Her eye caught the edge of the Polaroid, being used as a bookmark.

Greyson punched in the numbers. "Come on…answer…"

----------------

Dan pressed the phone between his pilot's headphones and his ear. "Who's this and how'd you get this number?"

*"Yes! Dan! It's Greyson, and I'm on my friend's phone. I don't have much time."*

Dan surveyed the horizon as he listened. They were approaching their landing in Florida. "You landed safely? Thank, God."

*"Yes, yes. But I need your help. We're on a cruise ship. A big white one."* There was a pause and more young voices. *"The American Dream it's called. And the Plurbs are doing stuff to the satellite dishes. And they have smart watches. And…we don't know, but there might be an attack soon!"*

Dan caught Greyson's urgency and punched in a few buttons on the control panel. "I can't turn back now. Low on fuel and about to land. Do you know where you're headed?"

*"We're just leaving Nassau, but I can't tell which way…"*

"Then listen. Find a safe place to hide. Don't rush into something stupid, but if you're able, find out what you can. I'll contact Grover and see what he can do." There was a long pause. "Greyson? Are you there?"

The call had ended.

Dan glanced at Asher, who had fear plastered on his young face. The plane shook, but their stare was unfazed.

322

"He'll be okay, Ash."

---------------

The sparks flew again, and this time it worked. The control panel's lights flicked off and the electric hum dimmed to silence. Suk nodded at his partner and pocketed the screwdriver. Their job was done. There would be panicked passengers for the next few minutes, but nothing like the panic that would ensue shortly after.

He snickered to himself as they descended the spiral staircase, but he stopped suddenly. He'd heard something.

He peered to his right, down the deck's perimeter railing where the lifeboats were suspended off the side. The wind was whipping a loose rope about, but there was nothing else. His narrow eyes glowered at the boats, like he wanted some enemy to show himself, but to no avail.

"Suk."

Suk followed his partner, but not without one look back.

---------------

"Geez, that was close!" Jarryd squealed, pressed against Sydney in the small alcove. He wished he had been pressed against Avery, but it hadn't happened that way. Somehow Avery was smashed against Greyson with only her forearms between them. She was staring at him with scared, puppy-dog eyes.

"That *was* close," she whispered slowly, her hands on his chest.

Greyson stared at her, more confused than scared before squirming free and peeking around the alcove's corner. Suk and his friend were gone.

"Come on," he said, motioning them to follow. "We have to find a better place to hide."

Sydney pushed Jarryd away and joined Greyson, but Nick stepped out of the alcove, defiant. "To hide?"

"Yeah."

"Why? We didn't come here to hide."

Greyson dropped his eyes. Did he have to explain that he was taking Dan's advice? "I know. But we can't rush into anything stupid. We need a place to regroup – a place to launch our attack – like a base or something."

Nick nodded his agreement and wiped his glasses on his wet shirt.

"Avery," Jarryd started, "how about your parents' room? They can help us."

She shook her head no. "I can't find them. They grounded me to the room before we ported, left for the spa – I still can't find them. I was still lookin' when you called."

The kids didn't say what they knew everyone was thinking. They'd been taken – or worse.

Nick finished wiping his glasses and put them back on, though they were still streaked. "We can't go back to our rooms. We have to go where they wouldn't think to look for us." He waited for their agreement and then peered toward the hull. "I think I know a place."

# Chapter 56

Mark, a husky man of thirty-six years, watched the television screen above the bar's rows of alcohol. His eyes and lips drooped, a weight of sadness weighing him down, pulling his shoulders deeper into the bar stool's cushion. A storm during vacation was depressing enough, but the news made it even worse. Details about the attack in Georgia kept coming in. The terrorists had killed over a dozen soldiers, several civilians, and caused millions of dollars of damage. Old images of the slain soldiers before they had been killed, video of their grieving families, and stories of their heroism brought up old, unwanted memories for Mark – memories of the attack in New Orleans that had taken his cousin.

"Another shot."

The bartender filled his glass and returned to wiping the empty bar. Mark was the only one inside. A few others had been with him, but when the ship had begun moving, they had panicked, yelling something about leaving too early and leaving someone behind. Mark had just shrugged with a "don't ask me" face. When the bartender didn't have any answers, they had made for the front desk.

Suddenly, the TV news anchors disappeared, replaced with static fuzz. The bartender rushed to it and punched it with the butt of his palm, but nothing happened. He moved it up and down the channels, but they were all the same.

"Friggin' TV. Must be Darryl messing with the reception."

Mark shrugged. "I'd seen enough anyhow."

"I'm with you there!" the bartender replied, shaking his head with frustration. "Friggin' government lets the thugs kill American soldiers…on our own soil. Despicable," the bartender said to himself, shaking his head.

Mark shrugged again and rotated the drink in his cup. "Yup."

"Foster's a weak-kneed idiot. Thinks these half-hearted random roadblocks and gun control laws can solve this? Never Again Act is a joke! A real man would find these thugs and wipe 'em all out – and anybody who's with 'em. Wouldn't you say?"

Mark shrugged again, still resting his elbows on the bar. He took another swig of his drink. "Need that Reckhemmer guy."

"The Hammer? Now you're talking. He'll do what it takes."

The intercom clicked on and the sound of the TV's static automatically muted.

"Heeeeellooo guests of the American Dream. I'm afraid that Darryl has made a change of course. Because of this, we have had to leave the harbor for safety reasons. The ship will be safer out at sea. Those guests that are still on the island are being escorted to secure shelters, and I assure you that we will reunite with them as soon as Darryl leaves. Until we are fully out of harm's way, you must now report to your nearest muster station. This is mandatory for all guests and staff. You will find your station written on your doors, along the hallways, and in the staircases. Once there, we will answer all your questions — and who knows? There may even be *prizes*! Thank you for your cooperation!"

Mark rolled his eyes.

The bartender gestured toward the door. "We better leave."

"I didn't pay for mandatory meetings." He downed the last of his drink in one gulp. "Another shot."

A new voice broke from the doorway. "Sure!"

Mark turned just in time to see the muzzle flash; the bullet's impact sent his body careening off the barstool. His shot glass shattered on the floor as more muffled gunshots dropped the bartender and pierced the bottles behind him in splatters of alcohol.

When the echoes of the shots had faded, the shooter lowered his pistol and sneered at the bodies. His free hand hovered around his crooked nose.

Orion had received the same message on his smart watch as the rest of them.

Communications down. Proceed with
round-up after announcement.

Another teenager smiled from his side. His face and hair were wet with rain; drops slid over the jagged scars on his discolored face, curling left and right before falling to the floor at his feet. A third boy with glasses stood astonished behind them. "Did you have to do that?"

Orion scoffed. "No. But it's easier than escorting them to their muster station."

Buzz laughed a snorting, choking laugh, and shrugged. He followed Orion outside to Central Park's winding path, peeking inside each store where several

326

guests had sought refuge in the storm. Most were on their way to their muster stations, but those that lingered were not to be tolerated. He would put them down like he had the ones in the bar. In the back of Orion's mind, he was hoping he would somehow see Greyson inside. He knew Greyson had been heading to Nassau – but the likelihood was slim to none.

Still, he had the right to dream.

------------

The announcement had taken Greyson off guard. Suddenly, a mass of people filled the hallways, employees barked orders and ushered them like cattle down a stairway. The kids marched with the crowd, grasping at each other to stay close, panic beginning to take hold.

"This is the wrong way!" Nick whispered, pulling on Greyson's arm.

A warning siren was going off in Greyson's mind. If there were an attack, this might be it. "We gotta get out of this. This way!"

Greyson darted through the rustling crowd and shimmied through an "employees only" door. His friends followed suit, hushed – on the edge of panic. He led them through the small drink-service kitchen that had been hastily abandoned by its staff and exited through a narrow swinging door in the back. After a moment taking in his surroundings, Greyson judged they were on a small balcony of a lavish auditorium. He could immediately sense the tension. A great murmuring of voices was below. Hundreds of voices.

Greyson's pace slowed to a crawl as he knelt along the empty balcony's railing with his friends trailing behind. They leaned over him, eyeing the scene below.

"We stay here," Greyson whispered. "Let the people clear the halls."

They waited for several minutes, peeking at the crowd below as they nearly filled the auditorium. Finally, when it seemed the last stragglers had arrived, the doors were shut and locked. Screams followed only to be interrupted by angry shouts and the clicks of bullets being chambered in rifles.

*No....*

The kids crawled close to the railing, mouths agape.

Men with automatic rifles spread about the room, barking warnings and removing the contents of frightened passengers' pockets. Some resisted but were struck down with a butt of a rifle. When some would scream, tape was shoved over their mouths.

327

Avery and Sydney turned away, and it was hard for Greyson to watch – especially the families with young children being prodded by gun barrels. Parents tried to pretend it was a game, but the kids were too smart. Their cries were not easily stifled.

Greyson's heart raced, a sinking feeling pushing his heart toward his gut. But the worst thing was knowing he couldn't do anything about it. From what he could see, there were at least twelve men – each with the same smart watch the others had told him about. They were each armed with an automatic rifle that held enough bullets to kill him thirty times over. And even if he were to attack, most of them wore body armor that would reflect his slingshot ammo like rocks off a turtle's shell. His aim would need to be perfect, but he was tired, a little seasick, and bruised nearly everywhere. He'd miss plenty, and one miss would be enough for it all to be over.

Suddenly, a terrorist took to the stage. "Cooperate, and you'll live!" he shouted loudly, waving some sort of remote in front of a row of hostages. "Try to escape, we blow the ship!"

The crowd shuddered with desperate cries and moans.

"This is unreal," Avery said breathlessly, at the edge of panic. "This c'ahn't be happening. What are they going to do to them?"

Seeing her panic, Jarryd smirked. "I know, right? It's so weird when it first happens – but your first time is always the hardest, mate. It gets easier." He pulled her into a reluctant side hug.

Greyson's thoughts pulled him in two directions. On one hand, Dan – an experienced soldier – had told him to observe and hide. On the other hand, he *had* to fight. He couldn't let all these people down like he had at the fair. Back then, he had delayed and wavered until it had been too late, but now he was being given a second chance. He had to give it his all – even if he did fail.

And he couldn't give up on them like he'd given up on Liam.

"Quick. You guys find that hiding place you were talking about. I'll keep an eye out here."

He'd made his decision. It felt right – at least for a moment.

Sydney pushed at his shoulder. "Don't be dumb. Why would you stay?"

*Don't be dumb.* Her words sounded like Dan's advice. He had told him not to do anything stupid – just to gather information until…until something. The call had ended before Dan had finished.

Greyson was still thinking when another voice came to his ear.

"We can't win this fight." It was Nick. "We need you – like we always do.

So, come with us. We'll get rest; we'll regroup; and then we'll hit them hard later."

He read Nick's face. He wasn't suggesting – he was telling him. There was a new confidence in him – and it wasn't just the red glasses and fanny pack. Wherever that confidence came from, it was effective.

Nick gestured toward the employee exit. "We have to go before they come around here. It's a few floors down."

Greyson took one more glance toward the auditorium and realized he was right. There hadn't been any shooting. Whatever the terrorists were doing would probably involve the hostages. They'd have time before the terrorists made their demands. And then they'd strike.

"Fine. But we aren't going to *hide*," he stated, mostly to himself. "We're going to *wait*."

Nick nodded, and together they slunk away.

---------------

Greyson wasn't pleased with Nick's idea of a waiting place at first, but it was growing on him. The adult-only Serenity Club was at the back of the ship. There were only two entrances, one on either side of the bar. There was a roof over the bar, but a few glass doors led to the roofless balcony with additional seating, three hot tubs, deck chairs, and a beautiful ocean view. The view at the moment was not beautiful, though. The clouds bubbled down in dark blues and purples, and rain lashed the glass doors.

After a quick survey of the area, Greyson led them behind the bar where they sat with their backs against the wall, listening for footsteps behind them.

"Well, at least we won't get thirsty back here," Jarryd chirped, looking at the rows of other bottles that were hidden under the bar. Avery laughed nervously from his side.

Greyson sighed. "We're not drinking any of it…unless some of that clear liquid is water."

Jarryd scoffed. "No, Brainless. It's all vodka. You can use it to make Bloody Mary's, martinis, Jell-O shooters, and lots of other ones I can't remember."

The other kids looked at him. "How the heck do you know that?"

He shrugged. "Step-Dad taught me. He has a book with pictures."

Greyson frowned. "That stuff ruins your mind. We kind of need our minds right now. Did he teach you anything more…useful?"

Jarryd thought for a moment and then raised his finger with an eyebrow pump. "A Molotov cocktail."

"Ugh. I told you. We're not drinking any of it. None. We're not 21 and we're surrounded by terrorists and…and…"

Jarryd was giving him a goofy smile. "It's a fire-bomb. Not a drink."

"Oh. Really? A fire…"

"Bomb."

"I think I'd rather you make a drink."

Sydney nodded her agreement, but Nick shrugged. "I think he might be right. He kind of knows this stuff."

Jarryd gave his brother a surprised and pleasantly grateful look. "Thanks, little brother."

"Doesn't mean you won't screw it up," he said.

"I can help," Avery interjected. "I saw it on TV. I'll find a rag." They got up together and set to work.

Greyson shared a helpless look with the other two. "It'll keep them busy," he whispered with a shrug.

"But…now what?" Nick asked. "How long do we hide…I mean *wait*?"

Laying his head against the back wall was surprisingly comfortable. Sleep fought for his attention. "I don't know. I…just don't know."

Sydney scrunched her face in thought. "If Sam had picked up, he'd have called in the whole army on them. They'd go all Navy Seal on their butts."

"But he didn't," Greyson stated sternly. "And phones don't work anymore."

Nick chimed in. "We could find their bombs. Disarm them…"

"You know how to disarm a bomb?"

Nick dismissed the idea, but his mind kept triggering. "We could take them out one by one."

Thinking it over, Greyson rubbed at his eyes. "We could…but we'd have to…" He stopped rubbing his eyes and let them shine with an idea. "We'd have to lure them to us. Of course." He turned to them both. "A deadfall."

"What?"

"A trap. We set a trap, lure them in, and then steal their watch. We use it to contact Sam."

Nick's face lit up as bright as Greyson's. "Yes. Let's do it."

Catching a short third wind, Greyson immediately put them to work on a trap. First, they broke a drinking glass just outside each door so that they'd hear footsteps if someone did come looking. Then, Greyson took his hoodie and dressed a cardboard cut-out of the ship's captain with it, placing the cut-out on the bar's deck outside so that it was visible from the doorways. It would be the bait. If a Plurb were to come inside looking for someone, it would appear as though someone was on the deck.

If all went as planned, the Plurb would ignore the bar and go toward the bait on the deck, where Greyson tied fishing line across the doorway to the outside. Finally, he spread more broken glass around the projected landing area to slice their hands and knees to delay them long enough for the kids to attack with their new weapons they'd found in the janitor's closet.

Sydney broke a mop in two for a jagged club, Nick found a heavy wrench, Avery wielded a plunger, and Jarryd held a bottle of vodka with a rag stuffed halfway inside in one hand and a lighter in the other. Greyson, of course, had his slingshot.

After all the preparations, they retreated behind the bar that would serve as their base. Greyson was the last to join them after one last check of the trip wire. He sighed and lowered himself with his back against the wall. They all took deep breaths as if they were slumped in a locker room at halftime, down fifty points.

Greyson put his hand on his dangling slingshot and closed his eyes. "Now…we wait."

# Chapter 57

Hours later, night had fallen. The hurricane seemed to have followed them, still nipping at the ship's heels with whipping wind and spitting rain. The rocking motion of the ship had lulled Greyson to sleep behind the bar, and Nick and Jarryd let him sleep, whispering to themselves. They snickered when Greyson's head slid to rest on Sydney's shoulder, but Sydney ended their snickers with a flash of murder in her eyes.

Greyson curled into himself and dug his cheek against her shoulder. She smiled and removed his hat for his comfort. Kindness passed over her eyes, but a gleam of sadness peeked in as well. There was a wall of guilt between them. She had felt it for months, ever since the attack. It was a deep wall, made stronger and wider with every call she made to Sam. She knew she was building that wall, but something inside of her wanted to. There needed to be a wall.

Way back at the church so long ago, Jarryd had been right. He loved her.

She knew it, because he'd shown it. He had dived from the truck for her. He had let the bomb go off…for her. He had chosen her over Liam. And now he was being punished for it. The chains of guilt weighed on him. She had heard it in his nightmares; she saw it in the way he looked at her with both longing and sadness.

He had chosen her, but it had brought him suffering. If there were a wall between them, maybe it would spare him more pain. And it would spare her the guilt – the thought that she had perhaps been the reason the bomb had gone off. How could she be worth it? How would she ever live up to that?

She would always be thankful, though. At times she had been overcome with gratitude – she had rushed to thank him – but she had seen his face and the pain hidden beneath it – and the guilt had removed her words before they could escape.

A distressed smile crossed her lips as she eyed his chopped hair, the slope of his cheek, and the rising and falling of his back with each breath.

Sydney wasn't ready for him or his love. She wasn't worthy of him, and perhaps never would be. He deserved someone so much better. Someone like Avery.

Avery sat to Sydney's left, staring into space. She was still struck by shock from the whole thing, her fingers tapping at the tile floor or pulling at her white beach dress. Sydney watched her for a moment, the guilt and unworthiness still choking at her throat. Perhaps one day she would be worthy of Greyson. But not yet. She was fourteen, judgmental, and fiercely jealous.

A determined thought peppered her mind until the words finally stammered free. "Wh-what's your favorite color?"

It took a second take before Avery realized the whispered words were for her. "What?"

Sydney almost retreated but continued after a sigh. "What's your favorite color?"

The worry on Avery's perfect cheeks faded. "My favorite col'ah? Uh…blue I guess. Like the ocean."

Sydney nodded through the awkward silence that followed. She glanced at the twins, who were still oblivious on the other side of Greyson.

"You?"

Sydney turned back to Avery, a little startled at the returned question. After too much thought for such a simple question, she answered. "Red."

"That's a good col'ah, too."

"What type of music you listen to?"

"Pop. Oldies, too – but anything that gets me dancing. Why?"

Sydney smiled to herself. "I…well…I've been a little…mean to you. And I don't even know you."

Avery watched her and then shyly looked at the floor. "Thanks."

"For what?"

"For wanting to get to know me. I'd like to be your mate. I don't have any girl mates."

Surprised, Sydney raised her brow. "Really?"

"No. I suppose I like being around boys too much. They make me feel smart'ah."

Sydney laughed silently. "Me, too. And I bet they like you a lot more than girls do."

Avery nodded knowingly, taking no offense. "Maybe not for the right reasons, you know?"

Sydney understood. Girls would only be jealous of her - intimidated by her – like she had been. Regret struck her again. "Well, I'm sorry I was mean. I like oldies, too, and dancing. You like country?"

"Which one?"

They laughed quietly, but her shoulder movement must have awakened Greyson. He licked at his lips and picked up his head to look at her through squinting eyes. They stared at each other, his stare a deep, absent-minded one until he turned to the other side, putting his head on Jarryd's shoulder.

"Aww, bro…" Jarryd said, pulling Greyson closer. He even set Greyson's weary head down on his thigh for a better pillow. "There ya go, buddy."

Nick snickered and laid his own head against the wall. Before long he would be wanting to sleep, too. Until then, he kept the wrench firm in his right hand. He looked at his watch. There had been no attempts to enter for five hours. Once they had regained their strength they would have to go out and find a terrorist to lure. "Think we should wake him?"

Jarryd shrugged as he playfully stroked Greyson's sideburns. "Maybe. But he looks so peaceful."

"He's going to drool on your thigh."

"Greyson. Wake up, dude."

He shook him awake and helped him sit up. He rubbed his face and blinked until his eyes could open fully. "How long was I out?" he asked with a husky voice.

"A few hours. No one's come yet."

Greyson thought to himself, still rubbing the sleep from his eyes. He felt much better. Sharper.

Sydney and Avery had scooted further to the left and were talking to each other in whispers in the corner. They looked to be getting along. Furrowing his brow, Greyson turned to Jarryd. "What happened with them?"

Jarryd shrugged. "I don't know. But what do you think?"

"About what?"

"About *her*, dude. Isn't she like the hottest thing you've seen?"

"Umm…"

Arching his brow, Jarryd held out his hand palm-up. "That's it. I need your man-card."

"My man-card?"

"Yeah. If you don't think Avery's hot, you have *got* to give up your man-card."

He rolled his eyes. "O-okay." He unzipped his fanny pack and faked as if he was searching for it.

"Keeping your man-card in a fanny pack – strike two. Indefinite suspension."

Greyson glared at him and then glanced over his shoulder. Confident he wouldn't be overheard, he whispered back. "She's attractive, okay?"

"Out of 10 – what would you say?"

"I'm not ranking her. I barely know her."

"What's that matter? Need to see her in a bathing suit first?"

"No!" he whispered loudly, now fully awake. "Because I wouldn't want *them* ranking *me* based on how I look."

Jarryd looked him up and down. "Why not?"

Perplexed and looking for a distraction, Greyson shook his head and stood up, hunched, just tall enough to peek over the bar at the doorway to the right.

Jarryd scoffed. "You're like a 10, dude, on your good days. Maybe an eight or nine today with that haircut, but still."

Greyson stared at him. "Awkward."

Nick elbowed his brother. "Maybe you should give me *your* man-card."

"Ha. Ha. But seriously, she's a 10, right?"

"If I tell you, will you give it up?"

"Yeah."

"Then yes, she's a 10."

"I knew it! I've got a 10! And everyone at school thought it would be impossible."

"Your mom's a 10, too," Greyson added.

The twins jolted. "What?"

"And Sydney. And pretty much every girl."

"Dude, you've got…problems," Jarryd grimaced. "Too much testosterone or somethin'."

"No, I'm just sayin'. To somebody they're a 10. And that's what matters, right?"

Jarryd thought intensely, trying to make sense of his logic, but it hurt his brain.

"Even you, Jarryd. Someday *someone* will see you as a 10."

His smile widened gently. "Sweet. It better be another 10."

Greyson smirked and took another glance at the girls to make sure they weren't being overheard.

*Thud.*

The sound struck them into silence. No one breathed.

*Thud-thud-thud-thud. Errr-chunk-chunk-chunk-thup.*

They felt it more than they heard it – deep reverberations, like distance drumbeats. And then a jerk, like their ship had hit the brakes.

"Did we just stop?"

Their heads and stomachs swooned, as if the waves suddenly gained control over their bodies. They *had* stopped. Or at least the engines had.

No one spoke as they contemplated the meaning. Greyson rose above the bar and peered out into the dark. With just enough light coming from the ship, he could see the wake their ship made in the ocean trailing behind them. After a time, the wake dissipated until there was none.

They were dead in the water. And the hurricane was lurking behind them.

"THIS IS YOUR CAPTAIN, CHIP!"

The intercom blasted. They covered their ears.

"THANK YOU FOR YOUR COOPERATION. WE HAVE REACHED OUR DESTINATION OFF THE BEAUTIFUL ATLANTIC COAST. PLEASE FOLLOW YOUR CREWMAN AND THE LIGHTED PATHWAYS TO YOUR NEAREST DISEMBARKATION POINT WHERE YOU WILL BE LIFEBOATED TO SAFETY. IF YOU CHOOSE NOT TO, YOU WILL BE KINDLY SHOT. FROM ALL OF US ON THE AMERICAN DREAM, WE WISH YOU THE BEST. THANK YOU FOR TRAVELING WITH US."

The kids stared at each other.

"AND ONE MORE THING. AVERY REDMOND, REPORT TO THE TOP DECK, OR YOUR PARENTS WILL BE KILLED. THANK YOU."

*Cruuunch.* The sound of glass under foot.

Greyson slunk down like a shot, Jarryd grabbed his Molotov bottle, and the rest held their breath as tightly as they held their weapons.

*Cruuunch.*

Greyson's eyes latched on his friends, and then onto Avery, who was still struck by the terrorist's threat. Fear had grabbed her heart and frozen her muscles. Greyson, too, felt its icy grip around his neck – the kind that urged him to run as fast as he could. But he brushed it off and unsnapped the slingshot. His other hand found the ammo pouch.

*Cruuuunch.*

The door to the Serenity Club turned like the hands of a clock.

Their waiting was over.

# Chapter 58

The door burst open.

The kids held their breaths as the men entered the room with weapons leveled, searching. Greyson could feel their eyes scanning over the bar, their bodies just feet away – their fingers on triggers, itching for somebody to shoot.

"Why would she be here?"

"We have to check everywhere."

"Why? Just let her drown."

"They're not going to set 'em off til they find her."

"Oh, they will. It'll flush her out."

There were two men. Greyson's mind scrambled for a change of plan.

"There!" The man spotted the hoodie blowing in the wind.

They'd taken the bait.

Greyson waited a beat, nodded at his friends, and then rose from behind the bar. He leveled the slingshot and placed the back of the second man's head between the bars of the slingshot's 'Y'.

*Snap!*

The ball pelted the second man's skull just as the first hit the trip wire. The first flung hard onto the broken glass and the second was propelled on top of him in a mess of limbs and guns.

"NOW!"

Greyson leaped over the bar and put another ball into the mass of bodies as his friends circled around.

Jarryd let out a war scream that prompted the rest to do the same. In a moment they had reached their victims and rained lashes on the men as they screamed in pain. The first tried to block the blows with hands full of bloody glass shards. The second man tried to raise his gun, but Greyson put him down with a sharp kick. The first man went down shortly after with a solid clunk from Jarryd's vodka bottle.

Though Avery added a few extra muffled blows from her plunger, it was over. They stood over the two unconscious bodies, the adrenaline pumping in their hearts so hard that they shook. It took a few moments for them to collect their breath before they could speak. And even then, no one knew what to say. The wind and rain pelted them, but they didn't want to move.

337

The violence had been real. It had gotten ahold of them and turned them into something they weren't. It still wrapped them in its grasp, giving them spurts of excitement between the inwardly creeping guilt.

Suddenly, Sydney reached out with her broken mop and snagged a gun's shoulder strap. The others watched as she operated the handle like a crane, carrying the heavy gun to the ground beside them, safely away from harm. She then picked it up, marched to the railing, and threw it overboard.

"Hey!" Jarryd complained. "We could've used that!"

Ignoring Jarryd, Greyson snapped to action and started unlatching the second man's smart watch. Nick went for the first man's and Avery went for the second gun.

Avery hoisted the gun in her arms and looked it over. "Heavy."

"Let me," Jarryd said, putting down his vodka.

"Heck, no. Have the plung'ah. I'm going aft'ah my pah'rents."

Suddenly Sydney came back, snatched the gun from Avery and threw it overboard. "No. We aren't killers."

"They'ah going to kill my pah'rents!"

"No, they're not," Greyson said defiantly, stepping between the girls. "Because they need them, too. If they didn't, they'd be dead already."

She gave him a sharp look.

"We're going to stop them. Somehow."

Nick stood, reading the watch. "New message. It says, 'Distress Call Initiated. Five minutes. Next phase will bring her up.'"

"Any other messages?" Greyson asked, still thinking about the first.

"Nothing else. Each message is deleted a few seconds after it's sent."

"Why would they call for help?"

"Maybe it wasn't them. Maybe someone else escaped and called somehow."

Greyson nodded. "Text Sam anyway."

"On it. Got the number, Syd?"

While Sydney shared the number, Jarryd turned to Greyson in a whisper. "Five minutes 'til what?"

"I don't know. But we have to find out – and fast." He stood and jogged inside the bar. "Everyone inside. Hurry."

His friends followed and huddled by one of the tables.

"Listen, guys. We can't wait…we can't hide anymore. We have to find out how to stop them."

Nick got their attention with words that struck them cold. "The guys we

338

took down…we could…make them talk."

"What?" Greyson retorted, eyeing their unconscious bodies. "You mean…like…torture them? Who would do that?"

Nick shrugged with all eyes on him. He then watched the rain dribble down the windows outside. "If it has to be done…"

Greyson drew back. Would Nick really torture them? Or was he just playing tough? The skeptical look Greyson gave him assumed he was playing tough, but deep inside, where absolute trust had been before, a thin veil of doubt rose between them.

"We have to find out some other way," Greyson said at last. "Is there anything else we know about them that we can use?"

Sydney lit up and pounded the table. "The bottom level! Nick and I went down there and saw the Plurbs messing with the life vests. I bet that's where they'd put the bombs. And they're going to set them off to make us go up."

"The bottom level?" Avery whined. "But my pah'rents ah'r on the top level."

"They say go up, so we go down," Greyson replied. "We might be the only ones who can stop them – and I'm not…we're not going to let them get away with it again."

Sydney jumped up. "We can get there from here in a few minutes – if we move fast."

The group gave nods of approval.

"Do you dare us?" Jarryd asked with a knowing look.

Greyson's affirmative nod took on more energy as his smile grew. "I dare you. I dare you all to do whatever it takes to stop them. No matter how hard."

"We're in!" Jarryd yelled for the rest of them, standing. "Now, let's go light some people on *fire*!"

"Hold on, Rambo," Nick said. "I've got to send this text."

"Woooow. Talk about killing a moment."

-----------

Sam stuck the black thumb drive into his new laptop's port and peeked out from under the covers. His heart thumped inside his chest, but the dark hotel room was still quiet. The line of white light under the door was undisturbed.

He ducked back under and waited for the drive to load. When it did, he stared at the icon. His pointer hovered over it, and his finger rested on the

339

track pad. He hesitated. It was like the last step before diving off the high dive. After the click, there would be no going back. The free-fall that came from what he found would not be up to him. It was exhilarating and debilitating both.

*Buzzzz...Buzzz....*

Peeking out from the covers again, he snagged his phone from the bedside table. It was after 9 p.m., and he wasn't expecting any texts.

He didn't recognize the number, but his curiosity got the best of him. As he read the message, he threw off the covers. He slammed the laptop, hid the thumb drive and called out, "DAAAAAD!"

------------------

The narrow hallway felt like a swaying bridge beneath their feet as they snaked through the corridors. A ship, stopped in the middle of a turbulent ocean, was at the mercy of the waves that beat upon its hull – and the kids felt every wave in its depths.

"It's just around the corner," Sydney explained from the front of the group. She held up her hand to stop them.

"Two minutes," Nick reported.

Greyson took the lead and slunk toward the metal door at the end of the hall, bending down to pick up a ball bearing and adding it to his diminished supply. He then turned his focus to the door and what would be behind.

"Okay, guys," Greyson said, swallowing his fear. "Don't worry. No matter what's behind that door, just remember...they can only kill our bodies."

Jarryd gave Nick a look and Nick shrugged back. "Not very reassuring..." Jarryd whispered.

As Greyson approached, he motioned Sydney to the door and took his stance with both hands ready at the slingshot. "You open it. I'll be the first inside. On three."

His eyes met Sydney's. "One."

She grasped the handle, her eyes locked on his.

"Two."

He pulled back the rubber on the slingshot until it creaked.

"Three!"

# Chapter 59

If time had slowed down, Greyson would have had time to make a different decision. He would have seen the five terrorists wearing orange life vests. He would have seen the closest one setting the timer on the last bomb against the hull. His decision would have been to run, if he'd had the time to make it.

But instead, he only had time to raise his slingshot and scream his pubescent two-voiced squeak. "Fr-EEEEEZE!"

The terrorists startled and stared, but the one with his hands on the bomb was the first to speak. "Easy, boys," he growled to his men. He typed in the last few digits on the bomb's keypad and turned to the kids with his hands raised in surrender.

Greyson's friends took in the situation, exchanging glances with each of the terrorists in succession. Each of them had been reaching toward the life vests they wore, but now raised their hands with their leader.

After a long pause, the leader took two strutted steps toward the kids, chuckling. "Ah, a Georgia bulldog and his pups." He put his hands down.

Greyson held his aim straight and true, straight at the man's nose. His fingers begged him to let go, but something held him back. They were too confident. Though he couldn't see any of their guns, he reasoned that they must have them. "It's not a Georgia hat. Disarm the bomb."

"Oh, sorry," the man said sarcastically, taking another step forward. "What does the 'G' stand for then?"

Greyson let out a sigh and chewed his words before speaking. "Everyone asks what the hat stands for. But no one asks what I stand for."

The terrorist gave him a patronizing smile. "Hmm…let me guess. The 'G' is for girls?" His buddies laughed.

"Games?" Another one added.

"Ghostbusters?"

Frustrated, Greyson blurted, "Good."

There was a long, eerily silent pause before the man eyed Greyson's weapon. "Isn't that nice. With a slingshot? I haven't seen one of those in ages. And is that a broom handle – and vodka? What kind of crazy party is this?"

The rest of the terrorists laughed, joining the other one in taking a few steps forward.

Greyson's strained eyes darted to the bomb. He could barely make out the digits counting down. They darted back to the men. The man on the left's hands were resting inside the orange vest.

"Disarm the bombs."

"I can't," the terrorist stated, "but I might if you hand over the girl."

"Don't come closer!" Greyson yelled.

"She'll come with us either way. Or you'll all drown."

The other men grew anxious, glancing at the bombs.

"Disarm them! Now!"

The man smirked. "Why should I listen to you?"

*There was nothing else to do.*

"We have a bomb."

He heard Jarryd flick the lighter behind his back.

"Is that right? Well, we have a few of our own. They're not big, but they'll get the job done real soon."

Greyson snarled. "Just like us." He heard the flames take the rag. "Throw it!"

The terrorists reached inside their vests.

The bottle sailed through the air, the flames on the rag licking at the air.

Their hands came out of their vests with guns. Sydney ducked. Avery screamed. Greyson aimed.

The ball bearing pierced the glass bottle, blasting the flammable liquid into a fine spray. The spray caught the rag's flame and burst into a wall of fire that rained on the terrorists like a dragon's breath.

The kids turned and covered their faces as the heat swelled over them. They ran from the heat. They ran from the screams, and they ran from the bombs.

Only Greyson stopped to look back. The flames flickered in his eyes as he watched; his conscience burned along with them, searing his heart. The numbness – the callousness – returned, and he continued watching as his friends yelled for him. Their voices seemed distant. He could see the bombs on the walls beyond, but there was nothing he could do.

Even the explosions did not snap him free of the numbness.

Suddenly, like a dam had broken, a torrent of water blasted into the room from three directions. Most of the flames were wiped away with a flood of blue and white, and a small river rushed across the corridor to Greyson's feet. Soon it lapped at his ankles.

"Greyson!"

Sydney yanked on his arm from the stairs, and he jerked back into action. His legs churned up the stairs; he caught up with the twins on a landing after three flights. They huffed and puffed with hands on their knees, glancing down the staircase, expecting the water to be close at their heels. For now, they could only hear it, like a tossing waterfall echoing in the metal walls.

"I can't believe we did that!" Jarryd exclaimed, his eyes inward.

"I did it." Greyson stated. "I did."

Jarryd's eyes flickered in understanding. "Then, what now?" he asked.

Greyson's mind wandered elsewhere. He stared into a distant place, his eyes flittering about. *We failed again. Again! Or did we? Was that it? Why the whole charade? Why the round up before the sinking? Why wouldn't they just have bombed the ship earlier and been done with it?*

Sydney answered for him. "We've got to keep going! Get off the ship!"

Bouncing back to reality, he nodded his agreement. "Let's go!"

They bounded up the stairs just as the water gurgled to the landing. The ship rolled to the left and right, heavier than before, making their steps wobbly and pitching them into the railings as they escaped upward. Their path brought them through abandoned corridors and the giant kitchen filled with uneaten dishes and half completed entrees. There were few words exchanged between them – only frantic breathing and frantic thoughts. They knew their only chance to survive was to get to the top deck to the lifeboats.

After what seemed an eternity, they stepped onto the final landing, still sheltered from the rain and wind. Their legs burned and ached, but they had put the flooding water well behind them. A deep, metallic groan vibrated beneath their feet as they wearily stepped to the top deck's door.

Greyson was the first outside, plunging into the storm, using his hand to keep the driving rain out of his eyes. The rest followed out single-file, slipping on the glazed wood as the ship tipped one way and then the other.

"There!"

Just visible through the downpour was a crowd of people by the last two lifeboats near the center of the ship. A line of people was stepping inside one at a time, all wearing life-vests and civilian clothes.

"Hurry!"

Like walking on a bowling lane, they scooted as fast as they could. Deck chairs wobbled next to them and scratched as they moved. The hot tubs bubbled with rain and poured out as the pitching increased.

Greyson led them along the railing overlooking Central Park many floors below. A sudden lurch forced them all against the railing with a bang. Greyson hit the bars hard and was forced to gaze below. The bushes and trees in Central Park were protected from the wind on all sides by the rising balconies, but they still shimmered and moved. Blinking rapidly, Greyson's mouth hung open as he finally discerned what was making the foliage move. Rushing floodwater was engulfing the park's foliage from all sides.

The ship didn't need another pool, but it was about to get a giant one in its core.

When the ship tilted back toward being level, the kids continued their trek to the crowd at the lifeboats. There was a scuffle at the lifeboat's entrance. A man and a woman were being shoved toward it but were resisting. Avery was the first to recognize them.

"Dad! Mom!"

"Av'ry!" Her dad called out, reaching out for her.

Avery's voice caught the small crowd's attention, and they turned to face the kids with the anger of a disturbed hornet's nest. All at once, Avery's parents were shoved inside the boat and guns flew out of the terrorists' vests; Greyson didn't even have time to draw his slingshot.

Despite the change to civilian clothes, Jarryd recognized the man pointing the gun at him. "Ah, Suk…"

Backed against the railing, there was no escape. They were frozen, expecting the gunshots with clenched teeth and closed eyes.

"Wait!" A teenaged voice stiffened the terrorists' hands just in time. The gun barrels wavered in the rain, still leveled in Greyson's direction, but stilled by the command.

From the midst of the wet bodies, a broad-shouldered boy pushed his way out. The wicked smile on his face made Greyson's stomach drop.

"Greyson Gray. You've come a long way to die."

Greyson gulped, still clutching the railing behind him as the ship lurched, sending his side of the deck higher than the terrorists'. He wanted to respond, but the anger was boiling over so wildly, he couldn't express it in words. The hatred simmered in his eyes.

"And you're too late to interfere this time." Orion motioned for the men to lower their guns. "Keep loading and keep the Redmonds safe," he commanded, giving Avery a smile. "I'll collect the last one."

Two more boys stepped from the crowd as the men began filing onto the boat once again. One of the boys Greyson recognized as Glasses. The other's body looked like Buzz, but his face had been disfigured with ugly, scarred bumps and ridges. His smile was as crooked as Orion's nose, and his body like a troll's. Suk stepped to the side, his pistol aimed at Jarryd as the ship tilted the other way, sending the kids back against the railing and the terrorists grabbing a handhold.

"Avery," Orion said with a smirk. "Want to do this easy?"

Jarryd jerked forward, but Greyson held him back.

"Psst. I need a weapon," Jarryd whispered to Greyson. "You shot mine."

Greyson reached in his pack and handed him two ball bearings.

Jarryd watched them roll around his hand and then squeezed them with determination. "I get it, and I got this." He pumped his chin at Orion. "She's staying with us."

Greyson assured Avery with a determined nod, and then spoke to the Pluribus boys. "You'll have to go through all of us."

"How defiant. But so dumb. But I guess that's how you work. You came all the way here, looking for your dad!" Orion yelled over the screaming wind. "In the Bahamas!" He laughed to himself. "I have to ask. During the days on the road, did you ever once think that he wasn't...actually...there?" He laughed again, with Buzz joining in.

Greyson lowered his brow and gritted his teeth.

"Did you really believe," Orion asked, shaking his head in disbelief, "...that my dad told you the truth?"

Greyson's face rose as if he'd been stabbed with a fatal wound. He felt the blood draining from his body. The nausea from the rocking sea turned him pale, and his friends turned to him in concern.

"Don't believe him," Sydney whispered. "He's a liar!"

"Oh, yes," Orion said. "But so is my father. And he told a little white lie, thinking you would be dead in a few minutes. He thought you might appreciate thinking in your last minutes that your dad was safe in paradise."

Greyson's breath shuddered as he held the emotion back. It was welling inside of him, pressing against his ribs. His grip on the railing grew red and white as the ship rocked again. Sydney sided up next to him. "He's lying, Greys. Don't believe him!"

"I, on the other hand, think it's best if you know the truth before you die. Your father's dead."

There was a brief moment when Greyson thought he would surrender to the pain and tears that fought for control, but a sudden memory flashed into his mind. The story John told of the demon-possessed man and the herd of pigs.

"I don't care!" Greyson released the railing and took a sloshing step toward Orion. The ship had listed enough so that it was as though he were walking uphill on a waterslide. Suk swiveled his pistol toward him.

"I don't care anymore!" Greyson shouted, taking another step as the ship leveled out. His voice was weak, but he stressed it as much as it would go, cracking or not. "I'd rather have no dad than your dad!"

Orion's smile vanished.

Greyson took another step and leaned backward to avoid falling into Suk's gun. He glanced at the rolling waves behind the men. Lifeboats were scattered around like rubber toys in a tub.

"Your dad's a liar and a murderer! He's killed thousands of people!"

Orion sneered as Greyson stepped once more, halfway between the two railings. The ship leveled and Greyson eyed the terrorists getting into the last lifeboat. Only four were left aboard.

Greyson puffed his chest. "Your dad has demons! So do I!"

Orion raised an eyebrow and Buzz snorted.

Though he didn't have actual demons, he felt the power that hate gave him. He felt the regret, the urge for vengeance inside of him.

*A legion of regrets…a legion's worth of power.*

The ship listed, sending Greyson higher as if he were looming over them. The rainwater on the deck began trickling to the outside railing, splashing at Suk's feet.

"And you're pigs."

At the peak of the ship's tilt, Greyson suddenly dropped onto his backside; the wet incline propelled him downward at a speed faster than Suk was prepared for.

*BANG!* The shot missed and Greyson leapt up from his slide, slamming into Suk's chest. Suk's body curled over the top railing and spun over the side as Greyson grabbed onto the railing where Suk had been.

He didn't have time to gloat. He ducked under Orion's gun and put a fist into the boy's gut. Grabbing Orion's arm and the railing, Greyson raised both legs and kicked Buzz in the chest as Buzz lunged at Greyson from behind. Buzz's large body reeled into Glasses, sending both to their backs. As the boat listed the opposite way, their bodies slid toward Greyson's friends, who were still stunned to silence. In a matter of seconds, Greyson had taken out four of them.

Regaining his breath, Orion grabbed Greyson and whipped him around. Greyson latched onto Orion' life vest for all he was worth, pressing the gun sideways between their two chests. He let out a yell as he pumped his legs, pushing Orion down the sloped deck toward the center of the boat. Orion tried to look back as his feet churned to keep up with the increased speed, but there was nothing he could do other than hold onto Greyson.

Sydney screamed and rolled away from the boys' bodies as they hit the railing with a clang and jerked over the top. She watched as they flailed in mid-air over the ship's interior chasm, flashing by balcony after balcony in a free-fall, with Orion's pistol following them down.

"Greyson!" She followed their bodies until they hit the water, which was now well above the trees. And then she hesitated, scanning the water below, waiting for Greyson to surface. Behind her, the last lifeboat was lowering. Beside her, Buzz and Glasses were scrambling to their feet. Inside, a voice pushed her to act.

She climbed to the top rail and leapt off with a scream.

# Chapter 60

Greyson blasted from the water with a deep breath, treading water and spinning around. *Where is he? WHERE IS HE?*

Suddenly, he felt very dizzy. The massive pool was level, but the ship was not. As it rocked, its interior rooms seemed to twist around the pool one way, only to halt and slowly rock back the other way. Greyson felt the current take him toward one side of balconies only to stop and shift toward the other side.

It was a terrifying fishbowl. The ship's structure shrieked and moaned; the waves inside the bowl crashed against the sides and churned from underneath so strong that he could barely keep his head above water. One wave and then another crashed over him, took his breath, and blurred his vision. Worse yet, the churning water was full of debris from the restaurants below, looted by the first waves of the flood. The rooms' lights surrounding him flickered as the ship lost power floor by floor; they flashed with sparks when the water hit, blasting the darkness like strikes of lightning.

In the flashes he saw a table and chairs float by; another chair hit his shoulder. Miraculously, his hat had snagged on one of the chair's legs. He quickly snapped it to his belt under the water.

Just when he grabbed hold of the chair and spat out a mouthful of the warm, salty water, a scream suddenly rose above the din. A moment later, Sydney smacked the water twenty yards away.

"Sydney!"

Just as fast, arms wrapped around him and yanked him under.

---------------

The ship had leveled out again, giving Nick and Avery the opportunity to pummel Glasses as he tried to get up. Avery swung the plunger into his face, smashing his glasses to the deck. She smiled in satisfaction until Nick put him down for good with a wrench to the jaw.

Avery cringed at the sound of the crunching jaw; and as she turned, she noticed Sydney's absence. Far below, she heard a cry for Greyson. She was down there with him.

"Sydney!"

In a flash, Avery mounted the rail and dove off headfirst.

A few feet over, Buzz rose to his feet, his bear-like body looming over Jarryd. His evil smirk sent shivers down Jarryd's spine as he brushed his sopping wet hair out of his frightened eyes. He looked down at the ball bearings in his hand. With a yell, he threw them at Buzz as hard as he could.

The balls hit with a smack on Buzz's chest, and he let out an anguished scream, arching his back and howling. Jarryd gave a short, relieved laugh, pleased with himself, until Buzz twisted away, revealing Nick was behind him, wielding the wrench he had smacked into Buzz's spine.

Jarryd smiled. "You wrenched his back!"

Nick gave his brother a smile, but it was short lived. Buzz whipped the back of his hand around, striking Nick across the face. His red glasses broke in two as he hit the floor in pain. Blood dripped from his nose and dribbled over his lips. He spat it on the deck as Buzz went in for the kill.

---------------

The bubbles burst from Greyson's mouth as he fought with the powerful arms that held him under. He caught spinning glimpses of dark trees with leaves and branches suspended like puppets in the water, but he couldn't see anything else. Orion had him in a bear hug, and they were sinking rapidly.

He jerked and pulled at the arms, but they were too strong. His mind railed for more options, but there were none. He was helpless and losing air fast. Out of the corner of his eye, he saw Orion's pistol sink down toward the once pristine garden, next to drowning roses gyrating in the currents. In his mind he reached for it, but he needed both arms to pull at Orion's grip.

He felt the first wave of panic. His instincts told him to breathe, but he fought them away. He was going to die if he didn't. But he had to breathe. He *had* to!

*"I dare you to hold your breath for one minute," his father said with a smirk.*

*Greyson smiled, his two front teeth missing. "A whole minute?"*

*"The world record's somewhere around 20 minutes. But you've got to start somewhere."*

*"How long can you hold yours?"*

*"Want to find out?"*

*"Yeah!"*

*"Okay. We'll do it together. It's kind of scary the first time, but you can always go longer*

*than you think. The panic is just a warning. It's your choice to heed it or not."*

Greyson let the panic fade. When his feet hit something solid, he was ready. He pushed against it with both legs, propelling both of them into a bush. Greyson thrashed and kicked, scraping Orion's back through the bush's sharp twigs. He felt Orion's body twisting beneath him, his grip loosening just enough for Greyson to bring Orion's arm up to his teeth.

He bit. Hard.

Orion let out a silent scream, and his grip loosened.

With a mighty pull, Greyson yanked himself free and kicked off the ground. His lungs screamed for air – black spots filled his vision – he felt lightheaded – but a final kick sent him into the air and the rain with a panicked gulp. He spat Orion's blood into the pool.

---------------

Nick spat again and rose to his knees as Buzz grabbed his shirt collar, pulling him up. Buzz's thick arm drew back, but another set of arms wrapped around Buzz's throat.

Jarryd clamped on tightly as Buzz whipped his body around full circle. Jarryd felt his shoes hit something solid, but he didn't realize they had hit Nick until he saw his brother's body skidding along the deck.

Buzz was going mad with rage, bucking and twisting until he somehow got hold of Jarryd's flopping hair.

"Ow! No, no, no!"

Buzz pulled Jarryd by his hair and dropped him on his side with a thud. He kicked him in the ribs and then reached for his shirt, picking him up almost effortlessly and pressing him against the railing. Though Jarryd latched onto Buzz's neck to avoid his fists, Buzz pushed him away with one hand and raised the other.

*SMACK!*

The blow nearly knocked Jarryd unconscious. His vision blurred and his mouth tasted metallic. Through his tears he could see the second blow coming.

---------------

"Greyson!"

Greyson snapped to her voice and saw her treading water only twenty yards away.

Avery's voice rang out. "Get to a balcony!" She was already near one to the right. "Hurry!"

Just then Orion burst from the water. He gulped in air and shook the water from his face as he jerked his gaze around, searching for Greyson. He found him, but he'd also found Sydney. He shot Greyson a menacing smile and swam toward his girl.

----------------

The second blow to Jarryd's face never came. Instead, Buzz's entire body smashed up against him. At first Jarryd thought it was just the rocking of the ship that had tipped him off balance, but then he heard Nick's grunts as he pushed at the mass of Buzz's body from behind.

Jarryd slowly regained his senses, but the blood dripping from his nose and Buzz's body smashing against him gave him too much to think about – until the ship actually did tip further in their direction.

He looked over his shoulder at the canyon below and gasped. His wet body was being squeezed, slipping out from between Buzz's body and the railing, toward the chasm.

"Nick…NICK! Stop!"

Nick grunted and continued shoving against Buzz's body, too enveloped in rage to hear his brother's pleas.

"Nick, no! Wait!"

As Buzz began to turn toward Nick, Jarryd screamed and popped free. He flailed backwards, disappearing over the rail. But Buzz went over as well, toppling toward the rising water.

Nick turned, breathing hard and heavy at the railing as it leveled again. He bent to grab the pieces of his glasses, but when he rose, he met eyes with Glasses, whom he had forgotten.

Nick blinked through the rain and his stomach flip-flopped. His vision was poor, but he could make out the shapes well enough to be queasy.

Glasses' jaw hung loose and awkward, broken in a permanent toothy gape. But his glasses-less eyes were piercing.

Nick stood defiant despite his bloody and bruised face. His workouts had been working. Each day he seemed to be able to lift more. He had seen more muscle definition in the mirror and his confidence had grown.

He clenched his fists and readied for battle.

But Glasses didn't attack. Instead, his limp hand slowly worked its way up to his life vest. He murmured something through his broken jaw, sending a trail of saliva from the corner of his mouth.

"Ermm gerwon…to kurrr ughhh."

Nick couldn't understand, but he saw the gun coming from the life vest. He had no other options.

With a running start, he vaulted over the railing and plummeted toward the belly of the dying beast.

# Chapter 61

The bodies hit the bubbling water behind Greyson, two at once and then followed by a third not long after, but he only gave them short glances, focusing instead on Sydney as she made it to a balcony with Orion close behind.

A wave rolled over Greyson's head, and he swallowed a gulp of saltwater. He was forced to stop and tread water, spitting and gasping for air.

*I'm not going to catch them.*

His mind raced as he watched Sydney pull herself up using the balcony's railing, kicking at the water that had risen to the balcony's level. To their left was the restaurant, with an entire wall made of glass, which had allowed the restaurant's customers a view of the park. The water was now lapping halfway up the glass, and Orion was near it.

Greyson made a snap decision. "Hold on, Sydney!"

He kicked hard at the water to keep himself afloat as his hands worked to load his slingshot. Taking another accidental gulp of seawater, he finally found a lull in the waves to take the shot.

*Snap!*

The shot hit the glass dead on, sending a ripple of cracks spider-webbing for yards in every direction. Orion was nearing Sydney.

Reaching into his pack, he realized he was almost out of shots. *Three more.* He had to make them count.

*Snap!*

The window shattered, and suddenly he felt the water turn from pool to river, sucking him toward the open restaurant. Orion grabbed for Sydney's shoes as she pulled herself over the balcony railing closest to the restaurant, but the current was too fast for him. He was sucked inside and rolled in the shallow water as it flowed onto the carpet, pushing him along.

Greyson swept along and called out to Sydney. "Stay there! I'm coming!"

He tried to swim sideways to Sydney's balcony, but the flow carried him through the broken glass window, just missing a jagged edge. He tried to get on his hands and knees on the restaurant's soggy carpet, but the water from the chasm was smashing into his side.

And then a kick slammed the air from his lungs.

"Get up!"

Orion stood over him, leaning against the current that pushed at his shins, nearly tipping him over.

Greyson coughed and gasped for air, but there were no more kicks. Hacking, he rose as if he were balancing on a surfboard, glaring at Orion and dripping hate as the saltwater cascaded from his clothes and face.

"Leave her out of this!"

Orion laughed and shook the water from his hair. "Like you left my cousin out of it? She's in a coma. I'll do worse to Sydney."

*The Redhead. In a coma?*

"I...I'm sorry," Greyson said, suddenly struck with regret. "I didn't mean..."

"*Sorry?* Think that's enough?"

The water was now up to their knees and still washing in. Greyson knew he had two more shots, but suddenly he regretted what the ball bearings had done to the Redhead. "We don't have to do this," Greyson yelled above the cracking of the ship.

Orion's face loosened with a hint of remorse. "I have to."

And with that, he flew forward with rage.

------------

Jarryd had just managed to snag onto a balcony's railing.

"Jarryd!"

It was Avery on the opposite side of balconies, several down from Sydney's. She had managed to climb inside a balcony, but the water was already up to her knees, tipped her direction. Soon enough she would be forced to climb higher.

"Avery! You okay?"

"They're all locked! Except the one above you!" Her face tightened and she gasped. "Watch out!"

He swung his head around just in time to meet Buzz's fist.

--------------

*Smack!*

Orion tackled Greyson and they toppled into the cascading water along the

354

sloping ground.

A table careened over them and its chairs bounced toward them like a wooden avalanche. Greyson scrambled to his feet and narrowly avoided one as he put the first hit into Orion's jaw; but he teetered off balance and fell onto Orion in knee-deep water.

His eyes burned as he went underwater and came out, frantically pulling at Orion's clothes and avoiding his fists. His feet couldn't find a decent foothold and more and more objects swirled into them.

As they fought, the one who gained the best balance took the advantage. They exchanged blows, threw each other down, wrestled for position and nearly drowned as the water rose.

Orion grabbed him by the shirt and swung him around with a splash. With a rip of his shirt, Greyson sprung free, throwing Orion off balance. Then, lunging through the water, Greyson jumped and punched, finding Orion's crooked nose with a sickening crack.

Orion fell backwards onto a floating table, his weight dipping it just below the water. Before Orion could shake off the hit, Greyson was close behind with more punches.

With mad thrashing, Greyson found himself throwing punch after punch into Orion's half-submerged body. He knew he couldn't stop. This is when fistfights were won.

Orion was a punching bag.

Greyson let out his hate – let out his revenge as one possessed. "Aaaghh!"

Water flung from his arms and fists like a sputtering fountain. He yelled out in fury until he was interrupted.

"Help!"

He stopped, fist suspended over Orion's bloody face. The pooling water rose to the boy's lips, pulling strands of blood into its blue.

"Help!"

Jarryd's voice. Panicked.

----------------

Jarryd had managed to kick Buzz away, but Buzz held on to his legs, trying to pull him from the balcony's railing into the chasm's pool. Jarryd held on with desperation. If he let go, Buzz would be sure to drown him.

His fingers screamed in pain, his knuckles cracked, and the skin on his calves burned as Buzz pulled with all his might.

His pinky fingers slipped first.

--------------

The current swept Nick toward the restaurant, but it had slowed as the restaurant filled. He swam and swam, kicking hard against the current to help his brother, but it was no use. He was too far!

And then the gunfire started.

*BANG! BANG!*

Amidst the churning water, he heard the bullets miss and hit the water with little *pluck, plucks.*

He took a panicked glance up to the top deck where he could barely make out the blurry shape of the gunman with a pistol aimed downward, shaking from the rocking of the ship.

Nick let out a yelp and dove under.

*BANG!*

----------------

Jarryd's ring fingers slipped next. His forearms burned and he felt the last ounce of his grip fade.

*NO!*

*Whiiiizzzz…thud!*

Suddenly Buzz let go. Jarryd regained his grip on the bars and hugged the railing like it was the side of a pool after a long swim. He turned to see Buzz drifting toward the restaurant with his hand covering a splotch of blood on his head where the ball bearing had struck.

-----------

Greyson stood waist high in water at the restaurant's window and lowered the slingshot. He was about to turn back to Orion when he saw Nick emerge for a breath. He saw Glasses on the top deck level squint one of his eyes for an accurate shot.

It was his last ball, but he had to. He fired it at Glasses, and it ricocheted off the railing bar directly in front of him. The boy jerked back with the pistol, and not knowing what had been fired at him, retreated from the railing.

"You alright?" Catching his breath from the fight, Greyson nodded at Nick as he paddled his way to the restaurant. Though Greyson's feet touched, they wouldn't for much longer. They had to get higher.

Out of the corner of his eye he saw Avery inexplicably floating on the water as it tipped toward Jarryd's side, moving fast and skimming over the water with hands out for balance. And then he saw it. She was surfing.

She deftly maneuvered the board, cutting through the waves and around debris until she swiped to a stop by Jarryd. Greyson watched them exchange words, treading water and holding onto the balcony railing as the water shifted once again.

As the ship tipped one way, the water would rise on their side, giving them the buoyancy and height to reach to higher levels. When the ship tipped back, the balconies would rise from the water, leaving them drier, but without the security of the water. And as the tipping grew more violent, they all knew at one time or another, the ship would choose a side and stick with it – turning on its side and taking them all under.

"Find us a way out!" Greyson yelled to them.

Avery and Jarryd nodded and ran through the open balcony door.

The water rose to Greyson's armpits as he glanced into the restaurant. A red light radiated brightly some distance away, giving an ominous glow to the debris that rolled nearer and nearer to the chandeliers. Greyson could swim through and search for an exit, but it would be too late for the rest of them.

And then he realized. Orion was gone.

"Greyson!" Sydney called out.

Nick pointed just as Greyson heard the splashing water and Orion's grunts.

Greyson cringed, preparing for the impact, but Orion wasn't going for him. He had chugged through the water toward the balcony where they had last seen Sydney. She already was making her way to the adjacent balcony, fleeing for her life.

"Sydney!" Greyson and Nick both jerked into action, swimming and kicking as if downhill. Suddenly the ship's creaks and cracks grew much louder, and the smell of smoke twinged their noses, burning a desperate urgency into their strokes.

"You…have any…shots?" Greyson asked Nick between strokes.

"No…all out!"

Greyson cursed under his breath. They'd have to do this the hard way. But eyeing Nick's fanny pack, Greyson couldn't help but to think that Orion didn't stand a chance. It was two versus one.

As they found the first underwater railings, the water seemed to suck out from underneath them, leaving them kneeling and balancing on the railing itself. Orion dangled from the balcony above and Greyson reached for his legs, wavering on the thin railing as it tipped to the side. Just as his fingers hit Orion's ankles, his feet slipped, and he toppled onto the balcony below.

"Greyson!" Nick shouted, dangling from the balcony above as the water leveled out.

Greyson grimaced and held his left shoulder, which had taken the impact. He used the railing to lift himself up to standing, watching the water rush toward the other side of the ship, where Jarryd and Avery had disappeared.

And then he heard the grunting above him. Sydney had nimbly jumped to the adjacent balcony and Orion was grasping its railing, pulling himself over with a smile. Nick was a balcony behind but climbing well.

Greyson had to be smarter this time. *Use the water.*

He began to count to himself as it smashed against the other side.

*One...two...three...four...five.* It began its retreat, leveling out.

Just as it leveled, he bounced to action; he rushed to the side and leapt from the railing of one balcony to the next. His foot hit the top rail and he stumbled to the balcony floor; but expecting the coming wave, he grabbed the railing, took a deep breath, and held on for dear life.

The relentless wave pounded him, but his grasp held.

*One...two...three...four...five.*

As he felt the current slow, he let go and swam upward with the rising water. When the retreating current began pulling him away, he kicked hard, pushing his body out of the water just in time for his arms to splash out and grab the balcony's floor a level higher. The wave retreated, leaving him hanging without the water to hold him up.

He wrapped his arms around the bottoms of the railings as the ship tipped further than ever. He looked below as his legs dangled, several feet from the water.

"Ughhh..." He was losing strength. He needed the water to lift him up if he hoped to climb any higher.

Another voice rang out. "Get away!"

Sydney was one balcony to the right, kicking at Orion as he tried to climb over her railing. He caught her leg and she fell backward. In a moment he was over the railing, looming over her.

"No!"

The wave hit his feet first, then his calves and waist. Waiting for just the right moment, Greyson pulled himself him up using the railings and jumped into the wave, swimming with every last ounce of strength.

The rising current took him where he needed to go. He turned just as it punched him against Sydney's balcony's railing; the water swept against him, pressing his cheek against the cold, metal railing and forcing him to watch as Orion dove on Sydney.

Orion straddled her, making her thrashing legs useless. He pinned her arms, even as the water lapped at her face, just shallow enough to allow her to breathe.

And then he slapped her.

"No!"

Orion's gaze jerked toward Greyson behind the railing, and a cruel smile curled at his lips.

"Don't!" Greyson cried, trying to pull himself up. But he didn't have the strength, and the water was already retreating. It would come back higher next time. But he had to wait.

Sydney recovered from the slap, reached for Orion's face, and clawed.

"Aaaagh!" Orion thrashed her hands away, slapped her again and then clutched her throat with renewed ferocity. Blood oozed from the wounds on his face, but he didn't care.

"Stop it!" Greyson screamed as the water left him hanging. He gazed at Sydney's face. It was bright red. Her eyes teared, her heart necklace dangled to the side, and her gurgling, choking sounds sent a wave of despair through his body. Tears welled in his eyes. "Stop! Please, stop!"

Orion turned to him and smiled. He choked her harder.

Her face was turning blue and her frightened eyes stared at him. Her hands, once grabbing for Orion's face, now slowly lowered to the floor. She reached for Greyson, her fingers curled and shaking, pleading for help.

*No! No!*

The water hit his shoes. Her hands jerked and the life slowly left her eyes. Water rose to his legs, and he kicked at it.

He reached through the bars for her hand and cried out. "SYDNEY!"

# Chapter 62

The water washed over Greyson's waist, and he pulled and kicked with all his might – but it wasn't enough. His muscles were jelly, his head thrashed with a headache, and he barely had the energy to hold on to the bars.

He reached for her hand and touched her fingers, but her hand washed away, floating limply in the wave. He had failed.

The tears of desperation and guilt poured out.

But when the water retreated, a new figure emerged from the railing behind Orion, moving stealthily through the ankle high water as the tide went out. He quietly approached and unclasped his fanny pack.

"Hurry!"

Nick lunged, swept his fanny pack's belt around Orion's neck, and pulled, yanking with a war cry so intense Greyson never would have thought it could come from Nick.

Orion wheezed and pushed backward violently, but Nick held on, pulling at the straps and tightening them around the bigger boy's neck.

Sydney hacked out a gasping cough, clutching at her throat.

Greyson let out a joyous whimper. "Sydney!" He exclaimed through his tears. "You okay?"

She couldn't reply. She rolled to her side, still hacking out shallow breaths and holding her throat as the two boys wrestled behind her.

Nick held on tight as Orion reached backward over his shoulders, pulling at Nick's arms and awkwardly punching at his face.

Eventually, Orion tried to stand, but the next wave hit, enveloping them all. Once it had retreated, Orion was lying face first with Nick on his back. Taking advantage of his weight, Nick straddled him with his knees on the ground, pulling at the fanny pack like he would a horse's reins.

Orion's face was blue, the veins on his temples throbbing and his eyes bulging red and desperate. His hands clutched weakly at Sydney's legs, but she crawled away.

Greyson watched in fear as Nick gritted his teeth and shuddered out an angry breath full of terrifying blood lust. He thought of nothing but ending Orion's life.

"No…" Greyson whimpered, still clutching the railing – his grip faltering. He glanced between Orion and Nick. "No! Nick…stop."

He didn't acknowledge Greyson.

"Nick, please!"

Nick turned, still tugging at the straps. Orion's hands stopped reaching; his eyelids wavered. He was dying.

"Nick," Greyson started pleadingly, struggling to hold on. "You…don't want…the demons…I have."

Nick's eyes flinched, and his brow lowered in thought. His breathing accelerated and he sucked at the saliva in his teeth, but just before the wave hit, a sudden release shuddered through him and he let the straps fall.

The wave hit hard, stronger and higher than ever, propelling Greyson up and over the tilting railing. He just managed to grab the top rail as the current flowed over him, pushing his body horizontally like a waving flag.

He held his breath and watched through stinging eyes as debris rushed by his head. The blast of water lasted longer – so long that he didn't know if it would be the last one, but it finally relented, eroding away, leaving their bodies crumpled against the corner of the tilted glass doors and the balcony floor.

For a moment they just lay there, gasping out deep breaths. Greyson also watched the water receding toward the other side with despair. When it came back, he didn't know if they could survive another bout. They had nothing left to give.

Nick looked over to him, his back against the doors. His eyes pleaded for sympathy – the guilt had already taken its toll.

But Orion was wheezing near their feet. He would live – at least for another few moments.

And then Sydney saw someone else and the gun he held. Across the churning chasm, Glasses leveled his pistol at them, standing in waist high water on a balcony. He had descended the stairs just to kill them, and now he had his chance. They were helpless – slaves to his aim.

He squinted his eye again for best accuracy, adjusting for the tilting ship as best as he could and wincing with the pain in his broken jaw.

But he never got off the shot.

A roar erupted from the room behind him. The dark shadow was large, loud, and fast. Only after it exploded from the open glass doors and knocked Glasses' body through the railing did Sydney realize it was, impossibly, a waverunner.

Jarryd's hair flung back as his waverunner sailed through the air with the railing's debris until the underside hit the water with a skid. He deftly swung the waverunner around debris and hopped the waves as the water leveled and then shifted toward Greyson's side of the ship.

Avery clutched at Jarryd's back and pointed in their direction.

In a flash, Greyson had stood and yanked at his friends. They put their backs against the doors as the gravity pulled them back.

"Watch out!" Jarryd yelled.

They moved out of the way just as the waverunner slammed through the railing and then the glass doors behind. The sudden chaos sent them falling through the tilting room with a tidal wave of water, following the path of the destructive waverunner as it upended a bed, toppled a dresser, and lodged halfway through the bathroom wall.

Greyson flipped through the wave, hit the mattress and landed back-first next to the waverunner. The water gushed over his body as he lay lodged in the plaster, but the tipping ship soon dropped the rushing water to the carpet and toppled him to the floor with a thud.

The powerful water dwindled quickly and curled through the carpet, around the debris, and out the hole where the glass doors had been.

Jarryd and Avery shook the drywall from their hair and sat in stunned silence as their waverunner remained lodged in the wall.

Still suspended, Jarryd muttered in surprise. "Job jobbed…"

Avery gave a tired laugh.

Shaking off the cobwebs, Greyson was the first to react. "Get up!" he shouted, pushing himself to his feet using the soaked mattress. He found Sydney and Nick and pulled on them. "We've got to go! Now!"

He took another glance around, but Orion was gone.

They braced themselves as the room inclined the opposite way. Greyson grabbed the bathroom doorway and tugged Sydney, who grabbed onto Nick. Jarryd and Avery yanked on the waverunner, trying to wrench it free.

"Leave it!" Greyson commanded.

"No!" Jarryd objected. "We wait for the water and ride through the halls. That's how I got it here from the casino."

"We can't all fit. Let's go!"

Once the room began leveling out, they scrambled out of the room with the wave of water crashing through the doorway close behind.

# Chapter 63

The ground shifted and the walls tilted as the abandoned ship lurched to the side. Gripping Sydney's hand tighter, Greyson pulled her up another flight of stairs as the staircase churned beneath them. Suddenly, the step was no longer a step as boards snapped apart underneath the carpet. Tripping on the gap, Greyson stumbled to his knees, pulling Sydney down with him.

Nick was right there, yanking them onward. "Get up or we die!" he scolded.

Suddenly, there was a deafening explosion. Splinters blasted over them as a giant chasm ripped a path across the beautiful mural of an underwater castle, as if a giant were tearing the walls apart.

They covered their faces for protection from the splinters but didn't stop their frantic staggering up the shifting stairs. The plumes of dust and debris seemed to cave in around them, as if plunging them into a smoking coffin.

"Keep going!" Greyson commanded.

Greyson led the group, coughing at the smoke and stumbling with the floor tilting at nearly impossible angles. Navigating with only the fuzzy yellow emergency lights glowing at his feet, his adrenaline was working overtime, numbing the pain from the blows to his body, giving him hollow strength. Reaching another landing, Greyson glanced at the sign dangling from a screw that barely kept a grip in the plaster.

*The Empress Deck.*

"Two more!" Sydney shouted raspily, the red welts vivid on her neck.

No reply was needed. They saved their energy for the last two flights, ignoring the heat wave and crackling fire coming from the landing. He wanted to shed his soggy shoes, but there was no time to stop. Looking back, he saw the lobby to the Empress Deck crack in two, swallowed by the level below with a plume of flame and smoke rising from beneath.

Another shuddering lurch sent them sprawling into a wall.

"Come on!"

He tugged on their arms until they were back on their way. They would not be left behind, and he didn't have the strength to carry them. He barely had enough to carry himself.

"Through here!" Sydney pushed at the door and the storm raged in their faces with lashing wind and stinging rain. But it was friendlier than what was behind. They stepped into it, onto the sloping main deck, trailing single file as the wind whipped at their clothes.

As the colossal ship lolled to the side, slamming the kids against the railings, they were suddenly very aware of the fact that the sinking was almost complete. The waves, once twelve floors down, were now splashing over balconies of the rooms beneath, only a few floors down.

Greyson searched for an escape route, but the last lifeboat was already gone. At least the passengers had escaped.

"Watch out!"

A deck chair came sliding toward them, and Greyson grabbed it just in time, pushing it away, keeping its trajectory toward the ship's bow.

More chairs came careening toward them with a rush of water overflowing the deck's pool.

"Hold on!"

They grasped the railing, rocking with the waves as if standing up on a roller coaster. Nick and Greyson battled with the deck chairs, but Jarryd, Avery, and then Sydney saw something. Their eyes went wide, searching, their fists clenched white to the railing. They shared a look as another blast of lightning bathed the storm clouds with a blanket of light. There was something illuminated. Massive. Powerful.

"Greyson!"

The ship tipped the other direction, sending the chairs back toward the pool. Greyson managed to stagger over one last chair to join the others at the railing.

"We have to…" he trailed off, catching a glimpse of the massive battleship, its guns gleaming with rainwater, its steel hull piercing the hurricane's waves like they were nothing. Most of the orange lifeboats had gathered near it, bobbing in the storm swells.

Greyson's mouth hung open and fear stole his breath. The realization cut at him, slicing an icy blade along his spine.

*It can't be. All of it. All of it for this.*

*The life vests. The change of clothes. The distress call.*

Greyson gulped, letting the rainwater wash over his trembling lips as the words formed and reformed.

"It's…it's a deadfall."

# Chapter 64

"A deadfall?" Sydney asked.

"A trap!" Greyson yelled, angry with himself for not seeing it. How could he not have seen it? "They're going to attack the battleship! The soldiers will rescue them, take them on the ship thinking they're the hostages…and then…"

Nick drooped his shoulders with defeat. "Oh no…"

"What?" Jarryd asked. "I don't get it."

Greyson gave him an annoyed sneer. "The sailors will rescue them, but the terrorists will use the guns in their life vests to take over the ship. It's the only way the sailors would ever let them on."

Nick squinted and chimed in through the deafening wind. "It's a destroyer. I think Arleigh Burke class." He drew a deep breath. "Over ninety missiles. Range of 1,000 miles."

Greyson eyed the dark ship's silhouette. "Nuclear?"

Nick shrugged. "I don't know."

Suddenly, there was a giant groan from within the ship, shaking the deck and sending cracks rippling under their feet.

"We gotta go!"

They set off running along the edge of the ship, searching for another lifeboat, but they were all gone. There was no way off except for one – and no one wanted to acknowledge it.

They reached the ship's bow, where the mini-golf course and the water park used to entertain happy guests.

"I'll jump," Greyson said, grabbing the railing closest to the destroyer. "I'll try to get help."

Sydney nodded. "We all have to."

"Not you. Stay here." Greyson remembered her falling from the moving van. Pulling her to shore. Thinking she was dead. "The last time you jumped, you almost died."

She shook her head and put her finger in his chest. "The last time you jumped, you needed someone to help you."

"Should have kept the waverunner," Jarryd mumbled.

Greyson shot him a look. But as they surrendered to the idea of jumping, a light flashed on them from afar.

They shielded their eyes and held on to the bars with one hand as the rocking nearly sent them toppling. They heard the beating of the chopper's blades over the howling wind. Greyson peeked through his fingers at the glaring spotlight beaming down on them as if from a UFO.

"Hey!" he shouted at the helicopter, waving with his one free hand. "Down here!"

The helicopter hovered directly above them as the ship finally seemed to succumb to the rocking. It leaned on its side, tried to rock the other way, but it was stuck, keeping the kids pinned against the railing – the only thing keeping them from falling to the ocean below.

They screamed for help, some of their limbs slipping between the railings. The churning, deep blue sea loomed closer, but the light was still on them.

Suddenly, two objects sent shadows over them from above. Ropes unwound and coiled at their sides with a zipping sound. Then, they were there. Two masked men dressed entirely in black held the ropes and found footholds on the railing.

"Grab on. Now!"

It only took a moment for the kids to realize the men were there to save them. The kids reached out; the men pulled them into their strong arms, but Greyson drew back. Each man had grabbed two.

They could not carry a third.

"Stay here!" one shouted.

Greyson recognized his gruff voice. "Where else would I go, butthole?"

The masked man tugged the rope, and Sydney gave Greyson an odd look just before she was zipped up in the air with the men.

Greyson watched her as she disappeared into the rain.

The ship jerked, and he fell against the railing. It was nearly on its side now and still tipping. He had to climb. He knelt on the railing and envisioned the sideways railing like a ladder lying on its side.

Timidly at first, he stepped along the rungs toward the bow where the railing ladder began curving upwards – away from the water. He grew more confident and treaded along as the railing curved and tipped toward the ocean. The wind whipped at him and the rain blinded him, but he was numb.

He climbed the ladder, using each slippery rung, approaching the tip of the ship. The ship was now completely sideways. Water poured from the overflowing chasm, back into the ocean from where it had come. Deck chairs toppled out along with the debris from its interior.

Greyson clung on and pulled himself around to the other side of the ladder as the ship turned toward its back. It would flip over completely at any second, slamming him into the sea.

He fought for handholds and footholds, but it was growing awkward. How long until they came back? He had to hang on, just a little longer.

And then he slipped. His calf cramped, and his foot jetted off the railing. He let out a yelp as he hung from the railing over the thrashing waves below.

He'd been hanging on too long. He could only do so much. The railing was heading for the ocean. He would have to let it take him there.

The man's hands wrapped around his midsection.

"Gettin' tired of saving you, Orphan."

They were yanked upward, blowing free in the wind. The once massive ship grew smaller beneath his dangling feet – a spectacle lying on its side, dipping beneath the bulging waves. Its giant rotor blades emerged from the water, spinning like calm wind turbines.

"Lucky you kept the infrared tag on," Grover said, referencing the button the soldiers had put on him during the battle in Camden.

Greyson managed to yell despite the man's arms grasping hard around his lungs. "It's a trap!" he yelled. "You have to warn them. Warn the destroyer!"

"What? What trap?" Grover yelled.

"The Plurbs. They're dressed as civilians. You have to take me there!"

"We'll warn them. You're going nowhere."

A sudden urge made Greyson thrash at Grover's grip. He had to go! He had to save them! His Payback list was too long – but ninety missiles would make it unimaginably longer. He had failed the 8,000, but if he stopped the attack – maybe it would make up for the rest. The entire list, paid back – four times as much!

"Let me go! Let me go!"

Grover grasped him even tighter as they drew closer to the helicopter. Greyson bit at his arm, but some sort of hard armor hurt his teeth more than it hurt Grover. "Please!" he cried.

"Where do you think we're going, kid?"

Greyson stopped struggling, and the ropes swung them around until the destroyer came into view. Little muzzle flashes were popping all over the deck and inside the rooms on the ship's superstructure. The battle had already started, and they were headed straight for it.

# Chapter 65

Grover pushed Greyson toward an open seat. "Buckle, now!"

Greyson found the buckle and snapped in next to Sydney. She hugged him from the side, and he closed his eyes, still catching his breath.

When he opened his eyes, a man with a painted mask was staring back. His mask was mostly black, but a red skull with jagged bones was painted over it. Only his dark eyes were showing, and they glared at Greyson. It was only a momentary stare; the man turned again to gaze out the side door with his four-foot long sniper rifle pointed into the storm.

*Diablo.*

Inspired by the man's mask, Greyson unsnapped his soaking hat and fit it on his head. It wasn't as cool as a skull mask, but it'd have to do.

Grover held a handle on the cockpit's door. He leaned toward the pilot. "Get us to that ship, Forge."

Forge nodded. "They put out a distress call a moment ago, but now...nothing."

"Then we assume the worst. Hightail it before they gain control of its weapons systems."

Grover turned back and took his seat next to Diablo as the helicopter banked hard, letting whips of rain through the wide-open side. The kids grasped their seats. They'd had enough of unstable ground.

"Where's Kit?" Greyson asked through the roaring wind.

"Stack's got him," Grover snapped. "Now shuttup."

Sydney leaned to Greyson and whispered, "You know these guys?"

"They're my friends...kinda."

Jarryd had been eavesdropping. "You're friends with these guys?" He reached into his pocket and held something invisible in his hand. "You can have your man card back."

Forge piloted them near the ship's starboard side and then hovered at a safe distance. There were several lifeboats strapped to rope ladders that had been thrown over the side of the massive ship to aid in the rescue. Several soldier's bodies also lay about the deck, signs of the battle. But it had already been won – at least on the main deck. More gunfire was faintly audible, but Greyson knew the soldiers had been taken completely off guard.

"You're seeing right, boys," Grover said to Diablo and Forge, who was piloting. "Orphan says they're dressed as civilians. Do your thing, Diablo. Then we set her down."

Diablo raised his rifle. Greyson didn't even get the chance to spot the terrorists.

*POW! POW!*

Greyson leaned toward the side door and glimpsed two men collapse to the deck, dropping their flashlights.

*POW!* Another one fell from the superstructure.

Jarryd put his hand to his mouth and bit. "Beast..." he murmured.

Greyson nodded solemnly until Sydney's hand nudged his. He turned to look at her. She kept looking forward, but her hand shifted under his.

Catching on, he grabbed her hand and held it tight. He examined her face and the red finger marks on her neck. She was scared, near tears, but she was alive. And he had this moment no matter what – better than any picture.

He rubbed his thumb against her skin and took in a long sigh.

*POW! POW!*

"Set her down, there!"

Forge swung the chopper to the back of the destroyer and began to set it down between three bodies. Grover and Diablo jumped out even before the skids had touched, their rifles raised and night vision goggles lowered. Greyson watched as they light-stepped forward, each aiming at one side of the deck.

As soon as the skids hit, Forge exited the pilot seat and wheeled around to retrieve a large case from the interior. In a few moments he had unhinged and removed the same drone that had spotted Greyson on the roof at Meyer's Crossing. With a few strokes on his wrist pad, the drone rose from the case and hovered in the air at his shoulder.

Forge turned to the kids still buckled into their seats. "Look at the black strip and don't move."

Still wary of the machine, the kids did as they were told.

"It's recording your faces."

Jarryd made a face for it to record – his beaver-face, when he squeezed his front teeth out of his lips and scrunched his nose.

*Beep!*

"Now it won't shoot you while it's on overwatch. It still needs a name, Greyson. We'll be back."

The soldier pulled a pair of goggles over his head and joined Diablo with his machine gun leveled in front of him. Through the helicopter's windshield, the kids watched them move silently, disappearing through the wind and rain like ghosts. The drone maneuvered up and around the helicopter's blades, vanishing into the night sky.

And they were alone.

There was nothing but the dimming sound of the helicopter's blades. They were stiff with fear, their hearts still beating from the fresh thrills they'd been through. They stared out the sides at the raging storm, which was Darryl's strong arm. He was getting closer and stronger.

A minute passed without a word. Their eyes were locked on the ship's superstructure, its giant gun barrels and missile launchers, and the outline of the sinking American Dream. When Greyson finally sighed and rested his head on the back of the seat, the group's tension released.

Finally breaking from her fear, Avery attended to Nick and Jarryd's wounds, even popping open a first-aid kit she'd found under their seat. Sydney put her hands near the cuts on Greyson's face, but she didn't know where to start. He eyed the welts above her heart necklace, still visualizing Orion's big hands strangling the life from her.

"You okay?" he asked, reaching toward the welts.

She gently pulled his hand away from her neck. "Yeah. You?"

He paused, thinking about all his injuries. Most of his body was bruised or bleeding, but he was lucky. "I'm alive. But my shoulder hurts worst."

He rotated his shoulder and massaged it with one hand. Sydney gave him a look and added her hands to the massaging. "There?"

"Yeah," he moaned. "Thanks. And my calf. Cramp I think."

Sydney eyed him for a few moments. He returned a serious look and draped his leg over her knee. Still eyeing him, she began to massage his calf.

"Thanks," he said, feeling the muscle relax. He glanced at her. "And here…" He pointed at his lips.

She gave him a childish smirk.

"From Indiana Jones, remember?" he explained with a tired smile.

She tried to hide her grin as she reached to his lips and massaged them with her fingers. His laugh was muffled through kneaded lips as Avery wiped a sterile pad across Jarryd's bloody nose, which had crusted under his nostril.

"You took quite a beating from that bloke."

Jarryd shrugged. "Seriously. I need another spa day."

She smiled. "Maybe lat'ah. I'll need my dad's credit c'ahd, and he's…well,

371

somewh'ah."

"We'll find him," Jarryd reassured. "Right, Nick?"

Nick was lost in his thoughts, staring at the floor and then his hands. There were raw scrapes where the fanny pack's strap had rubbed off skin. His biceps were stiff from holding them as tight as he could.

He had wanted him to die.

He'd lost his mind for that moment, and the idea of losing it scared him.

*Beep. Beep. Beep.*

"What's that?" Jarryd asked, leaning toward the cockpit, where a red light blinked with each beep. Sydney stopped massaging Greyson's lips.

*Beep. Beep. Beep.*

Nick shook from his reverie and unbuckled; he made his way through the cockpit doorway where a small green screen revealed what appeared to be radar.

*Beep, beep, beep.*

"It's getting faster," Jarryd noticed.

Greyson unbuckled when he saw Nick's face.

"Something's coming," Nick whispered.

*Beep, beep, beep.*

The kids' faces dropped. *What now?*

Greyson heard the noises first and jumped from the side of the helicopter.

"Greyson! What are you doing?"

He ignored Sydney and padded onto the wet deck, craning his neck toward the sound in the sky. His eyes settled on the bulging clouds, hanging like loose sheets from the darkest bed.

The rain patted his face again, waking him and prickling the hair on his arms with its cold.

"Greyson!"

"Shhh!"

He walked further away, and his friends gathered at the chopper's doors, watching him in silence. Greyson listened to the beeping growing fainter with each step that brought him further into the storm. He heard something. He'd heard the exact sound before, while on the mountain with Kit. Helicopters.

*WHHHHHIIIIR!*

He jumped and spun around as the ship's missile launchers cranked into action.

The metal box whirred to face the clouds, and a panel zipped open from

372

the top, revealing the tips of missiles Greyson's size.

*WHHHOOOOOOSHHHHHHHHH!*
*WHHHOOOOOOSHHHHHHHHH!*
*WHHHOOOOOOSHHHHHHHHH!*

Greyson fell to the ground at the sheer noise and intense heat, but he couldn't take his eyes from the missiles as they erupted with spouts of fire, burning into the sky. They streaked, louder and faster than he could imagine, through the rain like a space shuttle launching into the atmosphere. The heat burned into the rain, evaporating it in trails darting for the underside of the clouds.

The three missiles struck the clouds and were enveloped in their mist, as if sucked into pudding. In an instant they were gone, leaving only their smoke trails behind.

Greyson knelt on the cold metal and gazed with open mouth at the spectacle, struck speechless by the missiles' power.

And then thunder struck, sending red and orange lights soaking through the clouds with deep drumbeats. There were three thunderous strikes in quick succession.

Greyson rose to his feet as the red light grew brighter, as if the clouds themselves were lighting on fire. And then the clouds spat fire in three bursts.

The kids gasped as fiery metal rained from the sky, into the ocean below like a fireworks show gone out of control. Huge chunks of debris spiraled down and Greyson recognized it. Falling through the clouds were the blades of a helicopter with only a jagged piece of fuselage, still spinning and leaving behind a trail of black smoke and ash.

The destroyed helicopters splashed into the rolling waves – their coffins. There had been people in them. Soldiers or rescuers. Killed before they could be heroes.

Greyson seethed in anger. He had been sitting, getting a massage while the terrorists took control.

He swung around, grimacing and limping as he hobbled toward the superstructure of higher floors and towers at the middle of the ship. "Stay here!" he shouted at Sydney as she jumped from the helicopter.

"What are you doing?" Sydney asked.

"They're too slow. They need help. You all stay here. Try to radio for help."

His muscles were seizing up and the adrenaline was wearing off, revealing his pain again. He knew he was most likely dehydrated, so he stopped, took off his shirt, and wrung the shirt over his mouth, sending a stream of rainwater onto his tongue – the trick he'd used throughout the journey.

Jarryd leaned down to Sydney, his eyes on Greyson's battered body. "I think we should do what he says."

Greyson held the bunched-up shirt out to her. When she refused, he put the half-ripped shirt back on and shrugged.

Sydney shook her head. "I'm tired of trying to stop you."

"Good. But you're not going with."

"I am to."

"No! I-I need you...here. Wait for me here." He paused, almost begging. "Please."

He couldn't lose her.

Her eyes narrowed at him, but they gave in. "I don't like being left behind."

"I don't care. You can't come with. Not this time."

Sydney, hurt and cowering, whispered back. "You blame me, don't you?"

Greyson sighed, obviously trying to hold in whatever else was trying to come out. Memories were forcing him to watch again as he leapt after Sydney, leaving behind the bomb. He had pulled her to the riverbank and watched the explosion, holding in his arms what he had traded. The explosion had etched itself in his mind – a permanent scar.

She had held him back. He couldn't let her do it again.

"I had the choice. I blame myself. And I can't fail again," he looked at the faint outlines of the sinking American Dream. But then he glanced at the helicopter, where Avery leaned out, watching them. *Avery.* They'd saved her. She was only one – but one was better than none. "We have to protect her. They wanted her, so we do, too." He gave Sydney one last look. "Please, stay."

With that, he jerked around, ran to the first steel door, and opened it with a creak. The hallway was long, narrow, and rocking back and forth with the waves, but the first thing he saw was the dead bodies. There were sailors, dressed in all white, terrorists dressed as civilians with orange life vests, and soldiers in blue and grey digital camouflage.

Greyson took a deep breath and turned toward Sydney and the helicopter. She glared at him and then glanced away. He didn't give her any indication of his fear, but it was cresting in shivers as the rain trailed down his neck and back.

He didn't know where to go, but he lunged into the hall.

*Just follow the dead bodies...*

374

# Chapter 66

As Avery, Nick, and Sydney argued in the cockpit, fiddling with the electronic controls, Jarryd put his feet up and listened to the radio static they had achieved so far. His brain would prompt him to do things – such as offer his help or to keep an eye out for the bad guys – but his body would reject the promptings with excuse after excuse. He deserved a little break; he'd saved them all with his Jet-Ski skills. Or should he abbreviate them to "Jet-Skeels"? He liked to *abbreve* things and he liked this one especially. He'd have to use it later when he told the story – if they *let* him tell the story to the world this time.

He sighed in frustration and closed his eyes, trying to drown out his brother's annoying voice and the even more annoying radio crackle. The wind peppering the side of the copter with pellets of rain was a much more relaxing sound. The big waves that smashed up and over the sides of the ship sounded just like they were on a beach. Even the steady rocking left, right, left, right of the ship felt as if he were on a hammock. It all added up to a pretty decent time for a nap.

He felt himself drifting off to sleep – all his cares flitting away, the muscles in his neck and shoulders relaxing – until the voices stopped. Sydney and Avery's voices. Nick's voice.

There was only static.

Fear pulsed through his veins. His eyes popped open; he sat up; he leaned toward the windshield where the others sat stiff and motionless, staring straight ahead. Bouncing lights came from both sides of the superstructure. Men were coming.

"What do we do?" Avery asked frantically.

"Do you guys know how to fly this thing?" Sydney asked.

Nick and Jarryd shook their heads.

The flashlights grew brighter.

"Hide!"

But they didn't have time to hide.

Before they could even duck their heads, the drone came swooping down, past their windshield, as if surfing on air. It made a wide arc to the left, past the corner and hovered to a halt. The flashlights lit the drone's armor with a yellow hue as its gun snapped in their direction.

*RATATATATATATATATATAT!*

The flashlights' beams went crazy, flitting toward the sky before jostling to the ground, no longer moving.

"Kill them!"

The kids' gaze jerked to the right as two more men with orange life vests came from the right, carrying automatic rifles. They managed to raise their guns at the helicopter before the drone buzzed at them at high speeds, firing a rain of bullets.

*RATATATATATATATATAT!*

The men toppled to the deck without firing a shot. Their guns clattered as they fell, and the drone simply swooped over them as if to check for more enemies. But there weren't any more.

It hovered back and forth, undecided for a few moments as the kids tried to breathe their hearts back to normalcy. Jarryd's mouth still hung open wide, his big front teeth pointed right at the drone as it approached their windshield. It came so close that they could see the *714-M* and the red light inside its black band.

Its gun swiveled toward Jarryd.

Suddenly remembering, Jarryd made his beaver-face.

The drone's light turned green, and as if it had decided all was safe, it lifted into the sky.

"Wallaby d'ahned," Avery exclaimed with a huff.

Sydney let out a long sigh and slumped into the pilot's chair as Nick turned to Jarryd, astonished. "That thing just killed those guys. In, like, a second."

"Yeah," Jarryd said matter-of-factly. "I think we should keep it around."

Nick nodded to himself until an idea made him smile. "So…it's a friend that watches over us, right?"

Jarryd nodded as if pushing for more.

"Then I think I have a name for it."

Jarryd perked up. "The Drone-Ranger? The Glazed Dronut? Drone-ton Abbey?"

Nick's face said *you're an idiot.*

"No? Then what, genius?"

Nick smiled and shrugged. "Liam."

------------

Greyson stepped over a body's arm and then its torso, trying to move as quickly as he could without making a sound.

He could hear them – the echoes, vibrating through the pipes that ran the length of the metal corridor. The gunshots rang out like pans dropping to the floor, shouts and screams like children stuck inside a locked car in the summer. The echoes enveloped him from every angle.

With each corpse he encountered, a lump rose higher in his throat. The bodies – contorted, bleeding – made him sick to his stomach. He hated looking at them, but he had to, lest he trip over one and land on another – staring at the blank face of a dead man. The nausea rose higher and he began to panic. His face flushed and he let out a whimper.

*Concentrate on finding the voices.*

His eyes settled on the next corpse. A young man – clean-shaven, wearing camouflage and holding onto his rifle. His legs were curled toward his chest, almost as if he were sleeping. And his eyes were open. Green eyes – like his own.

Suddenly woozy, he steadied himself against a pipe, shutting out the light from his eyes. His trembling hand wiped at his eyelids, brushing away the fear.

*Shoulders back. Chin up. Eyes forward.*

He continued on, down another hall, up another bullet-ridden stairway, and the gunshots grew louder – ominous with each clanging echo.

His foot hit something, and before he knew it, he'd tumbled on top of a corpse. Panicked, he pushed off the man's abdomen to his elbows, scrambled to find footing, but stopped. He held himself up on his elbows, on top of the dead soldier. His eyes had latched onto something and his mind's gears were churning.

Finally working past his reluctance, Greyson reached and snatched what he had, up until now, resisted using. With a groan, he pushed off the corpse and rose up with the pistol in hand. He hated the heaviness of it. In his mind, heavy things were more dangerous, capable of more harm.

But a gun would have to do. He was out of slingshot ammunition and needed something. Eventually he would have to grow up and use a man's weapon. *What am I so afraid of? Killing someone? It wouldn't be the first time.*

He licked his dry lips and nodded reassuringly to himself as he continued hobbling down the hall with the gun at his side. The noises grew louder and louder. He grimaced as he ascended another flight of stairs that was riddled

377

with bullet holes and discovered that he had reached the top floor. No more stairs. And the voices were loud and clear. Angry. Threatening.

*This is it.*

But none of the voices were Grover's or Forge's. Perhaps it was Diablo, but that wasn't likely.

Greyson backed against the wall and shimmied to the corner. The voices and gunfire were just down the next hallway. What would he see? Would he have to shoot? Could he pull the trigger if he had to?

He held the gun in front of him and took a deep breath.

*Okay. On three.*

He blinked slowly.

*One.*

The terrorists were cursing, firing, and cursing more.

*Two.*

He placed his finger against the trigger.

*Three!*

# Chapter 67

Greyson swung around the corner, but a dark shape lunged from below, grabbing his arms and slamming him against the wall. He felt an ice-cold blade pressing against his Adam's apple.

"Dumb kid!"

The soldier swung Greyson around and sheathed his blade in one of his body armor's many pockets. It was Forge.

"Almost killed you."

Greyson didn't have time to say anything. Forge pulled him hard down the hall like he was being dragged to the principal's office. As he stumbled beside Forge, Greyson saw Diablo, Grover, and two soldiers in blue camouflage kneeling by a metal doorway that shook as bullets rang against it. The sound was near deafening and Greyson cringed as he was thrown to the ground.

"Stay close and don't move!" Forge yelled as he joined the others on either side of the door.

Greyson read the door sign. *Bridge. Fire Control.*

And then he understood. It was a standoff. The terrorists had the weapons' systems and the bridge under control on the other side of the door. Maybe even hostages. Grover and the rest were debating on how to take it back.

"Diablo – could you get a shot from outside?"

The skull-masked man spoke – his voice as scary as his face. "Only from the bird."

Grover turned to face the ship's soldiers. "Is there another entrance?"

"Yes, on the opposite side, but it's heavily guarded. Windows face the bow, but they're shatterproof."

"Nothing Forge can't take care of."

Forge nodded. "I'll need a few minutes."

"They may already have control!"

Greyson had to interrupt. "They shot down three helicopters. I – I think they have control…already."

The soldiers turned to him. Greyson nodded convincingly.

Grover stared a hole into him, but he turned back to the others. "The EMP grenades must have had no effect. We're going in and we're going in hard. Prep gas and flash bangs. And get that drone around to paint the windows. It'll give them something else to think about."

The soldiers went into a flurry of preparation. Canisters popped off belts, ammunition was checked and loaded, goggles were lowered, and Forge typed at his wrist pad. It took a moment for Greyson to realize what Grover had meant.

"Wait. The drone is leaving my friends? What if...?"

Forge shoved him farther away. "Our lives – their lives – are secondary. Stay here. Keep that gun on the doorway. If someone other than us comes out..."

Greyson gave a tiny nod. Forge accepted it and rejoined the others. They stacked at the door, crouched and ready.

*Our lives are secondary.* Greyson let it sink in.

Grover's left hand was on the door's lever – his other wrapped around some sort of cylindrical grenade. He spoke in a husky whisper. "We don't know who's friendly. Let God sort them out."

Putting his back harder against the metal as if he could get farther away, deeper into the wall for safety, Greyson remembered his agreement and pointed the gun at the doorway.

He aimed down the handgun's iron sights, but the sights shook and wobbled. It was heavy, and his veins pumped with adrenaline. He added a second hand to the grip to steady it, but it wasn't enough.

Down the wavering sights, he watched as Grover jerked the door open just a foot. In the same motion, Forge rolled in a canister and Diablo underhanded another. Grover closed the door as bullets blasted sparks over the opening.

Shouts rang out from inside, followed by two sharp bangs that reverberated through the floor and in Greyson's chest.

The soldier's dropped gas masks over their goggles.

Greyson felt his heart thumping against his ribs. He licked his lips and tried to keep his chin from wavering. They were headed into a barrage of bullets. He didn't want his friends to die.

Another door opening and more grenades. The door closed.

The soldiers' feet inched forward. The sound of the drone's gunfire sang out loudly, joining in with the drumbeats of the bangs and drowning out the chorus of voices inside.

Greyson couldn't even hear his staggered breaths as Grover opened the door and disappeared into the smoke.

# Chapter 68

The song called to him. It was in a mighty crescendo – a climax so loud and grand he couldn't resist. He had to see it.

Greyson found himself on his feet, inching to the doorway toward the hellish noise. The soldiers were already lost in the smoke inside. Taking a few deep breaths, he held the gun tight and fought his fear.

*Pay your debt. Your life is secondary. Pay it with your life if you have to. I dare you.*

Greyson waited for a pause in the barrage and then spun inside; he hobbled low and fast, sliding to a stop and putting a shoulder into a metal panel near the center of the large room. He was instantly surrounded by chaos.

The drone's firing against the glass set a clanging rhythm like crashing cymbals, the intermittent gunfire blasted like trumpets, and more grenades added a resounding bass that struck his eardrums numb. Suddenly a close explosion sent a violent ring that filled every sound with a hollow dullness – but the sights became the new sounds.

Time slowed as he took in the spectacle like a concert's final act. Smoke poured out like clouds, colored with flashes of yellow and red as muzzle flashes fired from underneath – left, right, far, and near. Bodies shifted from within the clouds, dipping and floating like dancers.

He rose to his knees – almost in a trance. He wanted to be a part of it, but he didn't know how. This was an adult production.

More bangs sent metal debris through the room. Showers of sparks bounced and popped. Bodies danced, like puppets strung in the air, spinning, flinging to the ground.

And he crouched on, suddenly drawn to the front of the bridge, some distance away. The smoke wafted over his vision, but Greyson could make out a figure at a control panel by the shatterproof glass. He, like Greyson, seemed unaffected by the choreography unfolding around him. His hands were at a control panel, fingers flitting away as if working a piano into a frenzy.

The numbness and the ringing anchored Greyson to the floor, but he rose up from behind the panel as the violence flurried around him. It ignored him as if he were the star of the show, appearing at center stage for the grand finale. He raised the gun and put the man in his shaking sights. He tried to hold his breath, but it escaped in short gasps. His finger pressed against the trigger.

*Do it. Pull the trigger. Stop him! Stop it all!*

A wash of smoke clouded Greyson's vision again, but when it faded away, the man had stopped playing with the panel. He still looked down at his hands, as if he were listening to the final resounding notes, but a time came when he turned to his audience.

His eyes seemed to search for Greyson amidst the clouds.

His eyes.

His Dad's eyes.

All at once, a powerful surge of frozen energy swelled in his lungs, pressing tears to his eyes – but a worldly caution beat back the joy, tensing every muscle in his neck. It couldn't be true. It hadn't been true so many times.

"D-dad?"

The man stared as if transfixed by the boy amidst the clouds and violence. His brow twitched, as if he were fighting with a thought – a memory – but confusion reigned.

Greyson's own memories were flashing through his mind, matching the dad he knew to the man at the panel. The twitch of his brow, the vivid, green eyes, the broad shoulders and thick hair.

*It's him! It has to be! He's alive, alive, alive!*

The emotion swarmed inside, spawning tears and shaking his limbs. The gun fell to his side and slipped from his hands.

Though only a few seconds had passed, Greyson feared the worst – that he wouldn't recognize him. He'd been forgotten.

"It's me." The tears streaked down his cheeks. "It's me, Dad."

The man's eyes gave nothing. No recognition. No love.

Greyson gulped hard and tried not to cry, but it was futile.

Suddenly a wave of smoke rushed over him and another blast of gunfire erupted from the opposite side of the room as a swarm of men entered, firing into the smoke.

Searing pain – like a knife had gone completely through his hand. A spatter of blood hit his shorts.

His blood.

Another knife blade sliced through his left shoulder with a thump. He screamed and fell backward to the floor.

The shock sent him reeling. *What just happened? I can't move my arm!*

The smoke rippled past, and shapes moved like shadows from the control panel to the opposite door. Several heads moved past, but only one stopped, looking back. A gap in the smoke revealed he had a gun in his hand, and his eyes searched for an enemy.

"DAAAAD!"

His dad looked toward him, but not for long. The swarm of men fired into the smoke as they ushered his dad toward the exit. Greyson jerked up but was suddenly slammed back down. Forge stood over him with his rifle raised in one hand and his other pressing against Greyson's shoulder.

"DAD! WAIT!"

Greyson's bloodshot eyes watched the doorway, expecting him to come back – to fight off the men who pulled him away. But he was gone.

Suddenly, a ripping pain bit at the inside of his shoulder like a small animal was feeding on his muscle; he winced and cried out, but the pain was secondary.

"Dad! Wait! It's me!"

He reached toward the door with his bloody hand and gasped at the hole through his palm. He'd been shot.

He snapped his hand back to his chest and cradled it.

"Stay down, kid!"

There were two men around him, but he could barely hear them. The lights were fading. He was so tired and nauseated.

He heard Grover calling from the control panel. "We're locked out of fire control! They've programmed the launch. Get on the com and tell them to take this ship out, now!"

Forge's voice blended into the ringing in Greyson's ears. He cried out for his dad again, but his voice grew fainter. Black edges blurred into his vision.

"Four minutes!" Forge yelled. "Disable missile defense!"

"Done! Get out of here!"

The voices around him grew fainter and he felt someone tug him up, swinging him over a shoulder.

The soldiers took him away. His eyes, glazed with pain, stared at the floor bouncing below him, but his thoughts were beyond. They were searching his memories – searching for an explanation. But he was so tired. So very tired. Even his mind was weary. He thought about odd things. His farm in Iowa. The corn swaying in the wind. Kit's weak bark in Forge's arms.

"Two minutes!"

The rain pattered his face, and his eyes rolled upward, toward the storm. A helicopter rose through the rain and wind, carrying men with orange life jackets; its rotors beat at the grey clouds as it disappeared into them.

"Dad…"

Forge swung him around. The sky was dark, filled with sideways rain, but a lightning flash lit the bulbous clouds and revealed the American Dream, broken in two. Its gigantic pieces were nearly submerged, engulfed by the dark splashing waves.

The lightning ceased, pulling a curtain of dark over the world.

He closed his eyes.

Another flash and he opened them. Everything was bright, except for a singular shape – like an ink blot in the sky. While he jostled, the ship rocked, and the sky poured, the shape did not move. The shape was that of a drone. But it wasn't Forge's drone. It was…it was…

"Get us up! NOW!"

The helicopter. His friends' voices. Sydney's hand in his.

He felt his body drifting upward, lighter than air.

"Oh, God."

Jarryd's voice.

Greyson's head turned as the helicopter banked. He saw the destroyer below, still surrounded by black waves, lit with the streaks of fire as missiles blasted from the launchers – numerous streaks searing into the rain, disappearing into the clouds.

But another streak came from behind.

*WhhhhhhhhiiiiiiisssSSSHHHH!*

The missile struck the ship's hull. A giant flash lit the entire world and then another flash enveloped the destroyer. It reappeared in three pieces, jutting from the fireballs that tore it apart as if it were a plastic toy. The waves rushed over the top, pulling the pieces into the ocean's abyss.

"HOLD ON!"

Their helicopter shook violently with the shockwave. Alarms went off and there were screams, but Greyson could only watch out the side as they turned, leaving the wreckage behind. He saw only the ocean and the spectacular storm front – a wall of circular clouds deeper and thicker than he had ever seen.

*Darryl.*

He'd finally caught up to them.

Darryl lashed at their helicopter out of anger, but they were gone.

*Gone.*

Greyson tried not to cry. He hated to. It hurt to breathe. It hurt to think. And he didn't want to die. Not yet.

"You're gonna be alright." Sydney spoke over him, crying as well. "They're going to take care of you."

"That's right, kid." Forge was over him as well. He pricked Greyson with a syringe and unwound bandages.

Greyson nodded, taking shallow gasps as the syringe sent a wave of relief through his veins. He felt the burden of pain lift from his shoulder. A sudden euphoria made him smile.

He had almost forgotten something. "I ate the cream corn," he whispered.

There was a long pause and then Sydney squeezed his hand. "Yeah? How was it?"

"It was…it's good."

"You're lying."

"So?"

Sydney scoffed through her tears. Behind her the soldiers were talking in worried tones. The radio chatter was intense. Ten missiles. No one knew where they were going. The fear was palpable. The aftermath would bring a firestorm of revenge and Foster wouldn't let even one Plurb live. It could be all-out war.

Forge cut Greyson's shirt away and pressed at his shoulder. Greyson only felt the pressure.

"Where'd he go?" Greyson asked sleepily. The euphoria was wearing into exhaustion.

Sydney and Forge shared a confused look, as if they thought he was hallucinating. "Who?"

Greyson swallowed hard and tried to open his eyes. His eyelids were too heavy. "My…my dad."

There was a long pause. Sydney whispered, "He was there?"

Greyson nodded as Forge applied some sort of bandage around his armpit and chest.

Sydney squeezed his hand. "He's alive? That's amazing. And you knew it! You knew it all along!"

Swallowing, Greyson fought off the chains of sleep. He couldn't fight much longer. He was too numb to be happy, too numb to be angry. "My…hat?" He hadn't been able to give it back to his dad yet. He still needed it.

Forge pressed it into Greyson's good hand. "You'll have some pretty wicked scars. Your hand especially."

His hand was a cold fire. Sticky. His fingers could barely move, and each time he tried, a shiver of pain would force its way through the numbness.

Jarryd blurted out toward the front. "Where are we going now? They took our parents – and our brother!"

Grover shouted back from the cockpit. "Shut up!"

Jarryd huffed and leaned back in his seat. Forge answered his question once Grover had turned back to the front. "We've got a safe place where we'll meet some friends and hide out until we figure out what to do."

"Hide out?" Jarryd asked. "We don't hide. We *wait*."

Forge's smirk was weighed down by concern. "Then we wait."

The kids' minds wandered off in separate directions, all wondering what they were waiting for. Avery thought of her father and mother. Hostages. Frightened.

Jarryd eyed the blood-stained bandage on Greyson's shoulder. He didn't want his best friend to die. He was his only real friend.

Next to Jarryd, Nick rubbed around the scrapes on his hand, wondering how he had missed it. The plot made complete sense now. The Plurbs weren't senselessly killing people. Perhaps the missiles would strike military assets – surveillance satellites, maybe, or the drones that blanketed the skies, able to kill American citizens on command. Maybe the Plurb's strike would bring the government to its senses. To show them *it* was not in control – the *people* were – free people who would not stand by and let tyranny control them. Nick nodded solemnly to himself.

Beside him, Sydney was watching Greyson wince as he struggled against sleep and pain. He was pale, shivering, and weak, but she was angry at him – for leaving her…for blaming her. And now for thinking about leaving her altogether. He couldn't die. *Don't leave me again.*

But she remembered something. He had left her weeks ago, but he had taken something with him.

"You…you took my picture – the Polaroid."

Greyson nodded, smirking as he fought off sleep.

"Why?" she asked, gripping his hand.

He took a stuttered breath. "I…admire you."

It took everything for Sydney not to cry. Tears still escaped, but she brushed them away as fast as they came. She didn't know how to respond, so she just held his hand tighter.

Under his shifting eyelids, Greyson's memory jumped back to the destroyer's bridge. The gunfire, the smoke, his dad. He remembered calling out. Walking forward. Seeing him.

"He…" Greyson whispered.

Sydney leaned in and squeezed his hand.

Greyson coughed and smacked his lips. With a calming breath, he whispered again. "He's one of them."

The helicopter rocked in the wind, rubbing the back of Greyson's head against the headrest. His hair made a scratching sound against the plastic that mesmerized him. Though Sydney began to say something, the scratching was all he heard as he lost consciousness.

-------------------

Under his bedcovers, Sam closed his laptop with a shuddering sigh. His eyes were lost in a present nightmare, and his fingers curled around the black thumb drive.

He had to destroy it. Burn it. Make it disappear. But no matter what he did to it, it would never disappear from his memory. The knowledge was now his, forever. He couldn't burn a secret, but he could keep it hidden from the world, trapped within his mind's vault.

But he hated hiding things. Especially this. He hated it. It ate a hole in his stomach. He wanted to punch something, throw something, scream and yell, but he held it in, just as he would hold in the secret. It couldn't be told. It would be as devastating to the nation as it was to him.

Footsteps in the hall. Rushed. Loud voices and radio static.

They were coming for him!

He never should have told his dad about his friends' text. Or maybe they had been monitoring his new computer – watching and waiting. He should have known!

Sam pulled the thumb drive out, flung his covers off, and vaulted to the window. He pulled open the window and flung the thumb drive out just as the door burst open.

Secret Service agents stood in the doorway. Sam was frozen, his arm still partially outside. They gave him a suspicious look.

He prepared himself to be taken.

*WAAAAAAAAAAAAAAHHHH!*

A siren blared through the open window, coming from down the street. It was like a tornado siren he'd hear in Iowa – but this was Washington D.C.

"Sam! Come with us. We've got to hurry."

"Wh-what's going on?"

One of the agents rushed inside. "It's a precaution. Missiles have been fired. Now!"

Sam's heart flopped inside his chest. They weren't out to get him. They were here to save him. He turned and leaned out the window with the flapping drapes. From thirty floors high, he could only make out individual cars.

A tiny black thumb drive was down there. Somewhere. But as far as he was concerned, it was gone.

As the agent whisked him down the hall in his pajamas, he contemplated the secret. Heat rimmed the outsides of his eyes.

His father had kept a horrible secret, and the secret was the truth.

Pluribus wanted his father to win.

They wanted him to be President.

The attack at the fair had been planned to further that purpose. The documents had said so. There were mentions of deals, of plans, of phases. And they wanted his father to lead. *Why? What did it mean?*

*What else could it mean except his father was in on it? Could there be any other possibility?* Whatever the possibility, his dad had seen the same evidence and had hidden it from the public.

A sudden realization streamed like energy through his veins. What he knew was devastatingly powerful. It was a powerful secret, and he held that power. Maybe that's why his dad was becoming so powerful. Though he had his own secrets, maybe he had other people's secrets, too. Some people would do anything to keep a secret from being told.

They made it inside an elevator, and the agent hit the button.

As the hum of the elevator droned on, he eyed the agent.

*Does he know? If he doesn't, what will happen if I tell? Would I be 'plucked?'*

"Don't worry, Sam," the agent said. "Your dad is already in a bunker. He's safe."

Sam's lips quivered into a sneer. Of course he was safe. Sam had warned his father that there was about to be an attack on the cruise ship. And if his dad was somehow in on Pluribus' plans, he would have known what was coming even before the warning.

But if his dad was in on it...had he known Sydney and the others would be on the ship during an attack? Would his dad have really allowed his friends to die?

And if he was in on it, working with the likes of Emory, why had Emory carved the message on his back: 'Out of evil comes good'? What was Emory saying to Dad? If they were working together – why would Emory do that to his ally's son?

Fresh doubts swirled in as they exited the elevator, rushing through the lobby to a waiting SUV. Even as people were panicking around him, his mind was lost in thought.

There *had* to be an explanation. Or maybe the evidence was faked. It had to be. He knew his dad more than anyone, and his dad hated the terrorists. He wouldn't let them get away with another attack. So, maybe his dad was going undercover, pretending to work with them. Or maybe...or maybe this was why his dad kept these kinds of secrets hidden – because normal people like him wouldn't understand.

That was probably it. He just didn't understand yet. He was missing some explanation or piece of evidence.

So that's what he'd do. He'd find the answer for himself.

It would be just like Hide and Seek. Sam was the seeker who knew where the hider was hiding. Now the hider was at his mercy. He could expose his dad's secret, but he'd give it more time. He had to know why. Until he knew, he had to *hide* the secret and *seek* more evidence. In this game of Hide and Seek, he was both hider *and* seeker.

The game was in his control, but he wasn't sure he wanted to win.

As the SUV drove away, he peered out the window, searching the street for the little black thumb drive.

----------------

Men heaved a body off the floating debris and into the middle of the rocking lifeboat where it was instantly the attention of dozens of frightened onlookers. Though the women and children gasped as it fell limp at their feet, a middle-aged man jumped to his aid. A moment later, the men at the boat's side heaved up a heavier boy from the water who coughed and hacked as he rolled toward the other body. This one was bleeding from a head wound and his face appeared to have been mangled recently, but he was alive. He scrambled to his knees, slipping on the waterlogged bottom and pushing away the onlookers.

"Save him! Save him now!" the bigger boy rasped.

The middle-aged doctor unsnapped the other boy's life jacket and pressed his ear to the boy's chest. A thin, wheezing choke seemed to bubble from his throat. "He's alive. But his esophagus has been crushed. A knife. Who has a knife?"

Two hours later the boy wavered in and out of consciousness. He was on the shore. He could hear the waves crashing. A helicopter was landing, and his friend was calling for it. Guns fired. Screams of fear. Bodies all around him. People picked his body up. Time passed.

He woke lying on a gurney, being pushed through a rocky corridor in the wake of a helicopter's blades. The lights flashed overhead as they rolled him onto the perimeter of a gigantic, rocky chasm. His head lolled to the side, giving him sight of the men and equipment bustling about like insects below. Though it was dark, he could make out shapes of helicopters, towers of cargo containers, forklifts, and soldiers spread about the canyon as big as a football stadium. There were hundreds of men below, and more corridors were dotting the rock walls on every side. He knew it was the quarry, but the question of why they took him here only began to pester his wayward mind as he was swung into a cave.

Suddenly, the ground beneath him flattened. The ride was smoother; the walls became white and tiled. There was a bright light over him. He heard the voices of doctors, felt the syringe. The light faded, dimmer, dimmer, and gone.

Orion woke and clutched at his throat. There was something clogging his

390

throat! Like he had swallowed concrete, it had solidified – pressing cold and hard against the sensitive skin inside his esophagus. It choked him!

He panicked and thrashed about, ripping tubes from his skin and sending the electronic monitors into a beeping frenzy. He needed to breathe, but he couldn't! He couldn't swallow the metal! Doctors rushed to his side, soldiers grabbed his arms, and he felt inhuman groans and hisses escape from his own mouth.

And then his father stood over him, his hands behind his back. "Just breathe."

Orion couldn't; he felt the panic pull his thoughts every which way – toward death, fear, and spiraling to despair.

"You'll do it. Breathe."

The room was fading to black. He felt lightheaded, nauseated. His eyes pleaded with the doctors and the soldiers, but they landed on his father. He was smiling.

Smiling.

Orion breathed.

The sound that escaped was that of a hissing monster. It breathed for him, reaching into his lungs and pulling out a dark, metallic breath. A sound of a child's nightmares, under the bed.

He inhaled and felt at his throat. With each breath came a rattling hiss.

His head swooned as the oxygen gave him new life.

A doctor showed him a mirror.

He jerked back, eyeing the doctor as if he had shown him a great lie. But the doctor shook the mirror and pushed it closer. Orion dared to look again.

A black, metal, snake-like tube was dug into his chest, curling up the middle of his throat to the underside of his chin. Orion's fingers ran along its scales as he listened to the sound.

The doctor holding the mirror spoke to him. "We replaced your esophagus, but the hissing sound may be a result of an incomplete vocal cord seal. Test your voice."

Orion was afraid. He was afraid it wouldn't work, or worse yet, he'd sound like a freak. He hesitated, the breath coming up and down his new throat like a gasping python.

But he worked up the courage, thinking of the fanny pack squeezing around his neck, of Greyson watching from the side. The hate burned within and erupted in a scream both harmonic and hideous, churning within his throat.

The onlookers jerked back and released his arms. Only Emory didn't flinch. When the scream had echoed its last in the cave's medical chamber, Orion snarled viciously, looking at his father. Tears formed under his eyes and trickled out.

"I'm ssss-orry," he said with his new voice. It hissed and it rattled from the depths of his throat.

Emory stepped closer, his prosthetic forehead wrinkling with perplexity. "Yes. The missing Redmond girl may pose a problem. And it appears the Rubicon team were the ones to call in the strike on the destroyer before all the missiles were away. But as usual, we will adapt. Enough missiles hit their targets for the next stage to begin. They added Pluribus to the list. Soldiers are raiding houses in nearly every city, and the people will witness the evil hand of tyranny firsthand. Our army grows by the hundreds every day, whether through the borders or from converts within. It was a success."

Orion blinked hard, then his pained eyes squinted as if he could see Greyson somewhere in the distance. "He esss-caped."

Emory scoffed. "Intriguing." He paced around the edge of the bed. The doctors and soldiers moved from his path. "I had my nemesis. Now you have yours. Like father, like son. I conquered mine after so long; you will, too, in time."

"Yes. I will. I'll kill him!" Orion breathed deeper and deeper, finding the sound slipping through his robotic windpipe and more familiar. It had an ominous tone but was somehow rhythmic and comforting.

*Hehhhhhsssssssta-ta-ta-ta. Hehhhhhsssssssta-ta-ta-ta.* "How do I find him? Greysss-on?"

Emory put his hand to his chin in thought. "Now that he's with Rubicon, it will be more difficult. But I suppose he may come to us, now that he knows."

"Knows?"

"His father's with us."

Orion smiled through his pain. "Let him come."

# Epilogue

Yotty's Ice Cream Store had attracted a record number of people for an early morning at the Iowa City Mall. The crowd had come, little by little, pulled away from their shopping toward the little counter with 55 flavors displayed beneath glass counter tops. Instead of the usual one or two in line, the gathering only grew bigger as the crowd became a spectacle in itself, murmuring in tense excitement. But the customers weren't eyeing the flavors – their eyes were fixed on the store's television screen where Yotty's newest deals and flavor combinations were once being showcased. But someone had changed the channel, and the screen was filled with images from a 24-hour cable news network.

A young, college-aged man shimmied into the crowd, his heart already racing. Somehow, he knew it was another attack, but he hoped it was something else.

The images became clearer as he shimmied closer. A storm – a hurricane – being filmed from the beach. The camera shook, the image was blurry. The voice of the amateur cameraman was barely discernible, but it had reached a high pitch that only fear could emit. Finally, the camera zoomed in and found its focus on the outline of the remains of a sinking ship, with fires burning despite the downpour.

The young man gasped. "Is that a…?"

"USS Coronado," a bearded man said beside him.

A lump rose in the young man's throat, but the images continued. Another amateur photographer captured what looked like meteorites, falling in a cluster, streaking through the night sky.

"What's that?" one spectator asked.

"Are we being attacked? Is it starting already?" a woman asked no one in particular, grabbing on to the arms of those nearby.

"It's satellite debris," the bearded man stated definitively, pointing at the TV. "They shot 'em down."

The young man eyed the screen where streaks streamed through the night over another location – in another state – but he wasn't really watching anymore. His eyes had begun to glaze. His knuckles turned white as he gripped his shopping bag full of useless junk. He wouldn't need it anymore. He was done with this life.

"Where's the nearest recruiting station?" the young man seethed.

The bearded man turned to him. He arched his brow. "Going to sign up?"

The young man set his jaw. "I got to do something."

"Good for you. Good for you!" The bearded man pointed across the wide thoroughfare, where a makeshift recruiting kiosk had been set up to help meet the demand of the recent influx of volunteers.

"Looks like fate is helping you out today," the man said.

A few others were listening to their conversation, adding their bits of encouragement, but the young man was working up his own courage. It had been building for months. He'd nearly signed up after the bomb, but the ensuing uncertainty of whom he'd be fighting gave him second thoughts. Without a clear enemy, his anger had no place to rest. But after Camden...after this...he knew for certain.

"I'd be the first to cheer you on as you sign up," the bearded man said, "but, being a father myself, you might want to talk this through with your parents first."

"My father's a Marine."

The bearded man smiled and gave a light laugh. "Then, by all means, make him proud!"

The young man nodded to himself. His dad would be proud. He'd been proud of him after the attack at Morris – for playing a vital role in thwarting the Plurbs there – but the young man had known in the back of his mind that it was the kids who had stopped the terrorists. They had been the ones who had truly risked it all to do something about the evil. If twelve-year-olds could be that courageous, so could he.

He glanced to the posters on each side of the recruiting kiosk, where emblazoned red letters words aimed straight at his heart.

The land of the Free,
Home of the Brave, remains free
When brave men dare fight

*When brave men dare fight.*

He breathed in deep and long, suddenly very sure of himself. Fate had meant for him to see the words. He couldn't help but to obey.

"I'm going to do it."

The bearded man stepped back and announced to the crowd. "He's going to sign up! He's going to send the Plurbs to where they belong!"

The crowd erupted in cheers and applause, and the young man blushed.

"What's your name, son?" the bearded man asked amidst the cheering.

The young man leaned in to whisper. "Brandon."

Brandon left the crowd with a confident stride toward the recruiting kiosk, the cheers and applause buoying him along.

# END OF BOOK 3

---

Continue the adventure with

# *Greyson Gray: Rubicon*

---

## Here's a Preview!

Glancing behind as the soldiers abandoned the smoking Bradley Fighting Vehicle, Greyson eyed his DOC. "Liam! Stay with it," Greyson whispered as if it could understand. Then he sent the drone after its wayward kin once again.

"Too much heat here!" Windsor shouted. "But the door's around that corner!"

The corner was too far. They wouldn't make it.

If Windsor wanted in the building to the right, Greyson would have to make a door.

He pulled an explosive ball from its pouch, loaded it, and warned Windsor. Then he fired.

The brick wall exploded

with dust and debris, blasting his ears with a sharp ring. When he could see well enough, he guided Windsor through. Seeing the interior of the hotel made him feel guilty for making a mess of such a pleasant lobby. There was even brick in the fountain.

But soldiers' footfalls were right behind; they didn't waste any time while racing up the escalator to the second floor. Windsor knew exactly where to go, and Greyson understood why he'd taken him here.

A skybridge.

"Pedestrian Network. Connects half of downtown. Tunnels, skybridges. We'd take the underground trucking tunnels, but the Merks flushed those a week ago – took it for themselves."

Greyson eyed his DOC. "North. Then West. It's headed toward Thanksgiving Square."

"Perfect!"

Windsor sprinted to the first skybridge, and Greyson followed as the HUD's path-line **appeared above** its grey and orange industrial strength carpet. A plain-clothed man was laying in the middle of it, next to a potted plant with a pair of binoculars pointed to the east through the skybridge's glass wall. He glanced in their direction but turned back to the street without a word. Greyson slowed to a jog to look where the man was looking. On the street below, two more men were kneeling at sidewalks on opposing corners.

"Bogies," came the man's scratchy voice. "Armor and drones."

Greyson stopped and turned to the man, but he wasn't talking to him. It didn't look like he was talking to anybody.

But something had signaled the kneeling men on the street; they hightailed away, ducking into the same shop down the block.

*The man on the skybridge had signaled the others. He's a lookout.*

A moment later, Greyson felt the skybridge floor rattle as a Bradley churned underneath. Then a shadow fell over them as a drone swarm flew above, like bees from their hive toward a large mob of protestors three blocks away – an enticing target for the military.

For a moment, Greyson marveled at the swarm. It was made up of tiny drones the size of grapefruits, and they swam through the air, synchronized like a school of fish, bobbing, morphing, like a deadly cloud. And it descended toward the group, ready to unleash their fury.

Greyson saw the ambush about to happen, but he knew what the results would be. He wanted to scream and pound his hands on the glass to warn them. *Stop, stop!* But he couldn't.

When the Bradley reached the corner, bombs went off on either side, pummeling the armored vehicle with stone and dark dust. The swarm reacted instantly, breaking apart. Some were sent spiraling into windows, but the others veered to safety and searched for victims. The Bradley slowed to a stop, but a flaming bottle flew from a window and crashed on its treads. But even as it burst into flames, it turned to barrage the window.

Kit whimpered and Greyson couldn't stand to watch anymore.

The scratchy voice grated behind him. "E Unum Pluribus."

Greyson turned to glare at the lookout. The man was smiling.

"Greyson!" Windsor shouted. "Let's go!"

Greyson jogged and then ran, his feet thumping hollow on the skybridge, like the thumping of the Bradley's cannon.

"E Unum Pluribus!" echoed behind him.

# Find the rest of
# *Greyson Gray: Rubicon*
# at **Amazon.com!**

## ABOUT THE AUTHOR

B.C. has always longed to both edify and entertain the next generation all while staying behind the scenes. While he initially wanted to tell stories from behind a camera, he now writes them from behind the pen. It may be because of his love for movies that his books are often compared to them. He also loved reading as a child, especially the *Animorphs*, *Goosebumps*, and *Left Behind* series, so it is a joy for him to give young readers another beloved series to add to their bookshelves. Finally, he has thoroughly enjoyed brainstorming ideas while running, listening to epic movie soundtracks, and researching in exotic places like the Bahamas...and Iowa.